BROKEN ALIBI

LIES, MEMORY, AND JUSTICE

Tim Vicary

The fourth book in the series of legal thrillers
The Trials of Sarah Newby

White Owl Publications 2016

Copyright Tim Vicary 2016

This book is copyright under the Berne Convention
No reproduction without permission
All rights reserved

ISBN-10: 1535322578
ISBN-13: 978-1535322577

The right of Tim Vicary to be identified as the author of this work has been asserted in accordance with sections 77 and 78 of the copyright Designs and Patents Act 1988

Disclaimer
This is a work of pure fiction. There is a real village called Osbaldwick but there is no such place as Straw House Barn, which does not exist. None of the characters in this book are intended to bear any resemblance to any real person, alive or dead.

Other Books by Tim Vicary

Legal thrillers in the series 'The Trials of Sarah Newby'

A Game of Proof
A Fatal Verdict
Bold Counsel

Historical Novels

Nobody's Slave
Cat and Mouse
The Blood Upon the Rose
The Monmouth Summer

Box Sets

Women of Courage (3 historical novels)

Audiobooks

A Game of Proof
A Fatal Verdict
Nobody's Slave

Website: www.timvicary.com

For Sue

With love, as always

Part One

Operation Hazel

1 . Thunder

THE FIRST fat raindrops fell on the windscreen as the car turned off the road. But the driver did not turn on the wipers; there were only a few yards to go. The headlights pierced the dark tunnel between the trees, as the vehicle bounced slowly over potholes, and came to a halt in a patch of muddy ground near a fence at the end of the track.

There were no other cars there, but that was to be expected, this late at night. The driver opened the door, switched off the engine, and sat there for a moment, waiting, listening. It was that strange atmosphere before an electric storm breaks, when sounds carry weird distances, so that something a mile away can be heard like something next door. The driver sifted through the sounds cautiously, searching for danger. The swish of traffic on the road thirty yards behind; the staccato random patter of raindrops on the trees; the shriek of an owl; the pinking of the car engine as it cooled; and underlying everything, the faintest gurgle of water from the river running nearby.

Reassured, the driver got out, walked to the back of the car, opened the boot, and bent to lift something out. At that moment, a million volts of lightning lit the scene, like a celestial flash bulb. If there had been a camera in the heavens, it would have recorded the image of two human figures, not one – both in long dark coats, struggling together in a strange clumsy dance in the mud behind the car. One, it seemed, was trying to lift the other.

But there was no one else there to see it, so perhaps it didn't happen at all. As the night returned, darker than before, the rain began to fall more heavily, fat heavy raindrops crashing on the canopy of trees like a sudden urgent waterfall, drowning out every other sound, so that no one, even if they *had* been there, would have heard the sound of the driver's feet staggering across the muddy parking place to the footpath and the river beyond.

Then, like a colossal iron ball rumbling and rolling across the heavens, the thunder came, threatening to collapse through the clouds and crush everything and everyone beneath. God's punishment, perhaps - but for what, and to whom? The driver, staggering, slipping and sliding towards the water's edge, was too burdened and busy to care.

Because the storm was almost directly overhead the lightning came again soon afterwards, this time illuminating a second image, which the driver fervently hoped no one saw, of two figures, both in that instant apparently standing drunkenly at the edge of the river, one behind the other, facing out across the dark, swiftly sliding stream, its surface pitted by a thousand raindrops. The figure in front had two feet in the water and its left hand snagged in a tree, while the rest of the body sagged with bowed head and limp knees as though drunk, unconscious, or dead.

Only an instant, then darkness returned, so no one but the second figure saw or heard the snap as the twig snagging the hand broke off, or the smooth gurgling splash of the shallow dive as the first figure flopped forwards into the strong, black, powerful current which spun the body face down, eddying round and round away from the bank, out towards the centre of the river where in a few seconds it vanished not only from sight — had there been anyone to see — but also from the surface, down into the depths where the mud, dead leaves and detritus drifted slowly downstream towards the sea.

The next flash of lighting lit up only the car, its boot and doors now closed, lonely and abandoned under the trees, the torrential rainstorm pounding on its roof and windscreen. Long after the lightning had gone, the downpour continued, steadily, relentlessly obliterating all traces of footprints not just in the mud of the parking area, but also on the grass of the riverside footpath and the slippery, muddy bank of the river itself.

But if some celestial camera had been watching, recording each billion-volt flash lit up in the summer storm, it would have seen countless other things, some with relevance to the drama by the riverside, others with no apparent connection at all.

It would have seen the driver, shoulders hunched, collar turned up, hurrying along the riverbank towards the city, until the grassy path gave way to a tarmac cycle track with houses and gardens on the right hand side. A later flash would have seen the same person, emerging from the dark of a ginnel between those same houses into an area of the A19 lit by streetlights in the suburb of Fulford, where the driver gratefully got into the back of a taxi summoned by mobile phone.

Another flash, half a mile further upstream, would have lit up the sleeping city of York, with its cathedral, York Minster, gleaming like a beautiful white monument under the lowering midnight clouds of the storm. A little to the south, and nearer the river, the remains of the medieval castle, Clifford's Tower, and the neighbouring Crown Court glistened palely in the rain and lightning flash.

Across the river from there, at a window on the third floor of a block of luxury riverside flats, an astute celestial observer might just have picked out the face of a slim dark-haired woman in her early forties, the barrister Sarah Newby, wakened by the storm and staring out, marvelling at the power of nature, hugging her nightgown tightly about her, thinking with amusement about the visit of her new lover earlier that evening, and wondering what the future would bring.

A mile away across the river, Detective Inspector Terry Bateson stood with an arm round his two young daughters, watching the storm from an upstairs window. The two girls, Jessica and Esther, shrieked with terror and excitement as the lightning split the sky. Terry smiled, hugging them tightly as the rain lashed the windows and ran horizontally across the glass. A cyclist passed under the streetlight outside, shoulders hunched under his streaming cape as he pedalled forlornly home.

Towards morning, the storm moved on towards a police station in Harrogate, where a group of police and special constables gathered, yawning, for a briefing. They had been picked mostly for brawn rather than brains, and all wore stab vests and carried riot helmets ready to put on. As the police piled into their van, it occurred to one constable, at least, that the approaching storm would provide a welcome extra touch of drama to the night. Grinning, he searched on his phone for the track of the ride of the Valkries.

A few miles west of them the target of their raid, a lanky, bearded man in his fifties, lay peacefully asleep in his bed, snoring gently with his partner's head pillowed on his chest.

Much further north still, across the border in Scotland, the weather was calm. Stars shone silently in a cloudless night sky. A little after midnight, a car drove into the car park outside a hotel in Edinburgh. The man who had hired the car, tall, lanky, bearded, got out and strolled nonchalantly into the building. It had been a satisfactory evening, his body language seemed to say. Everything was as it should be, all was right with his world.

Or at least, that is probably how it would have seemed, had he been lit up by a lightning flash then and the moment recorded. But then, there was no storm in Scotland, no celestial CCTV, and no one was watching – so how can anyone know?

2. Night Visit

THE THUNDER woke Sonya Green at 3.45 a.m. It broke into a dream about skiing. In the dream she was skiing off-piste through the mountains, her three children, John, Linda and Samantha, following dutifully behind her. In real life none of them were expert skiers but in this dream, miraculously, she slalomed neatly across an endless landscape of powder snow. Then suddenly, everything changed. She looked up and saw, beneath the blue sky and Alpine peaks, a man, zooming across the snow above her, too fast, too LOUD, as if there were an outboard motor on the back of his skis, and then ... it happened. The slope broke up, the avalanche collapsed on her and the children with a sound like thunder, and ...

She woke, trembling. At home in bed in the dark. Beside her, Bob was asleep, snoring gently. A faint glow from the streetlight seeped around the curtains. She could hear the patter of rain on the window, hesitant at first, then louder, insistent, a downpour. Next a flash of lightning, followed after a minute or so by a second crash of thunder.

'Mummy!'

Quietly, Sonya slipped out of bed and padded across the landing to the bedroom where her two daughters slept. It was the eight-year-old, Linda, who had called; her older sister, Samantha, was still asleep. The child held out her arms and Sonya sat down on the bed, cuddling her gently. A second flash of lightning lit the room.

'It's just a storm, love. Thunder. Can you hear the rain pattering on the window?'

For a while they sat together, listening to it. Then, as the lightning came less frequently and the rumbles of thunder seemed to move away, she kissed her daughter and tucked the duvet securely around her.

'Back to sleep now, pet. All safe now.'

Crossing the landing she checked briefly in the other bedroom, where her son John had slept stolidly through the whole thing. Then she slipped back into bed beside her gently snoring partner, Bob. He stirred drowsily as she snuggled up against him.

'Kids ok?'

'Mm. There was a storm.'

'I heard it. Back to sleep now. Hm?'

There was a faint question in his voice, and she wondered whether to respond to it. He lay on his back and she rested her head on his shoulder, feeling his beard tickle the top of her head. She slid one hand under his pyjama jacket, playing with the hairs of his chest.

'Maybe. We'll see.'

For a while they lay like that, neither making a further move. He was only half awake and she was cold, wrapping herself closely around him to regain the warmth of the bed. Did he want more? Did she? They were still new to each other; he had only moved in with her a few months ago. In one way that meant the attraction was still fresh; she had never kissed a bearded man before Bob, and her previous partners – the fathers of her children – had both been stronger, more muscular men. Younger too, more sexually demanding. Bob Newby was not only older, but quite skinny, despite his age. Gentler, more hesitant in his love making. Still, he was a man for all that, and she knew what men wanted. Also, despite his shortcomings in physique, it was quite a turn-on to be lying here in bed with her arms and legs wrapped round her boss, the head teacher of the school where she worked. She smiled, thinking of the other women at work, and slid her hand lower, down his stomach ...

There was a soft clunk outside the window, like a car door shutting. Sonya lifted her head slightly, to check the green glow of the alarm clock on Bob's side of the bed. 4.38 a.m. This was a quiet street; the neighbours didn't usually start moving until well after six. At least, not in the street, she thought slyly – who knew what they got up to indoors during the small hours? Her headmaster, at least, was responding predictably. He groaned, turned towards her, and ...

The doorbell rang. A clear, penetrating chime, impossible to ignore.

'What?' Bob sat up, the excitement of a moment ago subsiding. Sonya moved her hand away. 'Who the devil can that be?'

'Some drunken idiot. Ignore it.' She touched his arm.

The doorbell rang again, urgent, insistent.

'Mummy?' Samantha called from across the landing. 'What's happening?'

'Don't worry, darling,' Sonya pulled back the duvet, swung her legs out into the cold. 'I'll go and see.'

'No, you stay here. I'll go.' Bob got out of bed, switched on the light, grabbed a dressing gown. 'You watch from the window. If there's any trouble, call the police.'

But when Sonya pulled back the bedroom curtain and peered out of the window, she realised that wouldn't be necessary.

* * *

'Robert Edwin Newby?'

'Yes. Who ...?'

'Detective Sergeant Starkey, North Yorkshire Police. Mr Newby, you are under arrest for the rape of an underage female. You do not have to say anything. But I must warn you that it may harm your defence if you do not mention when questioned something which you later rely on in court. Anything which you do say may be taken down and used in evidence.'

'What? What are you talking about? You must be making a mistake.'

'No sir, I'm afraid not. You are Robert Edwin Newby, currently employed as head teacher of St Asaph's Primary School?'

'Yes, of course, but – what on earth are you talking about?'

'You'll find out in due course, sir. I also have a warrant to search these premises. May we come in?'

'I ... but it's not my house. I just live here.'

'The registered tenant is Mrs Sonya Elizabeth Green. Is she here?'

'Yes. She's upstairs, in bed. For heaven's sake – do you know what time it is?'

'I'm sorry to call so early, sir, but we needed to be sure you were in. Now if you would stand aside ...' He was in the house, followed by what seemed like an endless stream of burly uniformed officers – six, in total – before Bob could think of what to do. One of these men gripped his arm.

'Stay with me, sir.'

'But ...' Bob struggled, ineffectually. 'There are children upstairs asleep. Sonya ...'

The grip on his arm tightened. 'We'll be very discreet , sir. If you'd just step in here with me.'

Bob found himself in the living room with the man – a very large man wearing body armour and what looked like a motorcycle helmet – between him and the door. He wore holsters, a radio and some sort of truncheon strapped to his waist, huge boots on his feet. Bob, barefoot in his pyjamas, spluttered angrily.

'This is outrageous! You can't just burst in like this!'

'We can and we have, sir. As the sergeant said, you're under arrest for the rape of an underage female and we have a warrant to search this building. So my advice to you is to sit down quietly and let us go about our business, otherwise I shall be forced to restrain you with handcuffs.'

The perspex visor on the man's helmet was raised, and Bob could see a smug patronising grin on the man's face, like a giant trying to humour a helpless child.

'But this is ridiculous! I haven't raped anyone!'

'You can explain that in interview at the station later on, sir. Remember, anything you say now will be taken down and used in evidence.' The man pulled a notebook and pen from one of the many pockets around his chest.

'But my partner – Sonya, the children!' Bob could hear Sonya's raised voice from the stairs, the children crying. 'Please, let me go to them!'

The man stood immoveable as a mountain between Bob and the door. 'All in good time sir. We have two female officers in the team. They'll reassure them.'

'Reassure them? After breaking into the house like this!' Bob could hear Sonya's outraged voice shouting upstairs, male and female voices replying. One of the children crying.

'What's this warrant for, anyway? What are you searching for?'

'Evidence, sir, of course. Pornographic material, I suppose. Do you have a computer here, sir?' The grin on the man's face broadened, as though he were inviting a confidence, hinting that he was a man, he understood.

'Yes, my laptop, over there, but ... oh God!' Bob sank down suddenly on the sofa, his head in his hands. 'You're not really suggesting that I ... I'm a head teacher, for heaven's sake! I haven't got time to use pornography – I've got a school to run!'

This statement, too, went down in the officer's notebook, with a large question mark in the margin next to it, and the words 'Confession? Illogical?'

'There'll be time to go into all that down at the station, sir, as I say. Now sir, we'll be taking you down to the station, so as soon as your partner is decent I suggest you go upstairs to get dressed. Choose the clothes you'll be most comfortable in, that's my advice. You're likely to be there for some time.'

'But this is ridiculous. Absurd, outrageous!'

'You'll be able to explain all that later in interview, sir. Now if you'd like to come this way ...'

Incongruously, the man opened the living room door and shepherded Bob upstairs, in his own home. From the landing, he saw Sonya in the girls' bedroom clutching little Linda to her as tightly as she could, while Samantha clung to her nightdress. A female officer held a drowsy little Johnny by the hand. Sonya's eyes, wide with fright, stared at Bob in shock.

'Bob! What the hell's going on?'

'I don't know. I don't understand it.'

'This way, sir, if you please.' A large hand urged Bob firmly into the main bedroom. Once there, the man closed the door and stood in front of it. Bob tried to confront him.

'For heaven's sake! At least let me get dressed in peace!'

'I'm sorry, sir. Regulations. I need to be sure you don't have a chance to dispose of any evidence.'

'Evidence? What evidence, for heaven's sake? I haven't done anything.'

'Just get dressed, sir. Take your time, we've got all day.'

'But I can't go to the police station! I've got a school to run!'

'Not today, sir, I'm afraid. So if you'd just get dressed.'

Bob shook his head from side to side, the enormity of the situation descending on him like an avalanche. His heart was beating wildly in his chest, and he wondered if he was about to have a heart attack. He sat down on the bed, feeling the adrenalin rage through his veins.

'You can't do this, you know. It's all wrong!'

This time the policeman didn't bother to reply. After a while, Bob got up, stripped off his pyjamas, and stood there naked, fumbling to retrieve his underwear from a chair. The officer watched impassively, immune to the distress he was causing. It was all part of the process. The official reason for making an arrest at 4.30 in the morning was because that was when the suspect was most likely to be at home, but it was also the time most suspects were at their lowest, most defenceless ebb. This man was lucky he wasn't having his clothes confiscated and being told to dress in a paper suit; the offences, his sergeant had conceded reluctantly, had occurred too long ago for that to be necessary.

Nonetheless, this part of the process, standing impassive in the man's bedroom watching him dress, would also help to break down his resistance, so that by the time of the first recorded interview he would well on the way to confession. This lanky bearded fellow in front of him, he thought, was neither an imposing physical specimen nor, it seemed, a particularly strong character. But then many rapists were like that – pathetically inadequate rather than scary. The shocking thing was that this one was a head teacher. Well, these paedophiles got everywhere nowadays. There were even little kiddies in the other bedrooms.

The officer, a father himself, shuddered. He was just one of the Tactical Aid Team, he seldom knew the details of the evidence against the suspects he was sent to arrest. But he would feel good at the end of his shift today, going home to his family proud in the knowledge that he had helped to lock away one of the perverts who, it seemed, infested society these days.

Bob dressed in his normal clothes, a crumpled suit and tie. He glanced in the mirror, dragged a comb through his hair, and realised he hadn't shaved.

'I normally have a wash in the morning,' he said defiantly, realising it was probably too late.

'That's all right, sir, you can have a shower at the station. Breakfast too, if you can face it. It's not all that bad.'

'I'll need to phone the school, tell them I'm not coming in.' He fumbled his phone from his pocket.

'I'll take that, sir, if you don't mind.' The man moved surprisingly swiftly across the room, taking the phone before Bob could use it. 'Regulations. It could be evidence, you see. The custody sergeant will phone from the station.'

'No!' The thought of what a phone call like that would do to his reputation, his teaching career, his *life* – flashed through Bob like lightning. 'I'll ask Sonya. You're not arresting her, too – or are you?'

'No sir, just you.'

As the man opened the door Bob saw Sonya on the landing, standing there dazed with the children clinging to her while uniformed officers searched the bedrooms.

'Bob, what's going on?'

'I don't know, I don't understand. They're arresting me for something, but it's all nonsense. Ring the school, will you, tell them I won't be in today, say I'm ill, anything.'

'But won't the police ...?'

'No, I hope not. This is some crazy mistake, it'll all be cleared up by this evening, I hope. Don't worry everyone now ...'

'All right, but why ...?'

The burly policeman had his hand on Bob's arm, guiding him firmly downstairs. From the foot of the stairs Bob's voice floated back.

'I don't know, I tell you, it's mad ...'

But at least, he thought as he was hustled outside, if Sonya rings the school and makes some excuse, I'll have time to sort this out before any news of this leaks out and panics the parents. His primary school was just starting to do well. An OFSTED report six months ago had lifted them out of 'inadequate' – the disaster grade he had inherited when he took over the school – to 'good', the second highest category. Recruiting was dramatically up and he'd had to turn away three sets of parents in the last fortnight, telling them the school was full. The new school term began on Monday, and his ambition was to raise their OFSTED grade to 'outstanding.' But if parents were to hear about this ...

The officer led him firmly across the street to a police van. It was still dark, but the lights were on in several neighbouring houses. Bob noticed a couple of people standing outside their front doors, gazing in bewilderment at the array of police vehicles and flashing lights. As the officer opened the back doors of the van a young man standing a few yards away lifted his mobile phone and pressed the button.

Click. Flash. Gotcha.

3. SOS

SARAH NEWBY had just got out of the shower when her mobile rang. Twisting a towel round her head like a turban, she wrapped herself in another, tucking it neatly under her arms, and padded across the living room to her desk, where her phone was flashing its light and trembling, having its little tantrum. She picked it up and frowned. The call was from a landline, not a number she recognised.

'Hello?'

'Sarah! Thank God you're there! It's me, Bob.' Bob, her ex–husband; she hadn't spoken to him for months. What on earth could he want, at this time of day? And why wasn't he ringing from his mobile?

'Bob? What is it? What's the matter?'

'I ... I'm sorry to ring so early, but I couldn't think of anyone else ...'

If that's his idea of flattery, Sarah reflected wryly, it's not going to get him very far. But the voice on the phone sounded desperate, anxious.

'I've ... been arrested.'

'*You*, arrested? Whatever for – parking?'

'No, it's worse than that. Much worse, in fact. It's embarrassing, ridiculous, absurd. It's about the rape of a schoolgirl. They think I did it.'

'What? *You*, Bob? I don't believe it.'

'No, well, neither do I, obviously. It's nonsense. But they raided the house at half past four this morning and took away everything, my computer and phone, everything. I had to beg them to look on it to get your number. So now I'm standing here in a police station and they asked if I wanted a lawyer so I said yes, of course, but I don't know any lawyers so I rang you. Sarah, I need help!'

'Yes but ... where are you?'

'Harrogate Police Station, I think.' She heard him talking to someone, the custody sergeant, presumably. 'Yes, Harrogate Police Station. How soon can you get here?'

For a long moment Sarah didn't answer. She stared unseeing out of the window, past her third floor balcony to the view of the river below and the footpath under the trees on the opposite bank, where the first early commuters were walking to work. She knew her answer would mean everything.

'Bob, I can't.'

'What? Sarah, *please*, this is serious. *I need you*!'

She closed her eyes, took a deep breath. 'I know, Bob, I understand how serious it is. But you don't need me, you need a solicitor. I'm a barrister, I don't do police station work.'

'You did it before, I remember. For that woman who tried to shoot someone. You left me in a restaurant – on our anniversary, for heaven's sake, to go and help her!'

'Yes, but that was different. It was a mistake, anyway, the whole case went wrong.'

'So you'll do it for some random woman but not for me? Well, thanks a lot, Sarah! I thought for once in a situation like this I could rely on you!'

'What you need is a good criminal solicitor, not me. Bob, I ...'

'I don't know any solicitors, damn it! Only that divorce lawyer, and I doubt if he's the right man for this, somehow ...'

'No, probably not.' Sarah shuddered, remembering the elegant, smarmy young man who had represented Bob in their divorce negotiations. She had conceived an intense dislike of him, but perhaps that was only natural in the circumstances. He'd done his job well enough, but this ... 'Look, Bob, why not try Lucy Parsons? She does crime, she's good.'

'I'm only allowed one phone call, damn it! This is it! If you won't help I'll have to rely on whoever the police dig up.'

'No, don't do that. I'll ring her, Bob, I'll get her to come. She'll be much better than me in a situation like this. And Bob?'

'Yes?'

'Until she comes, don't say anything. Don't let them interview you, insist on food and medical attention if you need it, access to the toilet if necessary ...'

'For heaven's sake, Sarah!'

'I'll ring Lucy straight away, she'll be in touch. If she can't do it for any reason I'll get someone else, someone good. They'll come to the station this morning. Until then don't say anything, nothing at all, so they can't twist it. And Bob ...'

'Yes?'

'What is this all about? I mean ...' *Heavens, I'm breaking my own basic rule,* Sarah thought. *That's exactly why I'd be no good at this. I can't ask him to explain, the custody sergeant's listening to every word.* 'No, don't answer that, don't say anything on the phone now. I'll get it all from Lucy later.' Which would be a clear breach of confidentiality, she realised. But then he's my husband. Was.

'I'll ring Lucy right now.'

'All right. But Sarah, I wish it was you.'

'Bye, Bob.'

Sarah clicked the phone off. *You don't want me, Bob, you really don't,* she thought grimly. Or rather *I* don't, which in this case is pretty much the same thing.

She stood there trembling for a second, astonishment and rage racing each other through her veins to see which emotion came out strongest. Bob Newby had left her over a year ago, using the most humiliating words possible. '*I want someone else,*' he had said. *'Someone better than you.'* He had used those exact words, standing opposite her in the kitchen of the house they had both worked so hard to afford. Their marriage was dead, he had said, finished. What had he called it? *A husk.*

So she'd thrown him out, and he'd gone to live with this *better* woman, Sonya or whatever her wretched name was, breaking up the family home, trashing their long years of marriage. Yet now here he was, ringing up at seven in the morning to ask for her help because he'd been arrested for what? *The rape of a schoolgirl?*

I don't believe it, Sarah thought. There's got to be something wrong here. Bob's always had his faults and he's changed since he met that woman but this ... surely not.

And yet why did he leave? Because of sex, presumably. Bob had never been the greatest lover – gentle, kind, a bit clumsy, never arousing the wild passion she'd felt for a few short weeks in her teenage years with her first husband Kevin. But that wasn't what she'd married Bob for, anyway. His virtues had been the opposite – reliability, intelligence, thoughtfulness, common sense – all of which had seemed to abandon him in middle age, first in an affair with his secretary Stephanie and now with this supply teacher Sonya.

But that's miles away from the rape of a schoolgirl. Presumably what he was seeking with these other women was excitement, a reaction to the male menopause, some proof that he was still desirable in a way that I clearly, failed to give him. Maybe this slut Sonya gave him something of what I experienced with Michael Parker – *after* Bob had left me, though, not before. The sort of dangerous scary romantic sexual thrill that takes over everything, blinds you to common sense for a while. She closed her eyes for a long moment, reliving the joy and fear Michael Parker had given her, then swiftly overlaying the nightmare images of his death with the thrilling, healing memories of last time with Terry Bateson. *But both of those are love affairs between adults, after all. I'm not a child, I knew what I was doing.*

At least, I thought I did, with Michael. And this time I do. Don't I?

Anyway that's not this problem, that's not what Bob faces now.

Can a grown man fall in love with a schoolgirl? A man in his fifties like Bob, a head teacher, a father? Surely not. It doesn't make sense. And yet how old was I when he married me? Eighteen, by one day. No, that's different, has to be. There must be something wrong.

Anyway I was right not to go to the police station, I couldn't possibly defend him. I'd be too confused, too conflicted, it would be awful, impossible. Never again.

She found Lucy Parsons' number on her phone, dialled.

'Lucy? Sarah. You're not going to believe this ...'

* * *

'Oi! Is that yours?'

'No.'

'Yes.'

'We was just looking, mister. Anyway, what's it to you?'

'Well, clear off out of it then. Go on, get lost! Unless you want this round your backsides!'

'You can't do that! That's child abuse! We got rights, you know!'

'Max! Here, boy!' The man blew a whistle – a tiny, high-pitched sound, almost inaudible to the adult ear. Instantly, two of the boys ducked, clutching their hands over their heads, while the third yelped indignantly. A second later, a dog loped out of the woods – a large, powerful German shepherd, its bright red tongue lolling out between rows of gleaming white teeth. Ears pricked, two bright eyes focussed eagerly on the man. In two smooth leaps the animal was at his side, gazing up expectantly. Then it turned to where he was looking, saw the three boys, and growled.

'All right, mister, we're just leaving.'

'We didn't mean any harm. It was open anyway.'

'Call that beast off. If it comes near me I'll ...'

The dog didn't move. It just looked. When the boys were out of sight the man dropped the tailgate of his four by four, and nodded. The dog crouched, leapt, and was in. The man fastened the tailgate, said 'Stay', and smiled as he always did at the sight of the intelligent, eager face of the dog staring down at him to see what he would do next. Eyes bright, nose sampling all the hidden scents of the light breeze by the river, ears swivelled to catch the distant protests of the retreating boys, now out of sight round the bend.

The man turned to the car. He had noticed it when he set out on his walk and it had still been there when he came back. Not the sort of car he usually saw down here – a smart, powder blue Mercedes, nearly new, to judge by the number plate, and beautifully polished. The few flecks of mud behind the front wheel looked wrong, out of place. He was tempted to get out a tissue and wipe them off. Not the sort of car that was used to driving through puddles on unmade roads, then – as it must have done to get here. Not a dog walker's car either – the seats were clean, uncluttered by dog hairs or mud or protective mats. No child car seat, crumpled crisp packets or used tissues either, the usual detritus of family life.

So what was this car doing here? *It was open*, that boy had said. Had they broken in? But no windows were smashed, the lock didn't seem broken, no alarm had gone off. Cautiously, he pulled the door open and looked inside.

They had been trying to steal the radio, he thought. There were scratch marks, it was partly pulled out. The glove compartment was open too, but inside, what? Sunglasses, expensive woman's sunglasses in a flowery case; sun cream, lip gloss, a book. He eased himself into the seat, reached over, picked up the book, curiously. Not chicklit in a pink cover, as he'd expected, but poetry, an anthology of modern feminists.

So. I shouldn't have done that, the man realised, belatedly. He climbed out of the car, thinking *my fingerprints will be everywhere now*. My DNA too, quite probably, on the headrest behind me. And mud from my boots on the floor. Only two years into retirement, and I'm getting slack, forgetting crime scene protocol already. Ah well, I may be just an ignorant civilian, but there's definitely something here to investigate. Let's call this in, see how today's young constables cope.

He pulled his mobile out of his pocket, made the call. Then leaned against his muddy four by four, reached over the tailgate to ruffle the ears of the dog, and waited.

4. Operation Hazel

THE DOOR of Harrogate Police Station crashed open. The elderly constable looked up from his computer to see a woman approaching him, a determined look in her eye. In her late forties, she might easily have been mistaken for a vagrant or a bag lady. Her ample figure was encased in a crisp white blouse, loose sleeveless embroidered jacket, and long black ankle–length skirt over comfortable Doc Martin boots. Her shoulder–length hair was bleached white, with a defiant purple streak at the back. The elderly constable smiled.

'Mrs Parsons, isn't it? What can we do for you today, madam?'

Lucy Parsons smiled – a business–like smile in a chubby, motherly face. 'You've arrested a Mr Robert Newby, I understand. I'm his brief.'

'Ah yes.' The welcoming smile faded to a serious frown. *'Operation Hazel,* that is. You'd better come through, then.'

Operation Hazel, Lucy thought, as the man opened the security door and beckoned her in. That sounds as if more than one case is involved. A senior criminal solicitor with a dozen active cases on her books, she had been leaving for work when Sarah phoned. She would not have changed her plans at short notice for anyone else. But Sarah was one of her closest friends in the legal profession, and they had worked together on several high profile cases. They had met when Sarah had first qualified. Lucy, let down at the last minute by a senior barrister whom she'd engaged in a tricky burglary case, had decided to give this unknown beginner a chance; and Sarah, to her surprise and satisfaction, had achieved an unexpected success. Further cases had followed, including the dramatic trial of Sarah's son Simon for murder, and their friendship had blossomed.

Lucy had never particularly warmed to Sarah's husband Bob though, and thought she was well rid of him when the divorce came through. Strange incidents seemed drawn to Sarah Newby like moths to a flame. But for a respected head teacher to be arrested for child abuse – well, that seemed totally out of character.

'Ah, Mrs Parsons. Detective Sergeant Starkey.' A slim, dark–haired man greeted her, and opened the door of an interview room. 'I'll bring your client to you. He's been fed, washed and watered, finger–printed, seen the medical officer, read his rights. Here's the disclosure sheet.' He went out, closing the door.

There were four chairs in the room, either side of a table which was screwed to the floor. Lucy sat down, spread out the sheet of paper on the battered, scratched plastic table top, and began to read, with growing astonishment.

Officers from Operation Hazel are conducting investigations into a number of historic sexual offences. As a result of information received in connection with these investigations Mr Robert Newby was arrested at 4.38 a.m. by Detective Sergeant Starkey at his home address in Harrogate for the following offences:
1. *Indecency with or towards a child – section 1 Indecency with a Child Act 1960.*
2. *Indecent Assault – Section 15(1) Sexual Offences Act 1956*

First Victim
A 39 year old woman by the name of Clare Fanshawe states that in 1991 when she was 15 she was a pupil at Wellborough Comprehensive School in Leeds, where Robert Newby was employed as an English teacher. Mr Newby had sexual relations with her on three occasions, once on the school playing field and once in a classroom after school hours. On the first two occasions he kissed her and touched her intimately, and she gave him sexual relief with her hand. On the third occasion Mr Newby invited her to his home, a flat in central Leeds, where he had full sexual relations with her per vaginam.

Second Victim.
A 40 year old woman by the name of Eleanor Wisbech states that in 1991 when she was 14 she was a pupil at Wellborough Comprehensive School in Leeds, where Robert Newby was employed as an English teacher. She states that on

one occasion he kissed and touched her intimately in a classroom after school hours.

Both victims also state that he was known amongst their school friends at the time to be a man who would approach under-age girls for sex, so they believe there may be other victims who have not come forward.

It is proposed to interview Mr Newby about these allegations.

Lucy groaned. As she put down the paper the door opened and Bob Newby walked in.

* * *

'That'll be it, there,' Terry Bateson said. He stopped the car at the end of the muddy track, and gazed at the powder blue Mercedes parked under the dripping trees.

'Looks like it's well guarded,' said his colleague, Detective Sergeant Jane Carter. A burly man in an old anorak stood a few yards away from the Mercedes, next to a mud-spattered four-by-four. An Alsatian sat obediently beside the man, ears pricked, tongue hanging out, eagerly studying the new arrivals as they climbed cautiously out of their car.

'Was it you that called the police, sir?' Terry asked.

'Yes, that's right. Who are you?'

Terry held out his warrant card. 'DI Terry Bateson. This is DS Jane Carter. And you?'

'Robert Deacon, sergeant, dog section, retired. What brings CID out on a call like this?'

Terry shrugged. 'Breath of fresh air.' He hadn't felt like paperwork this morning so when he'd learnt that none of the area cars were able to meet this call because of a road traffic accident on the A64, he'd leapt at the chance of getting out. An abandoned car by the river: could be serious, could be nothing.

'So what makes you think it's suspicious?' he asked the older man.

'Well, I come here most mornings and I've never seen it before. It was here first thing this morning when I walked the dog, and it was still here an hour later when I came back. The only reason most people drive here is to go fishing or walk the dog, but it doesn't look like that sort of car, does it? Too neat and tidy.'

The two detectives examined the car curiously. A powder blue Mercedes, gleaming paintwork with a few flecks of mud, lemon yellow leather seats inside. A different beast altogether from the muddy four by four belonging to the retired sergeant.

'Also, it was left open,' Robert Deacon added helpfully.

'Have you been inside, sir?' Jane Carter asked suspiciously.

'Yes, I'm afraid I have. I caught some kids in there. They were trying to nick the radio, I think.'

Jane peered inside, and saw some scratches on the fascia where the radio protruded slightly.

'You shouldn't really have done that, sir,' she said officiously. 'You'll have left fingerprints. Contaminated the crime scene – if there is a crime, that is.'

'Don't worry, lass, you'll have my prints on record.' Robert Deacon said patronisingly, irritated by the criticism. 'What would you have me do? Let the kids trash the car?'

'No sir, of course not. All the same ...'

'Looks like a female owner, doesn't it?' Deacon added, watching as Jane pulled on a pair of latex gloves, before opening the glove compartment. She pulled out sunglasses, sun cream, lip gloss, and a book of poetry.

'Yes, I had a look at that,' Deacon said. 'Quite literary stuff, as it happens. The page is turned down at a poem by Sylvia Plath. You might think that is significant.'

'I might? Why exactly, sir?' Poetry had never been Jane Carter's thing.

'Well, she committed suicide, didn't she? Head in a gas oven. There's a poem on that page about death. Take a look.'

Jane passed the book to Terry, who read a few lines of the poem. 'Gloomy stuff, I agree. So you think the owner may have done something similar?'

Deacon nodded. 'No gas ovens here, but we're right by the river. Just a few yards, if you wanted to jump in.'

Terry Bateson studied the car thoughtfully. The older man had a point. The Mercedes was clearly out of place down this muddy, potholed lane. This place, Landing Lane, on the edge of Fulford just south of York, was a favorite area for dog walkers, amongst other things. Only a few yards off the busy A19, it was quiet, sheltered by trees, a place where people could park their cars and walk their dogs onto the bank of the river Ouse, turning south towards the Archbishop's Palace or north into the city itself.

But the owner of this car didn't appear to have a dog. Not unless it was an exceptionally neat and tidy one. And even then, it would only have to have ventured a few yards down the lane to have left muddy paw marks all over the immaculate fawn car seats. No, this car had been driven here for some other reason.

An expensive car like this – why had it been left open?

'All right,' he said. 'Sergeant, call in the registration, will you?' While Jane Carter was doing that Terry walked around the car, eased himself into the driver's seat, and drummed his gloved fingers on the steering wheel. Everything inside felt comfortable, luxurious, clean. He glanced down self-consciously at where his shoes had left traces of mud on rubber mat in the footwell. Had anyone else done this before him? Probably the retired sergeant, damn him.

As he got out he heard Jane Carter speaking on her mobile: 'This is a message from York Police, trying to contact Mrs Victoria Weston. Mrs Weston, a car registered to you has been found apparently abandoned by the river Ouse, in possibly suspicious circumstances. Please contact the police as soon as possible, on telephone number ....'

'No answer then?' Terry asked.

'No sir, just voice mail.'

'All right. Let's check the boot.'

Like the rest of the car, the boot was unlocked. Terry opened it, and the two detectives studied it for a while, conscious all the time of the older man peering between them. Like the interior of the car, it was clean with a pale blue carpet. The only contents were a plastic folded umbrella with a pink handle, and a reusable shopping bag from Morrisons, with pictures of fruit on the side.

'I always forget to do that,' Terry said wryly.

'What's that, sir?' Jane asked.

'Take my own shopping bag. Always mean to, always forget. You're destroying the planet, Dad, my kids say. Hello, what's this?' As he picked the bag up, a trickle of water flowed out of it onto the carpet that lined the car boot. 'Where did that come from?'

Apart from the water, the bag was empty. He felt the carpet gently with his fingers. It seemed damp all over, not just where the water had flowed. He looked at Jane.

'That's strange, isn't it?'

'There was that big storm last night, sir,' Jane said. 'Maybe the boot leaks.'

'What, on a flash car like this? No chance. Unless it was left open. And even then ... that would be odd in itself.'

He closed the boot thoughtfully, and glanced at Robert Deacon. 'All right, sir, I agree, this does look suspicious. We'll take a few details from you, if we may, in case we need a statement. Jane, ring the station to see if we can get someone down here to secure this car as a crime scene. While you're doing that, I'll just take a look by the river. And then we need to find out more about the owner, Mrs Victoria Weston ... '

5. Interview

'IN HERE sir, if you please.'

Detective Sergeant Starkey ushered Bob Newby into a room with a table bolted to the floor, four chairs, and two windows high up on opposite walls. Bob took one of the chairs, with Lucy Parsons beside him. Starkey and another man, DC Keith Nixon, sat opposite.

Bob stared straight ahead, stunned; Lucy looked around, all her senses alert. Through one window she could glimpse spiders' webs, dust, and a distant blue sky; in the other was a smooth pane of clear dark glass behind which, she guessed, were a number of other officers and a camera watching and recording each word, reaction and facial expression.

She hoped so; she had something to say.

DS Starkey took two sealed audio cassettes from a box, tore open the wrapping, and inserted them into a recorder fixed to the wall at the end of the table. 'Ancient technology, Mr Newby, I apologise,' he said with a flash of his smile. 'The police service is starved of funds so we're still back in 1980s. Not like all the hi–tech stuff you have in school classrooms today, eh?'

Bob Newby stared at him blankly. Then, practising the advice Lucy had given him, he said 'No comment.'

Starkey sighed and raised an eyebrow. 'Just a friendly remark, sir, we haven't started yet.' He pressed *record*. 'Now we have. Interview begins at 11.13 a.m., Harrogate Police Station, North Yorkshire. Present in the room are myself, Detective Sergeant Starkey, Detective Constable Nixon, Mr Robert Edwin Newby, and his solicitor Mrs Lucy Parsons. As you know, Mr Newby, you have been arrested in connection with two allegations of sexual assault.'

He repeated the words of the caution. 'At the end of this interview these audio tapes will be sealed and one given to your solicitor. Now ...'

'Before we start,' Lucy interrupted firmly. 'I would like to ask something. I understand my client has been arrested in connection with two allegations about events in 1991, twenty five years ago. Why was he arrested at 4.30 a.m?'

'Why ...?' Starkey stared at her. 'Because we needed to be sure he was at home, Mrs Parsons. That is normal procedure.'

'For common burglars and thieves, maybe. My client is a respected professional man in his fifties, a head teacher with no criminal record whatsoever. Did you think he was going to run away? This arrest has probably terrified his partner and her children, quite unnecessarily. Why didn't you simply invite him to call at a police station? This arrest was a deliberate public humiliation and you know it.'

Starkey scowled, his left hand wavering towards the cassette recorder as though he would like to switch it off. *Too late, boyo*, Lucy thought. *I'm wise to your tricks.* She could easily have protested about this earlier, but had deliberately waited until the interview was being recorded. On video too, probably. *Let's hear your answer to this, then.*

Starkey drew a deep breath, regaining his composure. 'These are very serious allegations, Mrs Parsons. As you say, your client is a head teacher in a large primary school, who until this morning was responsible for several hundred vulnerable young children. We have only received two complaints from victims so far, but this investigation, *Operation Hazel*, is in its early stages. There is every possibility that further victims may come forward, giving information about more recent offences, perhaps even from children at this school. We needed to take action to safeguard them as soon possible.'

Lucy and Bob stared at him. Both were shocked, but for different reasons.

For Bob, the suggestion that the police suspected him of harming the children at his own school was appalling, an outrageous insult. But at the same time he knew that this was exactly what the parents of the children would fear, the moment they heard why he had been arrested. The detective, he realised, had spoken of his job in the past tense. A man *who until this morning* was responsible for hundreds of children. Of course, he thought desperately, he's right. My career is over now. As soon as this news gets out, I'll never go back to work again.

He had only been allowed one phone call this morning, so he hadn't been able to call his deputy to explain why he wasn't coming in. Anyway he'd had no idea what to say. He'd asked Sonya to make an excuse but he doubted that would last five minutes. And if that neighbour who'd taken a photo of him being loaded into the police van had posted it on the internet, well ... that would be it.

He felt stunned, shell-shocked. *I used to be* a head teacher, he thought. Not any more. The detective said *was*.

Lucy Parsons was shocked for a slightly different reason. She was so annoyed that she found it difficult to formulate her words.

'I'm sorry,' she muttered, leaning forward across the table. She raised a hand towards DS Starkey, to retain the initiative, stop him speaking. 'Did I understand you correctly? Are you saying you deliberately arrested my client in this provocative way in order to create publicity to invite further allegations? Ones that haven't been made yet?'

'That is a possible result, I suppose.' DS Starkey shrugged, as though it hadn't occurred to him.

'This is a fishing expedition! You have nothing at all against my client from recent times.'

'That remains to be seen. As I said, until yesterday Mr Newby was in daily contact with a large number of potentially vulnerable children. Our job is to protect the public. Now if you don't mind, Mrs Parsons, I'd like to proceed with the interview. Mr Newby, you have read the disclosure sheet with the two allegations on it. The first is from a 39 year old woman called Claire Fanshawe. You were her teacher in 1991, she says. Do you remember her?'

'No. Of course not. It was over twenty years ago.'

Lucy shook her head. She was still appalled by the whole situation. *Bob Newby, a paedophile?* It didn't bear thinking about. But anyway, she had made her protest on tape and camera and the police were ignoring it. So now she had to guide her client through the minefield of questions over the next few hours, however long it took. She had advised him to say as little as possible. Unfortunately, like most teachers, he was not only naturally talkative but in her opinion, fairly naive.

'This may help you.' DS Starkey pushed two photographs across the table. The first was a typical school photograph, several hundred pupils sitting on chairs and benches facing the camera. In the front row sat a number of teachers. The photograph was mounted in a frame which bore the caption *Wellborough Comprehensive School 1991*.

'Is that you, sitting in the front row, third from the right?'

Bob peered at the photo. The man DS Starkey was pointing at was thin, with a full head of unruly hair and very dark full beard. He wore a Harris tweed sports jacket with several pens sticking out of the top pocket, and was grinning happily at the camera. *So long ago, he thought, in another world. I am the same person, yet totally different.*

'That's me, yes.'

'You were employed as an English teacher at that school, were you?'

'Yes. I only worked there for a couple of years. Then I left to retrain as a primary school teacher.'

'Why was that?'

Bob shrugged. 'I prefer younger children.'

No, don't say that. Lucy touched his arm in warning.

'In what way, sir?' DS Starkey smiled encouragingly.

'Well, they're more spontaneous, uninhibited. You can be more creative, get to know them better. Not in the way you mean, obviously,' he added hurriedly.

'Oh? What way is that, sir?'

Bob glared, realising he had been tricked. *Already.* 'You know very well what you meant. I have no *sexual* interest in children whatsoever, and never have had.'

'I see. Interesting that your mind jumped so quickly to that, sir. Is that something you feel strongly about?'

'Of course it is. It's revolting.'

'I see. And that would be the same for children of any age, would it? I mean, would you feel the same sexual attraction – or lack of it – towards a child of say, ten years old, as you would towards a young girl of fifteen?'

Bob thought about the question. In more academic circumstances it might have provoked an interesting discussion, but here it was clearly a threat. Remembering Lucy's advice, he said, 'No comment.'

'You don't see any difference between the sexual attractiveness of a child of ten and a young girl of fifteen, then, sir? They're both the same to you?'

'No comment.' Bob glanced at Lucy, following her advice, then changed his mind. 'Oh for heaven's sake, man, of course it's not the same!'

'Really? Could you elaborate on that for me, please sir?'

Bob sighed. 'Obviously a girl of fifteen is more sexually mature than a child of ten. That's common sense.'

'Sexually mature, you say. I understand. So in your case, sir, would you say you find fifteen year old school girls attractive, then? More attractive than girls of ten?'

'I'm sorry, I'm not going to answer that question. You're trying to make me say things you can twist to look bad. I am not and never have been sexually attracted to any of my pupils, of any age whatsoever.'

'Very well, sir. That's clear then.' The detective pointed to another figure, a smiling girl's face in the back row of the school photograph. 'Do you recognise that person?'

Bob peered, shook his head. 'No.'

'All right, what about this?' He passed over a smaller photograph, an individual portrait of a pretty dark–haired girl in school uniform. She had turned slightly sideways on to the camera, looking over her shoulder with her chin turned down, her eyes peering up in a seductive way she had probably copied from a magazine. 'Do you recognise her?'

'No.'

'That is a photo of Clare Fanshawe. It was taken at the same time as the other photo, when she was fifteen years old and a pupil in your English class. She's a pretty girl. Are you sure you don't remember her?'

'Look, Detective – what's your name, Starkey, isn't it? I have spent a long career in the teaching profession, during which I have taught literally thousands of young people. I can't be expected to remember them all, can I?'

'No sir, I understand that. But I thought you might remember this young lady, because she remembers you. I've spoken to her, you see, and she remembers you very clearly. You told her she was a good student, she says, you gave her high marks for her essays. You asked her to stay behind several times in the classroom at the end of the school day to talk about poetry and literature. She liked you, she says, in fact she admits she developed what she now calls a schoolgirl crush. Surely you'd remember something like that, Mr Newby, wouldn't you?'

Bob stared at him, shaking his head slowly. 'Not necessarily, no. It's not that uncommon, after all, for a pupil to have a crush on a young teacher. Especially teenage girls.'

'Oh, I see. So are you saying you attracted this sort of attention from a lot of young girls? They saw you as a sort of pop star, did they?'

'Don't be ridiculous, you're twisting things again. Of course I encouraged pupils from time to time and talked to them individually about their work. I'm a teacher, that's part of my job. It's nothing to do with sex.'

'But you admit some of them might have had a crush on you? Found you sexually attractive?'

'Possibly.' Bob shrugged. 'I don't think it's very likely. After all I don't exactly look like Mick Jagger.'

'Not everyone would say *he's* handsome either,' Starkey smiled briefly. 'It's a mystery, sexual attractiveness. But anyway, you were aware that some of these girls found you attractive? You must have enjoyed that.'

Bob drew a deep breath, trying to keep his temper. Negotiating his way through these questions was like dodging tripwires in a minefield. He understood more clearly now why Lucy had advised him to say 'no comment.' But that made him sound guilty, somehow, as though he had something to hide. He wanted to explain; if he answered honestly surely these men would see that they were making a hideous mistake.

'Look, I might have enjoyed it a little, perhaps. I was young, it was all so long ago. But if I did enjoy it, I was also embarrassed. Every teacher experiences something like that occasionally, it comes with the job. You just have to discourage it, pretend you haven't noticed. And that's what I did at that school. Nothing else.'

'I see. So you may have had this slightly sexual – what shall we say? – flirtatious relationship with a number of pupils? Is that what you're saying?'

'No. You're twisting it again. I didn't say that.'

DS Starkey looked down for a moment at the photograph of the teenage girl, smiling in her naive seductive way at the camera. 'It's quite a striking photograph, isn't it? Are you sure you don't remember this particular girl, Clare Fanshawe?'

'No, I'm sorry, I don't. Look, Mr Starkey, I don't know how many people you see in a day but in my job as a secondary school teacher I taught about a hundred and twenty different children each week. It's very difficult to learn all their names in a job like that, let alone have a meaningful relationship with each child. That's one of the reasons I left to become a primary school teacher, where I had just one class of thirty pupils. You get a much closer relationship that way.'

'I see. Well, perhaps we're getting to the heart of the problem here. You see this Clare Fanshawe, she says that's exactly what you were looking for with her too. A relationship. At first she thought you were keeping her behind just to praise her school work, but what you really wanted was something different altogether. A sexual relationship, Mr Newby. She says that on two occasions you put your arm around her, touched her intimately, and forced her to give you sexual relief with her hand. Then later you raped her in your flat.'

'No!' Bob shook his head vigorously. 'This is nonsense, I never did anything like that!'

'Really? So what *did* you do then, Mr Newby?'

'Nothing! It's all nonsense, it never happened!'

'But you did praise this girl and encourage her work? Kept her behind after school?'

'Only to talk about her school work. Nothing else.'

'So you do remember her now?'

'No, I didn't say that either. If she was a pupil in my English class it's possible I encouraged her and talked to her about her school work. But I'm sorry, I don't remember her name or her face.'

'That's quite insulting, isn't it?'

'It's not meant to be. It's a simple fact.'

'But you do admit that's the sort of thing you did with a lot of girls. Girls who may have found you sexually attractive? You kept them behind and talked to them individually about their work? Just you and a young girl alone together in a classroom?'

'It wasn't just girls – there were boys too, obviously. And the classroom door was probably open, that's certainly what we're advised to do. Now.'

'Oh, it was different back then, was it? In 1991?'

Bob sighed. 'I was young then, that's what was different. When you're young, you don't think anything like this is going to happen to you.'

Detective Sergeant Starkey contemplated Bob calmly for a moment. There were tiny beads of sweat, he noticed, under his hairline. His face was pale, with bright spots of colour in his cheeks. We're getting there, he thought. It won't be long now.

'All right, Mr Newby. Let's turn to the statement of your second victim, shall we? Eleanor Wisbech. Remember her?'

6. Tom Weston

FOLLOWING UP the case of the abandoned Mercedes, Terry Bateson and Jane Carter decided to visit the owner's home.

Straw House Barn, Osbaldwick, turned out to be a large two storey building set back from the village street down a farm track. For the first fifty yards the track was fully tarmaced with no potholes; after the house a muddy track continued into the countryside. Outside the house an ornamental wall flanked a pair of black and gold wrought iron gates which stood invitingly open. Terry drove straight through and pulled up with a satisfying crunch on the gravelled parking area beside a dark green Range Rover.

He got out and stood beside the car for a moment, looking around. In the middle of the parking area was a circular ornamental pond with a stone statue of a naked mermaid kneeling on a plinth in the middle. A steady stream of water issued from a jug which she clasped coyly between her breasts, while a snail crawled slowly across her face. Large goldfish flickered between water lilies in the pond below. The two storey brick built building behind, the length of five or six terraced houses, featured a central arch, wide enough in its former life for cattle and large farm machinery, which had been filled in up to roof height with double glazed windows and a glass door.

Terry knocked, marvelling at the huge candelabra, made out of a wagon wheel, which hung down from the roof in the stone flagged hall he could see inside. The man who answered the door was tall and thin, in his early fifties, Terry guessed, from the way his sandy hair was beginning to recede. He wore a crumpled white shirt, tieless, with black suit trousers over which a male paunch was beginning to bulge. He had a short goatee beard in the centre of which his lips were set in a thin, unwelcoming line.

'Mr Weston?'

'Yes. I'm Tom Weston. Who are you?'

'Detective Inspector Bateson, York CID.' Terry showed his card. 'And this is Detective Sergeant Jane Carter. We're looking for Mrs Victoria Weston. Is she at home?'

'No, I'm afraid she's out. What the devil do you want with her?'

'Would you mind if we came inside?'

The man thought about it, then shrugged. 'If you must.' He stepped back and they followed him through the hall to a kitchen, in which they saw an ironing board with a large pile of un-ironed clothes heaped on top of it, uneaten food and unwashed dishes beside the sink, and what looked like fragments of broken china scattered all over the floor. A piece of it crunched under Mr Weston's foot.

'So. Why do you ask about my wife?'

'Mrs Victoria Weston – she does live here?'

'Of course she does. When she's at home.' The man's eyes met Terry's in a cold, unfriendly gaze. 'But you've come at a bad time, I'm afraid. What's she done – broken the speed limit?'

'No sir, not so far as we're aware. Does she own a powder blue Mercedes, registration KW998XP?'

'Yes, that's her car. Why?'

Jane Carter explained where the car had been found. The first hint of worry appeared on the man's face, but what sort of worry was it? Concern? Anxiety? Fear?

'Oh God. It's true then.'

'What do you mean, sir? What's true?'

Tom Weston sighed, scowling at her as though he would have preferred talking to a man. 'I might as well tell you, constable – what did you say your name was?'

'Detective Sergeant Jane Carter, sir.'

'Yes, well ... Detective Sergeant, eh? Congratulations. And your boss is an Inspector, no less? This must be serious. Well, it probably is.'

'It's about your wife, sir,' Jane persisted. 'We're trying to trace her.'

'Yes. Well unfortunately, Detective Sergeant, my wife's movements are as much of a mystery to me as they seem to be to you. I may be her lawful wedded husband but that situation is ... unlikely to last much longer. To say nothing of her mental state.'

'What do you mean, sir?'

His voice rose to a sudden shout. 'What do I mean? Just look around you – DO YOU SEE THIS HOUSE? You notice what a terrible mess it's in, do you? It's not the ideal home, is it? Not what a man might like to come home to after a weekend away? Pictures, books everywhere, broken china, dirty clothes, washing up not done! And where is the person who might be expected to do something about this, clean it all up? Parking her powder blue Mercedes down by the river, for Christ's sake! Where no doubt she screwed her latest lover on the back seat before taking him for a romantic walk to ... wherever she's gone! Talking about poetry before she fucks him behind a bush somewhere.'

'I'm sorry to hear that, sir,' Terry said carefully, as the outburst ended. 'But we need to be sure that Mrs Weston is all right, that's all. You're quite sure you don't know where she is?'

'No, I've been away in Scotland, at a conference. I only just got home about an hour ago.'

'So when was the last time you saw your wife, sir?'

'On Friday.'

'Did you speak to her while you were away? Send her a text or email?'

Tom Weston closed his eyes, and when he opened them he looked away from Terry, gazing past him at something outside the window. When he spoke he seemed less angry than nervous.

'Yes, I spoke to her once. Last night, as it happens, about seven o'clock.'

'I see. Was she ok then?'

'So far I could tell, yes. She seemed fine.'

'What did you speak about?'

Tom Weston sighed. 'Look, as I already told you, officer, we didn't part on the best of terms. I guess our marriage is going through what they call a bad patch; anyway, we had a quarrel before I left. When she rang me last night the quarrel started all over again.'

'What was that quarrel about, sir?'

'One of her students. She'd been screwing him behind my back. It happens all the time, she can't help herself. Anyway I caught her texting a message to this little wanker just as I was leaving, on Friday morning. Then it all kicked off. That's how some of this china got broken, things were thrown about. I would have thought she would make an effort to clear it up, but apparently not.'

'So she rang you? About seven, you say? Was that the last contact you had with her?'

A strange look crossed the man's face; an expression that Terry would try to recall and interpret more than once in the days to come. His lips twisted in a grim sardonic smile, yet at the same time Terry saw, or imagined, something quite different in the eyes that met his. Anxiety, grief, or was it fear, perhaps?

'Well no, not quite.'

'What d you mean by that, sir?'

The man let out another, deeper sigh. He dragged a phone out of his pocket. 'You asked if she'd sent any texts. Here, you'd better look at this.'

Terry took the phone, a small, black Nokia. On the tiny screen he read the message: *Everything ends and this is how it is for me. Love turns to hatred, hope to despair. No understanding, no one cares. Let the river wash away the pain.*

Received 21.37.07
28.08.2016
From Vicky.

A cold shiver went through him. It confirmed what he had expected. 'This is from your wife, sir?'

'Vicky? Yes. Hysterical nonsense I thought when I saw it at first. But now you come to me with this story about her car ... it begins to make some sense, doesn't it?'

'You received this message last night, did you sir? At 9.37?'

'Is that what it says on the screen? No actually, I didn't see it till this morning, when I was already on the train. I know it seems strange in this digital age, but I often ignore the damn thing. Still, when I did get the message I tried to call her, of course. *Number unobtainable,* it says. *Please try later.*'

'This looks a bit like a suicide note,' Jane Carter said cautiously.

'I do realise that, sergeant, I can read. Don't you think I'd have done something if I'd seen it before? I mean, look at it! *No understanding, no one cares.* Typical self-dramatising nonsense – poor tragic little me, no one cares so I'll do away with myself just to make everyone feel bad! It could be written by a teenager, couldn't it, not a grown–up woman, an academic. I suppose she's imitating those self–pitying feminist authors she reads. Thank God I never saw it before; it would have ruined my weekend.'

'So you don't take it seriously, sir, is that what you mean?'

'Well, I didn't at first. But now you're here, telling me about her car, it begins to looks more serious, doesn't it?'

Jane flipped open her notebook. 'Has she ever talked about killing herself before, sir?'

Tom Weston glared at her. 'Oh God, yes. She's always trying tricks like this, emotional blackmail I call it. I should have seen what was coming, and called in a psychiatrist, I suppose. But what sort of advice could he give her, eh? Keep your knickers on in front of your students? Only this time, if she's actually done it ...'

'We don't know that yet, sir. We've only found her car. Perhaps if you tell us her phone number ...'

'Yes, help yourselves, it's on there.'

Terry copied the number into his own phone and rang it. But just as her husband had said, he got nowhere. *'The person you are calling is unable to take your call at this time. Please try later.'*

'All right, sir. Is there anyone else you think we might contact? Friends, family – someone she might have gone to stay with, perhaps?'

'Family, no, not very likely. Her mother lives in London, but they don't get on, haven't spoken for years. Her father left, took up with a woman in Germany. She has one brother, Ranolph – he had a good job in the City, gave it up to work on a sheep farm on the Orkney Islands. Tosser. She hates animals, she'd never go there.'

'What about friends?'

'Oh sure, she's got plenty of those. Colleagues at the university, mainly, academics teaching literature. But which one of them she'd run to for sympathy after a row with me, I couldn't tell you. If you had her phone, of course, you could check her address book. But she's probably taken that with her, hasn't she? And she'd never let me see it, anyway. Guards it with her life.'

An unfortunate phrase, in the circumstances, Terry thought.

'You said earlier, sir,' Jane said. 'You thought she might have a lover. Any idea who that might be?'

Tom Weston scowled. 'If I knew, I might do something about it. But it'll be one of her wretched students, it always is. Ask around at the university, they'll know. Everyone probably knows except me.'

'All right sir,' Terry said. 'If she doesn't turn up by tomorrow we will. But in the meantime, we'll take a careful look at her car. Maybe that will tell us something.'

If it hasn't already, he thought. Missing woman, abandoned car, suicide message, fast flowing river. What's obvious is probably true.

* * *

Driving back to the station, Terry and Jane discussed the interview. Neither of them had liked the man much, but they were used to dealing with difficult people; it was part of the job. Still, Terry thought, if a man's wife was missing, you'd expect him to show more concern, less anger.

'Not a happy marriage,' he murmured drily. 'Poor woman. Perhaps he drove her to it somehow.'

'Maybe,' Jane answered. 'I might top myself too, if I was married to him.'

Terry glanced at her, wondering, not for the first time, if anyone would ever want to marry his colleague. She had been part of the team for over a year now, and he respected her as a hardworking professional. But her large, bony physique, big masculine hands, and most of all her hearty contempt for the male sex made it hard to imagine any man being sexually attracted to her.

He grinned. 'You'd throw the crockery too, would you?'

He knew it was a mistake as soon as the words were out of his mouth. Jane didn't do teasing. She frowned.

'How do we know that it was her that threw it, anyway? It might have been him. Maybe he beat her, that's why she did it.'

'Possibly,' Terry acknowledged. 'I'll run a check, see if she ever rang 999. But even if he is a wife batterer, he was in Scotland, wasn't he? Or so he says. Check that too.' He had noted down the name of the hotel in Edinburgh, and the conference Tom Weston claimed to have been attending: *Global Trends in Secondary Education*. A quick phone call to the hotel confirmed that this did indeed exist, and Tom Weston had taken up his reservation. He'd checked in at the hotel on Friday 26th, and checked out on Monday.

Back at his desk in the station, Terry took his next decision, about the car.

To his surprise the husband had not offered to collect it – perhaps he had no keys – and now he was glad of that. If the woman had disappeared that car was a crime scene that had to be preserved. But it couldn't just be left where it was: some kids had tried to nick the radio already. He picked up the phone and arranged for it to be transported to a police garage for forensic examination.

Then he rang the underwater search team. A woman was missing, her car had been found by the river, he told them. Would they be able to mount a search in the morning?

They would see what they could do, sergeant Lofthouse replied without enthusiasm. The Ouse was full at the moment, after the storm the other night, and if he had no definite witnesses who'd seen someone enter the water ...

That was it, Terry thought. This could be something or nothing. There was the woman's phone – he asked Jane to see if the phone company could trace calls and texts over the past few days. But that would take a day or two. In the meantime, presumably this Victoria Weston had friends and colleagues at her place of work – the university, her husband had said, she was a lecturer in English Literature – but by now, 6 p.m., they would all be at home with their wives and families.

Which is where I should be, Terry thought, thinking warmly of his two daughters and their Norwegian nanny, Trude. She had promised her special pancakes tonight, a family favourite, he remembered. And when the children are in bed, perhaps I'll phone Sarah. See if I can arrange something for this weekend.

Victoria Weston can wait till tomorrow, he decided.

7. Home from Home

'SO HOW did it go? Tell me!'

Sonya was waiting at the door as Bob Newby came home. He felt a brief surge of relief that she was still there, ready to offer comfort. But then he saw the pain and anxiety in her face and realised how much this morning's events had hurt her. He feared things might never be the same again.

She hugged him briefly on the doorstep, then turned and went swiftly inside. Bob followed, imagining the twitch of curtains in houses opposite. Lucy Parsons had driven him home, so there were no more police cars or flashing lights; but they had been here for much of the morning, carrying away bags of possessions for 'evidence'; and he saw inside how what they had left was strewn randomly in every room. Books and pictures were scattered on tables and sofas; shelves once full of DVDs and old videocassettes were half empty; Sonya's desktop computer, the one her children used for homework, was gone, leaving a gap like a missing tooth between the screen and printer which still remained.

'Where are the kids?' Bob asked as they came into the kitchen.

'They've gone to my mum's. I phoned her, she came here this morning.'

'Oh. So she knows too, then?'

'Everyone knows, Bob. The police were hardly discreet.' Sonya gazed at him, her face softening at the evident signs of strain. 'Was it really terrible?'

'About as bad as it could be. That solicitor, Lucy Parsons, helped a bit.'

She filled the kettle, switched it on. 'Tell me.'

Bob slumped in a chair and leaned forward, his elbows on the kitchen table, running his hands through his hair. 'Well, as you see, they let me go. I'm released on police bail until 10th November.'

'What does that mean?'

'It means I haven't been charged, they're just investigating. On the 10th November I have to go back to the police station to see if they've found enough evidence to go ahead with the charges. Or let me go, I suppose.'

'Charge you with what, exactly?'

Bob sighed. 'It's all nonsense. It's all about two teenage girls – well they're not girls now, obviously, but they were when I taught them. Ages ago in 1991, it's ridiculous. Anyway, they've made these statements, apparently ...' He handed her a folded sheet of paper. 'Here.'

The kettle boiled unheeded as she read. A cloud of steam drifted between them until it clicked off. Sonya glared at the paper as though furious with its contents.

'But this is terrible! It's not true, is it? Any of it?'

'No. None of it's true.'

'Thank God for that.'

She turned to the kettle, busied herself making tea. As she put a mug of tea in front of him she asked: 'Did you know these girls?'

'I was at the school when they were there. I probably taught them. I don't remember them, though.'

'My God.' She sat at the kitchen table opposite him, a mug of tea in front of her. 'You poor man.' Her right hand reached across, squeezed his arm tentatively, then fluttered back. She gazed at him, the strain in her eyes terrible to see. 'Bob, tell me. Is this true? Honestly.'

'None of it's true. Not a single word.' He studied her, watched her retreating hands seek comfort around the hot mug of tea. The response was not what he had hoped. For a second, unwanted, the memory came into his mind of Sarah's hands, his ex–wife's. He had lived with her for over twenty years before he met Sonya. He'd known Sarah's hands like his own. But he had rejected her, thrown her away.

'I didn't do this, Sonya,' he said, as firmly as his tired voice could manage. 'You must believe me.'

'Of course, if you say so, I do.' She attempted a smile, then shook her head despairingly. 'What happens now?'

'We wait, I suppose, until the police realise their mistake. That solicitor, Lucy Parsons, said she'd find out what she could. It'll cost money, of course. Legal fees.' He sipped his tea. 'What did you tell them at school?'

'The truth. What else could I say? There were eight policemen here, Bob, searching the house until lunchtime. Everyone in the street could see them.

There was even a reporter from the *Yorkshire Post*. He said it'll be in the paper tomorrow.'

'Oh God!' Bob buried his face in his hands, then got up and strode to the window and back, four manic, furious paces. The kitchen was no bigger than the police cell he had been in earlier. 'What did you say, for heaven's sake?'

'Just told him our names, who we are. The police may have said more, I don't know.'

'That's it then. My career is definitely ruined – over. I'll never be allowed inside any school again.'

'That's not my fault. You can't blame me for that!'

'No.' Bob drew a deep long breath, trying to regain control. 'Of course I don't blame you, I never meant that. But ... it's not my fault either, don't you see!' He thumped the table, spilling hot tea from the mug. 'I didn't do this, damn it! It's totally unfair! This is going to ruin my life! Those wretched women are lying!'

He crumpled the disclosure sheet into a ball, and flung it across the room. 'Why is this happening?'

'Bob, stop it.'

A sudden rage consumed him. He flung open the kitchen door and strode into the back garden. But that didn't help; Sonya's neighbour, an elderly man in a flat cap, a keen gardener, eyed him curiously over the back fence.

'Evening, Mr Newby. Bit of a to–do with the police here this morning!'

'Yes. I'm sorry, I can't talk just now.'

Bob turned abruptly and strode back through the kitchen into the hall. As he did so the front doorbell rang, the same chime that had started the day.

Oh no, not again. If that's the police I'll tell them to ... Furious, he opened the door. Outside stood a pretty young woman with long dark hair. He thought he recognised her but wasn't sure how. She held a microphone in her hand. Behind her was a man with a video camera on his shoulder, pointed directly at Bob.

'Good evening, Mr Newby. BBC local television, *Look North*. I was hoping you could give us an interview ...'

* * *

'So, what happened? Tell me.'

Lucy Parsons had called in at Sarah's flat on her way home. The flat was on the third floor of a block of new apartments on the banks of the river Ouse, just south of Skeldergate Bridge. It had two bedrooms, kitchen, bathroom and a moderate size living room with a balcony overlooking the river. To Sarah it seemed small, almost like a suite of hotel rooms if you compared it to the detached house she had once shared with Bob; but everything was luxuriously appointed and it was the best she could afford on her single income. *If* she could afford it, that is; the mortgage was draining her bank account every month, a constant leak she could only plug by more work.

Otherwise, she would have to find somewhere cheaper.

They sat outside on the balcony, sipping orange juice and enjoying the view. A jogger passed under the trees on the opposite bank; a little red motorboat, hired by tourists, puttered slowly upstream towards the city; beyond the elegant Victorian bridge, the white walls of York's medieval castle, Clifford's tower, reflected the light of the declining sun.

'Well, he's been released on police bail until 10th November,' Lucy said. 'He denied everything, of course.'

'Yes, but denied what exactly, Luce? For heaven's sake, what do they think he has done?'

'Well, there are two allegations.' Lucy studied her friend thoughtfully, wondering how much she could say. 'Look, I probably shouldn't tell you too much. The police will be making further investigations, they told me. They may well come knocking on your door. They didn't forbid me to talk to you but ...'

'On *my* door? Why?'

'Well, you were married to him, weren't you? They'll see you as a character witness. The best possible, presumably. If *you* don't know about his sexual tastes, who does?'

'Well, quite,' Sarah said dryly. 'So what are we talking about here?'

Briefly, Lucy told Sarah about the allegations. 'It all happened in 1991, they say. Were you married to him then?'

Sarah thought back. 'No. No, we married in 1992, on my 18th birthday. I met him in 1991, though, the last part of it. Which months did they say, exactly?'

Lucy told her.

'That was when we were getting to know each other. He was still a secondary school teacher, and I was doing my GCSEs at evening classes.'

'Did he show any interest in schoolgirls then?'

'Well, I was only seventeen myself.'

The two women's eyes met, as a similar thought occurred to them both. A cold, horrible suspicion was trying to insinuate itself into Sarah's mind. But she pushed it back out, closed the door firmly.

'He was very kind, understanding, thoughtful. I was an emotional wreck, after all. I needed help and he gave it. He was never at all pushy or trying it on. It wasn't really about sex. We spent a lot of time talking together; him listening to me and all my troubles with mum and Kevin, and then telling me about books and literature, stuff I was supposed to be studying. We didn't even have sex until ... well, a month before we married, I suppose.'

'Not in a classroom, I suppose?'

'Good heavens, no! It was at his place, a flat he had somewhere. It wasn't that great, not like with Kevin. It was just – I was so glad to find someone who was kind, who cared for me, and Bob did care. Back then.'

Sarah fell silent, remembering the teenager she had been all those years ago. *I was so young then, she thought, we both were. Are we still the same people, or does time change everything?*

'You never had any suspicions?'

'About Bob being a paedophile? No! For Christ's sake, Lucy, that's just ... ridiculous.' She met Lucy's eyes, shook her head vigorously, then turned away, staring at the trees across the river. 'Although ...' she murmured softly.

'Although what, lovey?' Lucy asked, when no more words came.

'Well ... I was only a teenager myself, when we met. Not much more than a schoolgirl, really, a young mother with a baby. And it was very flattering, to have an older man take an interest in me like that. You remember what it was like, Luce, when we were young. Didn't you ever have a crush on a teacher?'

'Oh yes.' Lucy smiled, remembering. 'Dai Williams, it was, our PE teacher. Welsh rugby international. The whole class swooned when he came in.'

'Well there you are, exactly. And you probably came on to him in any way you could, just to get noticed.'

'Of course. He even put his arms round me once, just for a second. It was on the main school staircase. We were going down and I tripped, accidentally on purpose, falling towards him. He caught me quick as a flash before I fell. Saved me from a broken leg. He blushed, too. The whole class was dying of jealousy for weeks! I still dream about it now.'

'Lucy Parsons! You wicked girl! I had no idea!'

'Oh, I was a tearaway back then.'

'Well, Bob was no rugby hero, but you see my point. I was seventeen and I felt flattered by his attention, honourable as it was. So young schoolgirls of fifteen, full of teenage hormones, might have behaved as badly as you. Probably did – he wasn't that bad-looking. So he probably faced some temptations.'

'No doubt,' Lucy said. 'He admitted that this morning. Said it was an occupational hazard, it happened to most teachers now and then.'

'But that's a million miles away from actually abusing his pupils,' Sarah said. 'I can't believe it. He may be stupid about a lot of things, but not that. It's just not like him.'

But then, he was a different person back then, a little voice whispered in her mind. We all were. *Look how naughty and randy I was, with Kevin.* A string of delightful, lustful memories flooded into her mind, and were dismissed as swiftly as they had come. They're not relevant, Sarah told herself sternly, not to Bob.

'What can have possessed these girls?' she asked. 'Grown women they must be now. Why make these accusations now, after all these years?'

'There's been all this publicity,' Lucy said. 'The world's changed, since the Jimmy Savile case. The police are encouraging victims to come forward, telling them they'll be believed.'

'Yes, but why Bob? He's not a pop star or TV personality. Why would they think of him?'

'Because they knew him, I suppose. He was a teacher at the school when they were there. If it's true it all makes sense. It's only if it's not true that it's a mystery.'

'But it can't be true. I don't believe it!'

'Well, good. I agree, it seems wildly out of character. But you know him better than I do. Just tell the police that when they ask.'

Sarah shook her head, despairingly. 'Oh Bob, Bob. I thought I'd got the wretched man out of my life and now this! Just when I've got a new man, too.'

'Sarah?' Lucy put her glass down on the little table between them, almost spilling it in surprise. 'You're a dark horse! Who is it?'

Sarah felt herself flushing with mingled pleasure and embarrassment. She hadn't meant to blurt the news out like that; it was a sign, perhaps, of her current fragile state of mind. Still, having started ...

'Terry Bateson. You remember, the detective.'

'Oh yes. Tall, handsome, rugged. But he has two children, hasn't he?'

'True. But I'm not ... necessarily planning to be a stepmother, Lucy. It's not gone that far, not yet anyway.'

'So how far *has* it gone? Come on, lovey, don't blush! You have to tell me now – I won't leave until you do.'

'Well ...' And so for the next half hour Sarah confessed to some, if not all, of the intimate details of her new relationship.

8. Therapy

IT WAS a confession in confidence; Lucy was her best, if not her only, female friend at work, and she was a lawyer too, used to keeping secrets. And having blurted it out, Sarah found delight and relief in the telling. It was a relief to think about this, instead of the disaster with Bob.

The affair, if that's what it was, had started a week ago, after a court case, one Sarah had lost. It had only been a brief trial, lasting half a morning, and her client had been guilty as hell. Sarah had done her best but the result had never been in doubt. On her way out of court she had been accosted by her client's girlfriend, who blocked her way, refusing to let her pass.

'Fat lot of use you were! You ought to be struck off! Useless cow.'

The confrontation had last less than a minute before the security guard cleared her way, but it had left Sarah unaccountably shaken. Outside the court her wheeled briefcase, the one she used to carry her files, slipped from her hand and fell clattering down the steps where it was retrieved by two youths who had been smoking there. When she had thanked them, waving away the security guard's suggestion that she might wish to press charges of assault against the woman, Sarah had crossed the road by Clifford's Tower and sat on a bench in the riverside park.

She raised her hand in front of her. It can't be true, she thought, but it is. The hand was trembling. However hard she tried to hold it still, there was that slight, infinitesimal movement which she couldn't quite control. And there was a fluttering in her stomach too.

What's happening to me?

She knew, deep down, what it was. It was the result of her accident, six months ago, when she'd nearly been killed. Her lover, Michael, *had* been killed – murdered by Sarah's client, who'd then tried to murder her too. She would never forget those wild, terrifying moments as she fled from him on her motorbike, the icy wind slicing through her thin clothes as the murderer in the stolen BMW came ever closer, trying to catch her back wheel and force her off the road ... and then the crash, when she lay spread-eagled and stunned in the hedge, like a fly in a web, while the short powerful man strode towards her with murder in his eyes and the long metal spanner in his hand ...

The doctors in the hospital, six months ago, had warned her that this might happen. The broken arm and ribs would heal, they'd said, but her mind might take longer. Her counsellor had warned her about post-traumatic stress disorder too. But Sarah had refused to believe them. 'I'm not like that,' she'd said. 'I'll get over it, I'll be fine.'

'Maybe, let's hope so,' the consultant had said. 'But we're all different, no-one can be sure. The reaction can come back months, even years later. You've had a big shock after all, and the natural reaction of the body is to bury it, shut down all worries so you can survive. The fight or flight thing. Well, you've had a fight and flight, quite a big one, after all. A major shock to the system. So don't be surprised if you get some sort of reaction later, when you feel safe.'

And here she was sitting on a bench, her hand trembling, just because a stupid woman had sworn at her. *This isn't going to happen to me,* she told herself sternly. *I won't let it.*

It was then that her salvation had appeared. Perhaps – if that was who he was. Sarah laughed now, ironically, telling Lucy about this, aware of how feeble and feminine it sounded. Romantic, saved by a prince. But still, there were elements of truth, even in fairy tales. Weren't there?

'Hi.' A man's voice. Sarah had looked up, and seen a tall, handsome man in a loose-fitting double breasted suit.

'Oh, Terry. Hello.' They'd known each other for years; they were old colleagues and antagonists.

'Mind if I join you?'

'Be my guest.' She'd patted the bench beside her. 'What are you doing here?'

'Cameo appearance in Court Two. You?'

'Court One, burglary, defending. I lost.'

'Glad to hear it. One more villain locked away then. No peace for the wicked.'

Sarah shrugged. 'Well yes, in this case you're right. It doesn't feel great, though.' She smiled wryly, the trembling fingers subsiding.

'Same old Sarah. Battling for the bad guys. You should come over to us. Prosecute. Join the angels.'

'I do, when the CPS give me the chance.' Sarah sighed. 'This was my first moderately big case since ... you know.'

'Your accident. Yes.' Looking at her, Terry had felt a return of that same longing, the desire that she, almost alone among women, still woke in him. And with it, a surge of tenderness – the concern he had felt last year when she had almost died. He glanced at his watch. 'I'm not due back for an hour or two. How about lunch?'

'Well ...'

'Come on. Do you good. Me too.' He stood up and stretched out a hand. Why not, she thought, letting him pull her to her feet. I need some comfort, a friendly face. And Terry was an old friend and opponent in court. She had won cases for him on some days, and savaged him as a witness on others. He had alternately challenged her, rescued her, and put her in harm's way. They had a dramatic shared history. And he was handsome, too, in his tall, loose-limbed way.

They walked down to the quayside where several cafés were doing a busy trade. But just as they reached the first, a large coachload of excited chattering Japanese tourists came the other way. Sarah looked at the queue, the harassed, scurrying waiters, and had an idea.

'Look, my flat's just over the bridge. I've got bread, salmon, salad stuff. Why don't we go there? We can sit on my balcony and watch the river from there.'

'If you're sure?'

'Yes, why not? Even if we get a table here it'll take ages.'

They crossed Skeldergate Bridge, Sarah trundling her trolley behind her. It was not the first time Terry had been to her flat; he remembered a party six months ago, after the traumatic events which had led to the death of her lover, Michael Parker, and her own hairbreadth escape from his killer. Terry had played a part in that, first infuriating her by asking her to spy on the man she shared a bed with in case he was a murderer, and then helping her son to save her from certain death. The party had been to celebrate her release from hospital, with only a broken arm and several cracked ribs. He remembered how busy the flat had been that day; full of her lawyer friends, Sarah's son and daughter Simon and Emily, their partners, and his own daughters Jessica and

Esther, who had disgraced themselves by leaning over the balcony and dropping cake to the swans and humans below.

Now there were just the two of them.

Sarah bustled around in the kitchen, finding bread, butter, plates, smoked salmon, salad things. He offered to help her but the kitchen was too small really for two people, and he didn't know where things were. He bumped into her clumsily so that she almost dropped a plate.

'Ooops, sorry!'

He caught her arm to steady her and there was a moment when their faces were only inches apart and neither said anything. Then ...

'Look, Terry, there's a half empty bottle of wine in the fridge and the glasses are in that cupboard there. You take them out on the balcony and I'll bring the rest, okay?'

He obeyed, and the moment passed. A couple of minutes later she came out to join him. They sat on the balcony, a small garden table between them, looking out on the autumn leaves in the treetops over the river. A few hundred yards to the north across the bridge, they could see the Crown Court, the castle, Clifford's Tower, and the tourists milling like ants outside the cafés on the quay.

Sarah raised a glass, noting with relief that her hand was now steady. 'This is better, isn't it?'

'Much.' Terry smiled. 'You must love living here.'

'It seemed a good investment at the time.' Sarah wrinkled her nose. 'The question is, whether I can still afford it. I need the work, Terry, and that's not coming. It's okay for you, salaried civil servants.'

'The work will come. How are you, anyway?'

'Oh, so-so. Recovering.' She leaned back in her chair, stretching her arm over her head like a dancer. 'See? Perfect movement, almost. And it doesn't ache as much as it did, thank goodness.' She tapped her head. 'It's just inside here I feel a bit wobbly sometimes.'

'That doesn't sound like you.'

'Doesn't it? I have these dreams, Terry. Very colourful but ... not ideal.'

'Tell me.'

It was, it turned out, the right thing to say. Sarah was not naturally given to talking about herself; for most of her adult life she had been too driven, too focussed on her work to get in touch with her own emotions. But the events of the past few years had changed that. First she had had to deal with the shock of her son being charged with murder, and the possibility that he might be guilty.

Then her husband's infidelity, leading to their subsequent divorce and sale of their beloved family home, the treasured symbol of her success. Then, no sooner had she found a home and security with a new lover, Michael Parker, than she had seen him murdered almost in front of her.

Any one of these events, her awe-struck counsellor had gently explained, would have been enough to unbalance the strongest of women; so it was hardly surprising that Sarah had needed some therapy. She had initially been resistant to counselling, hoping that her own willpower would be enough, together with the amitriptyline prescribed by her GP to help her sleep. But reluctantly, she had been forced to admit that it wasn't so.

It was the nightmares that were the worst. She'd been embarrassed to admit that they were often about sex. It was that which led her into the dreams, which tempted her. Something in her mind seemed to crave it. And always, it went wrong.

The dreams were about Michael, not Bob. Sex with her husband had become a familiar, comfortable thing, no more exciting than wrapping herself in a favourite duvet – a security blanket whose every smell and crease she knew, and which sheltered her from the risks of the world outside. But Bob had left her. And in the shock of that desertion Sarah had rediscovered – not love, exactly, but the scary intoxicating thrill of emotions she had not known since she was sixteen. Sex with her new lover Michael had been exciting, dangerous, compulsive, and quite different from anything she had experienced with her husband. She still shuddered at the memory of that strange man, Michael: mesmerising, mysterious, demanding, domineering, and now – *dead.*

He still haunted her dreams at night – his smooth, muscular chest, his strong hands wrapping her in a towel as she climbed out of a steaming bath, his hands grasping her buttocks as he thrust into her, the seductive smile on his face shifting by stages into the grimace of ecstasy and then – *no please no not again* – morphing further into the rictus of the hanged man, face swollen, tongue lolling, bloodshot eyes bursting from their sockets ...

She had talked these nightmares through with her counsellor, who had mentioned post-traumatic stress disorder, and suggested a long break from work. A Mediterranean cruise maybe, a period of relaxation, reconstruction, pampering. 'But I'm self-employed,' Sarah had smiled wryly. 'I need to work to pay the rent.' Nonetheless, the talking therapy had helped, she thought. Slowly, she was returning to normal, though this morning's tremors outside court showed she was not there, not completely, not yet.

The counsellor was a woman, and discussing these sexual nightmares with her had helped, over time, to defuse them. Sometimes they laughed together; that helped quite a lot. So now, sitting in the afternoon sunshine on her balcony, Sarah felt confident enough to describe to Terry, a man, a polite, bowdlerised version of what she had felt. She hoped, expected, that he would laugh too. Which would be a further step on her road to recovery, a way to finally exorcise her demons.

He had laughed, a little. But less than she had expected. And as he'd sat there, listening with a concerned look in his eyes and a warm breeze ruffling his hair, a different memory had surfaced to trouble her. Terry was not just a friend and colleague, after all; she had once invited him into her bed.

It had happened long before she met Michael; she had still been married back then. But she and Bob had quarrelled and one evening, at her colleague Savendra's wedding, Sarah had kicked off her heels, twirled barefoot in the dewy midnight grass, and stretched on tiptoe to slide her arms around the neck of her tall policeman and kiss him, before taking his hand and leading him through the last few revellers on the dance floor and up to the hotel room she had booked especially in the hope that this might happen.

That invitation had been so out of character that she had only dared to issue it after copious glasses of champagne. Which had been her downfall. Her spirit had been willing but her flesh had been horribly, embarrassingly sick. Now, looking at Terry, she flushed slightly as she wondered if he, too, was recalling that night.

He'd been a perfect gentleman back then, holding a cold flannel to her forehead as she puked into the toilet bowl, and leaving politely before sending a huge bouquet of flowers next morning. All for nothing, she'd told him later. A missed opportunity, a mistake never to be repeated. An illusion.

But now? What did she feel about him now?

'So,' she said brightly, rising to her feet. 'That's my story. It's kind of you to listen to my dreams.' *And you don't know the half of them.* She began to collect the plates and glasses and carry them indoors.

'I'm honoured. Here let, me help you with that.' Terry had been fascinated, bewitched not just by her story, but by the look in her eyes as she told it. He too, got to his feet, picking up the empty wine bottle and a plate she had missed.

As they entered the kitchen he'd somehow collided with her, coming out. He tripped, she lost balance, and they clung onto each other for support. Afterwards, thinking about it, neither of them could quite recall how it had happened or which of them took the initiative.

But neither had wanted to let go. Their embarrassment had melted into an embrace. As they kissed Sarah thought, perhaps this is it. *The final act of my therapy. Or another terrible mistake.*

In bed Terry's body was lean, slim, muscular; his chest was hairy where Michael's had been smooth. Not just his chest, but his back and legs too – it was like being caressed by a long slender ape. Her husband Bob had been hairy too but not strong, lithe, athletic as this man was. Or as virile; Terry's need for her was as great as hers for him. As though he, too, had been waiting too long for some therapy, some cure he feared might never arrive.

Afterwards they lay entwined, gazing into each other's eyes across the pillow. Terry's face was flushed, anxious, amazed.

'I ... didn't hurt you, did I?' Sarah had cried out, more than once, not always with obvious pleasure.

'What? No. Only my ribs. They're not used to such activity.'

'Your ribs? Oh. There?' He stroked gently below her breast.

'Mm. It's okay.' She lifted her arm cautiously, to put his hand on the place. 'There. That one. *Ouch.* Not quite healed yet.'

'I'll be more careful next time.'

'Promises, promises.' They lay silent for a while, then she laughed softly. 'Next time?'

'If ... you like. If it was ... acceptable.'

Her fingers played with the hairs on his chest. Her eyes smiled into his. 'Oh, I think so. My tall policeman.' She raised herself on her elbow and kissed him, long and luxuriously, her hair falling like a curtain around their faces. Her fingers wandered lower.

* * *

'So was that it?' Lucy asked, fascinated. 'A single dramatic lunch date?'

'Good heavens, no!' Sarah smiled, her face slightly flushed with the joy of confession. 'What do you take me for, Luce? This is ... serious, at least I hope it is. More than a one night stand, anyway.'

'Serious for him too, you think?'

'Oh yes, I think so. Hope so, anyway. He's always been a ... distant admirer. Made it clear more than once. In fact if I hadn't met Michael when I did, just after Bob left ... a lot of things might have been different.' Sarah flexed her fingers as if examining her nails, secretly searching for that slight tell-tale tremor. Nothing now; good. 'Still, that's water under the bridge.' She smiled, looking out over the balcony at the reality behind the metaphor.

'So he came again, did he?'

Sarah burst out laughing. 'Lucy, you're dreadful! But yes, since you ask, he did. Last night too, as a matter of fact.'

* * *

The second time, a day later, they made love in the evening. Terry was home by six, and spent two hours with his children, before they met in a restaurant at 8.30. Both he and Sarah were nervous; they had the emotions of teenagers with the experience of adults. They gazed into each other's eyes over the candlelit table, laughing self-consciously and toying with their food. Sarah goosed him wickedly with her foot while the waiter watched him sample the wine. She longed for the meal to be over so she could drag him home. Terry had never seen her like this – or only once, that disastrous time in the hotel long ago. He wondered if once again he was taking an unfair advantage. Back then, she had been drunk because of a quarrel with her husband; this time, she was in therapy after an attempt on her life. But surely, something that made her glow and smile like this must be good for her. And for him – well, it was what he had dreamed of for years.

For nearly twenty years there had been only one woman in Terry's life, his wife Mary. She had been beautiful, sexy certainly, but also, as the years passed and the children were born, a maternal figure – not just to their two girls but to him too, in a way. After their second daughter Esther was born Mary had not, perhaps, seemed so interested in sex. It was something she submitted to or indulged in companionably rather than with the passion of their younger days. Perhaps that was normal, as you grew older, Terry had thought. It was pleasant enough, after all.

And then, quite suddenly, his wife had died, leaving her memory frozen in time, like the photo he kept on his bedside table.

Terry had been frozen too, unable for years to relate to any other woman. None compared to Mary; they were beings of a different species, unreachable, behind a glass screen. The very idea of being involved with one, physically or emotionally, had seemed alien, unimaginable, repugnant.

Until Sarah Newby shattered the screen. Terry could never fully explain to himself what it was about her. She was pretty, but no more beautiful than other women – forty-two years old now, with faint lines beginning to deepen around her eyes and mouth. The slender body, which had entwined so passionately with his, was fragile in places, the ribs and arm still healing: smooth, soft and curvy but not toned or glowing with youthful muscular health like that of Trude, his young Norwegian nanny.

Sarah Newby wasn't even a particularly nice person. The controlled aggression, the bloody-minded argumentative skills that made her a good barrister were not always attractive and could be downright infuriating. As a mother she'd been erratic – tiger-like at times in defence of her children, but casual, even ignoring them at others. Her obsessive devotion to her career had been one of the reasons her husband had left her.

Terry had long understood all that and dismissed it. It didn't count against the simple fact of her existence. To him, she was the one – the only woman in his life since Mary. He'd hoped, for several years now, that she might feel the same; but there'd been little sign of that until now. Just that one disastrous time in a hotel long ago, when she'd been drunk after a quarrel with her husband. Nothing more had come of it, and the morning after she'd told him quite firmly that nothing ever would. Her career, and his, had been too important to risk in some casual, adulterous fling.

Now he had another chance. This second lovemaking when they returned from the restaurant was slower, more fully enjoyed, more satisfying than that first time in the afternoon. They were beginning the process of knowing each other's bodies. It was a joy, something to be treasured. Terry was only the fourth man Sarah had ever had sex with. Each had been wonderful in different ways. Her teenage husband Kevin had been rough, demanding, drop-dead handsome; Bob kind, thoughtful, funny, gentle; Michael smooth, masterful, controlling, scary. So now, what was Terry like? Certainly virile, athletic, strong, but also kinder and more cautious than either Michael or Kevin. Surprisingly, he even seemed afraid of her at times, as though she might break. 'Come on!' she cried, wrapping her legs round him, 'Oh, yes, *yes*!'

Terry *was* afraid, though, that he might hurt her. Physically, because he was strong and her ribs were not healed. And emotionally, because she was recovering from trauma, still in counselling, and for that reason perhaps unbalanced, needy, lacking in judgement.

So when she encouraged him to be more forceful he held back, being deliberately gentle. And that led to tension between them.

'I'm not a woman on a pedestal, Terry,' she said. 'I won't break.'

'You might though,' he answered, stroking her cheek cautiously. 'You don't know your own weakness.'

'Well, show it to me, soldier. I'll let you know when I've had enough.'

And so he did. Afterwards, when they lay there exhausted with the sheets on the floor and the moonlight silvering the room, projecting ripples all around the walls and ceiling in reflections from the river outside, she started to laugh. And then cried.

'What is it?' he asked, raising himself on an elbow to look down at her. 'What's the matter now?'

'Nothing.' She wiped her tears on a pillow and smiled. 'I'm just happy, I suppose. In this moment which won't last. Time is fleeting, like that river.' She gestured at the ripples on the walls. 'And you must go.'

'I know, soon.' He leant down, kissed her eyes. 'Esther still wakes in the night sometimes. She comes looking for me.'

'Yes. A good father.'

They lay there for a while longer, prolonging the moment. The ripples of moonlight faded, as clouds covered the moon. They heard a spatter of rain on the window, and the rumble of distant thunder. Terry swung reluctantly out of bed, and began to search for his clothes. Sarah lay on her side, watching him dress. He smiled back at her.

'You'll come and see them soon? Spend a day with me and the girls?'

'I will. If you invite me. But we can't do this in your home.'

'No. But there are other pleasures. And you must get strong.'

'I *am* strong, Terry. Always have been.'

'True. We just proved it.' He came back to the bed, kissed her again, and felt the words *'I love you'* forming in his throat. But instead he said: 'You're beautiful,' which seemed less risky and more appropriate somehow. He was a little afraid to commit himself.

She laughed. 'Only in the moonlight, and that's gone. Get out of here, Terry, go home. You've got kids to care for and I have a case to prepare in the morning. After my beauty sleep. Go.'

As Terry came out of the flats a gust of wind buffeted his face, and he heard the raindrops hissing on the water. He hurried across Skeldergate Bridge, turning up his coat collar as the growl of thunder came closer.

9. Invitation

'BOB?'

'Yes?'

Bob Newby looked up. He was sitting at the kitchen table, his elbows resting disconsolately either side of a half-eaten salad. Sonya's home cooking was, or had been, one of the many attractions he'd found on moving in with his new partner. She was only a part-time school teacher, not particularly ambitious for her career. But it was in a domestic setting that her real talents shone. She was a natural housewife, proud of the way she kept her house tidy, baked her own bread, changed all the sheets once a week, sent her children to school in clean, well-ironed clothes, and welcomed them – and Bob – home to an appetising, nourishing meal every evening.

All of which, Bob had told her, was a welcome change from his former wife, Sarah Newby.

But tonight, Sonya noticed, her cooking was not appreciated. He had only eaten a few mouthfuls, it seemed. Her home-baked roll lay torn and crumbled into fragments on the side plate. He looked tired, haggard, his face pale, his fingers distractedly rubbing his forehead.

'A policewoman came today,' she said.

He groaned. 'Not another one. Why? When?'

'When you were out. At school.'

'Clearing my office, you mean? The final disgrace.'

Bob had been lucky, in a way, that school did not start until next week. He had been told very firmly by the education office, that he should stay away from school during teaching hours. Until this unfortunate business, as they had put it, was resolved, he should have no contact with children whatsoever. Purely a precaution, the voice on the phone had insisted, but the safety of the children was paramount, and any breach of this rule would be considered a disciplinary offence. So until further notice he was not only suspended from teaching, but also banned from the school premises. His offer to stay in his office and run the school from there was instantly rejected. His deputy was appointed acting head teacher forthwith. When he'd protested that he had personal possessions in his office, they had checked with the police who had agreed to allow him to remove them today, since no children were present.

So he had spent the day clearing his office, handing over his keys, and explaining to his shocked staff what had happened. It had been an excruciating meeting. Everyone said they didn't believe it, but Bob didn't believe their protestations. How could he? None of them had known him when he was young; three of them had not even been born in 1991. Many of them hugged him when he left, but then their eyes slid away, and he could imagine the flurry of chatter which had erupted as he drove away.

Presumably the policewoman had called when he was out doing that. Sonya had tactfully stayed at home.

'What did she want? Did you tell her where I was?'

'Yes, but she knew already. She came to see me, not you.'

'Why?' Bob shook his head wearily, watching Sonya walk to the fridge and pour herself a glass of juice. Something about the way she did it, avoiding his eyes, made him close his own in anticipation. *This is going to get worse*, he told himself.

Sonya closed the fridge door, took a long swig from her glass, and turned to face him. 'She was worried about the children,' she said.

'Which children?'

'Mine, of course, which do you think?'

'What, you mean Samantha ..?'

'Yes, and Linda and John.' She tossed her hair out of her eyes. 'That's curious. Why do you mention Samantha?'

'Because ... I don't know, she's the eldest. What did this policewoman want?'

'She was worried about them. She thought they might be in danger.'

'What? Oh no, Sonya, you don't mean that, they can't mean that! You're not telling me ...'

'She asked if I thought it was safe for them to be sharing a house with a man suspected of child abuse.'

Bob stared at her, then closed his eyes. He had a sensation of being punched in the stomach by a tree, shortly followed by a sense of falling endlessly through a void. There must be a poem about this, a tiny dreamlike part of his mind said, by Dante perhaps, where a man falls into the lowest depths of hell only to find another, deeper pit opening up beneath his feet.

After an age he opened his eyes and asked: 'And what did *you* say?'

'I told her I trusted you. I thought it was ok.'

'Thank you.' The words came out in a whisper, no more. He was watching the agony on her face.

'All the same, she said ...'

'She said *what*, Sonya?'

'She said it was better to be safe than sorry. She asked how I would feel if I was wrong. She wondered if ...'

There were tears on Sonya's face now. But under the tears, a cold, terrified look he had not seen before.

'Why did you think of *Samantha* just now, Bob? Just Samantha, not Linda or Johnnie?'

'I don't know! It was nothing, just a name, it came out first! Sonya love, please, don't do this! They're poisoning your mind! Don't think like this!'

'I don't know what to think, any more. I don't know what to do.'

'Don't do anything. You say you trust me ...'

'I do, Bob, I do, only ... well, I've sent the children to my mum's for the night ... for another day or two ... just so we can think ... until all this blows over ...'

That falling sensation again. I have no parachute, he thought. *Further and further down. Alone into the inferno.*

'It's not going to blow over in a few days,' Bob said bleakly. 'That solicitor woman, Lucy Parsons, she said weeks, months maybe.'

'But we can't ... I can't ... live with this hanging over me for all that time. What about the children?'

'They'll be fine. I'll explain to them.'

'No! I've told them something already, and ... they're really upset, Bob. Policemen bursting into the house like soldiers and arresting you. It's awful. Johnny was terrified, Linda couldn't stop crying.'

'And Samantha?'

'She was better. Said she didn't believe it.'

'Good.'

'Why is that good, Bob?'

'Because at least someone trusts me, that's why. I've been a bit short of trust today.'

'Yes, well, maybe. She's only a child, Bob. Thirteen years old.'

Again that cold, frightened look that sent shivers down his spine. As if an alien had invaded her mind, and was staring at him through the eyes of the woman he loved. It hardly seemed possible. Yesterday they had been so happy, himself, Sonya and the children – his comfortable, loving new family, making plans for the future. He'd been going to buy them a house. Now this.

'I know that, Sonya. For Christ's sake – there's nothing between me and Samantha, all right? Don't be ridiculous! *I didn't do this! Any of it!*'

'I know, Bob. I believe you. But ...'

'Do you? Do you really? Then why don't you show it?'

For a wild, terrible moment he was consumed by rage. He felt like hitting her. He saw the frying pan on the stove, imagined himself picking it up, swinging it round his head, smashing up everything in sight, the chunky ethnic plates, the spice rack, the rows of coloured mugs, the mobile in the window, the children's drawings on the wall, the glass door ... He saw Sonya's tearstained face, half–hidden by her curly chestnut hair, and he wanted to grab handfuls of that hair and shake her stupid head from side to side, smash it against the fridge until she saw reason, until she understood ...

But he didn't do any of this, of course, he wasn't that sort of man. Even so, the adrenalin surged through his brain like a tsunami. He watched his hands clench on the table beside the plate, like claws, trembling claws that had nothing to do with him ... and then he regained control.

'I'm sorry. I know it's a shock for you too. But if you don't believe me, what is there left?'

She sat down, cautiously, on the opposite side of the kitchen table. 'That's just it, Bob. It's destroying us both. But, if this isn't going to break us apart, I need to understand. *Why is this happening?*'

* * *

Next morning, crossing Skeldergate Bridge, Sarah paused to lean on the parapet. Behind her, the last of the morning rush hour traffic grumbled and queued its way towards the city centre; a journey she had once made daily from the country on her motorbike, zooming in and out of cars to gain an advantage whereever she could. Not any more though. From her flat to her chambers in Tower Street was just a five minute stroll, ten minutes if she dawdled, as now.

She folded her arms on the wrought iron Victorian parapet and leaned forward, rising on tiptoe to peer down at the broad river Ouse flowing below. A pair of swans paddled in an eddy by a warehouse on the left bank; a rowing eight swished its way silently upstream. A fresh breeze ruffled a lock of hair across her face, obscuring the contented smile on her lips.

Something clicked behind her and she turned, surprised, to see a tall man in black leather with a camera in his hand.

'What the ...?'

'Perfect! And another!' The camera clicked again.

'Oh my God! Savvy! What are you doing?'

'What does it look like? Snapping my perfect model! Here, see.' He passed her the camera, and she peered at the screen, holding her hair out of her eyes with one hand. But it was hard to see in the sunlight. All she could make out was a smudged dark figure, hunched over a railing.

'It'll look better indoors. I'll show you.'

'But where's your bike? I don't see it.' The man, Savendra Bhose, was clothed from head to foot in jetblack motorcycle leathers, with heavy boots. Not normal gear for a pedestrian crossing the bridge.

'Just down there.' Savendra pointed to a road junction at the edge of the bridge, where the Honda FireStorm rested on its stand partially blocking the pavement. 'I saw you when I was coming from Bishopthorpe Road, and thought this is my moment! And it was!'

'But Savvy, you can't just sneak up on women like that. You'll be arrested!'

'For you, it would be worth it. Hop on, I'll give you a ride into chambers.'

'What, in a skirt and no helmet? No thanks, I'll walk. Everyone's watching.'

They were, too, which made the idea oddly tempting. Motorists and taxi drivers, stuck in the queue, were gawping at the mini drama on the bridge. As the heavy booted Savendra stumped back to his bike she nearly ran after him, taken with the idea of riding pillion behind him to chambers, hair blowing in the breeze like a teenage rock chick. But there are laws against that, it's not worth the risk, she decided regretfully.

Still, she told herself smiling as she walked across the bridge, that's my second boost in two days. I must still have something men like, after all.

Savendra was her oldest friend in chambers, a young Indian barrister who had qualified at the same time as her. Until her accident Sarah, too, had commuted to work by motorbike, and she and Savendra had spent many happy hours comparing their shiny machines and the adventures they had had on them. Sarah had sold hers after her accident, to help pay for the deposit on the flat. But now, waving as Savendra rode past her, she thought maybe, one day when I'm earning again ...

You need confidence to ride a motorbike when a crash has nearly killed you.

Well, my confidence is returning too, isn't it? This new thing with Terry, that's another boost ...

Or is it?

She had spent much of last night reflecting on her conversation with Lucy. She hadn't planned this new relationship with Terry; it had just happened, seemingly by chance. And yet explaining it to Lucy had put it in a new perspective. Things like this weren't just random, surely; there was an emotional meaning behind them, a cause. This new, passionate affair was a spontaneous expression of ... what?

Joy? Need? Loneliness? Loss of control?

Three of those four seemed scary but so far the first was winning the battle to interpret the events in her mind. Yes she'd felt lonely over the previous few weeks in her flat. That was hardly surprising, with her lover dead and her children grown and now her pathetic ex husband entangled in God knows what. Yes she also knew she was still fragile and needed the reassurance of human contact. This time she had had it from a man instead of the counsellor's talking therapy. But is that a mistake, did I lose control? Not really, she decided. I just lost my inhibitions. It was a spontaneous outburst of something that I *wanted* to do, *chose* to do, and could have stopped at any time until well ... the time when it was too late and our bodies took over and neither of us wanted to stop anything.

But that's what sex is like, isn't it? Good sex between friends, anyway.

And that's the point. Terry Bateson is my friend, he has been for years, I've resisted him so often but I've always known he fancied me. But now we've done it and it was nice – more than nice – so what is there to worry about?

Nothing, unless I get pregnant – God, that would be stupid at my age – but I can't because I stayed on the pill even after Michael died and why was that? Because I knew, deep down, something like this might happen or rather I *wanted* it to happen and now it has. So the proper response is joy – as well as gratitude too and relief that I've found a man *who isn't Michael*, that's his most important quality. Terry's just as handsome and virile in his way but slimmer and hairier so he'll drive Michael out of my brain.

Is that why you did it? The voice of her counsellor whispered in her mind.

Well yes, in part? So what? It was fun. Lucy was impressed, as well.

Is that fair to Terry? Aren't you just using him for entertainment?

Oh come on! He wanted to be used, he loved it.

So where do you go from here?

That will depend on him, as well as me. Regular repeat performances, perhaps. We're friends, we're adults, we'll work something out.

So long as you don't get hurt. Either of you.

Stop fussing. I'm cured. Starting afresh. New life, new man, no regrets. I may not need counselling much more.

Still smiling, she strode into her chambers where Savendra was waiting with his camera. 'Look, you can see them better on the computer screen.'

With a few clicks of the mouse he brought up three pictures of her of which the first, a woman gazing across the river with her hair drifting across her face partially obscuring a secret contented smile, was clearly the best.

'There, perfect! A lovely lady on a bridge. What were you smiling about, anyway?'

'Ah, Savvy, that would be telling.'

'Well, whatever it is, you look beautiful. Honestly.'

'I thought, Mr Bhose, that you were a married man.'

'Oh I am, most definitely yes. Soon to be a father too. But that makes me safe, you see. Belinda knows me much too well to feel the slightest twinge of jealousy.'

'She's a lucky woman then.'

'So I tell her, every day. Are you still on for the weekend?'

'What, on your boat? Yes ...'

Savendra had recently acquired a thirty foot river cruiser in settlement of his fee for defending a well-known fraudster. Since his client had been convicted, he would have no need it for the next five years; the only open water he would see would be the duckpond in an open prison. But he was still grateful: if Savendra hadn't succeeded in getting two more serious charges against him dismissed he would have been locked away for three times as long..

Savendra was delighted with the boat and longed to show it off to everyone. He had invited Sarah to join him and his wife on this trip a week ago, but in the excitement of the last few days she had forgotten. Now, an idea sparked in her mind. Terry's a widower, he has children, two young daughters. If this new relationship is to last, I should get to know them better. A river trip might be the perfect way to spend time with his family without it seeming too oppressive.

'Can I bring a friend?'

'Of course. The more the merrier. Let's make it a party.'

'That's very kind, Savvy. Tempting. Leave it with me, I'll let you know.'

10. A Sentimental Education

TERRY'S PHONE rang as he was getting out of his car. Seeing who it was, his heart beat a little faster.

'Sarah? Hi. How are you?'

'Oh, not too bad. How about you?'

'I'm ... fine. More than fine. No regrets, I hope?'

'Why, should I have?'

'I don't know. I wondered ...'

'Terry, *I have no regrets,* okay? None at all. Do you?'

'Of course not. Quite the opposite.'

'Good. Glad to hear it.' He held the phone close to his ear as he locked the car. Sarah's voice sounded warm, intimate, cheerful. He imagined her smiling

'Terry, I've got to be quick, I've got a client waiting outside. But I've got a proposition to put to you.'

'Really? Sounds tempting.'

'Not what you're thinking, not this time. But you know how you said we should spend more time together. Apart from ... you know.'

'Yes, that's difficult. I've got the kids ...'

'Yes exactly, that's what I was thinking. We should do things together, fun things. Well, this weekend I've been invited on a boat trip, by my friend Savendra, you remember him? So I thought maybe you and your girls ...'

She described her idea for the next few minutes, as Terry made his way through crowds of students down to the university lake, where a fountain played and Canada geese paddled contentedly.

'Just a day out together having fun,' she said. 'No strings. They know me as your friend already; they won't see anything more in it than that.'

It sounded great to Terry. After all, this new relationship of theirs was in its infancy. Neither of them knew where it would lead. He dreamed about Sarah moving closer into his life, but could it actually happen? Did he really want it to? Did she? They hadn't discussed such questions yet; the idea needed to be crept up on carefully, stalked as if they were children playing grandmother's footsteps.

His daughters had met Sarah several times though, and liked her, as far as he knew. Agreeing to meet on Saturday, he switched off his phone and approached the reception desk of the English department in Derwent College.

'I'm looking for a Dr Victoria Weston. Is she here?'

Surprise and concern appeared on the face of the woman at reception. 'Vicky? I haven't seen her today. Why, has anything happened?'

'She's been reported missing, that's all. When did you see her last?'

'Thursday, I think it was. She's not in every day, you see. She often works from home or at the library. The academics just come and go as they please. They don't keep regular hours.'

'Would you mind if I looked in her office? She may have a diary, something like that.'

'Oh, I'm not sure. That's private. I'll call professor Stephenson, the head of department. He'll be able to deal with this.'

While he was waiting Terry watched the flow of students going past. More girls than men nowadays, he noted with interest. Quite a few ethnic minorities, several Chinese. All looked young, eager, healthy, a different flow of humanity from those you would meet elsewhere. As he watched, a thin man in checked shirt and jeans, slightly older than the rest, strode briskly up to the desk.

'Yes, how can I help?'

'You are ...?'

'Alan Stephenson, professor. I'm head of the English department. I hear you're asking about Victoria Weston?'

'Yes, that's right.' Terry explained, taking in the lined, friendly face, grey hair, and wiry, athletic looking body. This man couldn't be more than forty, yet apparently he was head of department and happy to come to work in faded jeans, lumberjack checked shirt and trainers. 'We're making enquiries in case something has happened to her. Her car was found abandoned by the river, you see, and her husband can't find her.'

'Good Lord. Well, let's hope there's a reasonable explanation. She doesn't come in every day, after all. Have you tried her mobile?'

'I have, sir. It doesn't answer.'

'Oh. Well, that does sound strange. But how can I help?'

'Well, I'd like to talk to anyone who knew her, her work colleagues. And if I could look inside her office?'

'Yes, I don't see why not. I doubt if she locks it, but if so, security will have a key. This way, I'll show you.'

The office, a small square room, had just enough space for a desk, a computer, a leather office chair, another upright chair beside the desk, a cheap Scandinavian armchair, a tiny coffee table, and a grey filing cabinet. Two large wall-to-ceiling bookcases, full of books, covered an entire wall. A small window looked out onto a patch of grass covered with goose droppings, with part of a lake visible about twenty yards away. On the pinboard above the desk, printed notices vied for place with a number of portraits of severe, intense looking women whom Terry could not identify.

'What do you hope to find, exactly?' Professor Stephenson stood by the door, watching Terry look around.

'Hard to say, really, sir,' Terry said. 'Did she keep a diary, do you know?'

'No idea,' the man shrugged, looking at the desk. 'If she's like me, she'll use her phone.'

'No doubt. But she's probably got that with her, and it's not accepting calls. What exactly was she working on here, do you know?'

'Apart from her normal teaching, you mean? She was working on a critical analysis of feminist writers. She'd published quite a few articles already. Hence the dreary pin-ups.' He cast an ironic glance at the portraits above the desk. 'Not my first love, I'm afraid. I was pulling her leg about them last week.' Meeting Terry's puzzled frown, he guessed further explanation might be necessary. 'That's Virginia Woolf there, and her friend Vanessa Bell. And Sylvia Plath, in the corner. Very important feminist writers.'

Terry remembered the last name from the book of poetry they had found in the abandoned car. He'd checked it out on Google.

'Didn't she commit suicide, sir? Sylvia Plath?'

'Yes, that's right. Tragic; stuck her head in a gas oven. Can't do that nowadays, thank God – wrong sort of gas.' He peered over Terry's shoulder as he studied the other portraits. 'Virginia Woolf, of course, she killed herself too. Walked into a river and drowned, with her pockets full of stones. You did say ... Vicky's car was found by the river, is that right?'

'Yes sir, exactly. At Landing Lane, in Fulford.'

'My God. Well, I see why you're worried. But what can we do? ... I say, Adrian! Come in here a minute, would you?'

He turned, beckoning to someone passing outside in the corridor. A young man stopped and, somewhat reluctantly, came towards them.

'This is Adrian Norton, one of Vicky's graduate students. If anyone knows where she is, he's your best bet. Adrian, this is Detective Inspector - sorry, what did you say your name was?'

'Bateson, sir. Terry Bateson.'

'Yes, I apologise. Well, it seems there's a bit of a panic about Vicky, and the police are trying to find her. Do you have any idea, perhaps?'

It was unfortunate that the young man was wearing a red shirt, because his face flushed a similar colour. He was a short, stocky young man, only about five foot nine, but broad shouldered, with strong muscles showing under the short-sleeved shirt. He had curly fair hair, cut short around his scalp, and a round, babyish face with a faint stubble which the sudden blush on his fair skin made almost invisible. He wore faded blue jeans and was carrying a couple of hardback books under one arm.

'Vicky? Missing?' he said. 'Since when?'

Terry was used to the startled looks which crossed people's faces when suddenly confronted by a police officer. Occasionally it was just surprise, but more often than not there was guilt somewhere below the surface. The guilt was not always connected to the case he was investigating; quite a few people seemed to believe he could see into their souls, uncovering petty childhood offences committed years ago. The dramatic blush burning the young man's cheeks might indicate no more than that.

But on the other hand ... Terry remembered the bitter comments Tom Weston had made to himself and Jane Carter. *It'll be one of her wretched students, it always is. Ask around at the university, they'll know. Everyone probably knows except me.*

'She wasn't home when her husband returned from Scotland yesterday,' Terry said coolly. 'When did you last see her, sir?'

'I ... it's hard to remember.' The young man shook his head, staring at Terry intently, then away out of the window as though something out there might help him recall. Terry said nothing, waiting.

'On Thursday,' he said at last. 'That was the last time I saw her.'

Five days ago, Terry thought. A little alarm bell rang in his mind. *Why did he find that so hard to remember?*

'I see. Do you remember where you met her, and what time it was?'

'Yes, it was, er ... at her house, in the afternoon.' The young man shook his head earnestly. 'What do you mean she's disappeared? What's happened?'

'That's what we're trying to find out, sir. You see, her car was found by the river.'

'What? Oh God, no!' Terry noticed how his eyes, just like the professor's, moved involuntarily towards the portraits pinned to the board above the desk. 'You don't think she killed herself?'

'I hope not. But it's a possibility, of course. That's why we need to find her.'

'God no! If she *has* it's all my fault!'

'Oh? What makes you say that?'

'Well, it's difficult.' The young man glanced at professor Stephenson, as though wishing he was not there. 'It's just, well ... personal, you see.'

'Look, I've got a lecture in five minutes,' the professor said tactfully. 'So if you don't mind ... I'll be free after twelve, Inspector, if you need me later. Our administrator, Linda, can show you my office.'

Terry waited until the professor left, then closed the door and pointed to the upright chair beside the desk.

'Adrian? Why don't we sit down? It might be easier.'

The young man moved to the chair slowly, like a schoolboy expecting punishment. Terry sat in the padded leather swivel chair at the desk, took out his notebook, and attempted a faint, reassuring smile.

'You said it was personal, just now?'

'Yes. Well, I don't want everyone gossiping about it.'

'Gossiping about what, sir, exactly?'

The blush had faded from his face now, leaving it pale, but there were still ugly red splotches on his neck. Almost girlish, Terry thought, remembering teenage embarrassments of his own.

'Well, Vicky is my supervisor, you see. I'm doing a Phd in, well ... certain aspects of feminism in twentieth century literature. You probably wouldn't know ...'

'Studying writers like these ones on the wall, you mean? Sylvia Plath and Virginia Woolf?'

'Amongst others, yes. But that's not the main point. I mean ...'

'She's a good teacher, is she?'

'Who, Vicky? Oh, yes. Well, we get on pretty well ... *were* getting on, that is. Until ...'

'Until ...?'

Terry waited. Silence, and a steady stare, could be useful weapons at times, he knew. Let the boy tell his story in his own words at first, if possible.

The more he said now, the more details there would be for Terry to check later.

'Yes, well, what happened I suppose, is that we ... she ... both of us took it too far. I mean, as you say, she's a good teacher, it all started quite well, and because of the work we get ... got ... to spend a lot of time together, sitting in rooms, talking, like this.' He smiled faintly. 'In fact she usually sits just where you are now, swivelling that chair. Well, she's a good-looking woman, older than me of course, but quite sexy in a way and ...'

He glanced towards the door, grateful perhaps that Terry had closed it. '... I don't want everyone to know but, well, we had an affair. I suppose that's what you call it, isn't it, when an older woman seduces a young student? It was fun at first, I was flattered, I mean, who wouldn't enjoy something like that, but ...' He shook his head. The blush, Terry noticed, was returning. ' ... I don't know why I'm telling you this, really ...'

'Because she's missing,' Terry said softly. 'We're trying to find her.'

'Yes, well, that's just it. You see if she *is* missing and has done something to herself it may be my fault. Unfortunately. That's the only reason. It's terrible but ...'

'What makes you say that? That it may be your fault?'

'Well, because of what happened. On Thursday. When we met that last time.'

That *last* time, Terry thought. Telling phrase. 'What *did* happen, Adrian? You met at her house, you said.'

'Yes, well, I go ... used to go there sometimes. To borrow books, talk, and well, have sex, obviously, when her husband's away. She has a huge bed, queen size, and a hot tub in the garden, too, really cool ... but I went there on Thursday to end it. To tell her we couldn't carry on like this anymore.'

'I see. Why was that?' Terry asked quietly.

'Well, because of Michaela, mostly.'

'Michaela?'

'Yes, my girlfriend. You see, she's just come over from Czech ...'

'From where? Sorry, you've lost me.'

'From the Czech Republic. I had a summer job there, you see, teaching English in Prague. I've been there before, and I met Michaela last time, but ... well I really got to know her this time, and well ...' The blush was returning, as strong as before. '... Michaela came back with me. She's pregnant, you see, so ... we're going to get married ....'

'Congratulations,' Terry murmured drily, writing *Michaela, Czech, pregnant* in his notebook.

' ... so I thought, I can't carry on like this with two women, I'll have to see Vicky and explain ... I mean, she's my supervisor after all, she ought to understand ... I thought she would, anyway ...'

'Did Michaela know about this?'

'About my affair with Vicky? Christ, no! That's the whole point, you see, she mustn't know ...' The boy glanced at the door, to reassure himself it was still closed. 'You won't tell her, will you? I'm telling you this in confidence ...'

What does he think I am, Terry wondered, *a counsellor, a psychiatrist?* 'I'm afraid I can't promise that, son,' he said stiffly. 'It depends on the enquiry.'

Adrian half rose from his seat, the returning flush darkening his face. 'But *why?* She'd be terribly upset – it's not necessary, is it?'

'I didn't say I'd *have* to tell her,' Terry said peaceably. 'It depends on the enquiry. My job is to find Victoria Weston, that's all. If I can do that without talking to your girlfriend Michaela, I will.'

'Please do.' The young man sat down again, relieved. One hand drummed nervously on the side of the desk.

'But if you want my advice, son,' Terry continued, thinking he sounded like a Dutch uncle. 'It's probably best to tell your fiancée the truth. It's nearly always best, in the long run.'

'It's not that easy,' Adrian said. 'You don't understand. Michaela, she knows what she wants ... she's very passionate, and ...' He shook his head ruefully. 'I seem to attract passionate women.'

Lucky you, thought Terry, with a twinge of jealousy, remembering his own student days. *But I only slept with other students – anyway, all my tutors were men.*

'Let's go back to the beginning,' he said, suppressing a smile. 'You say you met Victoria Weston on Thursday. At her house in Osbaldwick, is that right?'

'Yes.'

'What time was that?'

'Oh, about half past one, two maybe. Lunchtime.'

'I see. So what happened when you got there?'

'Well, I'd brought back some books she'd lent me, so I gave her those, and then ... well, it was awkward.'

'What do you mean, awkward?'

'Well, she knew I was coming, and she was excited, I think. She'd laid out some open sandwiches in the kitchen, she was good at those, and she'd opened a bottle of wine. I think she'd been drinking already. She was wearing these tight jeans and this sort of open blouse thing. It was quite seductive, she obviously thought I'd come for, well, sex.'

'And?'

'Well, in fact ... I guess this doesn't sound good, but she was very hard to resist when she was like that, she's an attractive woman, so I thought ... I guess I thought why not, one last time ...'

'You had sex with her, you mean?'

'Yes. Yes, we went to bed together.'

'And after that?'

'Well, it was then that it all kicked off, rather. You see, afterwards ... I got out of bed and ... told her.'

'Told her what, exactly?'

'That this was the last time, that we weren't going to do this anymore. That I ... was engaged, so it wasn't right ... I tried to explain. I said she was my teacher, after all, in a position of authority, and I suppose I'm not masochistic enough, I didn't want to be controlled and ... I don't know ... used. I said maybe it was fine for her but it was messing with my mind. I wanted to go back to how we were before. Otherwise I'd ask for a new supervisor. Anyway it was over between us, I told her, that was it. The end.'

'How did she take it?' Terry asked, thinking *this woman Victoria Weston doesn't seem to have had much luck with men.*

'Not well. Not even slightly well.' The young man shook his head again, wondering. 'Hell hath no fury like a woman scorned, they say. That's Congreve, sorry. I guess you wouldn't know ...'

'I can imagine,' said Terry drily. *Even if I didn't study literature.*

'Yes, well, that doesn't say the half of it. She went berserk, screaming, yelling, throwing things. I wasn't sure I'd get out of there alive. I guess I didn't time it well – it was really dangerous.'

'She assaulted you?'

'Well, she tried to. Luckily Vicky isn't a very good shot and not that strong but even so ... I was trying to get dressed and keep out of her way ... it developed into a terrible screaming match which seemed to go on for ages. It was a horrible scene. Like a sort of Restoration comedy gone wild. Quite funny looking back on it but believe me it didn't seem funny at the time.'

'So she tried to assault you but you weren't injured?'

'No. A couple of bruises, that's all. Like I say she isn't a very good shot.'

'But she was attacking you so you had to defend yourself. Did you hit her?'

'No, of course not! I was just ducking to get out of the way.'

'You didn't touch her at all?'

'Well yes, of course I touched her. I held her arms a bit to stop her scratching me. Pushed her away once or twice. But that's all. I didn't hurt her, she was trying to hurt me!'

'So what happened next?'

'Well, after about half an hour of this she ran out of steam and started sobbing. I'd rejected her as a woman and a teacher, she said, I'd ruined her career and her marriage so she might as well kill herself because her life was over. Stuff like that. I thought it was rubbish at the time, I told her not to be so silly. I even laughed, God help me!'

A strange look, like the memory of a smile, passed across the young man's face. Terry watched the odd, ghostly expression form itself briefly from the smooth, unlined skin, the boyish stubble, the earnest eyes. Then it vanished, and he wondered. *What did that mean? Is he glad she's disappeared? Would he laugh if we found her body?*

'So you see that's why it's so scary when you come here saying she's missing, and you've found her car by the river,' Adrian continued. 'I mean I just thought she was upset because of what I'd said, you know, dumping her. I thought that was it, you know, just a mega tantrum to get it all out of her system; that's why I laughed. It was impressive and scary but a bit silly, too, in a way. All very predictable; I knew she'd be unhappy.'

Unhappy. Terry thought of the suicide text Vicky Weston had sent to her husband's phone. *Love turns to hatred. Hope to despair. No understanding, no one cares.* Was that how this student's rejection had made her feel?

Subduing his distaste, Terry was trying to analyse how this story seemed to the young man; how he felt about what he was saying. Was there an element of pride there, somewhere – pride in proving to this female authority figure that he didn't need her after all, that she couldn't control him? Pride that his words had reduced her to screaming and tears?

If that was all he'd done.

'She did mention suicide, you said?'

'Yes. It wasn't the first time. But I never thought she'd actually go ahead and do it!'

'These suicide threats. Did she say how she was thinking of killing herself?'

'No. It was just wild talk. When we discussed writers who'd killed themselves, like Virginia Woolf and Sylvia Plath, she explained why they'd done it. She sympathized; she said she sometimes felt the same. It was partly to do with her husband ...'

'What about her husband?' Terry asked, poised to take a note.

'Nothing in particular. Just ... they were getting divorced. She didn't like him. There was some sort of nasty secret about him which she'd discovered.'

'Did she tell you what that secret was?'

Adrian shook his head. 'Sorry, no. I didn't ask and ... I don't think she wanted to say, really. She seemed embarrassed and ... guilty perhaps, to be talking about him in bed with me.' The young man grinned, as to share a pleasant memory.

'So what time did you leave?' Terry asked coolly.

'About four, four thirty, on Thursday afternoon. I got on my bike and cycled home.'

'Ok. Did you contact her again, after that meeting? Speak on the phone, exchange texts, emails?'

'Well, yes, she sent me a text, next morning. I can show you if you like.' Adrian pulled a mobile out of his pocket, tapped the screen a couple of times, and passed it over for Terry to see. It was a short, dignified text.

Storm is over, sweet boy. For now, at least. Meet next week? We can be adults, look and not touch. If you insist on changing supervisor, I will accept, with fond regrets.

Received 09.17.09
26.08.2016
From Vicky.

No hint of suicide there, Terry thought. His sympathy for the missing woman increased. 'Did you reply?'

'Yes.' He tapped the screen again, and showed him.

'cool. c u then. no regrets.'
Saved 11.08.10
26.08.2016
To Vicky.

'That's it?' Terry noted down the texts and times and handed the phone back. 'Nothing else?'

'No. Well, I thought we'd said enough already.'

'And did you contact her again after that, in any way?'

'No. I was expecting to meet her here, yesterday. But she wasn't in so I came back today.'

'So you have no idea why her car was found by the river?'

'No.'

'And just for the record, where were you on the night when it was left there? Sunday evening?'

'I ... I don't know, really... yes I do! I was at home all evening with Michaela. We went to bed early – I'd been showing her round York and we were tired. Well, sort of – you know.' A sly grin crossed his face.

'And she'll confirm that, will she?'

'Of course. But you won't need to ask her, will you? I told you, she doesn't know ...'

'I understand, Adrian. If we do need to speak to her I'll be as discreet as I can. But I gave you my advice. Just be honest.'

'Yeah. Easy enough for you to say ...'

Terry wasn't interested in being a marriage guidance counsellor. 'All right, son,' he said briskly. 'Just give me your address and phone number, in case I need to get in touch with you again. And a list of Dr Weston's other friends and colleagues, anyone who might have an idea where she's gone. That'll be all, for now at least.'

11. Limbo

Yorkshire Post

Head Teacher arrested

*M*R ROBERT *Newby, the Head Teacher of St Asaph's Primary School, Harrogate, has been arrested by police investigating child sex abuse. North Yorkshire police arrested Mr Newby at his home early on Monday morning. He was taken to Harrogate police station where he was interviewed for several hours, before being released on police bail. The allegations relate to historic sexual abuse committed in the 1990s.*

A spokeswoman for Harrogate Education Department said: 'Mr Newby has been suspended on full pay pending further enquiries. We understand from the police that this arrest relates to complaints received from two former pupils whom he taught at a secondary school in Leeds. Mr Newby has been barred from the school premises until further notice. We wish to reassure parents that all necessary precautions for pupil safety have been taken, and the school remains open as normal.'

Detective Sergeant Starkey, leading the investigation, said: 'Mr Newby has been interviewed in connection with serious allegations made by two former pupils whom he taught in the 1990s. The alleged victims, both female, were teenagers at the time. So far as we are aware, no complaints have been laid against Mr Newby in his present post. Anyone who has further information should contact North Yorkshire Police.'

'Look at that!' Bob Newby said. He flung the *Yorkshire Post* on the desk and paced furiously across the room, too fired up to sit down. To Lucy Parsons, sitting behind her desk in her Leeds office, he looked like a caged panther, burning with rage and adrenalin, unable to escape the trap.

'I know,' she said. 'I read it this morning.'

'So?' His pacing came to a sudden abrupt halt. His knuckles, white with fury, gripped the back of the client's chair, as he stood glaring across the desk at her. 'What are you going to do about it? It's got to be stopped!'

Lucy shook her head sadly. 'There's not much I can do,' she said. 'I rang DS Starkey this morning, before you came in.'

'And? What did he say?'

'What *I* said was that this was a fishing expedition and if he makes the slightest unsubstantiated allegation he's in danger of being sued for libel, but ...'

'Yes? And?'

'Well, I didn't get very far, I'm afraid,' Lucy said diplomatically. *He burst out laughing,* would have been a more accurate answer, but not helpful. 'The fact is he's well within the law, and phrased everything carefully. These are only allegations, and that's all he's actually said.'

'He called them *victims*,' Bob raged. 'They aren't victims, they can't be! There was no crime, this never happened! They're lying!'

'Yes, well, quite. I'm afraid this is what happens, sadly. Try to ignore it, if you can.'

'Ignore it? I can't! This is my name they're destroying, my reputation! We should ring the newspaper and protest!'

'Well, maybe but ...'

'Will you do it or shall I?'

Lucy sighed. 'Look Bob, sit down. The best way to protest is to draft a statement. Calm but clear. Don't go into details, just say you absolutely deny this. Is that what you want to do?'

'Yes, of course. Why not?' Bob paced across the room again, came back to the chair, and stood beside it, staring intently into Lucy's face. *'What?'*

'Nothing.' Their eyes met. In Bob's eyes Lucy could see the distrust, mingling with fury, turning his rage still more toxic. *Do you doubt me too?* he was wondering. *Does even my solicitor believe the police?*

Looking at him, Lucy could see that Bob Newby was no violent criminal. A skinny, middle-aged schoolteacher, with thin arms, narrow chest, the hint of a pot belly and narrow face half-hidden by a greying beard, he was probably the least likely of all her clients to threaten violence, or to know *how* to hurt someone physically even if the idea occurred to him. Normally, that is. But just at this moment he was so aflame with rage, resentment and fury that he stood there like a candle, consuming himself, ready to set the world on fire if it touched him.

And the lack of trust Lucy saw in his eyes fed on something in her own. For a millisecond she wondered *do I believe him really?* Or is this anger all confected, his rage not that of innocence, but of fury at being found out? Lucy was a criminal solicitor after all, and few of her clients were innocent. More than half of those convicted of sexual offences were not burly, strong men at all; those were in the minority. Many rapists were skinny, insignificant looking men – often youths – who were physically, mentally and socially inadequate. That was why they did it, because they couldn't sustain a normal sexual relationship, so in frustration they sought to – well, steal one, any way they could. Force themselves on victims, vulnerable teenagers.

Was Bob Newby one of those? Not now perhaps, but once, long ago?

These thoughts, which she'd pondered before, now flashed through her mind and were dismissed. It was not her job, after all, to believe her client or judge him, but merely to prepare his defence. To use the walls of law to protect him, insofar as she could, from the hordes of media raging rampant outside.

'Right,' she said. 'We'll draft a statement. Sit down, Bob. This needs some thought.'

* * *

Half an hour later the statement was ready. Lucy read it through carefully before she picked up the phone.

I understand from the police that allegations of sexual misconduct have been made against me by two women who say they were pupils of mine in the 1990s. On legal advice I am not allowed to name those women, although my name has been released to the media by the police.

I strongly deny these allegations. At no time in my teaching career have I ever had inappropriate sexual relationships with any of my pupils, male or female, of any age whatsoever. I have no idea why these women have made these allegations, but they are not true.

It seems to me wholly unjust that my name has been released to the public, while my accusers are allowed to remain anonymous. This is not justice. I have been suspended from a job that I love, my family relationships are strained, and I face accusations in the media of the most hurtful kind.

I wish to assure parents that these allegations have no connection with children at St Asaph's Primary School, and that their children are as safe there as they always have been.

I hope that when these allegations are proven to be untrue, as they will be, that I will be able to return to a normal life. Until then, I ask that the media respect my privacy.

Robert Newby.

'This will stir things up even more,' she said thoughtfully. 'You're sure you want to do this? You're bound to get a reaction; you should be prepared for that. It may not be very pleasant.'

'I've already got the reaction. Look at this!'

Bob pulled his ancient laptop out of his rucksack, scrolled clumsily down to the school's Facebook page, and passed it to Lucy. She read: *'When I think of that pervert grooming my child in his school I want to vomit. My wife's been weeping all day. He should be castrated and fed his balls for breakfast.'*

'There's half a dozen like that. It's probably trending on Twitter.'

Lucy frowned. 'You should show this to the police.'

'What's the point? It's because of them that this is happening.'

'All the same, it's intimidation. That's a clear threat of violence.' She hesitated, looking at him carefully. 'How are things at home? Have there been any threats so far?'

'Threats? Not yet. Just dirty looks from all the neighbours. And silence. Gossiping no doubt. When I walk down the street I can almost hear them, *whispering* like starlings in the trees.'

'How is Sonya taking it?'

Bob snatched his laptop back, stuffed it in his bag, and stood up. His fingers twitching, he paced across the room. This hurts so much he can't stand still, Lucy thought. *Is this what a nervous breakdown looks like?*

'Badly, is the answer. She's sent the children to stay with her mother. For safety, she says. As if I was some sort of threat. Christ!'

'Does she believe you?'

'She tries. I truly think she's trying, she wants to believe me. But she doesn't know what to think, poor woman. I mean I love her, at least I thought I did, but we've only been together for what ... a few months. She knows nothing about my past, how can she?'

Whereas Sarah, your former wife, knew everything, Lucy thought. *But you left her, didn't you? Abandoned her for a younger woman, this Sonya.* 'It's very difficult for her, of course,' Lucy said tactfully.

'Yes, I understand that. But even so, she could show a bit more loyalty. It didn't help when the police sent a constable round, a family liaison officer, they called her, to suggest I might be a danger to the kids. I think, honestly, she wants me to move out.'

'Who, Sonya?'

'Yes. She hasn't said it yet, in so many words but ...' Bob stopped pacing and stood behind the chair, gripping its back tightly. 'Maybe she's right, at that. I mean, so long as this lasts, I won't have a job, will I? If ever again. So I'll be the one at home all day while she goes out to work. And when the kids come home, it'll be just me. Normally that would be nice, something to look forward to, but now ... Christ! She's especially worried about Samantha, her eldest, I know she is. It's nonsense, of course, but it's something I said. Sonya's latched onto it. I mean, Sam's a lovely kid, I like her, we get on fine, but now ...' Bob ran a hand through his hair, shaking his head violently. His voice rose to a shout. 'I'm a *PERVERT*, aren't I? That's the truth of it. That's the worm that's got into everyone's mind, that's what they see now when they look at me – a child abuser!'

The worm's in my mind, too, Lucy thought, secretly. *Is it true? Did he really do it?*

With a face and tone as calm and sympathetic as possible, she said: 'Look, what we have to do, is go through these allegations carefully, line by line, to seek out the best way to refute them. It's going to have to be partly an exercise in memory, Bob, since it happened – or didn't happen – so very long ago. I can help you with that, up to a point, but what you really need is evidence, character testimony from people who knew you back in 1991. Teachers at the school, colleagues, friends, people who knew you well and you may have kept up with ...'

'Sarah ...' Bob muttered, shaking his head grimly.

'Well, yes, Sarah of course ...'

'She knew me better than anyone, back then. But now ... I doubt if she'll even talk to me.'

'The police will be interviewing her for certain,' Lucy said. 'Do you think she'll support you?'

The brief smile on Bob's face was wistful, wry, bitter, anxious. 'Of course. Well, I suppose she will. Surely. After all, what else could she say?'

* * *

'We've found nothing so far,' Sergeant Lofthouse said. 'But then we wouldn't expect it. The river's up after those storms last week, and there's a full moon too.'

'What's the moon got to do with it?' Terry asked. He had seen the big yellow moon last night, low over the trees by the river as he crossed Lendal Bridge, driving home from work. Moonlight had rippled along the surface of the water, and he had thought, she's down there somewhere, poor lady. Perhaps she'll float to the surface at midnight, when no one is there to see.

'A full moon means high tides,' the man on the phone said now. 'And correspondingly low tides as well. That means the river backs up towards the weir at Naburn twice a day, and then drains away quickly downstream six hours later.'

'She wouldn't drift past the weir, would she?'

'Not likely, no. But even as far as the weir, it's a long stretch of water to search. And if she went in on Sunday she won't come to the surface for a day or two yet. If she ever does.'

'Why do you say that?'

Patiently, Sergeant Lofthouse explained. 'When a person drowns their lungs fill with water and they sink, right? Then as the body begins to decompose the bacteria excrete gases, which eventually bring it back to the surface. That can happen quickly or slowly depending on a number of factors, like water temperature, body weight, health, clothing and so on. Any idea what physical condition your missing lady was in?'

Terry shuddered. 'No, sorry. Just that she was in her mid thirties, I believe. She looks quite slim in the photo.'

'Well, the water's relatively warm at this time of year, so it shouldn't take too long. We'll give it another try tomorrow. You're fairly sure she's there, are you?'

'There doesn't seem to be any other explanation.'

Sergeant Lofthouse's team of frogmen were a costly resource, as Terry's senior officer, DCI Will Churchill, was sure to point out when he returned from holiday next week. But the evidence was pointing increasingly towards suicide by drowning. There was the suicide text, for a start, and the concern of her student lover, Adrian Norton. And the car, left unlocked beside the river. It had been transported to the police garage where an initial search had revealed nothing unusual except the book of feminist poems with a page turned down at a poem by Sylvia Plath about suicide. There was no sign of Victoria Weston's car keys, handbag, or phone.

Sad. She'll turn up sooner or later, Terry thought, driving slowly home.

12. Oysters

IT WOULD have been fine if not for the oysters. And the champagne, perhaps that was unwise too, Terry admitted ruefully.

But then who can predict the future? If a butterfly in the forests of Brazil can clap its wings and set off a chain of consequences which brings down the Roman Empire, then what hope is there for humans to control their own fates? Terry remembered debating such ideas as a student; he had seldom seen a better example than today.

It all started so well. The sky was blue, the early morning air was crisp with the promise of later warmth. As they set off from the boatyard at Naburn, bright sunshine sparkled off the ripples on the river, and seagulls and swans bobbed prettily in their wake.

Terry's youngest daughter Esther had made a skull and crossbones flag out of an old pillowcase, which Savendra attached to the radio aerial. Her 13 year old elder sister Jessica, who'd arrived in jeans and a sweater, surprised everyone by diving below into the cabin and emerging in a teeshirt, sandals and the tiniest pair of pink shorts which displayed her long skinny legs to perfection. She proceeded to display these by lounging on the foredeck in a style clearly copied from TV adverts. Terry raised his eyebrows, but decided any paternal protest would ruin the day permanently.

The girls waved gaily to passers-by on the riverbank and other boats. Sarah and Belinda chatted gaily to both of them, Sarah telling stories of her own daughter, Emily, now in her early twenties, while Belinda, eight months pregnant, encouraged them to feel the baby's movements in her huge tummy, and listen to its heartbeat through a stethoscope which she had bought for the purpose.

Terry knew Savendra of old, both as an antagonist in court and as a friend of Sarah's. It had been at Savendra's wedding reception when Sarah had so disastrously invited Terry to her room, though he hoped Savendra did not know that. The two men were not close friends, but Savendra, an enthusiastic motor cyclist, was clearly delighted to have a man on board to whom he could show off the workings of his new toy. He explained the engine, the various throttle speeds, the steering, the depth of the keel, the rules of the river, the costs of mooring and maintenance, and his ambitions to take the cruiser downriver to Goole and the Humber mouth, perhaps even further one day. As soon as they were north of York he gave Terry the helm, a friendly gesture which Terry, after a few hairy moments, found himself enjoying thoroughly.

Ten miles north of York they tied up at a jetty near Aldwark and Belinda unpacked the picnic she had prepared. French bread, salad, paté, cheese, smoked salmon – and oysters. Dozens of oysters, carefully packed in canisters of crushed ice. Terry was not used to oysters – they were a rarity in the police canteen – and he and his daughters set about them cautiously. Esther shrieked with delight as one slid down the front of her sister's teeshirt, and both girls pulled faces and made gagging noises before the slippery food went down. But the adults washed them down with champagne, and Belinda in particular swallowed nearly a dozen.

Savendra tried to stop her but she only laughed. 'I get these cravings, darling, it's a mummy thing. Better than lumps of coal, surely! What did you long for when you were pregnant, Sarah?'

'All sorts of things – tomatoes, I remember. Those little cherry ones – I ate fifty at a time.'

'There you are, darling, you see! It's your son I'm feeding, not just me! Come on girls, look – I'll show you what do with the shells.'

Belinda was not particularly good at skimming the oyster shells across the water, but she was certainly in high spirits. After the picnic they sailed on further upriver. The engine purred smoothly, the sun shone, a herd of black and white cows lifted their heads and lowed at them as they floated past. The food and champagne had made everyone happy. Sarah, who was leaning over the bows with Jessica looking for fish, turned back to catch Terry's eye, and winked.

Then Belinda screamed.

Savendra, who was nearest, looked at her in alarm. She was crouched on a bench in the cockpit, doubled over, staring at the floor.

'What is it, darling?'

She looked up, her face white, clutching her stomach. 'Nothing. I just felt this pain – here.'

'Oh my God, I hope it's not ...'

Belinda smiled faintly. 'No, it can't be. There are three weeks to go.' She struggled gamely to her feet and leant on the rail, gazing forward. 'Look! under that tree – is that a kingfisher?'

A few minutes later, she screamed again. Savendra put his arm round her, glancing at Terry with concern. Sarah came aft.

'What is it?'

'I think ... it might be ...' Belinda looked at Sarah. 'Did you get twinges like, this, a few weeks before?'

'Not painful ones.' Sarah sat down beside her. 'Where do you feel it, exactly?'

'Here. I ... ooooooh! *No*, what's this?'

This time there was no doubt. A damp stain was flooding the crotch of her jeans. 'It's all wet. I'm so sorry, I ...'

'Her waters have broken,' Sarah said, looking at Savendra, seeing the concern on his face. She put her arm round Belinda. 'Come on, love. Let's go into the cabin and get these off. You'll be all right, it's quite normal.'

As the women disappeared Savendra gazed at Terry in alarm. 'But she can't have it here! She needs a doctor, a midwife, a hospital!'

'Yes, of course. Where are we, exactly?' Terry looked about him, at the willow trees bending over the quiet winding river, the cows grazing peacefully on the wide empty water meadows.

Savendra glanced at the Satnav on his phone. 'We're coming up to a bridge in five minutes. The road on the bridge leads to ... where? Wetherby – do they have a hospital there?'

'It goes to York the other way.' Terry pulled out his mobile. 'Look, I'll call for an ambulance. They can meet us there and take her to Maternity. It'll be all right.' He smiled at Savendra who was looking panic-stricken. 'Don't worry, women do these things all the time.'

'I know, but Belinda ... Terry take over the wheel, will you? I want to go inside.'

So Terry steered the boat to the bridge, where they moored and he called for an ambulance. When it came, Belinda clung onto Sarah and insisted she went with her. Reluctantly, the paramedics agreed, but drew the line at taking Savendra as well. As they drove away, the two men stared at each other.

'It's our first, I said I'd be there. She needs me,' Savendra said. 'I can't just ...' He waved his hand at the boat despairingly.

'Okay, look, I'll call a taxi,' Terry said. 'We can all follow on.'

'But what about the boat? I can't just leave it here.' Savendra drew a deep breath, pulling himself together. 'Of course, Terry, you're right, a taxi's a great idea. But look, would you mind ... if I just turn the boat round, do you think you could take it back to the boatyard at Naburn? I've shown you what to do, it's dead easy. And you seem to have the knack.'

* * *

And so it was that two hours later Terry and his daughters found themselves approaching the city of York by boat. So far, the return trip had gone smoothly. Truth to tell, Terry was enjoying it. He kept to a moderate speed, leaving only a slight wash on the river banks and keeping religiously to the right of approaching boats. Jessica stood next to him, admiring her father's new skill and watching how the throttle and the rudder worked. On a quiet stretch, he let her hold the wheel for a while. And when that went well, Esther had a go too.

And if they hadn't met the rowers, Terry thought ruefully afterwards, nothing would have gone wrong at all.

Approaching the city, they passed under the iron railway bridge, with a train rumbling loudly overhead. Then they passed two medieval towers between which, Savendra had told them this morning, a huge metal chain had once been slung across the river to keep out marauding water-borne Scots – and pirates, as Esther insisted with delight. Then under Lendal Bridge, the first of York's three road bridges. Tall buildings, both ancient and modern, rose on either side now; the children waved to families sitting on the balcony of the Coney Street cinema, while Terry steered them carefully to the right of a large red-painted tourist ferry. Then under Ouse Bridge, past King's Staithe which was so regularly flooded that the riverside pub, the *King's Arms*, had a marker inside the door to show how high the flood water rose each year – well above a man's head, quite often. And so on to Skeldergate Bridge, with the Crown Court and medieval castle, Clifford's Tower, on their left, and on their right, modern blocks of flats with balconies overlooking the riverside walk.

'We've been up there, Dad, haven't we? There, that one at the end!' Esther pointed to a balcony, three stories high. 'That's where Mrs Newby lives, doesn't she? She showed us this morning.'

'Yes, I remember,' Jessica said. 'We went to her party after her motorbike accident, and Esther threw cake down from the balcony for the ducks. It landed on an old lady's umbrella – it was SO embarrassing! We had to hide behind the railings!'

'Jessica, you pig! It was an accident!'

'It was not. You were aiming for her!'

'I wasn't! I slipped. There was a swan, I was aiming for that!'

'Pretty poor shot, then.' Jessica turned away from her sister, gazing up at the balcony thoughtfully as the block of luxury flats drifted slowly astern. 'Dad, what exactly happened to Mrs Newby when she fell off her motorbike? You never did say.'

'I know,' Esther burst in. 'There was a man chasing her, wasn't there? Her daughter Emily told me.'

'Yes, that's right.' Terry sighed, thinking back. 'But there was no great harm done. Her son arrived in time, and we arrested the man.'

'But what had he done? Why was he chasing her?'

Terry shook his head firmly. 'You know I never talk about things like that.'

'But why not, Dad? It's interesting.'

'When you're older, perhaps. Look, there's a swan over there, right ahead. Two of them.'

The distraction worked, this time. They passed the swans, and moved on downstream, the banks of the river turning green and quiet once more. Birdsong replaced the bustling noise of the city, and then another sound appeared – a whooshing sound like the sea, growing steadily louder. They turned a bend and there in front of them was the source: the concrete road bridge carrying the dual carriageway of the A64, cars and lorries swishing by overhead. Beyond that, there were just trees, meadows, and ahead on their right, the palace of the Archbishop of York.

As they approached the palace, they saw the rowers. Two teams of coxed fours, in light racing shells, coming towards them upstream. Terry had been letting Jessica steer the boat for the past few minutes, but now he moved to take over the helm.

'It's all right, Dad – I can do it!'

'Well, keep to the right – starboard bank, remember? Give them plenty of room. Those are long oars!'

'Ok, Dad, here we go!'

The manoeuvre went well at first. But the river ahead of them was beginning to narrow slightly and on the right bank willow trees hung low over the water. As the rowers approached Terry lowered their speed, already slow, to a crawl in the hope of reducing their wash; but the rowers were coming on fast, much faster than either he or Jessica had expected. As they approached, the cox in the leading boat raised an arm and yelled. His words weren't clear but his meaning was aggressive and impatient, which flustered Jessica. She turned the wheel sharply to give them more room, but almost immediately the rowers were alongside, lean muscular bodies stretching and pulling in unison, the cox waving his hand in a slightly more friendly gesture of acknowledgement. Esther waved her pirate flag. Terry smiled in relief and glanced ahead to look for the second boat, just a dozen lengths behind the first.

Then their bows crashed into a willow tree.

Jessica screamed. Branches bent and cracked and scraped along the side of the boat as it drove steadily in under the overhanging canopy of leaves. The boat slowed with the resistance, but the current, still carrying them steadily downstream, began to push the stern out into the middle of the river in the path of the oncoming rowers. Terry grabbed the wheel and switched off the engine, watching in horror as the racing shell swished ever closer, the oblivious oarsmen with their backs to him leaning into each stroke, the cox swearing and tugging on his tiller ropes as the thirty-foot cruiser slowly swung broadside across the river in front of them.

'Pull – HARDER!' the cox yelled in a voice like thunder, and to Terry's astonishment, just as the collision seemed inevitable the racing shell leapt forward even faster, the outer oars shaving the stern of the cruiser by a few millimetres at most.

'Stupid wankers! Keep off the river if you can't steer!' yelled the cox, and the astonished eyes of the rowers glared back at Terry and Jessica for a moment before – to Terry's intense relief – they bent to their next stroke and raced on upstream, around the bend and out of sight.

'I'm sorry, Dad, I didn't mean ...'

'Don't worry, we'll get out of this, somehow. Just sit down and let me – Esther, get back here!'

With the two girls sitting meekly beside him in the cockpit Terry switched on the ignition and put the engine into reverse. He had to rev hard to counteract the drag of the current, but eventually the bows began to pull away from the trees where they were snagged. Willow branches dragged and scraped along the deck, holding the boat back, and then they were free – but with the bows pointing upstream.

'Dad, I'm really sorry. It's all my fault ...'

'Don't worry, I'll get this sorted out. Look, if I let the boat turn with the current, like this ... you see, we'll swing round and be pointing in the right direction again.'

They almost made it. Terry was feeling quite proud of the manoeuvre but the river just here was fairly narrow and as they came round eventually facing downstream another huge overhanging willow tree loomed ahead. To avoid it Terry put the engine into full speed astern. The boat moved backwards, into an eddy of branches and flotsam just under the bank. When he judged they had room to move out again and miss the trees, he engaged forward gear.

But something was wrong. The engine roared but the propeller was only turning sluggishly. Jessica leaned over the stern.

'Dad, I think there's something caught! You've snagged something in the water!'

'Bloody hell fire.' Terry almost never swore in front of his children but the afternoon was threatening to end in a nightmare of incompetence. He should never have allowed Jessica to steer in the first place; now she was blaming herself and he looked like an idiot.

Come on Terry, he told himself sternly. *You're the adult here. Get a grip.*

'All right, I've switched the engine off. Let me see what it is.'

Before leaving the wheel he took a nervous glance over his shoulder, trying to estimate how much time he would have before the boat drifted downstream again, into the willow tree he had just avoided. But they were close under the bank now, the current wasn't so strong here, thank goodness. They might even be in a back eddy, which would explain why all that litter which he had just backed into had got here. He leaned over the stern and looked.

'It looks like ... I don't know, leaves ... bits of branches ... a cloth of some kind, a coat. How the hell did that get here? Give me that long hook thing, Jess – the boathook. That's it. I'll try and reach it here. If it doesn't come loose we'll have to moor somehow against those trees and I'll get into the water. Christ, I hope not.'

The idea was hardly attractive. The river might be a lot less polluted than it had been ten years ago, but it was still cold and wet and its very name – Ouse – suggested what it would be like, wading into deep brown mud close to the shore. Terry leaned over the stern and began to search for the obstruction with the boathook.

It was definitely that cloth, that coat or whatever it was, which was causing the trouble. Three times he hooked it and almost pulled it loose before it snagged on something beneath the boat; the propeller presumably. It was pale brown like sacking; on the third try he saw a pocket with something lumpy in it. Definitely a coat then or a jacket. How did a thing like that get here? He searched again, a little bit further under the boat this time, and felt the boathook catch around something firmer; a branch maybe, a piece of wood. It was hard to lift it up. Terry leaned out further, reaching his arms down as far as he could.

'Dad, be careful! Don't fall in!'

'I'm okay. Grab my feet if you can. I've nearly got it! Yes, here we go!'

'Have you found something? What is it, Dad?'

Oh my God.

To his daughters' surprise, their father didn't answer. Clinging onto his legs as they were, they couldn't see what he had found. Which, in Terry's opinion, was just as well.

The cloth, he had decided, was definitely a long coat or jacket of some kind. He knew that for certain now, because what he had hauled up was the sleeve. The sleeve had been hard to pull up, because there was something inside it. Protruding out of the end of the sleeve, directly in front of Terry's horrified eyes, was what remained of a human hand.

Part Two

Alibi

13. A Pocket Full of Stones

THERE WERE stones in the pockets, that was the first obvious thing that they noticed. The dead woman had been wearing a long, rather stylish three quarter length fawn jacket or housecoat – DS Jane Carter wasn't quite sure what to call it – which fastened with two buttons at the front and a long loose belt like a dressing gown cord around the waist. It was probably very fashionable, she thought, the sort of thing you might see on a film star or a model in a Sunday colour supplement, perhaps. She couldn't imagine wearing such a thing herself; it was too ... elegant, somehow. On a slim, slender woman it would look fetching, like a man's shirt on a girl. But if you were tall, unusually strong for a woman and well, chunky and tomboyish in appearance then a garment like this would just not work.

Not that the woman inside the jacket looked particularly attractive now, Jane thought grimly. Face bloated, wrinkled and puffy with the water, long straggly fair hair tangled in knots with weeds and small twigs in it, hands scratched, limbs swollen and floppy, long past the stage of rigor mortis.

'Death by drowning, almost certainly,' Andrew Jones, the duty doctor said. 'Linda will do a full post mortem on Monday, but my guess is she'll just confirm that. Looks like suicide to me, but that's your call, isn't it, sergeant?'

Wearing gloves to avoid contamination, Jane, the doctor, and Detective Constable Harry Easby stripped the body and lifted it into one of the long refrigerated drawers to await full examination tomorrow. Jane and Harry laid out the dead woman's clothes on a table to see what they could tell from them. As Jane picked up the jacket she felt the weight of the stones in the pockets. They clinked together as it moved. She upended the jacket and tipped them out

– six large pebbles, three on either side. Carefully, so as not to disturb any fingerprints that might have survived the river, she collected them in a plastic bag and put it on a weighing scale.

'Six pounds, almost half a stone,' she read from the display. 'How much would you say that woman weighed, doc? Seven stone, eight?'

'Somewhere around that,' Dr Jones agreed, looking down at the body in the drawer. 'Light bones, around five foot six. In her mid thirties, probably. Good condition, no sign of obesity. Pretty lady, before she did this to herself. What a waste.' He slid the drawer shut.

Jane was still looking at the pebbles. 'So with another six pounds of dead weight in her pockets, that was quite enough to inhibit her swimming, wouldn't you say?'

'It would have made it harder, certainly, in a strong river current,' the doctor agreed. 'But if she'd wanted to live, she'd have shrugged the coat off, wouldn't she?'

'I read about someone who did kill herself like this,' Harry Easby said thoughtfully. 'Someone famous – I can't recall the name just now.'

'I can guess the name of this one,' Jane said. 'Still, we need to be sure.' But although they searched, there was nothing obvious in the clothes, no labels, nametags or receipts, to confirm who the woman was. Apart from the loose jacket, she'd been wearing a blouse, slacks, bra and pants, all from Marks & Spencers. The blouse had been torn and the bra twisted, one shoulder strap broken, the left breast out of the cup. That had probably happened in the water, Jane thought. She remembered how the dead woman had been tangled in tree roots below the surface, with her arm and part of the housecoat snagged in the boat's propeller. But the real shock, of course, had been seeing her senior colleague, Terry Bateson, leaning over the stern of the boat. With his two daughters, their faces white as sheets.

He'll be in on Monday, she thought, wanting to know how I've dealt with all this. So I'd better get it right.

'Nothing on her feet,' Harry Easby noted. 'That's odd.'

'Odd, why? Her shoes probably floated away in the river, don't you think?'

'Yes, but if she'd gone to all this trouble to drown herself, putting stones in her pockets to weigh herself down, why not put something heavy on your feet as well. Welly boots, for example – they'd fill with water, pull you down.'

Jane shrugged. 'Maybe she didn't have any. An elegant lady, she probably just wore something light. Slip–ons that slipped off. Anyway the stones did the job.' She picked one of the stones out of the bag, and examined it carefully in a gloved hand. Smooth, round, shiny, with attractive veins of red and grey in the rock. 'These aren't local. They're quite pretty really. I wonder ... Where would you get stones like these?'

Harry Easby shook his head. 'No idea. Ask a stone merchant – a geologist, perhaps?'

'Maybe I will.' Jane tossed the pebble in her hand and smiled. 'If only stones could talk. Looks like this is the best clue we've got, at the moment.'

* * *

'But how long had she been there, Daddy?'

'Not very long, Jess. A few days, perhaps a week.'

'It's so horrible. I don't want to go on a boat again.'

'You don't have to, love. We'll do something else next time.'

'I keep seeing it. A hand coming out of the water. They don't tell you about that, do they, in the boatyard. If they did people wouldn't go on boats.'

It had been a dramatic afternoon – life and death in twelve hours. He wished he had handled things better than he had.

Ever since his wife Mary had been so shockingly killed in a car accident, one of Terry's principal aims as a father had been to keep a clear wall between his family life with his children and the grimy world of crime in which he spent his working days. Now the two had, quite literally, collided.

As soon as he had seen the pale hand poking out of the sleeve in the water under the stern of their boat he had ordered the girls to go below into the cabin, but it was already too late. Jessica saw it first and before Terry had managed to clamber back on board from his awkward position, head down over the transom, Esther had seen it too.

They were shocked, horrified and delighted all at once, and Terry feared afterwards that he had made everything worse by hustling them down into the cabin and insisting on pain of dire punishments that they stay there and *not come on deck whatever happened.* Then when Esther *had* come on deck, mischievous and apologetic but not really looking frightened or upset as he had feared they both might be, he had yelled at her to *get back below at once, do you hear?*

Admittedly he had been on the phone to Jane Carter asking her to call the police diving team at the time while simultaneously trying to moor the boat to a tree so they didn't drift out into midstream dragging the body behind them, but it was still, he reflected when they finally got home, a pretty poor performance by a father. After all, Jessica would have been willing and eager to help him moor the boat, which would have given her something positive to do instead of spreading panic. But he was still flustered by his own lamentable judgement in allowing Jessica to steer the boat at a moment when he – as the vessel's captain – should have taken charge. Then after crashing the boat himself he had given a textbook example of anger and emotional loss of control in the face of an unexpected crisis.

By the time the divers had arrived he'd calmed down and explained things to the children as best he could. Then there'd been a long wait until they'd agreed to let him take the boat on to the boatyard which was just closing when they arrived. The one positive moment on the drive home was when Sarah Newby phoned, to tell him that Belinda had been delivered of a healthy boy, and mother and baby were doing well.

'It's just the father who's looking a bit shocked,' Sarah said, laughing cheerfully. 'I'm taking him out for a meal to calm him down. Everything okay with the boat?'

'Yes, we've moored it safely. Just driving home now.'

'Good. No incidents on the return trip then? Savvy was a bit worried about letting you sail it on your own.'

'What? Sorry, can't hear you. You're breaking up.'

'I said how was the return ...'

'Can't hear. I'll ring you later, when the kids are in bed. Bye.'

Terry switched his phone off. On the way home they bought fish and chips and then, since Trude was still away watching her boyfriend Odd playing for Leeds United, Terry got the girls ready for bed. There was school tomorrow and they needed sleep, he insisted.

But that was not how they saw it. Twice he sent them to bed, and twice they came down, the second time just as he was about to ring Sarah to explain. The events of the day were too exciting. So now they sat cuddled together on the sofa in the living room, drinking hot chocolate and discussing things. They were pleased about Belinda's baby but what fascinated them was the body in the river.

'It doesn't happen often, hardly ever, in fact,' Terry said. 'Careful – you'll spill that on your nightie.'

Esther sipped her hot chocolate thoughtfully. She was calmer now – the wide, dark pupils in her eyes had shrunk to normal size.

'Yes, but it does *sometimes*, Daddy – you said. How often?'

'How often do people drown in the river?' Terry considered his answer carefully. What was the right amount of information for a child of eleven? He believed in being honest with his daughters, not lying to them, but he wanted to shield them too, from the horrors he had to confront in his job.

'It varies. Maybe one or two people a year, that's all. Sometimes less.' *And sometimes more, too*, Terry thought. *Quite a lot more, but you don't need to know that. You don't need to know any of this.*

'Do you think she just fell in?'

It was not the first time little Esther had asked this question. She seemed to feel a need to go around in circles, time and again, checking if the answer was still the same. It was a psychological process, Terry supposed, a way of coming to terms with a traumatic event. But it was eerily like the process he was familiar with at work; the way detectives obsessively circled around a crime, asking the same questions again and again until they felt sure of the answers.

'That's what we'll have to find out, my love.' He yawned, stroking her hair fondly as she snuggled closely under his arm. 'She may have fallen in, tripped over something, had an accident. We don't know yet.'

'But if she fell in, she could swim to the bank, couldn't she? That's what I'd do.'

'You were wearing a life jacket, remember? And the river's very strong, it's not like a swimming pool. Maybe she was drunk, or ill, or just couldn't swim.'

'Alison said sometimes people kill themselves, too,' Jessica said. 'If you do that you go straight to hell, Alison says. You burn in hell forever.'

Thanks, Alison, Terry thought, remembering a thin schoolgirl with pigtails, Jessica's classmate. *That's just the sort of help we needed, at this time of night.* 'There isn't a hell,' he said firmly. 'At least I don't believe it. Nobody knows for sure.'

'If you're not sure, that means it might be true.' Jessica shuddered, took a long sip of hot chocolate. 'But Mummy's in heaven, isn't she?'

'Yes. If there is a heaven, Mummy's there for sure.' Tears prickled in Terry's eyes. There'd been many conversations like this since Mary had died, but they always touched him.

'Why are you so sure, Daddy?'

'Because heaven is for good people, and Mummy was very good – the best.'

'So where do the bad people go?'

'They, well ...' Terry sipped his drink, thinking how to answer.

'Do they turn into zombies and vampires?' Esther asked.

'No, of course not!' Terry spluttered, and put his hot chocolate down carefully to avoid spilling it. 'Look, there's no such thing as vampires or zombies, okay? Trust me – that's one thing I am sure about. That's just a silly story.'

'But heaven and hell?'

'Jessica, we've been through that, you know we have. If there is a just, kind God – like the vicar, the people in the Church, all say there is – then good people like your mother get to rest in peace in heaven, whatever that's like. And the others ... they're probably at peace too, but not in hell. If there was a hell God would be cruel, and he's not like that. There are no zombies either. Definitely.'

It sounded thin even to him, but it was very late, and what *do* you say to children when their mother dies and you think there's nothing after death, nothing at all? You make it up, just as the priests have been making it up for thousands of years. Why? Because it's comforting, a fairy story, and the alternative is too hard to think about or focus on for long. Especially when you're eleven years old.

If there's nothing after death then there's nothing to be afraid of. What are you afraid of? Nothingness. Exactly. Try explaining that.

'Come on, young lady, it's too late to talk about this now. You've got school tomorrow morning and I'm going to work. If we don't get some sleep neither of us will be good for anything. Drink up now.'

Thoughtfully, Jessica got to her feet and Terry picked up the yawning Esther. As they climbed the stairs quietly, Jessica whispered: 'You'll tell us about the lady in the river when you know, won't you, Daddy?'

Terry nodded wearily. 'When I know more, I'll tell you. Now off to sleep.' He tucked them both into bed and kissed the tops of their heads.

'Sweet dreams.'

He went downstairs to ring Savendra, to congratulate him on his baby and warn him why his boat might be in the news.

* * *

'Yes, that's her. It looks something like her, anyway.' Tom Weston stood, irresolute, staring down at the body. 'My God, is this what we all come to?'

The pathologist had cleaned the weed and mud from the dead woman's face, but it was still pale and bloated, the skin soft and puffy like a decaying mushroom. The cheeks were expanded, as though inflated from within, the lips blue, the eyes within the dark sockets mercifully closed. It was a long way from the photographs Jane had seen in the Weston's house – of a slender, pretty woman, her eyes alight with laughter, her fair hair tousled by the wind, not limp and dank as it was now.

'We'll take a DNA sample anyway, sir, to compare with one from your home. But you're quite sure, are you?'

Only the face of the body was uncovered on the metal trolley. He reached out for a moment to touch it, then moved his fingers away. 'Yes. Well it has to be her, doesn't it? We've been expecting this all week, after all.'

'Would you like to stay for a moment? I can wait outside.'

'No.' He glanced around the room – the rows of impersonal fridges with their sliding drawers all down one wall, the tiled floor sloping slightly towards a drain in the middle, the metal examination tables, the array of knives and saws arranged neatly beside the sink, and shuddered. 'No, let's get out of here, now.'

As Jane opened the door he took a final glance at the body, lying forever still on the metal trolley with the green cover drawn up the neck, and lifted a hand as though in farewell. 'Silly, silly bitch,' he muttered. 'You should never have done that.'

The words were whispered softly but Jane was sure she heard them correctly. Almost sure; she was only a few inches away. As she escorted him outside she waited, wondering if he would say any more. But he said nothing until he was in her car, and she was driving him home.

'So what happens now? There'll be a post mortem, I suppose.'

'Yes, first thing Monday morning.'

He shrugged. 'What's the point? She drowned. She was found in the river, wasn't she? Silly woman, killed herself, threw herself in. And that's how she ends up.'

'Yes, that's how it looks, I agree,' Jane said. 'But we have to do everything properly, all the same. There'll be an inquest, then a funeral for you to arrange.'

'Hm.' He slumped further into the passenger seat, staring away from her out of the window. 'Wonderful.'

'Do you have friends or family, someone who can be with you this evening?' Jane asked, as they approached his home. It was part of the job, driving bereaved relatives to and from the mortuary. She could have let him drive himself, but that wouldn't have been wise.

'What? Oh, yeah, my sister, I gave her a ring. Don't worry, Mrs policeman, I can cope. I've been living without a wife for nearly a week now. I'm starting to get used to it.'

The car scrunched across the gravel around the statue of the naked mermaid in the fishpond, and came to a halt outside the front door.

'You'll be okay then, sir?'

He opened the car door, then gave her a weak smile. 'I'll be fine. Enjoy your post mortem, sergeant. Cheers.'

'Sweet dreams,' Jane whispered, watching him walk alone towards the house.

But as he put his key in the front door another car drove across the gravel and parked the other side of the fishpond. A woman got out. Jane watched as Tom Weston held the door open and escorted her inside.

His sister, she presumed. At least he'd have some company, then.

14. Post Mortem

'So, THIS is our suicide, is it, Jane?'

'More yours than mine sir, after your efforts yesterday. The frogmen were well hacked off; they'd been searching the river all week before you turned up.'

'They should do their job properly,' Terry said. 'Then my kids wouldn't have had nightmares.'

'She was snagged on the propeller of your boat, I hear?' Linda Miles, the pathologist, smiled sympathetically at Terry. A friendly, extrovert mother of two, her youngest daughter was in the same school as Esther. She and Terry met, on happier days, at children's parties and parent's evenings. Like him, she had probably driven her children to school this morning, before coming to work at the mortuary. He wondered, looking at the corpse on the slab, what she told her children on the subject of death. But then, it's only when it's personal that the subject really gets under your skin.

'She was drowned, anyway, to state the obvious first. No other injuries that I can see so far. Just a few cuts and grazes on her face and arms and legs, But that's what you'd expect, if she'd been in the river some time. Do you know when she went in?'

'Last Sunday, we think,' Jane said. 'Sometime in the evening, probably. Her car was found at Landing Lane last Monday morning.'

'So that's why she wasn't floating yet,' Linda said. 'I'd have expected her to stay under for a few more days even without the pebbles in her pockets. How deep was she?'

'Two or three feet under water,' Terry said. 'She was tangled in some tree roots by the bank. Don't remind me. Jessica saw me dragging a hand out of the river.'

Linda Miles raised a sympathetic eyebrow. Under the white protective cap she had a mild, motherly face. 'I didn't know you were a boating man. How long has that been going on?'

Terry, who hadn't slept much, forced a grim smile. 'It's a long story. Tell you later. Have you found anything significant?''

'There *are* a few details, as a matter of fact. If you look carefully enough. See here.' Linda Miles lifted the dead woman's hands, spread out the fingernails. 'What do you see?'

'A graze on the back of the knuckles. A wedding ring.'

'True. anything else?'

Terry peered closely. 'Well ...'

'It looks very clean,' Jane Carter broke in.

'Very good, detective sergeant!' Linda Miles beamed. 'Examine the fingernails, for instance.'

They did so. The dead woman's fingernails were not cut short; they were trimmed to an elegant oval shape and protruded a couple of millimetres beyond the end of each finger. The third nail was broken, the rest in good shape.

'They're not varnished, are they?' Terry said.

'There are traces of varnish yes, but transparent. I guess it looks natural to you.' Linda's smile this time meant *'to a man.'* She darted a conspiratorial grin at Jane – a look largely wasted on a woman whose use of cosmetics was minimal. Brains, not beauty, were DS Carter's strong point.

'Did you search under the fingernails?' Jane asked now.

'I did, and found very little. Which, in the circumstances, seems rather surprising, don't you think?' The pathologist watched to see their reaction.

'It's a fairly muddy river,' Terry said. 'If this is a suicide, however much she may have wanted to drown herself, most people clutch at straws, in the end. It's a physical reaction, isn't it – a panic which is hard to control.'

Linda Miles nodded. 'Impossible, I'd say. When you take that first breath and your lungs start to fill up with water ...' She shuddered. 'Try holding your breath in a swimming pool and see how you feel. So most drownings I've seen, suicides included, have mud, tree bark, leaves, whatever – under their fingernails. Whereas this lady's nails were clean. Unusually so.'

'Really?' Terry said. 'You're telling me this lady washed her hands before ending up in the river?'

'And then didn't panic when she drowned?' Jane Carter added.

'So it would seem.' The pathologist nodded, a curious smile on her face. 'But that's only the start of this mystery, my dear detective friends. My *hors d'oeuvre*. Here is the *pièce de resistance*.'

She lifted a large dish containing two reddish, slippery objects. She lifted them out of the dish in her blue, latex-gloved hands. 'These are the poor lady's lungs. Notice anything unusual?'

Terry swallowed, shaking his head. 'No. should I?'

'If you held them you might, but I'll spare you that.' She moved her hands up and down, testing the weight. 'They're much heavier than I would have expected. Slippery too – whoops!'

Terry closed his eyes as the lungs slithered back into the metal dish. 'Is that significant?' he asked grimly.

'Sorry about that, but yes it is actually. Very. I would have expected them to be lighter, and more doughy, not jelly-like like these. And if you look at the lining ...' she opened one of the lungs where she had made an incision before – '... you can see they're red, not as grey as I would have expected from someone pulled out of the river.'

'So what does that tell you?'

'Well, the last time I saw lungs like this was in a Russian sailor who was pulled out of the sea near Whitby.'

'What?' Terry and Jane looked equally puzzled.

'You see, the symptoms of drowning in salt water are different from those of drowning in fresh water. To put it simply, if a person's lungs are filled with fresh water, that water quickly passes through the lining of the lungs to enter the bloodstream, where it causes your red blood cells to swell and burst, so they can't supply oxygen to your brain and heart. But if a person's lungs are filled with salt water, the opposite happens. Instead of the water passing through the lining of the lungs into the bloodstream, the blood is drawn out of the veins and into your lungs. So your lungs fill up with a mixture of blood and water. Which I think is what we have here.'

The pathologist turned and lifted a large jar from a shelf. It was full of a pinkish brown frothy liquid. 'This was the actual contents of the lungs. Again, rather more than I'd expected. The reddish froth is proof that she did indeed drown – it's blood from the lining of the lungs which has combined with water instead of air as it's supposed to do. I've run one simple test already. Guess what I found.' She paused expectantly.

'Poison?' Terry asked.

'Not this time.' Linda smiled. 'Salt.'

'What? *Salt?* But there's no salt in river water is, there?'

'Not usually, no. Not unless there's been some sort of catastrophic pollution which would hit the national press.'

'So what you're saying, Linda ...'

'What I am saying is that very little if any of the water in this lady's lungs came out of the river Ouse. Which means ...'

'She wasn't drowned in the river at all!' Jane said. 'You're saying she was drowned somewhere else! So this isn't suicide at all!'

'That does seems to be an inescapable conclusion.'

'So where then? In the sea?'

'Well no, probably not. The salt concentration is high but not as high as sea water. It's more likely to have come from a jacuzzi, a hot tub, something like that.'

'So if she was drowned somewhere else, in a jacuzzi or hot tub or somewhere where she could get salt in her lungs and had clean fingernails, then ...'

'She couldn't have driven her car to the river, ' Terry said. 'Or put those stones in her pockets! And she's very unlikely to have drowned herself in a bath or a jacuzzi either. That doesn't happen, does it, doc?'

'Oh yes, it can. Much more likely in a hot tub or jacuzzi than a normal bath. They're a lot bigger, for one thing, and in a jacuzzi you've got all those jets of water swirling around. There's a fair number of those deaths each year in the States, where hot tubs are more common than here. Most of the people who die like that are either drunk, or faint because the water's too hot. A combination of both, sometimes. Or they have a heart attack.'

'Does any of that apply here?' Terry asked.

'Not obviously, no. There was no alcohol in her blood, no sign of drugs. Her heart looks healthy; it stopped because of drowning, not the other way round.'

'Even if she did somehow manage to drown herself in a jacuzzi,' Jane pointed out. 'She certainly couldn't have driven herself to the river afterwards. She'd need help to do that.'

Terry met her eyes grimly. 'So I didn't haul a suicide out of the river after all. This is a murder victim.'

15. Bad News

THE CAR scrunched to a halt on the gravel outside Straw House Barn. As the two detectives got out, they noticed how silent and secluded this place was. Their car doors slammed in the silence. There was no hum of traffic here, just the pleasant gurgle of water trickling into the fishpond from the jug between the ornamental mermaid's breasts. The snail had gone from the statue's face, Terry noticed, and fish hid beneath the water lilies.

Tom Weston stood in the stone flagged hall, watching through the tall glass windows as Terry and Jane approached. He opened the door reluctantly.

'Now what? Not more bad news, I hope.' He looked pale and strained, as if he would rather be left alone with his grief.

'I'm afraid there has been a development, sir. Could we come inside?'

'If you must.'

The man stood back from the door and led the way across the hall which, Terry noticed, was tidier than on his previous visit. No broken china underfoot, no heap of un-ironed clothes or newspapers scattered across the floor. Noticing his glance Tom Weston said: 'Looks better, doesn't it? That's my sister's doing. She's in here. Audrey! It's the police.'

He led the way into a cavernous, oak-beamed living room. As they came in a woman stood up from a sofa. A tall well-built woman, in her late thirties perhaps, in jeans and a blue cardigan, with a strong, horsey face and brown hair pulled back in a ponytail.

'My sister, Audrey,' Tom said. 'She's been a godsend, found a new firm of cleaners. Vicky drove the last lot away. She's been giving me moral support too. As you can imagine it's very welcome. We're still trying to understand why she killed herself.'

His sister smiled briefly. 'Yes, it's tragic. Poor Vicky. Can I offer you tea? Coffee?'

'No, thank you,' Terry said. 'I'm afraid there's been an important development. It might be best if you both sit down.'

'So serious? We've had enough shocks already.' An anxious smile flickered across the woman's face as she resumed her seat. Tom Weston lowered himself slowly onto the sofa beside her. Then, with deliberate brusqueness, Terry dropped his bombshell.

'We've had the results of the post mortem this morning. It seems your wife may not have killed herself after all. It's more likely she was murdered.'

As he spoke he watched Tom Weston closely. If this *is* murder, he thought, I'm looking at the obvious suspect, and his reaction may tell me something.

'Murdered?' Tom's eyes widened, the blood draining from his face. 'But that's absurd! How? By whom?'

He turned to his sister beside him who looked equally stunned. She clutched his hand with both of hers – whether to give comfort or receive it was hard to tell. For maybe ten seconds they stared into each other's eyes, ignoring the two detectives. Then Tom turned back to face them. His left hand – the one his sister was not holding – was trembling. He closed his fist to stop it.

'But how can that be true? She threw herself into the river, didn't she? Left her car there, jumped in, and drowned.'

'Yes sir, that's how it appeared at first. But the results of the post mortem have made us question that idea, I'm afraid.'

'Well ... how? Who could possibly have done it?'

'That's our job to find out, sir. It will involve collecting evidence and taking statements from everyone who knew her. Including yourself, I'm afraid.'

'Me? But I was in Scotland, for heaven's sake! I've already told you that!' He glared at Terry, then glanced at his sister, who sat beside him on the sofa, still apparently shocked. He freed his hand from hers, got to his feet, and strode across the room. 'This is absurd. It's terrible.'

'Yes sir, I understand. But it has to be done. What were you doing in Scotland, exactly?'

'I was at a conference in Glasgow. It was about the changes to the education curriculum the government is bringing in.'

'I see. That's part of your work in some way, is it, sir?'

'Yes, of course. I work for a small publishing company that produces school textbooks, syllabuses, that sort of thing.'

'And you went away when?'

'Last Friday, I told you!' He glared at Jane Carter, who had discreetly taken out her notebook and was writing things down. 'I was away in Scotland from Friday morning until Monday afternoon, when I met you both here. That was when you told me Vicky's car had been found. I showed you her suicide text, for heaven's sake!'

'Yes sir. You first noticed it on your phone that morning, you said, although it was sent the evening before, at 9.37. And you spoke to your wife earlier on Sunday evening. About seven, I think?'

'Er ... yes ... something like that, yes.' Tom shook his head, flustered, apparently still shocked by the news.

'Did she call you or you call her?'

'She ... called me, I think.' He looked away from Terry, at his sister. 'Yes. Yes, that's right. I was in a restaurant, having supper. She called me.'

'Would you mind showing me your phone, sir, so that I can check the time of that call?'

'What?' A look of indignation crossed the man's face – or was it fear? 'Why do you need that?'

'As I said, sir, just to check. The more information we have, the better.'

'Yes, well ...' Tom's hands patted his pockets. 'I ... haven't got it on me. It must be in my bedroom. Wait there, I'll get it.' Quickly, he left the room.

While they waited for his return Terry smiled at the woman on the sofa. She looked pale, a little shocked, but met his eyes with a gaze that was calm enough. This is a woman with strong self control, Terry thought. Either that or she doesn't care very much.

'You're Victoria's sister-in-law, is that right?' he said.

'More or less. I'm Tom's half-sister actually. We had the same father.'

'I see. Your full name is ... ?'

'Audrey. Audrey Adair. That's my married name.'

Terry wrote it down. 'Do you live here in York?'

'In Sherriff Hutton actually. Just outside.'

'So when was the last time you saw Victoria?'

'Oh ... it must be ten days, a fortnight ago. I can't remember, exactly. I've been away on holiday. But I could check my diary, if it would help.'

'Did she have any enemies, as far as you know?'

'No.' Audrey Adair frowned, her expression sad, thoughtful. 'Nothing like that. But she was always very highly strung, neurotic. So when Tom told me she'd committed suicide, that didn't come as a complete surprise. Tragic of course, but ... now you say it's murder, well ...' She shook her head sadly.

Tom returned and handed Terry his phone, a small black Nokia. 'There. You can see I received Vicky's call at 19.15 on 28th August. Sunday.'

'Thank you.' Terry noted the time and scrolled through the call log briefly, but saw no other calls to or from Vicky on the 28th, or the two days before. He wrote down the phone number and passed the phone back. 'And you were in Scotland at the time, sir?'

'Indeed I was.' Tom slipped the phone into his pocket. The colour had returned to his face. 'So if Vicky really was murdered, it couldn't have been me, obviously.' He glanced at his sister, a nervous smile on his face; then strode irritably across the room, as though unable to control his energy.

Terry waited until Tom turned round, standing with his back to a large stonebuilt fireplace.

'Apparently not, sir. We'll be able to confirm the location of your phone if necessary, but it would help eliminate you now if you had any train tickets, hotel receipts and so on which you could show me. Do you keep things like that?'

'I suppose I've got them somewhere, yes. Why, don't you believe me?'

Terry looked at him coolly. 'We have to check everything, sir, that's our job. So if you could find those tickets it would be very helpful. Then, if you come down to the station, we'll take a proper statement there. You can have a lawyer present if you like.'

'A lawyer?' For a second time that morning the colour drained from Tom Weston's face. 'Why on earth should I need a lawyer? You're not arresting me, are you?'

'No sir. I'm just asking you to give a voluntary statement about the death of your wife. You don't have to say anything, of course, but since it appears she was murdered, I would have thought ....'

'Yes, yes, of course. Anything that will help catch her killer, if she really was murdered, as you say. Though it's hard to believe. Christ!'

'We'll need to take away your wife's computer, sir, I'm afraid,' said Terry firmly. 'And look around this house, especially the bathroom. The scenes of crime officers will be arriving shortly. Do you have a jacuzzi, by the way?'

'A jacuzzi? No. But there's a hot tub in the garden. You don't ... think she was drowned in there, do you?'

There was a slight, significant pause. Terry said nothing.

'She ... she *was* drowned, wasn't she? I mean ... she wasn't killed in some other way, and then ... thrown in the river to disguise it?'

I only told you she was murdered, Terry thought. *Not how.* But of course the pathologist told him she was drowned when he saw her body.

'I'm afraid I can't tell you any more at the moment, sir. But it seems likely she was murdered in this house while you were away in Scotland. And if it was murder as we suspect, someone else must have sent that suicide note from her phone. Her killer, presumably.'

'But this is terrible.' Tom Weston turned away from the fireplace, and strode blindly towards a window. As he did so, he caught sight of a van, pulling up outside on the gravel next to the fishpond with the statue of the mermaid. 'Now what? As if I didn't have enough trouble! Who the hell is this?'

'That'll be the SOCO team, sir,' Terry said, as three men and a women began climbing out of the van. 'I'm afraid we're going to have to treat this house as a crime scene from now on. So if you would like to accompany us down to the station, it might be a convenient time to take a detailed statement.'

'But ... what about her colleagues at work, her students? Aren't you going to interview any of them? I told you she was having an affair with one of them, the randy bitch! That's what we quarrelled about!'

'Of course, sir,' Terry said. 'We'll need statements from everyone who knew your wife or met her in the last couple of weeks, perhaps longer.' He glanced at Tom's sister, who had risen hesitantly to her feet, and was gazing out of the window at the men and women, climbing into white paper suits beside their van. Her face was still pale, her hands twisting anxiously together. 'Including you, madam, if you wouldn't mind. You won't want to be here while the SOCO team are crawling all over the house.'

16. Sarah and Bob

'SARAH?' A man's voice on the intercom.

'Yes. Who's that?'

'It's me, Bob. Don't you recognize ..'

'Oh God, yes of course. What are you doing here?'

'I was out for a walk, and I thought, maybe, if you're in ...'

'Yes, all right. Come on up.' Sarah pressed the switch that opened the front door of her apartment block. Then she looked around, flustered. Her flat was a mess – clothes drying on a hanger, court papers scattered all over the dining table in front of a half–finished plate of food. Quickly, she gathered up the crockery and took it into the kitchen, then checked her hair in front of a mirror – oh, what did it matter? This wasn't Terry, her lover, but Bob, her ex-husband, no need to look good for *him!*

What is he doing here anyway?

The buzzer chimed and she opened the door. There he was! So familiar, so alien, so strange. A tall thin man in a coat which hung loosely on him somehow, as though the lanky body inside had shrunk. That well-known face with the goatee beard, now flecked with touches of grey, dark crinkly hair ruffled by the wind, those once kind brown eyes scanning her anxiously.

What do you say when your ex comes calling?

Sarah stepped back, waving a hand vaguely towards the living room. 'You'd better come in.'

'Thanks. I hope it's not a bad time.' He shrugged his coat half off, then stopped, uncertain if he was presuming too much. She helped him out of it brusquely, hung the coat in a cupboard.

'Would you like tea? Coffee?'

'Um, tea, please. If you're making one.'

While she was in the kitchen he strolled around the room, gazed across the balcony to the river and the city beyond.

'Nice flat. Lovely view.'

'Yes. So long as I can afford it.' Sarah's response was sharp, pointed. She had seen her bank statement this morning; the mortgage was draining her account. The court papers on the table were a brief for a robbery, a two-day trial at most. Less if the defendants changed their plea at the last minute, as they probably would. Then nothing for the rest of the week. If she didn't find better cases soon she would lose this flat. Yet only a year ago, she and this man had shared a lovely detached four bedroom house in a pleasant village with views across open countryside. Her share of the mortgage had been less than half what this flat cost her now.

'So. What can I do for you, Bob?' She gave him his tea. No biscuits. Bob sat on the sofa, Sarah on a chair by the table, slightly higher than him. History crackled between them.

'Well. You've heard about this ... investigation.' As he said the last word Bob felt the rage surge back inside him, so strong that his hand trembled. He put the mug carefully down before he spilt the tea.

Sarah noted the reaction. 'Yes, of course. Lucy's told me some details. Is she doing a good job for you?'

'The best she can, I suppose. But you realise it's all lies, Sarah! I've lost my job!'

'Lost it? Surely ...'

'Okay, I'm suspended, technically, home on gardening leave, or whatever they want to call it. But I'm finished, Sarah, you do realise that? No school will ever take me back again, how could they? There'll always be that suspicion now – parents would run a mile! As it is I'm all over the press, the TV. All because of some wicked, malicious lies! Honestly, Sarah, it's hell!'

'I know, Bob.' Sarah put down her cup and leant forward sympathetically, looking into his eyes. No touching though, she wouldn't do that. 'But there's no truth in it, so one day ...'

He snatched at her words, like food in the desert. 'You *do* believe me, Sarah, don't you? You know it's not true?'

After only the faintest hesitation she replied. 'Of course I do, Bob. You may be all kinds of fool but you're not a paedophile. You'd never do that.'

'Of course I didn't. I'm not that sort of man, Sarah.'

'No Bob, you're not.' And then, when she saw how needy he was, how desperate, she added firmly: 'You're an idiot, but not a sex maniac. *I believe you*, okay?'

'Yes. Thanks, Sarah. It means a lot.' He dragged a tissue from his pocket and wiped his eyes. 'I *am* an idiot. I should never have left you, should I?'

Oh no, don't start that, Sarah thought. *You did leave and you're gone and I don't want you back. I have my own life now.*

'No, you shouldn't,' she agreed. 'But that's all in the past and can't be put back. Like toothpaste.'

'What?'

'Toothpaste.' She smiled, trying to lighten the atmosphere. 'You know, you can't put it back in the tube. How's Sonya? Is she supporting you too?'

'Yes. Well, she's doing her best. It's difficult for her, Sarah, she's got three young children ...'

Mistake, Sarah thought. *I don't want to hear about this.*

'... and she hasn't known me as long as you. She has no idea what it was like back then, when these things were supposed to have happened.'

'Yes, quite. Look, Bob, do you know the names of these schoolgirls – women now, presumably? Do you remember anything about them? Anything that might give you an idea why they might have made these accusations?'

'Not really. I've seen pictures of them and racked my brains but ... it was twenty-five years ago, Sarah. And since nothing actually happened – nothing sexual that is – what is there to remember?'

'Nothing sexual that is.' Sarah let the words hang in the air for a moment. 'So ... did anything else happen, perhaps? Anything non sexual that might have given them the wrong idea? They were teenage girls back then, after all. Full of hormones and fantasies.'

Bob drew a long, shuddering breath, trying to control the rage inside him and consider the matter rationally. 'Well, there must have been something, mustn't there? I mean I did teach them, so obviously we must have had conversations. But where they took place or what they were about – other than schoolwork, of course – I have no idea.'

Sarah considered this answer. *'Where they took place?* Are you saying you met them outside school, Bob?'

Bob shook his head in frustration. 'Who knows? I lived quite near the school, you remember my flat. I might have met them in the street, walking to or from school. It wouldn't be unusual.'

A sliver of ice slid down Sarah's spine. 'Bob, you didn't ever meet them in your flat, did you?'

Bob shuddered, then frowned. 'One of them claims I did, yes. But I don't remember anything about it, Sarah. Honestly, I swear it. If she ever was in my flat then it was only for something totally innocent, that's all.'

The flat where we first made love, Sarah thought. *When I was seventeen.*

Very quietly she said: 'What sort of innocent reason would that be, Bob?'

'God, Sarah, I don't know! Borrowing a teabag, perhaps?' He met her eyes and realised that this sort of answer wouldn't do. 'Maybe some question about homework? Borrowing a book? Just ... innocent friendliness, that's all.'

She watched him, shaking her head silently.

'The truth is I can't remember. *I don't know,* Sarah! I thought you said you believed me!'

'I also said you were an idiot, Bob. If you invited teenage girls into your flat ...'

'I invited *you*, didn't I? Nothing bad happened to you!'

'Bob, that's just it, don't you see?' Tears came to her eyes at the memory. 'You were an angel back then, a really kind man, the only person who really cared about me at that time. And I was really grateful, and we made love, on your bed, in that flat ...'

'And then I married you,' Bob interrupted firmly. 'That's the whole point, surely. I took you to a registry office, and we were married, and we stayed married for twenty-three years, which is a long time these days, and ... it's completely different, Sarah. Not the same at all.'

'Not the same as *what?* Oh come on, Bob, think! Listen to me – if you took one of those teenage girls back to your flat, to lend her a book maybe or discuss homework, whatever excuse you dreamt up – or *she* did – then what do you think was going through that teenage girl's mind, eh? I remember that flat, it was nice – full of books and pictures and candles and music, with a warm gas fire and the bedroom just there off the living room – what do you think a young girl would be fantasising about? You weren't that ugly back then, Bob Newby, trust me! And what were you teaching these young girls about? *Jane Eyre, Women in Love.* Christ, Bob, you should have been more careful!'

'The point is, Sarah, *it didn't happen!*' Bob got to his feet, and strode angrily across the room. 'I don't remember inviting any young girls to my flat. Only you, and you were different. Completely different!'

'I should hope so,' Sarah said, watching him coolly.

'Yes, well obviously you were. You were two years older for a start, much more intelligent, and you already had a baby, and ... damn it, I fell in love with you, Sarah!'

So long ago, Sarah thought, as she saw the angry, appealing look in his eyes. *The past is another country. You can't go back. Don't ask.*

'I know, Bob,' she said softly. 'I remember. I was there.'

Her mobile rang. She reached across the table, picked it up, and walked into the kitchen, her back towards Bob.

'Hello? Oh, Terry. Yes. Hi.'

When the doorbell had first rung she'd hoped it was Terry and her heart had leapt for a second before she'd seen it was Bob. Now Terry was asking if he could come round later this evening, to talk about the river trip, and maybe ...

'Not tonight, Terry, I'm sorry. I've got a trial to prepare for and a visitor here now. Maybe tomorrow? ... Yes, look forward to it. Bye!'

Bob noticed the way her voice had changed. Light, flirty, higher pitched. 'Who was that?'

'Oh, just a friend.' Sarah clicked the phone off and came back into the living room. 'Now, where were we?'

'A man friend?'

'Yes, as it happens. Terry Bateson, the detective.' Sarah glared at him. 'It's none of your business, Bob!'

'No, of course not. I'm sorry.' Bob got to his feet. 'I should go.'

'Yes.' She indicated the papers on the table. 'I've got all this work.'

'Same old Sarah.'

But as he moved towards the door she relented. 'Bob, I'm really sorry about this trouble you're in. I will help, truly, in any way I can.'

'Thanks. The police will probably ask you for a statement.'

'Don't worry, I won't shop you. Bob, have you told Emily?' Their daughter, Emily, was in her third year at Cambridge, studying environmental science.

Bob frowned. 'No. We ... haven't been in touch recently. And with all this, what should I say? Maybe it's better she doesn't know.'

'She's bound to hear sooner or later. Would you rather I told her?'

'Would you? It's ... not so easy for me to talk about this without getting angry. She won't want to hear her father ranting down the phone, poor kid.'

'You could write. Send an email.'

'Yes, good idea. I'll do that. But in the meantime maybe you could warn her?'

'Okay. And ... Bob?' He had nearly reached the door now. 'You haven't asked about Simon.'

'Yes, of course. How is he?' Simon was Bob's stepson, Sarah's first child from her teenage husband, Kevin. Bob and Simon had never been close.

'He's about to make us grandparents, Bob!' Sarah shook her head, amused and sad at once. 'Surely you remember? His partner Lorraine, she's due any time. You have met her, haven't you?'

'Oh. Yes, I think so. Once. Pretty girl, quite shy.'

'Yes, that's the one.' She passed him his coat, still bemused by this disconnection from the family they had once shared. She tried again. 'Bob, you're going to be a grandad! Isn't that something to celebrate?'

'Oh. Yes, I suppose so.' He shrugged his way into the coat and, for the first time on this visit, smiled. A brief ghost of a smile, a fleeting memory of the man she'd once loved. 'It makes you feel old, doesn't it? And you a granny, Sarah, at the age of what – forty two? It hardly seems possible, does it?'

'No. You will go and see them, won't you, when the baby's born?'

The smile fled as fast it had come. 'Perhaps, when all this is over. Until then, I'm a pariah – a leper. Goodbye Sarah. And thanks.'

She listened to the sound of his feet going down the stairs, then turned back to the table, to resume reading through a thick file of documents about a burglary which bored her to tears.

17. Prime Suspect

TERRY WAS surprised and a little hurt by Sarah's response to his phone call. When he had finally got his children to bed on Sunday night and finished speaking to Savendra he had decided it was too late to ring Sarah, so he had waited until Monday evening. He wanted to explain fully about the discovery of the body; it was too good a story to waste. He'd hoped perhaps she would invite him round to her flat, where they could discuss the boat trip at length over a glass of wine and ... whatever came after.

But when he had rung just now she had brushed him off, saying she had too much work and anyway, she had a visitor. What sort of visitor? Had he heard a male voice in the background? Surely ...

Don't be ridiculous, Terry chided himself. You have no right to be jealous. Sarah Newby doesn't belong to you and when she said tomorrow would be fine, she sounded quite happy about it. She's not promiscuous, she's not that sort of woman.

Nevertheless ...

At a loose end, he felt full of energy with nowhere to go. The children were safely in bed, Trude was there to watch them, and there was nothing good on TV, so he decided to go for a run. In his youth he had been a talented runner and it was his favourite way of keeping fit. After the stresses of the day a hard run cleared his mind, and the buzz of the endorphins afterward was pure bliss. 'Like tiny dolphins dancing in your bloodstream,' he had explained once to his daughters. 'Endolphins.'

Tonight he ran down through Fulford to the river, which he crossed by the graceful Millennium footbridge, and then turned right towards the city centre.

Half a mile along here were the luxury riverside flats where Sarah Newby lived. As he approached her home he saw a man, coming out of the rear entrance by the bridge. A tall skinny man in a long dark coat, who hurried away toward Bishopthorpe Road, hunched with his hands in his pockets. For a second Terry thought of following him, then dismissed the idea as absurd.

There are a dozen flats in that building, he could have come from any of them, he told himself firmly. Anyway, what of it? You're behaving like a lovesick teenager.

He crossed Skeldergate Bridge and headed downstream, pausing for a moment to gaze back across the river at the light behind the balcony in the third floor window. Tomorrow night, he thought, smiling. Then he ran hard, all the way home.

* * *

'So, Terence, I hear you've been messing about in boats!'

Detective Chief Inspector Will Churchill beamed delightedly. This was his first week back from holiday and his face was tanned from by the sunshine of Barbados, where, no doubt, he had been water-skiing and scuba diving with his latest bronzed girlfriend. It was clear from the photos and trophies in his office that Will Churchill fancied himself as the police force's answer to James Bond. Will Churchill was a small man, several inches shorter than Terry Bateson, and perhaps for that reason he lost no opportunity to needle his taller colleague whenever he could, calling him 'Terence' which he knew the older man hated. He was younger than Terry but senior in rank, and the tension between two men soured the atmosphere in the department.

Jane Carter had been aware of this conflict ever since she was transferred to York from Beverley. She hated it. So far she'd spent most of her time working with Terry Bateson, but she had reservations about him too. In her opinion he spent too much time with his family, and often went home when there was still work to be done. This absurd discovery of the body was an example of the wrong way to do things. Will Churchill might be cocky, bumptious, overconfident, but he had climbed higher up the greasy ladder of promotion than Terry had, and was rumoured to be angling for the rank of Detective Superintendent. If Jane wanted her own career to progress, she might one day have to choose which man to support.

'So what have you got?' Churchill asked, seating himself at the back of the room. He had no intention of becoming actively involved in the investigation at this stage, but he had a right to know what was going on in his department, and this tale of Terry pulling a body out of the river sounded highly promising.

Terry suppressed a sigh, annoyed by Churchill's presence but unable to do anything about it. He had assembled a small team of four, all he could find so far. Apart from himself and Jane Carter there were Detective Constables Mike Candor and Harry Easby. Terry stood in front of an incident board, where he had pinned photographs of the blue Mercedes, the riverbank adjacent to Landing Lane, and the opposite bank further downstream where the body of Victoria Weston had been recovered. He had also printed out the apparent suicide text which had been sent from Victoria's phone. For the benefit of Will Churchill and the two constables, he explained swiftly what they had learned from the post mortem.

'So from that evidence, this appears to be a murder disguised as a suicide. Victoria Weston must have been drowned elsewhere, in a jacuzzi or a hot tub with salt water, and her body dumped in the river afterwards. And since she has a hot tub in a gazebo in her back garden, it seems reasonable to assume that she was drowned there.'

'And you've only just suspected this?' Will Churchill asked from the back of the room. 'She disappeared when?'

'A week ago, sir. Last Sunday we believe.'

'I see.' Churchill sighed ostentatiously. 'Well, well. Carry on.'

Terry knew what he meant. The key time in solving any murder was in the 'golden hours' – the first 24 or 36 hours after the crime had been committed, when forensic scientists could crawl over the crime scene, finding tiny crucial bits of evidence before they vanished forever. He and Jane had missed that by over a week. Indeed, if this *was* a murder they didn't even have a definite crime scene yet, because they couldn't be certain where the murder had been committed.

'We know she was alive at 7.15 pm on Sunday 28th because she phoned her husband then. They spoke for nearly ten minutes and according to him she was fine. Then a fake suicide text was sent from her phone at 9.37 p.m. Our guess is the killer wrote it just after he drowned her,' Terry continued doggedly. 'The other main piece of evidence we have is the victim's car, which was found abandoned in Landing Lane on Monday morning, a week ago. Which begs the question: 'Who drove the car there if she didn't?'

'And your answer?'

'The most obvious suspect would be her husband, if he didn't have an alibi.'

'Why?'

'Well, he admits their marriage was going wrong, and behaved pretty oddly when we told him his wife was missing. He didn't seem to want to know.'

'What do you mean, he behaved oddly?' Will Churchill asked. 'How is a man supposed to behave in a situation like that?'

It seemed an innocent question but it wasn't. Churchill, like everyone in the room, was well aware that Terry had lost his own wife two years ago. It was because of Terry's grief, his inability to do his job properly for months after that, that Churchill, not Terry, had got the Chief Inspector's job. Terry met his young superior's eyes coldly.

'I mean he didn't seem worried, sir, in the way you'd expect. It was as though he didn't really care. He claims he never saw the suicide text until the next day. And when he did see it the main emotion he expressed was anger, not anxiety.'

'There were obvious signs of disturbance, too,' Jane Carter broke in, as Terry paused. 'The house was wrecked, broken china everywhere. He admitted there'd been a quarrel between him and his wife. So all that made us suspicious, even before we'd found the body.'

'But you say he has an alibi,' Churchill asked. 'What's that about?'

'He claims he was at a conference in Edinburgh. Left York on the Friday and didn't return until the Monday afternoon, when we called to see him. Which was several hours *after* her car was found by the river, where it had probably been all night.'

'Have you checked this alibi?'

'Of course, sir. He can't find his train tickets but we've established that he was booked in at a hotel in Edinburgh and did attend several seminars at a conference there on Friday and Saturday as he claimed. But the conference ended on Saturday evening and he didn't check out until Monday morning.'

'What was he doing on Sunday then?'

'Well that's just it, sir, he can't say. Or not entirely. He claims he hired a car and went sightseeing but he couldn't immediately tell me where he'd been. Eventually he came up with a tale about visiting a place called Abbotsford, Sir Walter Scott's house, but he got very aggressive when I asked him what it was like, or whether he'd bought any postcards or souvenirs there. Frankly, I don't believe him.'

'So where do you think he really was?'

'Back here in York, killing his wife. He could have driven south, drowned her in the tub, dumped her in the river, and been back at the hotel in Edinburgh for breakfast. There you are – perfect alibi, or so he thought. We'll know more when the Scottish police have traced the hire car and checked the mileage. Cell site evidence will tell us where his phone was too, when she called him. But that will take a while ...'

'Why would he do this?'

'Well, we know his wife was unfaithful, which gives him the perfect motive. And there's another thing ...'

'Which is?'

'His first wife died as well. Drowned in a boating accident in Devon nine years ago. Coroner's verdict, death by misadventure. But I wonder. To lose two wives by drowning looks careless.'

'Well, well. Good thinking, Terence. Are there any other suspects so far?'

'Just one, sir. A young lad called Adrian Norton, I met him at the university. He is – was – a graduate student of hers – the one she was having an affair with. He admits to the affair, but says he broke it off with her last Thursday, three days before we think she died. When I told him she was missing he said if she'd killed herself it would be all his fault. So we'll need to visit him again, pass on the good news that it wasn't suicide after all.'

To Terry's annoyance Will Churchill was checking his mobile. When he realised Terry had finished Churchill slipped it into his pocket and got to his feet. He smiled. 'Right. Well, it seems you've got your work cut out then, boys and girls. I'm sure you'll enjoy solving this one. Your own personal murder victim, eh, Terence? Just make sure you don't cock it up for once, eh?'

And with that, he was gone.

* * *

Later that day, Terry phoned Adrian Norton and asked him to come in for a second interview. 'It's basically to put everything you told me before into a proper statement,' he said. 'Everything about your relationship with Victoria Weston, the last time you saw her, and where you were on Sunday 28th. I'll get it typed up from my notes, then you can read it through, alter anything that isn't right, and then sign it. And we'll need to take your fingerprints and a DNA sample, just for elimination purposes. It shouldn't take long.'

The young man looked nervous when he arrived, paler than before, his eyes darting around anxiously. But police stations had that effect on people; Terry had seen it many times before. The boy had been surprised, but once in the interview room he seemed determined to be co-operative. He was relieved that Terry had managed to summarize his relationship with Victoria Weston in a couple of short paragraphs. Adrian accepted most of Terry's description of his last meeting with her, only quibbling at the words '*she tried to assault me*'.

'It wasn't really an assault,' he insisted, with a belated attempt at gallantry. 'It was just – hysterics, I suppose. I'd hurt her feelings and she was angry and upset. It was natural, really; I'd handled it badly.'

'Well, let's change it, then,' Terry suggested, deleting the words. 'How about this: "*She was angry and upset and threw things at me.*"?'

'Yes, all right, change it to that. And add something like '*I accept that this was natural because I had hurt her feelings.*' After all now she's dead it seems terrible to speak badly of her, especially when you're writing it down. I didn't know she was going to kill herself, did I?'

'Ah well, that's just it, Adrian,' Terry said, looking up from the statement. 'We're not quite sure she did kill herself now. This may have been murder.'

He watched the colour drain from the young man's face. It was a key moment; he had deliberately not forewarned him of this surprise. He wanted to see his reaction. Shock, certainly. But no obvious sign of guilt. Adrian met his eyes, appalled.

'Murder? But how? Who could have done that? I thought she drowned in the river!'

'So did we, at first, but now we have evidence to the contrary. Were you aware that she had a hot tub in the garden?'

'What? Er, yeah, I think so.'

'Did you ever use it yourself? Or see Victoria use it?'

'Oh. Well, yes, actually. Once. Before I went to Prague, it was. At the end of the summer term. Her husband was away and we ... sat in there one evening, steaming away, drinking wine. Very pleasant it was, lovely. Why? You're not suggesting ... you don't think she was drowned in there?'

'It's a possibility we're investigating, that's all. This hot tub, would you know how to switch it on?'

'No. I'd never been in one before. Vicky did all of that.'

'And you've only used it that one time? At the end of the summer term?'

'Yes, that's right.'

'Okay. Well, I'll add that to your statement.' Terry typed for a few minutes then said: 'The reason why this statement is important, you see, is that you were one of the last people to see her. Now the next page mentions the text she sent you on that Friday morning, and explains that you never saw her or contacted her again. Are you happy with all that?'

Adrian read it through carefully. 'Yes, of course. It's all true.'

'Ok. And then I need a little more detail about where you were on Sunday 28th. You were with your girlfriend Michaela, according to my notes. *'I showed her round York and then we went to bed early.'*

'Yes, that's right,' Adrian's previously confident expression became more anxious. 'Oh God, you're going to ask Michaela about this, aren't you?'

'Probably, yes.'

'Does that mean you'll have to tell her about the first part of this statement – my relationship with Vicky?'

'Meaning you haven't, Adrian?'

'Not yet, no. Christ, it's difficult! I mean that's why I broke up with Vicky in the first place – I told you!'

'Yes, well, I gave you my advice, son. Honesty is your best policy.'

'That's all very well for you to say. I love Michaela but she has a terrible temper. Do you really have to tell her?'

Terry considered the young man in front of him. He felt slightly more sympathetic to the boy than the last time they had met. After all, if Tom Weston *had* killed his wife as Terry suspected, then this boy was innocent. Adrian was young, trying to be helpful, and, it seemed, deeply in love. Terry knew what that was like, both from memory and from present experience.

On the other hand, if Tom Weston *had* been in Scotland all weekend, then this boy was the obvious suspect. Could *he* really have killed Vicky Weston? He was strong enough, certainly, but devious and cunning too? Terry wondered. Those soft, downy cheeks – the boy was hardly old enough to shave. Like me when I was a student.

He doesn't look like a murderer. But then what have I learned over the years? Murderers don't look different to other people. They look just like everyone else.

'Well, we'll see. All we need from her at the moment is confirmation of your movements that Sunday.'

The young man looked inordinately grateful. 'Thanks. I know what you're saying. I will tell her about Vicky, of course, but ... I'd rather choose my own time. When all this is over, if possible, and we're married. It'll be in the past then, and seem less important.'

It may not be that simple, Terry thought. We'll see.

18. Witness Statement

'Mrs SARAH Newby?'

'Yes.'

Sarah had agreed to this interview only if it was conducted in her office. Ignoring the proffered hand, she showed the man to the client chair in front of her desk. The two armchairs either side of a coffee table were for more friendly conferences; not this. She sat behind her desk and waited. Her visitor took a small Sony voice recorder out of his pocket.

'Do you mind if I record this?'

Sarah shrugged. 'If you must.'

'Thank you.' Ignoring the frosty atmosphere, Detective Sergeant Starkey pressed *Record*. 'Sarah Newby, you were, until last year, the wife of Mr Robert Edwin Newby, school teacher. Is that correct?'

'Yes.'

'As I expect you know, Mr Newby was arrested recently in connection with some historic allegations of illegal sexual activity with under age females in 1991. Did you know Mr Newby at that time?'

'Yes, I did.'

'I see. When did you first meet him?'

Sarah turned her chair slightly, to avoid looking directly at her interrogator. She could see the top of a plane tree in the riverside park outside her window. A blackbird landed on a twig, detaching a yellow leaf which floated slowly to the ground.

'In that year, 1991. I was studying for my GCSEs in evening classes at a technical college. He was a teacher there.'

'I see. Was that his full-time job, as far as you know?'

'No. It was a part-time job in the evenings. He was employed full-time as a secondary school teacher during the day.'

'How old were you then?'

'Seventeen.' Sarah gazed at the blackbird, which cocked its head, its beady eye focussing on something far below.

'What subject were you studying?'

'I was studying a number of subjects. Mr Newby taught English literature.'

'Was he a good teacher, would you say?'

'Very good.' The bird flew away. Sarah focussed her eyes on the distant clouds, far above.

'So you wrote essays for him, did you, as part of the course?'

'Yes.'

'Presumably he read these essays and wrote comments on them. Did he discuss these essays with you, after the class?'

'Sometimes. Mostly he discussed the essays in the class, with the other students. We were only a small group, about six of us. We had some very good discussions, as I recall.'

'But did he sometimes ask you to stay behind, to discuss your essay with him individually?'

'Sometimes, yes. As we got to know each other better.'

'Yes. You got to know him very well, obviously. You married him.'

'Indeed.'

'When you married him you were ... how old exactly?'

Reluctantly, Sarah turned her gaze away from the window, and focussed her cold stare on the detective. 'I'm sure you know the answer to this already, Mr Starkey. I was eighteen. We married on my eighteenth birthday. January 23rd 1992.'

'Very romantic.'

'It seemed so to me, yes.'

'I believe you already had a child by that time?'

'I did, yes. My son Simon. But for the avoidance of doubt, Sergeant Starkey, Robert Newby is not Simon's father. His father was my first husband, Kevin.'

'So ...' Starkey peered up from his notes, not sure if he had got this right. 'By the age of eighteen, you had already been married, had a child and were divorced?'

'As you say, yes.' *It's no good trying to ignore this man*, Sarah decided reluctantly. *In a minute I'm going to have to take control.* She turned her chair to face directly at him for the first time. Starkey smiled apologetically.

'I'm sorry if some of my questions seem personal, Mrs Newby, but the allegations against your husband – your second husband – are very serious and in their nature quite personal, I'm afraid. And these events took place – are alleged to have taken place – during the autumn of 1991, when you first met Mr Newby.'

'Do you have specific dates for them?'

'I'm sorry?'

'I understand my husband is alleged to have had sexual relations with two underage girls. No doubt each of these events occurred at a specific time and place?'

'Well, yes, they did, but I'm not at liberty to divulge precise details ...'

'Have you told my husband?'

'What?'

'Presumably my husband has been informed of the precise nature of the charges against him. Which must include a time and place.'

'They are only allegations so far, Mrs Newby, not charges. Mr Newby has been told where each of the events are said to have taken place, but it's a little harder to obtain a precise date, given the length of time since ...'

'So you haven't got precise dates?'

'No ...'

'So if these girls – middle–aged women I suppose now – cannot give a precise date on which these alleged rapes took place, it will be impossible for my husband to defend himself by saying he was elsewhere on that particular date or time. Even if he can unearth a diary or school timetable from that year, the defence of alibi is denied him?'

'Well, obviously it's understandable after such a long period of time, that precise details such as dates may not be accurately remembered ...'

'Why stick at dates, Mr Starkey? If these women can't remember dates properly, perhaps their memories are faulty in other ways too?'

Starkey, Sarah noted coolly, was looking a little less confident now.

'These are the difficulties we face in all historic enquiries, madam.'

'Quite. Is there a reason why these women have waited until now to make their complaints? Twenty five years after the events are alleged to have happened? Why didn't they complain before?'

'It's the Jimmy Savile effect, I'm sure. The public realise that we are taking child abuse more seriously than we used to, which gives victims more confidence to come forward. They know they'll be believed.'

'*Believed*, you say?' Sarah's voice was sharp, swift as a rapier. 'Are you telling me you automatically *believe* every allegation which is made? That's a change, isn't it?'

'What I mean is we take every allegation seriously, and treat the victim's story as believable and worthy of investigation until proved otherwise. That's what I'm doing now, trying to collect evidence.'

'What about the presumption of innocence? Or are you saying that you regard my husband as guilty, unless he can prove his innocence?'

'He has all his legal rights, madam. He has simply been remanded on police bail.'

'As a result of which he has been suspended from his job,' Sarah said angrily. 'He's not allowed anywhere near his school because everyone thinks he's a paedophile. That's hardly a presumption of innocence, is it? He hasn't even been charged yet but his life is being ruined.'

'These are very serious allegations, Mrs Newby. The victims claim that they have suffered the consequences for many years ...'

'*Victims*, you call them! Not complainants. What are their names?'

'I'm sorry, I can't tell you that.'

'Does my husband know their names?'

'Yes. He and his solicitor have been told. But they are not allowed to make them public, as I'm sure you know. Victims of sexual assaults are guaranteed anonymity.'

'But my husband isn't, is he? His name's out there in the media; I read it in the *Yorkshire Post*. It's probably online, *Facebook, Twitter*, everywhere. No anonymity for him – the whole world thinks he's a child abuser.'

'Mrs Newby.' Starkey shifted in his chair uncomfortably. 'I'm not here to argue the rights and wrongs of the law with you. I'm sure you're an excellent lawyer, but today I'm just here to take a witness statement. As the former wife of Mr Newby, you are an important character witness. Now, if we could proceed?'

'All right. Go ahead.' Sarah swivelled her chair away, turning to gaze out of the window.

'Thank you.' Starkey sighed, noting the insult. 'Now, back in 1991, when you first got to know Mr Newby, you were seventeen years old. How did you feel about him?'

'I thought he was a very nice man.'

'Did you feel – I apologise for this – sexually attracted to him?'

'Not at first, no.'

'So, what *did* attract you to him?'

'He was a good teacher; very funny, witty. He made the subject come alive. He was very kind, too.'

'How did this kindness show itself?'

'Well, I was very unhappy at the time. I was young, I'd already been divorced, and I was under a lot of pressure to give up my baby son for adoption. Bob was very understanding and sympathetic. He listened to me and took me seriously.'

'You had a number of personal conversations with him, then?'

'Obviously.'

'Where did these conversations take place?'

'In the classroom. In the canteen at the college.'

'And during these conversations, you got to know him better?'

'For goodness sake! Of course I did.'

'So ... I'm sorry to have to ask this, Mrs Newby, but when did you first have sex with your husband?'

'I don't think that's any of your business, really, do you?'

'It's relevant to these allegations, that's all. Let me put it another way. There you were, a young girl of seventeen. He was a teacher ten years older. At what point did you realise that his interest in you was not just understanding and sympathetic, but sexual?'

'You expect me to give you a precise date?'

'That would be helpful, of course.'

'Obviously I can't. Are you married, Sergeant Starkey?'

'I am, yes.'

'Well, could *you* answer that question you just put to me? When did *you* first realise that your interest in Mrs Starkey was not just friendly, but sexual? You tell me and I'll tell you.'

Turning back to face her tormentor, Sarah was surprised to notice a faint twinkle of respect, perhaps amusement, in his eyes. *Not a total robot, then.*

'Hm. Well, to be honest, I think it was from the very first day I saw her, as a matter of fact. She's a beautiful woman, my wife. Or was then.'

'Oh dear, you spoilt it.' Sarah smiled coldly. 'Well, I can't tell you what my husband saw in me, all those years ago, I'm afraid; all I know is what I saw in him. We talked a lot, about literature and my problems with my mother and the Social Services. He made me laugh, too. That was a great thing. It wasn't really about sex, strange as that may seem to you.'

'So you didn't feel pressured into having sex with him?'

'No. It was probably my idea more than his, when it first happened.'

'And that was before you were married?'

'Yes, if you must know. A month or so before.'

'And – forgive me again – was that at the college?'

'Of course not. What do you think? It was in his flat.'

'And when you were in his flat, or anywhere ... during that time, that autumn, did you get the impression that he was interested in other girls, not just you? You know he was teaching in a secondary school, not just the college where you met him for evening classes. He must have talked about his work, his other students perhaps. Looking back, do you remember anything like that? Any suggestion that ... he was attracted to young female pupils?'

'No.' Sarah could feel the bubbles of grief and rage rising within her. Any moment now they would boil over.

'You're quite sure, Mrs Newby? You don't look very sure.'

'I am perfectly, one hundred per cent sure. You mistake me, Mr Starkey. These tears are because you have been asking me extremely personal questions for a very long time, and the only result has been to take me back twenty five years to a time when I met and married the kindest, most understanding, wise and witty man I had ever seen at that point in my young life, and I loved him. I loved him then and for many years afterwards. The fact that we are now divorced is a very great sadness to me, and possibly to him too, but it doesn't make any difference to the fact that we fell in love and married all those years ago. I believed in him and trusted him.

'So now for these girls, these wretched women, to come up with their ugly allegations and besmirch all that – it's obscene, quite horribly disgusting. My husband, Bob Newby, did *not* interfere with or sexually abuse any of his pupils, either at the college or the school or anywhere else, at any time whatsoever. He is not that sort of man and he did not, would not do it. I was married to him for twenty three years and *I know!* All right? So you put that in a draft statement and I'll sign it when I'm sure it tells the truth, ok?

'And I suggest you drop these allegations as soon as possible. Now, if you don't mind, I'm a busy woman.'

So busy that when he'd gone, Sarah put her head in her hands and wept.

19. Michaela

AS THEY drove towards the university, Terry Bateson was humming. Jane Carter glanced at him curiously. 'Is it your birthday, sir?'

'What? No. Why do you ask?'

'Just that you seem quite cheerful. You're humming.'

'Nothing wrong with that, is there? Lighten up, sergeant. It's a sunny day.'

'True. Fair enough.' Jane Carter shook her head, bemused. It wasn't an especially sunny day; there had been rain earlier and a strong wind was chasing dark clouds across the sky, letting occasional flashes of sparkling sunlight through in between. She couldn't think of any particular reason to be happy; she was investigating a murder, her love life was non-existent, and there was a nasty conflict between her two senior officers at work.

So why Terry should be humming she couldn't understand. He, after all, had pulled the body out of the river, right in front of his two little girls, and then been sniped at by Will Churchill yesterday. She would have expected him to be surly, irritable, but he seemed quite the opposite this morning.

Terry stopped humming, but smiled to himself. It was the memory of his evening with Sarah which inspired him. This was strange, in a way, because they hadn't ended up in her bed, as he had anticipated. When he'd got there it was late and she still hadn't eaten, so they'd bought fish and chips and sat together on the quayside in the twilight, eating it out of greaseproof paper and throwing scraps to the ducks. It had been a time out of time, friendly, relaxed and intimate in a way Terry had not known for years. He had told her of the discovery of the body and his daughters' reaction, and she had described the birth of Belinda's baby – the panic in the ambulance, the parents' bliss when it was born. She'd talked a little of her cases – the burglar she had defended today, the shoplifter she was prosecuting next week – but then told him of what he hadn't known: her ex–husband's arrest for child abuse, her shock and belief in his innocence, and her embarrassment and pain during her interview with DS Starkey.

'It has to be a mistake, Terry, surely. I rang Emily today, our daughter. You can imagine how appalled she was, poor kid. Even though it's nothing to do with me it still hurts. It hurts like hell.'

He'd put his arm round her and felt the tension in her slender frame. She was not an easy woman to comfort: there was too much self-reliance, too much stiffness in her spine to imagine her simply letting go; but when they'd got up to put the wrappers in the bin and walk downstream towards Skeldergate Bridge and her flat she'd leant into him and they'd adjusted their pace together and strolled side by side, like a couple in love.

Which we are, Terry told himself ecstatically this morning as he drove toward the university. *Isn't that what this means?*

At the door she had thanked him for listening and then, reaching up and sliding her arms around his neck to kiss him, whispered: 'Not tonight, my lover, I'm too tired. But next time, I promise. Better than ever before.'

Terry had guessed that was coming and strangely it was all right. For an angry second walking back to his car he'd thought *I'm being played for a fool*, but then: *No, that's not it at all.* We're still learning to be together; after all she's still healing from that murder attempt last year. And this problem with her ex which she spoke of this evening. But although she's still fragile she's given herself to you already. *Remember that, Terry, and rejoice! This could be your future and hers starting here. Cherish it, don't throw it away.*

All night he'd relived the memories of the evening, and this morning Jane Carter had caught him humming at work. Well, why not? The sun *is* shining, look out the window. My glass is half full, not half empty.

He smiled at his colleague tolerantly. Jane Carter was a thorough, efficient detective but there was a puritanical, plodding side to her character which made her hard to like. It was partly to do with her looks – she was nobody's pin-up – but it was also to do with the way she distrusted people, particularly men. Perhaps the two traits were combined, Terry thought: she attracted so little male attention that she resented it, and blamed others. If she would just lighten up a little, make a few jokes, men might like her more.

He himself had tried flirting with her once, just out of politeness, but been instantly crushed. Feminism ruled ok, and don't you dare forget it. Perhaps she's a lesbian, he wondered. But if so, what did that matter to him? Three times in the last week Terry had spent time with a woman who was very clearly *not* a lesbian, and who seemed – joy of joys – to actually find him attractive. And promised to see him again.

Isn't that something to hum about?

Adrian Norton's flat at was on the ground floor of a small house on a student housing estate within walking distance of the university campus. It was part of a row of two–storey terraced houses, brick built on the ground floor but faced with fading wood shingles on the floor above.

Terry knocked on the door. 'Good morning. We ... er ...'

'Yes?'

'Um ...we are ...'

Jane had never been particularly impressed by any of her male colleagues' attitudes to gender equality and Terry's response to the young woman who opened the door just added to her disgust. He seemed to lose the power of speech, and gawped at the girl like a happy idiot. But then, even Jane had to admit, she was quite strikingly beautiful. If this was Adrian Norton's fiancée, it was clear why he didn't want to lose her.

They were faced by a lithe, willowy figure in a beige, tight-fitting teeshirt and skintight white jeans, balancing lightly in the doorway on the balls of her bare feet. She wasn't conventionally pretty, but looked at once strong, athletic, and intensely feminine. She was tall, about five foot ten, with a turbulent mane of tangled red-brown hair which she flung back slightly as she tossed her head to meet Terry's eyes. It was this, perhaps, which had struck him dumb. She looked a little like a gypsy, with light, coffee coloured skin, a wide sensuous mouth, and unusual, pale green eyes alight with curiosity and amusement.

'Yes?' she said again.

'We are police officers, miss,' Jane explained at last, to cover her colleague's silence. She held out her warrant card. 'Does Adrian Norton live here?'

'Yes, but he not home. At lectures. Why? What is problem?'

'No problem, exactly, miss, but you are his girlfriend, is that right? Michaela Konvalinka?'

'You know my name? Yes, I am his ... what you say? *Fiancée!*' She brought out the English word proudly. 'We are to marry.'

'Congratulations,' Jane said drily. 'We're investigating the death of his supervisor, Dr Victoria Weston. Has he told you about that?'

'Oh yes.' The girl frowned, her forehead crinkling in a way which did nothing to ease Terry's fascination. 'Very sad. She drown, in river, right? Murder, Adrian say!' Her eyes widened, showing irises which had traces of blue as well as green. 'Is terrible, scary. Who can do thing like that?'

'Yes, well that's what we're trying to find out. We have a few questions, maybe you can help us.'

'Me? What you think I know? I only met her once.'

'Yes, well it's just routine, miss. I could explain better if we come inside.'

'Inside? I don't know ... ok, come.' Somehow the girl's uncertainty gave way before Jane Carter's firm body language, and they entered a small, cluttered living room. There were books and magazines scattered on a table next to a bowl of cereal, a vase of flowers and a laptop. An array of clothes was drying on a rack in front of a radiator. She waved her hand around apologetically. 'All mess, I'm sorry. Cleaning later.'

'Don't worry. My home's the same.' Jane smiled. 'Do you mind if we sit down?'

'No, please.' Hurriedly, the girl pulled some socks and newspapers off an old green sofa, and plumped up a cushion. She perched nervously on the arm of the only armchair, giving herself a slight advantage and, to Terry at least, an entrancing view of the shapely legs inside the tight jeans. She had red painted toenails and wore a thin gold chain round one ankle, he noticed.

'What you want to ask?'

'Well, as you know, Dr Weston's body was found in the river a few days ago ...'

'Yes, Adrian told me. I saw in paper. Terrible, poor woman. But first we think she kill herself – how you say – suicide? Why you change now, say is murder?'

'We have uncovered some more evidence,' Jane said, glancing at Terry to see if he wanted to take over. Not yet, it seemed. 'I'm afraid we can't tell you what it is.'

'Hm. Typical police. Secret, eh?'

'Yes, well I'm afraid that's the way we conduct enquiries. Anyway, her car was found beside the river a week earlier, on Monday 29th August, which makes us believe she went into the river sometime the night before, on Sunday 28th August. So we're asking questions of anyone who knew her or might possibly have seen her that night.'

'Did you know Victoria Weston, Michaela?' Terry asked, breaking his silence at last.

'Me? No. I met her once, I think. Adrian introduced us, in library cafeteria. Small skinny woman. Funny glasses.'

'She wore glasses, did she?'

'Yes. On string round neck, for reading, I guess. Clever lady, reads many books.'

'But that's all? You just met once?'

'Yes.' A cautious, slightly anxious smile, perfect white teeth. 'She was Adrian's teacher, not mine.'

No sign of jealousy, Terry noticed. *Is it my job to tell her, inject the poison?* He was fascinated by this young woman but felt sorry for her too. He remembered his interviews with Adrian, and the young man's anxiety about his fiancée learning of his affair with his supervisor. Every girl would hate that, of course, but this one glowed with an inner vitality which no man would want to see turned against him. And here she was, alone in a foreign country, building all her hopes on a young man who, Terry thought, was quite probably innocent of the crime they were investigating. But for all his foolishness, Terry had gained the clear impression that Adrian Norton was in love with this girl. Having met her, Terry could understand that only too well. Adrian's story, after all, was that he had gone to see Victoria Weston to *end* their affair, so that his fiancée, Michaela, would never know of it.

Of course the boy should have been honest with her, Terry thought, *I told him that twice.* But Terry could see why Adrian had been afraid. His fiancée wasn't just stunningly beautiful, she exuded a sexual magnetism that had probably addled the boy's brains. Adrian was a nice enough lad but this young woman could eat him for breakfast.

Right now she was looking suspicious.

'Why you ask me this?'

'It's just routine, miss. We have to check lots of details, to build a clear picture of what happened. Now, I've already interviewed Adrian, and he said he was at home with you on the evening of Sunday 28th August. Is that right?'

A frown crossed the young woman's face. Her green eyes widened, she peered at Terry suspiciously. 'Why you ask this? You think I do something wrong?'

'No one thinks you did anything wrong, love,' said Terry kindly. 'We're just asking questions of everyone, that's our job.'

'I not your love,' the girl hissed. 'My love is Adrian.'

'It's just a phrase, love .. I mean ...' Terry laughed, then subsided into silence, quelled by a glance from Jane. 'No offence.'

'Of course I do nothing wrong, and Adrian neither! What right you have coming in here, calling me *love*?' The indignant young woman appealed to Jane. 'You think that's right? Acceptable? Cheeky bastard!'

'It's the way Yorkshire folk talk,' Jane explained. 'When we say *love*, it's polite, friendly. It doesn't mean anything bad.'

'Well, not in Czech.' She considered this. 'A man say that in my country, my father ...' She drew a finger across her throat, expressively.

'I see. Well, it's different here,' Terry resumed peaceably. 'Ask your boyfriend to explain it to you. Now, about that evening, Sunday 28th August. Think back. Was Adrian here with you?'

'Of course he with me!' She tossed her hair back, irritated and perhaps a little embarrassed by the conversation. 'He sleep here every night!'

'So he was here then? All evening, is that right?'

'*Yes.*'

Just one word, accompanied by a stare that, as it persisted, made Terry strangely uncomfortable. Those eyes, he realised, blazed with an intensity he had seen somewhere else. Not in a human, but a tigress, watching its prey.

'You and Adrian are engaged, aren't you,' Jane said, trying to cool things down for a moment. 'Have you fixed a day for the wedding yet?'

Michaela relaxed, responding to the easier question. The tigress glare faded slightly; she smiled. 'In December, I hope. Before Christmas anyway. I want – wanted – York Minster, fine church, but I am Catholic, so tomorrow we have appointment with priest there, right next to Minster. Also beautiful church. More colour.'

'Are your parents coming over?'

'From Czech? Yes. And my brothers. Will be fine day. Perfect. But a lot to prepare ... organise.'

'I'm sure. Especially in a new country. Look, just to help with our enquiries, can you think back, remember a few other things about that day – the Sunday before last. Did you go to church perhaps, do anything special?'

This time the frown was more thoughtful, less defensive. 'Not church, no. I think ... we visit *Jorvik Viking Centre*, busy place, lots of tourists. Good history but bad smells – stink!' She wrinkled her nose, laughed. 'Life today much better. Then ... shopping in town, back here, study ... I remember, Chinese food, takeaway.' As the memory appeared to crystallise in her mind she stared fixedly at Jane and said firmly. 'Yes, I told you. Adrian here all evening. As normal. Why? You think something bad?'

'We're just checking,' said Jane calmly. 'You're sure, are you? Adrian was with you all day? In the evening too?'

'How many times? *Yes, all day, ok?* Why? You think he has some other girl? No chance!' She tossed her red-gold hair back, lifting her chin and looking down at the two detectives with a sort of haughty self-confident gypsy amusement which suggested that the very idea was absurd, no man could possibly choose anyone else. *But if one did, she'd have his scrotum for a purse.*

'All right,' said Terry, shifting on his chair uneasily. He wasn't wholly convinced, but her answer was clear. Crystal clear, in fact.

So this was his moment to decide. Jane hadn't interviewed Adrian; *he* had, both times. If Tom Weston's dodgy alibi worked out, then clearly Adrian was a possible suspect. He knew the victim well, he was possibly the last person to see her.

But was that enough to justify challenging this girl's story by telling her of her fiancé's affair with the dead woman? Perhaps, but it would certainly cause an upset, a huge emotional explosion. And it would be very cruel. It would ruin this girl's plans for a marriage and her hopes for a new life in England.

Is that any concern of mine? Not really, Terry thought, but all the same ...

He tapped his pencil against his notebook, debating what to do. Adrian Norton claimed he had spent all day on Sunday 28th with his fiancée, and this girl had confirmed it, three times now. No doubt Adrian had prepared her for this interview, told her the questions he had been asked, but Terry hadn't been able to prevent that. There were only four officers on the case, they hadn't been able to interview her and Adrian at the same time. They had no reason to arrest either of them. So he had to take the girl's word for it.

If he'd had a single piece of evidence to suggest that this alibi was false, Terry would have challenged it. But he hadn't. Adrian's story was credible and this young woman had confirmed it.

'Well, that's all we wanted to know, really,' Terry said, glancing firmly at Jane, ignoring her frown. 'So I'll write this down as a statement, and you can check it's all correct. Then, after you've signed it, we'll be on our way.'

And I hope we don't have to come back, he thought, as the clouds outside parted, and a flash of sunlight briefly lit the room.

20. Broken Alibi

JANE CARTER had been disappointed by Terry Bateson's decision not to challenge the Czech girl's statement. It was the obvious thing to do, she thought. Confront the girl with the evidence that her fiancé had been regularly screwing his dead supervisor, and see how she reacted. If she still maintained he had been with her all day on Sunday 28th, all well and good. Her evidence would have been the stronger for it. If not, not.

But Terry had ducked that opportunity. In the car on the way back to the station, he explained why.

'I've seen too many people's lives ruined by heavy handed police investigations,' he growled, somewhat defensively Jane thought. 'You'll see it too, if you do this job long enough. We go in, turning over all the furniture in people's lives, dragging skeletons out of the closet, and sometimes all we leave behind is the mess, while the villain gets clean away. That girl told us three times young Adrian was with her that Sunday night, and we haven't a shred of evidence to prove her wrong. Or him, for that matter.'

'With respect, sir, we have. He was in Vicky Weston's bed three days before. We could have challenged her with that.'

'Yes, and ruin the poor girl's life. Look, sergeant, I gave the lad my advice when I interviewed him. Be honest with your girlfriend, I said. Make a clean breast of it. Tell her you had an affair with your supervisor but it's over and you're sorry. Then hope she sticks by you. That's what I would do if I were him – at least I hope I would. But if we, the police, tell her first, what hope is there then?'

Jane shook her head. 'You sound like a social worker, sir.'

'Or a decent human being,' Terry snapped. 'Look, sergeant, this was my call, and I made it. If I'm wrong, I'm wrong. But for my money, it's the husband whose alibi will fall apart. Not Adrian Norton's.'

* * *

Over the next few days more evidence began to trickle in. The first development came from Mike Candor, a solid, dependable detective constable, who had spent the morning knocking on doors near the Westons' home in Osbaldwick.

'I spoke to a neighbour, sir, Mrs Bishop,' he told Terry. 'She lives in a cottage on the main street, at the end of the track which leads to the Westons' house. She knows the family quite well, she says, and she saw Mrs Weston leaving her house in her car just before ten that Sunday night, the 28th.'

'Saw her leaving in the car? How?'

'Driving it, sir. That's what Mrs Bishop says, anyway.'

Terry leaned back in his office chair, surprised. Jane Carter, sitting at a desk a few feet away, was listening intently.

'She saw Vicky Weston driving it herself?' Terry asked. 'How sure is she of this, Mike?'

'Pretty sure, sir. She knows Vicky Weston well, recognises the car, and she gave her a wave.'

'Sorry – who gave who a wave?'

'Mrs Bishop waved to Vicky Weston, she says.'

'Did Vicky wave back?'

Mike Candor frowned. 'Not sure, sir, I didn't press her on that. But she only caught a brief glance. I asked if she sure it was Vicky and she said she assumed it was because she'd never seen anyone else driving that car.'

'All right. But what about the time? She may have got that wrong – or even the date. How do we know she's not remembering a completely different event?'

'I did test her on that, sir, of course. She remembers it because of the storm, she says. There was a thunderstorm that night, I checked.'

'Yes, yes. Go on.'

'Well, her daughter had come over from Manchester with her grandkids that Sunday. They'd had lunch in the garden and played football with the kids. Then when her daughter left Mrs Bishop and her husband were so tired they fell asleep in front of the fire – they're both in their sixties, I'd say. So they didn't clear up until later in the evening when they saw the storm coming. Mrs Bishop remembered she was getting things in from the garden when the first drops of rain started to fall. And that's when she saw Vicky Weston drive past. It must have been just before ten, she says, because that's when she went inside to watch the news.'

'Okay,' Terry said slowly. 'So if it *was* her, where was she going? And how could she end up drowned in the boot of that same car, later that evening?'

The damp area of carpet in the car boot had been analysed and found to contain traces of salts similar to those dissolved in the hot tub.

'Maybe she went to see lover boy,' Jane suggested. 'And was drowned in a hot tub elsewhere.'

Mike Candor burst out laughing. 'Two lovers with two hot tubs! She was quite some goer, this lady!'

Terry frowned, annoyed by this levity. It was just the sort of insensitive wisecrack his boss, DCI Will Churchill, encouraged.

'No, that can't be right. Look at what we know from forensics so far.' He began counting off facts on his fingers. 'First, the lining of her lungs was red and jelly-like, which is how they get from drowning in salt water, not fresh. Second, the damp carpet in the boot of her car contained salts similar to those used in the Westons' hot tub. Third, she had unusually clean fingernails. It all tells the same story. She was drowned at home in the hot tub and driven to the river in the boot of her own car. So whoever Mrs Bishop saw driving that car, it couldn't have been Vicky Weston, who was already dead. Did you get a closer description, Mike? Could it have been her husband, perhaps?'

'I asked her that, sir, and she didn't think so. But she admits it was dark and the windows were misty. She's more reliable about the time, I think, than the driver.'

Terry drummed his fingers on his desk. 'Okay, thanks, Mike. Good work. Write it all up and give me the report.'

'The pathologist's quite sure about this salt water drowning, is she, sir?' Mike Candor asked tentatively. 'Because if she's wrong, Mrs Bishop's evidence fits in perfectly. Vicky Weston sent her suicide text at 9.37, then got in her car a few minutes later to drive to the river. With stones in her pockets to help her sink.'

Terry shook his head. 'Linda Miles is our best pathologist. I've never known her wrong yet. No, that's what the killer wants us to think, not what really happened. This is a murder, not a suicide. The question is, who did it?'

* * *

'Adrian Norton,' Jane said. 'I bet it was him in the car.'

'Why?'

'Well, this book of feminist poetry, for a start. I mean there it is in the front of her car with his fingerprints all over it.'

'True,' Terry acknowledged. 'But that's not enough on its own. The fact that he studied that sort of poetry with her, gives a perfect reason for his fingerprints to be on the book. If his prints were on the steering wheel itself, that would be a different matter. But they aren't. Nobody's are. Which suggests ...'

'That the killer was very careful. Probably wore gloves and wiped the steering wheel to be sure.'

'Exactly. So if he went to such care with the steering wheel, why leave the book there with his prints all over it? There are more of his prints too, but all on the passenger side. To my mind, that argues *against* it being young Adrian, rather than for him.'

'Maybe he was just careless. Took great care with the steering wheel, but forgot about the book.'

'Yes, well what about her husband? His prints are all over the house, and in the car too.'

'Her husband was in Scotland, sir, we know that. He has an alibi.'

'So does young Adrian. We met the young lady, remember? She was adamant he was with her all day. Whereas Mr Thomas Weston, on the other hand, has so far failed to produce anyone who will substantiate his claim that he was driving around Scotland on Sunday visiting popular tourist sites. I looked up Abbotsford, Sir Walter Scott's home, the place he said he visited. It has a gift shop, restaurant, guided tours, entry fee, all the usual works. But can he show me a ticket? No. Describe what he saw? Not really. Sir Walter Scott was a writer, remember, a famous historical novelist, the first one ever, apparently. And what did his wife Victoria do? Taught English literature at university. So wouldn't you think, if he'd been there, he'd have bought some sort of souvenir for his wife, at least? A book, a poem, a postcard perhaps. But no, nothing, nada.'

'Maybe she didn't like Sir Walter Scott, sir. I've never read him. Vicky Weston was a feminist, remember? Perhaps old Sir Walter was a nasty male chauvinist.'

'So? Even if he was, that would give Tom Weston a good reason to buy his wife a souvenir, just to wind her up. No, the man's lying, that's what it is. He never went there at all.'

'Why would he lie about that?'

'Because he's got something to hide, that's why. Remember how he behaved, when we first went to see him. Did he show concern that his wife was missing and had sent him a suicide text? Not really. He was angry, he thought she was being selfish. Grief when he learned she was dead? Not a lot.'

'Oh, that's not fair, sir. He was shocked when he saw her body. I was there, you weren't. Stunned, I'd say. A fairly normal reaction.'

'All right. But I'll tell you when he was really shocked. When we told him she was murdered. That really rattled his cage – don't you remember? His face went white, his hands shook, he would probably have fainted if his sister hadn't held his hand, poor lamb. And then next minute he was marching around the room like a maniac. What does that tell you?'

'He was upset, sir, it was a shock.'

'Yes, but a shock that looked a lot like guilt, to me. Look, he didn't behave like that when we thought it was suicide, did he? He was okay with that, he could cope with it. But when we turn up saying she was murdered, different story.'

'But we can't even prove he was in York that night,' Jane insisted stubbornly.

'Not yet, no. But we'll find something.' A cynical smile crossed Terry's face. 'What I want to know is, *cui bono?*'

'Sorry sir? Come again?'

'*Cui bono?*' A faint smile flickered on Terry's face. *'Who benefits?* It's Latin, one of the few bits I remember. So who does benefit from this poor woman's death? Her husband, I would suggest. Look at that house; it's not your average semi, is it? You could fit my house in the drive, and still leave room for that fishpond and a mermaid. They didn't have any kids, so now she's dead it's probably all his, to say nothing of any life insurance. And how do you think he got a house like that?'

'Bought it, I suppose, sir. Like everyone else.' Jane, who had grown up in a large farmhouse on the Yorkshire Wolds, saw nothing unusual about the size of the Weston's home. Terry, she thought, had a chip on his shoulder.

'Wrong. I googled him, just to check up. He works for a small educational publishing company, and they have what they call a *'friendly, holistic human-centred policy'*. Which means they give each of their employees a web page to fill with smiling photos and biographical details. Take a look. It seems that our Mr Weston grew up in a poor working class area of Birmingham. His father left when he was two years old, and his mother worked as a cleaner until he was ten, when she married a soldier. That's when his step-sister Audrey must have appeared.'

'So? What's wrong with that?'

'Nothing. It's a heart-warming story, that's why it's there. To show that someone like him, born into poverty, could still advance through education. He loved books, he says, worked hard at school, went to university, and became a school teacher and worked abroad for a bit before he got this job in publishing. That's why he's so 'passionate' about his work, it says. Everyone's 'passionate' about their work nowadays. Even burglars and rapists, God help us.'

'Really? I don't see what's wrong with this sir, honestly.'

'The point, dear Watson, is in the dog that didn't bark. I checked this self-serving biography and managed to fill in a few blanks. In particular about his first wife, a woman called Christine Fleetwood, the daughter of a wealthy West Country farming family. For a wedding present, her father gave the happy couple a five-bedroomed house by the sea, near a small town called Budleigh Salterton in Devon.'

'And?'

'Two years later she drowned, in a boating accident. Young Tom not only inherited the house, but quarter of a million in life insurance.'

'Well ...' Jane thought about this. 'If it was really an accident ...'

'That's what the inquest said. Death by misadventure.'

'Then it has no relevance to now, does it? I mean, we don't even know if Victoria Weston had any life insurance. But even if she did, would it pay out for suicide?'

'I don't know,' Terry admitted. 'I suppose it would depend on the policy.'

They sat in silence for a moment, watching the wind blow the first few autumn leaves from a tree outside the window.

'Just because his first wife died, doesn't make him guilty,' Jane said at last. 'After all, he does have an alibi, of sorts.'

'I know. And if we can't break that, none of this is relevant, of course. We follow the evidence where it leads. But if you add in the fact that they quarrelled, his attitude to her death, that phony visit to Abbotsford, the fact that he hired a car and still can't say where he drove it to on Sunday ... this man's got something to hide, I'm sure of it. You know those old coppers, Jane, the ones you meet sometimes in the pub, with the pot bellies and bloodhound faces, close to retirement or already on the shelf ...'

'I think we move in different circles, sir,' Jane murmured.

' ... old blokes with no idea how to use a smart phone, send a text, or switch on a computer? But those guys talk about instinct sometimes, how they could smell a wrong 'un at twenty paces. Well, it's probably all bullshit ninety per cent of the time, but in this case ... I feel a bit like them.'

Jane shrugged. 'That's why they're retired, sir. They're out of date. What we need is solid evidence, not instinct.'

* * *

Within a couple of days, Terry's instinct-based theory started to unravel.

The first blow came with the cell site report from *Hi-Tech Crime*. This confirmed that at 7.15 pm on Saturday 28th August, Thomas Weston's phone had been in contact for nine and a half minutes with the phone registered to his wife, Victoria Weston. The radio mast nearest to Vicky's phone had been in Osbaldwick, York. It had picked up her signal and forwarded it northwards to her husband's phone which at that moment in time was within two miles of a mast in the picturesque town of Melrose, in the Scottish borders.

'Shit,' said Terry. 'Well, maybe he was on his way south. He could still have made it to York by 9.30, couldn't he?'

'Only if he had his foot to the floor all the way,' Jane protested. 'And he wasn't caught in a tailback somewhere.'

'Still, it's an outside possibility, isn't it?'

'In theory, perhaps,' Jane said diplomatically. *A hare-brained fantasy,* is what she was thinking. *Where does he get his ideas from – Hollywood?*

The theory was finally knocked on the head an hour later, by the report from the Edinburgh police. Tom Weston had indeed hired a car, they confirmed, an Audi saloon, at 10 a.m. on Sunday 28th August. Scotcar, a small backstreet outfit who apparently had difficulty returning phone calls, particularly those from the police, had finally been persuaded to produce records showing that the Audi had travelled 97 miles during that period. It had been returned just before 10 a.m. on Monday 29th with no damage and a full tank of petrol.

Reading the report, Terry clicked his tongue irritably. 'Anyone know the distance between York and Edinburgh?'

Jane checked on her computer. 'Two hundred and two miles, sir. '

'Ah well.' Terry met her eyes thoughtfully. 'So it couldn't have been him after all. Damn!' He heaved a deep sigh. 'Whatever the bastard was doing in Melrose, he wasn't driving south to murder his wife. So, we move on to our second suspect, it seems. What have we got on that front now?'

By the end of the day they had plenty. Like London buses, all the reports came at once, forming a traffic jam on his desk. Forensic examination of Straw House Barn had already shown plentiful fingerprints and DNA traces of Adrian Norton, mostly in the bedroom, kitchen, and living room. But now another print, the most significant of all, had been found. On the back of the blue Mercedes, two inches to the right of the handle which opened the car boot.

The evidence against Adrian increased later that day, when Harry Easby, who had been set the thankless task of trawling through CCTV videos, found something at last. 'Coming up now, sir,' he said, pausing the tape at a grainy black and white image. 'Osbaldwick village street, taken from the camera on the front of the pub. The private road to Straw House Barn is about fifty yards that way, just round the corner. You can see the time and date in the bottom right hand corner, there. 8.22 in the evening on Sunday 28th August. It's not the best technology but we're lucky they kept it this long. I retrieved it from their wheelie bin.'

'What? They threw it away?'

'Yes. Well on the first of September they installed a new system and took this one down. That's why this film wasn't recorded over when I went to ask for it. They just slung it in the trash.'

'Very environmentally friendly. Haven't they heard of recycling? Anyway, what have you found?'

'This.' Harry clicked *Play* and they watched a couple of men come out of the pub and stand smoking beside a lamp post. Then, from the right of the screen, a cyclist appeared. As the cyclist reached the lamp post something caught his attention and he looked to his right, at the pub. Harry paused the video at the point where his face was clear, or as clear as the primitive camera could make it. He used the computer mouse to draw a little circle around the figure and enlarge it. As the face reached its maximum magnification Terry and Jane stared at it, entranced. Terry gave a low whistle.

'It could be him, couldn't it? Adrian Norton. What do you think?'

Jane Carter bent down to peer closer at the screen. After a long moment she nodded. 'It's not brilliant but yes. I'd say that's him. Maybe the techies can enhance it a bit to make sure.'

She checked the time and date on the bottom right of the video. '8.22 p.m. Sunday evening. That puts him in the frame all right, doesn't it.'

Terry breathed a deep sigh. 'Adrian Norton. Well, well. Fifty yards from Victoria Weston's house on Sunday evening, when he swore he was home on the sofa with his lovely Czech girlfriend. Looks like you were right, Detective Sergeant. That young man's going to have to answer some more questions. And so is his girlfriend. And this time young Adrian may need a lawyer.'

21. Emily

THE SECOND bedroom in Sarah's flat belonged to her daughter Emily. When Sarah and Bob got divorced Emily, a student at Cambridge, had been upset not just by the rift between her parents but also about the sale of their house. That house, a comfortable four bedroomed detached house with beautiful gardens on the outskirts of a village just outside York, had been Emily's home for all of her teenage years, and like her mother, she loved it. But the divorce meant it had to be sold, no longer a home but a financial asset split between her warring parents.

To Emily, it seemed that she had been cast adrift. Packed off to university with no home to return to. For a while she'd been encouraged by her mother's affair with Michael Parker, only to be traumatized by its terrible end. But then – thank goodness! – her mother had not only survived but bought this lovely riverside flat with a bedroom to which Emily could return whenever she chose.

She decided to do so now. The news of her father's arrest had come as a further horrible shock to her. What was the matter with her parents, that they made such a mess of their lives? Not to mention her brother Simon, who had once been arrested for murder! To Emily, as she related these lurid tales to her fascinated student friends, it seemed at times that she was the only sane person in her family. And if so, perhaps she had a responsibility to do something about it.

She was in her third year at university, finals looming but still some distance ahead. Her time was largely her own; essays could be written anywhere, tutorials skipped or postponed. So she got on a train to York.

Sarah was, of course, delighted to see her. The spare room, with the posters, the giant teddy bear, the books and clothes that Emily had forgotten or grown out of, was there ready and waiting. It was also, Sarah thought wryly, divided by one thin wall from the main bedroom in which she and Terry Bateson had recently been indulging in such passionate, abandoned love-making.

Well, time for a change. Her daughter, she was astonished to see, was taller than her now, by a clear couple of inches. It was only Sarah's killer heels, which she loved and Emily scorned, which had given her the advantage before. Together with age, wisdom and sobriety, of course.

'Mum, what are you going to do?' Emily asked, when their first happy greetings were over.

'Do, darling? About what?'

'Dad, of course! You're a lawyer, you've got to help him!'

'He's got a lawyer already, Lucy Parsons, I told you.' Sarah had explained this over the phone, in the long conversation which had precipitated Emily's arrival.

'Yes, but you're a better lawyer, a barrister, you're good at it. And you *know* Dad better than anyone else!'

'That's exactly why I can't represent him, even if I wanted to.'

'Why not? You represented Simon, didn't you? You acted for him in court!'

'Yes, but that was different, it was special and very unusual. I had to get permission from the judge.'

'So? That's my point. If you did it once, you could do it again! Come on, Mum – Dad needs you!'

'I can't, darling, you don't understand. I'm a witness.'

'What? *A witness?* My God, you don't mean you actually *saw* him doing these things? You can't have, surely – it's not true!'

'No, of course I don't mean that – do you think I'd have married him if I had? I've had to provide a witness statement for him. A policeman came to see me – a wretched man called detective sergeant Starkey.'

'My God! Does that mean you can't ...'

'I can't be a witness and an advocate in the same case, darling. Even if I wanted to. There's a conflict of interest.'

'Oh.' Emily digested this for a moment, flicking her long hair out of her eyes. They were sitting outside on the balcony, gazing across the river to the castle and law courts. A little further away, the gleaming white stone of the cathedral, York Minster, crouched like a huge sheepdog keeping watch over the huddled flock of houses in the city below.

'What do you mean, *even if you wanted to?* Mum, you don't *believe* any of this nonsense, do you? Dad, having sex with fifteen year old school girls? That can't be true? Can it?'

'No, I don't think it can be.' Sarah shook her head, distressed. 'I said that in my statement. Very clearly.'

'Then why did you say you didn't want to. *Mum?*'

'Because ... darling, it's difficult. We've gone through a divorce, and it hurts when that happens. It hurt me, anyway, a lot. Your father came to see me recently, and ... he's a different person. Not the man I married, not any more. Look, I gave a statement and of course I don't believe it – don't *want* to believe it – but ... he's got to fight this battle on his own. Lucy's a good solicitor, and she'll get him a top barrister if he needs one, a QC probably, but it may never come to that anyway. It's just that for me, Emily darling ... I don't want to be any more involved than I already am. If that makes sense. That probably makes me sound heartless, doesn't it?'

Emily thought about this, winding a strand of her untidy frizzy hair round her fingers. She frowned, but then smiled, and stretched a hand towards her mother across the table. 'A bit, maybe. But after all he was the one who left you, wasn't he? And it's a hard thing to face, for me too. Just think, if my Dad really did do these things ...'

'Emily, he didn't, I'm sure. But even if he did, it was long before you were even born. It's not your fault, don't ever think that.'

'No, I don't think that.' Emily laughed. 'Of course not, how could it be? But Mum ...'

'Yes?'

'Would you mind ... I'm sure you wouldn't mind, would you?'

'Mind what, darling? Come on, spit it out!'

'If I went to see him? Maybe I can help somehow, in ways you can't.'

* * *

My father, Emily thought, has become an old man. Even as he smiled when he caught sight of her she noticed the lines, somehow etched deeper into his face; and the hair – what had happened to his hair? Last time she saw him it had been going grey, but now it was a sort of odd gingery-brown colour, cut very short at the sides but loose and spiky on top; it looked awful. His beard had gone white.

It was still her Dad, but a parody somehow.

She smiled uncertainly and ran towards him, holding out her arms for the embrace she felt sure he expected. As she did she thought, he's smaller too, he's thinner, he's shrunk! Or have I become a giant overnight?

'Dad! Good to see you!'

'You too, Emily, you too!' After the initial embrace they stood back looking at each other, a little rock in the stream of pedestrians on the pavement.

'Well, what a pleasure!' He smiled. 'Shall we go in?'

He had insisted on meeting at *Betty's*. If you're coming to Harrogate, where else? he had said. He had booked a table to avoid the queue. *Betty's Tea Rooms* were famous all over Yorkshire – worldwide, in fact – and Harrogate was the place where it had all started in 1919. Tourists, business folk and locals filled the place, day in, day out, treating themselves to expensive, exquisitely served tea, sandwiches and cakes, served on silver cake stands by uniformed waitresses at tables with crisp white tablecloths and bone china cups and plates. Emily followed her father to a small corner table, bemused.

'Now,' he said when they had ordered. 'Tell me all about Cambridge. And Larry. How is he?'

So for half an hour Emily talked about her studies and Larry, her boyfriend, who was deep in his doctoral thesis at Birmingham, all the time watching her father and thinking *he's dyed his hair*, that's what it is. But he's only what – fifty something. That's not so old, *why does he need to do that?*

At last she got to the reason why she had come. 'Dad, this story about you and the police. It's terrible!'

'Yes, of course. More than terrible, in fact. I'd hoped you wouldn't hear.'

'I was bound to hear sometime, Dad. It's even been in the newspapers, Mum says.'

'Yes. Bloody journalists.' Bob's face grew hard, angry. 'You've talked to your mother then?'

'Of course; she phoned me. I'm staying in her flat.'

'So you've discussed it, I suppose. What did she say?'

'She doesn't believe it. Dad ...' Emily leaned forward, forcing herself to gaze intently into her father's eyes. It wasn't easy; she gripped one of the elegant expensive teaspoons so hard in her fingers that it began to bend. 'Dad, is any of it actually true?'

His face flushed – with anger, she hoped. 'No, it bloody well isn't!'

'None of it?'

'Not a shred, no. It's all lies.'

The silence lasted for five, ten seconds. As Emily smiled, she felt tears prickle her eyes. 'I thought so. But I had to ask.'

Bob shook his head, his ever-present rage and embarrassment stilled for a moment by pity and admiration for this, his only daughter. 'You've got your mother's eyes.'

'Have I? Hers are hazel, Dad; mine are brown.'

'I wasn't talking about the colour,' Bob said, quietly. 'I meant the way you look at me, straight to the heart of the matter. Like her.'

'Oh.' Emily looked down, flustered, and saw the spoon in her hands. 'Goodness, look what I've done with this!' Awkwardly, she tried to straighten it.

'Of course I *knew* those girls, way back then. They were my pupils, I taught them English. But that's all. No sex, for Christ's sake – that's all rubbish!'

'So why do you think they're saying it?'

'I wish I knew, Emily, I wish I knew. Either they've got me mixed up with someone else, or they're living in a fantasy world. Madwomen, mentally ill. But look, this is my problem, not yours. You haven't travelled all this way to be troubled with my nonsense.'

'Dad, don't be silly – that's exactly why I've come! I want to help, if I can! To understand it, at least.'

'Do you? Do you really?'

Even his voice has changed, Emily thought. I've never heard it break like that before.

'Yes, Dad, of course! I'm your daughter, I'm on your side!'

'Well, thank you, darling. That's really very ... very kind indeed.'

He turned away, to stare out of the window, where a crowd of well-dressed pedestrians were strolling past, some peering through the plate glass window to see if there was an empty table. It's like we're on stage, Emily thought. But no one can hear what we're talking about, thank goodness.

'Dad, you're not crying, are you?'

'No.' He wiped his eyes with one of the napkins. 'Of course not. It's just that ... I don't hear a lot of kind words these days. None at all, in fact.'

'What about ...' Emily searched for the name in her memory. '... Sonya? Isn't she supportive?'

'Not really, no.' Bob drew a deep, shuddering breath. 'It's all been too much for her, I'm afraid. She's asked me to leave.'

'What?'

'Well, you can see her point of view. We've been together less than a year and she never expected this to come up. She's got three young children and the TV and press banging on the door asking why she's living with a man who ...

well, you know. The kids go to my school, after all, she works there ... what *was* my school, that is. Not anymore.'

'But you've only been suspended, haven't you?'

'*Only?*' Bob shook his head bitterly. 'I'll never get another job teaching again, how could I? I'm a *former* head teacher.'

'But that's so unfair!'

'Of course it's unfair. Even Sonya knows that. She tried, really she did.'

'But she asked you to leave? That's so cruel!' Emily had only met her father's new partner once, and the occasion had not been a success. She had hated the woman for replacing her mother, and despised her for having three fatherless children and for looking so ... well, *ordinary,* in Emily's opinion. A bit frumpish and frazzled, slightly overweight; eager to please, perhaps, but homely, not especially bright – with none of the fire, the sparkle, the challenge of her own mother.

Nonetheless, for her father's sake, Emily had been prepared to make an effort. But now, in this crisis, *she had asked him to leave?*

If fifty demons of hell drag the woman down to a lake of burning fire, it won't be enough.

'So what ... where will you go?'

'Don't worry, love, I've found a flat. Just a student bedsit, really, but it's all I need for now.'

'Dad, *you're living in a bedsit?* Where, for heaven's sake?'

'Here, in Harrogate. The rent's pretty high, but it's just for six months, then we'll see. It's a lovely town. I go for long walks on the Stray – ranting and cursing my fate.'

'Dad, I'm so sorry.'

'So am I. But it's my own fault. I should never have left your mother.'

'Won't she have you back? Perhaps ...'

'No.' Bob reached across the table, patted his daughter's hand. 'Don't get your hopes up, that's not going to happen. I went to see her, and she promised to support me, up to a point, anyway ... But we're divorced now, and we've grown apart. We had a long marriage, longer than most people these days. But we're different people, and ... I got the impression she's found someone else. She's an attractive woman, your mother.'

And my father is a lonely old man, Emily thought. She shook her head sadly.

'Come on, eat up!' Bob said. 'This is my treat! And those cakes cost an arm and a leg. Would you like some more tea?'

'Yes, okay.' Forcing down a cream cake, Emily stared at her father, with that determined gaze which reminded him so much of her mother. 'But look, Dad, when I said I'd come here to help, I really meant it. I want you to tell me everything you know about these accusations, everything. All about what it was like when you were young, before I was born, when they say this happened. And especially about these two girls – women – so we can find out what's wrong with them.'

'My solicitor's already doing this, Em. It's not so easy.'

'Well, maybe she's not trying hard enough, or doesn't really care. I'm your daughter, Dad, and I'm not going to let this happen. So after this, we'll go back to your flat, okay? Then you can tell me everything.'

22. Arrest

THE CCTV evidence wasn't conclusive, but it provided a sufficient reason to arrest Adrian Norton. Since Terry Bateson liked to take his daughters to school in the morning, he delegated supervision of the arrest procedure to Jane Carter. It was her idea to arrest Michaela Konvalinka at the same time.

Jane arrived outside the student flat at 6.30 a.m. She had a search warrant in her hand, and was accompanied by DC Harry Easby and four uniformed constables. As she had expected, the student village was deserted at that time of day. A single male jogger gazed curiously at the police van as he loped by. Everywhere else was silence.

A grim smile of satisfaction played around Jane's lips as she rang the doorbell. This was the part of police work she found most satisfying. All the evidence pointed to Adrian, and with any luck he would confess before the day was out. Another case solved, another star on her career record.

It took several rings before the door was opened by a young man who, as she had expected, looked bemused, tousled and sleepy.

'Hello ...?'

'Police. Are you Adrian Norton?'

'Yes. What the hell ..?'

'Adrian Norton, I am arresting you for the murder of Victoria Weston. You do not have to say anything, but it may harm your defence if you do not mention when questioned something which you later rely on in court. Anything you do say may be given in evidence.'

'What? I don't understand.'

'I'm arresting you, Adrian Norton, for the murder of your tutor, Victoria

Weston. Do you understand now? I also have a warrant to search this house. Stand aside, please. Is anyone else here with you?'

'Yes, my girlfriend, but ...'

Michaela, her auburn hair ruffled, appeared at the door of the bedroom, hurriedly shrugging herself into a thin blue dressing gown. 'Adrian, what is this?'

Jane led her team purposefully into the flat. 'You remember me, Ms Konvalinka, don't you? Detective Sergeant Carter.'

'Yes. Why you break in here like this? What the hell time you think is?'

'Michaela Konvalinka, I am arresting you on suspicion of obstructing enquiries into the murder of Victoria Weston. You do not have to say anything, but ...' As she ran through the arrest formula Jane watched as shock, fear and fury crossed the young woman's face in rapid succession, like clouds in a hurricane.

'You arrest *me?* You cannot do this, you crazy!'

'I can do it and I am. Now, if you would just go inside with this female constable to get dressed ...'

'Adrian! Stop them! Is terror, fascism!'

But Adrian, though he looked equally shocked, was stunned into immobility. This was part of Jane's plan. The reason for the early morning arrest was not just to ensure that the suspects were at home, but to shock them into compliance, surrender, and with luck, an admission of guilt. The first two objectives seemed on the way to being achieved – with Adrian, at least. With Michaela, not so much.

'This my house, my room! You can't come here! Get out!'

It was fortunate that there were two female uniformed constables in the team. Even with their presence and firm steady persuasion, it took more than half an hour before the Czech girl, dressed and handcuffed, was persuaded to join her stunned fiancé in the back of the police van.

* * *

At York's Fulford police station they were booked in and processed separately. When Terry arrived he was surprised to find Michaela had been arrested too. But by the end of the day he understood why.

All morning Adrian stuck stubbornly to his story. He waived his right to a lawyer; he didn't need one, he said. He was innocent, so it wasn't necessary; this was all a crazy misunderstanding. If the police would just listen they would realise they had got things all wrong.

Terry, sitting this time with Mike Candor, took him painstakingly through the history of his relationship with Victoria Weston. It was all much as Adrian had told Terry before. Yes, he had been to her home many times, so if they found bodily traces – fingerprints, DNA, hairs, sperm, whatever – in the house it was hardly surprising. Yes, he'd been in the bedroom, bathroom, kitchen, living room, and in the hot tub too – though only once, he recalled, in late June or early July, shortly before he left for his summer job in Prague where he met Michaela. Vicky actually drove him to the airport.

When he'd returned in the autumn, things had been different. He'd visited Vicky's house two or three more times at most – the last time being the day he'd described before, when he'd told her their affair had to end. Perhaps he'd done that unkindly but that was all he'd done wrong. And that day, Thursday 25th August, was the last time he'd seen her. She'd been very much alive then.

It was totally absurd to suggest that he'd killed her, Adrian insisted – why would he? He liked her, after all, they'd been friends as well as lovers, and she was a good teacher – excellent, in his opinion. He just didn't want to have sex with her anymore, because that would threaten his planned marriage to Michaela.

'Well exactly,' Terry suggested. 'Isn't that a motive? You killed her to keep her silent, so Michaela would never know.'

Adrian denied that, leaning earnestly forward across the table to impress his interviewers with his sincerity. 'That's nonsense, I couldn't do that, I'm not that sort of person. Anyway, I wouldn't know how!'

'All right. So for the record, you're absolutely sure that the last time you saw Victoria Weston was that Thursday afternoon, the 25th? You didn't go back to see her later? On Sunday perhaps?'

'No! I was with Michaela all day Sunday, I told you!'

'Quite sure about that, are you? You don't want to change your story?'

'No.'

'Very well.' It was at that point that Terry produced the CCTV images. The pictures he showed Adrian were stills, prints from the best magnification they had got from the video. They showed a young man on a bicycle outside the pub in Osbaldwick, less than fifty yards from the entrance to the Westons' drive. The date and time – 8.22 p.m. Sunday 28th August – were printed at the bottom of the screen. The cyclist's face was fudged, fuzzy, but the hair and features were clearly similar to Adrian's. As though he had been photographed through a bathroom window, the pixels blurred.

Adrian's real face turned pale when he saw it. His lips trembled, his fingers shook.

'Is that you, Adrian?' Terry asked. There was a long, pregnant pause.

'No,' he said at last. 'It can't be. I wasn't there, I told you. It must be someone else.'

'And that isn't your bike?'

'No. Well, obviously not. I mean I do have a bike like that, but if it isn't me it can't be my bike, can it? You've got the wrong person.'

And that was as far as Terry got. Until Jane came in.

* * *

DCI Will Churchill was watching both interviews on adjacent screens fed from cameras in the interview rooms. Every word and image was being recorded, and Will Churchill was drawing cynical amusement from what he was watching. He disliked and despised Terry Bateson, who had caused him such trouble in the past. He longed to gain his revenge, and saw an ideal opportunity unfolding in front of him now.

On the left-hand screen was Terry, interviewing Adrian in what seemed to Churchill a quiet, unnecessarily gentle fashion; not exactly as though he believed the boy, but more like a favourite uncle who is disappointed in his nephew. On the right-hand screen a much more fiery, confrontational drama was taking place. Jane Carter had disagreed with Terry's softly-softly approach in their original interview with the Czech girl, and she was making up for it now. As soon as she told the young woman about Adrian's affair with his tutor, the interview became compelling viewing. At first, Michaela refused to believe it.

'You lie! That's not true! He never do that!'

'He did, Michaela. He told us.'

'No. Not Adrian, never. Why you tell these filthy lies? You think he killed her, you arrest him for that? Rubbish! He just go there to study poetry, feminism, women's rights. Nothing you understand about that, lying fascist bitch!'

'It's no good insulting me, young lady,' Jane said patiently, glancing at the young female constable by the door. 'The reason you've been arrested today is because of this statement you made last week, remember? Now, let's go through it carefully, shall we? Maybe you got something wrong.'

'You call me liar now, are you? I tell truth, always. Not something police understand.'

It took several more exchanges like this and a break for a soothing cup of tea before Michaela condescended to even glance at her previous statement. But all the time she was protesting, Jane Carter, like her boss Will Churchill up in the control room, could see signs of the impact the revelation had had upon her. While she re-read her statement tears trickled down her cheeks. When the young constable offered her a box of tissues Michaela took one, wiped her eyes, blew her nose, and then flung the tissue angrily to the floor.

'What you want with this stupid statement?' she asked, shoving it back across the desk. 'I don't care about it anyway.'

'What I want to know, Michaela,' Jane insisted tediously, 'is how true this last part is. Look at these paragraphs here, where you describe what you did on Sunday 28th August. Adrian was with you all day, you said. Let's go through this word by word, shall we?'

* * *

The final act of the drama occurred later that afternoon, when Jane confronted Adrian with Michaela's new statement. That was the moment she felt sure she had got him. She sat beside Terry Bateson in the interview room. Will Churchill watched from the control room.

'Adrian, I have a signed statement from your girlfriend, Michaela Konvalinka. Would you like to know what it says?'

'Yes, I suppose. I thought she had already done that – made a statement, I mean.'

'She has, yes, but this is a new one. She's revised some of the things she said before. Perhaps you'd better read it. This is the key paragraph, right here.'

Jane slid a paper over the desk, with a section marked in yellow highlighter. It was a photocopy, to guard against the risk of Adrian ripping up the original in rage. But instead of anger, there was only shock, and resignation. When he'd read it he pushed the paper away, and slumped forwards with his head in his hands.

'She really said this?'

'She did, yes. That's her signature at the bottom.'

'So I see.' After a long moment he looked up, his face bleak, his eyes wide and despairing. 'I knew this would happen. And now I suppose she hates me.'

'It's not really a question of what she feels,' Jane said coldly. 'What matters here is the truth. You lied to us before, didn't you, Adrian? You told Inspector Bateson here that you were with your girlfriend all evening, but you weren't, were you? You went out about seven thirty, just as she says here, and didn't come back until late.'

There was a long, pregnant pause. At last Adrian turned his hands face up on the table, and nodded. 'Yes. Yes, that's true.'

'And you persuaded your girlfriend Michaela to lie for you, didn't you? She lied to protect you?'

'Yes.' A deep sigh. 'I suppose she did.'

Terry Bateson spoke for the first time. 'So where were you, Adrian, for those hours?' Will Churchill, watching, noticed the irritation in Jane's glance at Terry sitting beside her. *She* should be asking the questions now, he thought. *She* made the breakthrough. Not Terry.

'Where was I, you ask?'

'Yes.'

Adrian shook his head hopelessly. 'I don't know, I can't remember. We'd had a row, Michaela and me, and ... I just wanted to be alone for a bit.'

'For over four hours?' Terry was annoyed now. 'When she'd gone out to buy Chinese food? Oh come on, Adrian, you can do better than that.'

'I know it was thoughtless. I just ... needed some peace.'

'So where did you go?'

'On my bike. Cycling round. Here and there.'

'So this *is* you, isn't it?' Jane shoved the still from the CCTV across the table. Adrian stared at it glumly.

'Probably. It looks like me.'

'So there you are, outside the pub in Osbaldwick, fifty yards away from Victoria Weston's house, at 8.22 p.m. on Sunday evening. Where were you going, Adrian?'

'I went ... past Vicky's house.' The words were whispered, hardly audible. To ensure they were recorded, Jane said: 'For the benefit of the tape, you're saying you cycled past Vicky's house. Is that right?'

'Yes.'

'*Past* the house? Or did you go in it?'

'I just cycled past. I didn't go in.'

Jane closed her eyes, and drew a deep breath. *Almost there,* she thought. *I've hooked the fish; now land it.*

'Did you see Vicky, when you cycled past?'

'No.' Another whisper. 'No, no.'

'Think carefully, Adrian. Are you sure? Did you see her through the window, perhaps?'

'No, not there. I didn't.'

'Not there, you say. Did you see her somewhere else, perhaps? Outside in the garden? In the hot tub?'

'No. Yes. I mean ...' He shook his head, apparently confused, though the question was clear enough.

'Which is it, Adrian? Yes or no?'

He stared at them, silently. There was panic in his eyes, Jane thought.

'Did you see her in the hot tub, Adrian, is that it? When you cycled past the house, did you see her in the hot tub, and go into the garden to join her? Is that what you're saying? Did you go in and drown her there?'

No answer. He shook his head violently, side to side, then got to his feet. The door was closed, it was unlikely he would escape. He paced across the room, once, twice.

'Sit down, Adrian,' Terry said quietly. 'Just sit down and answer the question.'

But he didn't sit down. Instead he stared at them wildly, then said: 'No. I won't sit down, I don't like these questions, they're wrong. I need a lawyer – I can have one, can't I? I want a lawyer now.'

* * *

While they were waiting for the lawyer Will Churchill made his decision. 'Checkmate, Sergeant,' he said, smiling at Jane. 'You've got him now. Even if the lawyers try to drag it out for a bit, the kid's only real choice is when to confess. The sooner the better, if he comes to his senses. But if not, you've got a slam-dunk trial ahead of you. Another feather in your cap.'

'Thank you, sir.'

But while Jane beamed, pleased but a little wary and embarrassed as she always was when dealing with Churchill, Terry looked on quizzically. This was *his* case, surely? It had nothing to do with Churchill, so why was he here at all? Praising Jane in front of him?

He soon found out. Churchill turned to him, a devious, innocent look on his face. 'Only fair, don't you agree, Terence? Our clever Sergeant Carter here should be SIO on this case? After all, she's done the work, made the breakthrough, and I'm sure you'll agree, we need to encourage the junior ranks when we can – especially bright young country lasses like our Jane!'

'Well, yes sir, but ...'

'Anyway, it couldn't be you, Terence, could it? You found the body, so you're a witness in the case. We can't have our Senior Investigating Officer in court describing how he crashed a boat with his daughters into the riverbank, can we? It wouldn't look right. In any case, this spate of burglaries now. We've had fifteen cases in the last month, all in posh houses, and I'm getting grief from the Chief Constable. I know you've been supervising that but it needs more attention from a senior detective, not one distracted by this murder. So I'll leave that in your capable hands, ok? Must dash.'

And then as usual he was gone, before Terry could think of any protest that would not make him look undignified and mean. But it was typical of Will Churchill's warped style of leadership to use this case to simultaneously undermine him and patronise Jane Carter. Jane was clever, certainly; she'd been a successful detective for years in the rural part of East Yorkshire before transferring to York. But did that make it fair or even decent to call her a 'bright young country lass' – especially with the emphasis Churchill had put on the first syllable of the penultimate word in that phrase?

Perhaps I'm imagining things, Terry told himself as he went in search of a coffee. Jane hadn't seemed to take offense, and any protest I make will just worsen the atmosphere in the department. After all, we're here to catch criminals and it looks like we've done that today.

If the lawyer's got any sense, he'll advise young Adrian to plead guilty, and that'll be another case wrapped up.

Part Three

Emily

23. Google

'DAD, YOU can find anything on the internet.'

'I know, that's what all your generation think. But Emily, you have to realise that once upon a time there *was* no internet. No smart phones, no laptops or tablets, nothing. We're talking about 1991, remember, before you were even born.'

'Yes, Dad, we learned about it in school. The black and white years – no colour TV, and dinosaurs roaming the streets.'

'That sort of thing, yes.' A faint smile hovered on Bob's lips, the first small victory for Emily that day. 'That's why we should go to the library. They'll have old newspapers there, paper copies perhaps, or microfiche.'

'Micro – what?'

'You'll see. It'll take time, but that's all I've got, right now.'

'Ok, but I'll bring my phone. Haven't you got an Ipad, Dad?'

'I've got this.' Shyly, Bob produced a ten-year-old laptop, heavy as a brick and little more use. 'I've never really got on with it though. I think my fingers are too big.'

'Dad, you're prehistoric! What did you do in your day – hunt deer and wear animal skins?'

'Most of the time, yes.' *Except when I was raping young schoolgirls*, Bob thought bitterly. But the bitterness, always there in the background, was lighter this morning. He had always loved Emily, his only daughter, but never appreciated her so fully before. She'd arrived on his doorstep this morning full of ideas, energy, optimism, the medicine of life itself.

But Emily's heart sank as she looked around. It was the second time she had visited her father's new home, and it depressed her as much as the first. It was like a cheap parody of her own room in college. The rented bedsit was a similar size, but the furnishings and decor came from a different century. Where her own walls were freshly painted, these were papered with ancient woodchip which was peeling away in two places from the ceiling. A single battered armchair sat forlornly beside an ancient gas fire, which spluttered and popped dangerously when her father stooped to light it. The only other furniture apart from the single bed, which sagged when she sat on it, was a pair of upright dining chairs and a pine table scarred by the rings of a dozen careless coffee cups. There was a tiny kitchen, no bigger than a cupboard, with a cooker, sink and miniature fridge, and a bathroom of similar size.

'It's only for a while, until the case is sorted out,' Bob said, as he saw her looking round. 'It's a new life, quite liberating in a way.'

'But Dad, haven't you got money, to afford a bigger place than this?'

'Of course, if I want one. But that will take time; I need to look around first, before I buy. So this is just my launch pad, as it were.'

Some pad, Emily thought, comparing it to her mother's luxurious riverside apartment. How did my father come down to this? But she was here to help, not criticise. And her father was determined to be cheerful.

'If we have time after the library, I can show you the school, and the flat where I used to live,' he said, leading the way down the worn staircase to his battered front door.

'Cool. I'll take some photos of them too,' Emily said, brandishing her smartphone.

So they caught the bus to Leeds, and spent the morning in the Central Reference Library, Bob requesting huge folders of ancient newspapers which were hauled up by breathless assistants from the library basement. Emily watched him turning the yellow crackling pages, and scrolling his way through the microfiche viewer which looked to her like some ancient relic of the era of silent films, with Charlie Chaplin and Buster Keaton. She, meanwhile, searched through Google, Facebook and Twitter.

By mid-afternoon, both could report some success.

Bob had found, and photocopied, a dozen newspaper articles from 1991 in which his old school was mentioned. Most were about exam results, sports days and the building of a new sixth form common room. There were several yellowing photographs, including a couple in which he recognised a slim, slightly blurred version of himself. Shyly, he showed them to Emily.

'Well, you look okay, Dad,' she said, peering closely. 'That tweed sports jacket looks a bit naff, but I guess it was the thing in those days. Your beard's pretty dark and quite bushy too; I prefer the goatee.'

'Do you? Well ...' Bob fingered his chin. 'Fashions change, don't they? A lot of men had full beards back then.'

'Yep, there's another one.' Emily pointed to a tall, thin bearded man two rows behind her father. 'Looks a bit like you, too.'

'Uh huh. I don't remember him though. Anyway, what did you find?'

'Well, the library staff were a bit anal about letting me print stuff. It's easy back in college, I can do it there later if necessary. But I bookmarked a few pages and found this. See here.'

She passed him her smartphone and Bob read the sharp, crystal clear electronic print. At the bottom of the page he lost his place, fumbled, and had to ask Emily to find it again and scroll down. Then he looked up, amazed.

'My God, she's a criminal!'

'So it seems, yes. Assuming this is the right woman.'

'How can we check?'

'I don't know, I'll find out. But it's pretty spectacular, don't you think?'

The article was about a woman called Clare Fanshawe, the same name as Bob's first accuser. In 1995, aged 19, she had been arrested by a store detective outside *Next* in Trinity Shopping Centre, Leeds. Police had been called and she had been found to be wearing three sets of underwear, three blouses and two pairs of trousers, all new and with the store's labels still attached. A pair of faded jeans and the teeshirt which she had been wearing when she entered the store were found stuffed behind a cistern in the ladies' toilet. Entering a guilty plea in the magistrates' court, her solicitor explained in mitigation that his client had recently suffered a miscarriage and was mentally disturbed at the time of the offence. She was currently unemployed but had applied to train as a nursery nurse. The magistrates fined her £50 plus costs and gave her a conditional discharge for two years.

'Well, well. Presumably that put an end to her career as a nursery nurse,' Bob murmured. 'Who'd want their child cared for by a thief?'

'Some people do, apparently. Look here!'

She tapped her finger on the screen and brought up a page from 2003, with a picture of a single storey building beside a semi-detached house, in the place where a garage would normally be. It was from a local newspaper in Pudsey, a respectable suburb between Leeds and Bradford. A sign on the front of the building read *Tiny Tots Nursery*, and a cheerful banner was strung beneath it with paintings of sunflowers, elephants, and cuddly cartoon characters. The article –

an advertisement really – triumphantly declared that the nursery was now open for business, after a year-long struggle for planning permission. Proudly in front of it stood the joint proprietors, Ms Helen Bamber and Ms Clare Fanshawe.

Bob studied the picture. Helen Bamber, the older woman, was in her early thirties, respectably dressed, with a comfortable body and kind, friendly face. Clare Fanshawe, beside her, was much younger, a skinny girl in her late twenties with long dark shoulder-length hair. She wore jeans, trainers, and a pink teeshirt printed with flowers and animals. She too was smiling, but her face was thinner, more nervous looking than the older woman's.

'Do you recognise her?' Emily asked.

'No,' Bob shook his head. 'I don't think so, anyway. Maybe if we saw this next to the school photo the police showed us. But even then ...' A thought struck him. 'Does she still work there?'

'No. The nursery's still there though.' Emily tapped the screen again. 'Look, here's their web page. It lists the staff. Helen Bamber still runs it but there's no Clare.'

'I wonder how long she stayed?'

'We could always ask, I suppose. Ring them up or visit.'

'Hm. I'm not sure. What would we say? Hello, I'm the man accused of abusing your friend when she was a schoolgirl, and I'd like to get in touch? That won't go down well, will it?'

'I could do it, Dad. Say I'm a long-lost relative or something.'

'Let's be careful. Not tell lies unless we have to. Did you find anything else?'

'No, that's all. But look, Dad, we haven't done so badly, have we? Why don't we have some lunch, and then visit that school of yours, the scene of the crime. You could show me your old flat, too.'

* * *

Her father's old flat, Emily thought, looked little better than the one he had now – from the outside anyway. It was on the third floor of a converted Victorian villa, once a middle-class family house, no doubt, but now it had six separate bell-pushes on the front door. They stood for a while on the pavement opposite, contemplating it in silence.

'It's that one there,' Bob said nostalgically. 'The one with the giant rubber plant in the window. It used to be sunny in the late afternoon.'

'How long did you live there?'

'A year, eighteen months, I suppose. It was warm and convenient. Converted servant's quarters, I suppose. I liked it – we both did.'

'Both? You mean Mum lived there too?'

'She ... visited,' Bob said shyly. 'It was too small for a couple. We moved out when we married. Found somewhere bigger.'

'So, Mum climbed those stairs ...' As they watched, a girl – a student perhaps – in jeans and puffy anorak, carrying a plastic Tesco bag, climbed the three stone steps to the front door, which she opened by tapping in a security code. Emily imagined her own mother, seventeen years old, doing the same thing in the same place, climbing the stairs inside to meet a man – a youthful version of this man beside her – in that very same room. She gazed up at the window with the rubber plant, wondering if the light would come on and a girl's face, like her own but younger, would look out.

If so, whose face? Seventeen year old Sarah's? Or that of a different schoolgirl, still younger?

Emily shuddered, as if someone had stepped on her grave. No light came on in the window; the young student must live in another a different flat. She turned to her dad.

'Do you want to go in? Shall we press a bell?'

'No.' Bob shook his head, as if he too, had been absorbed in a dream, a memory of times past. 'No point, there's nothing to see. Let me show you the school. It's just five minutes' walk.'

The school had changed since Bob worked there. It looked cleaner, newer, bigger. The old Victorian science block, built in the 1890s, had been demolished and replaced with a light, airy, two-storey building with odd-shaped wooden cladding and one wall composed almost entirely of glass. As they walked across the playground towards the main entrance, Bob wondered if it was like a greenhouse inside in the summer.

'Can I help you?' The receptionist smiled through her glass screen.

'Yes. I used to work here a long time ago, and I'm showing my daughter around. A sort of nostalgia trip, really. You don't have a prospectus, do you?'

'I suppose we could spare one. They're for parents really, but since you're old staff. Retired now, are you?'

'In a way.' Bob took the glossy brochure gratefully. 'I wonder – you don't remember Dr Kenning, by any chance? Tall man, walked with a stoop, used to teach science.'

'Dr Kenning? No. Before my time, probably.' The woman turned to her colleague. 'Cath, do you remember a Dr Kenning, used to work here?'

'Dr Kenning! Yes, of course. Used to be headmaster.' An older woman, overweight and wheezing, lumbered to the window. 'I remember, him – kind man, real gent.' She smiled at Bob. 'Were you here with him?'

'Yes, in the 1990s. Only for a short time.'

'Pupil, or teacher?'

'Teacher. I taught English.' Bob dug his fingernails anxiously into his palm. Would she recognise him, from the newspaper perhaps? His picture hadn't been on TV, but his name and the nature of the allegations certainly had.

'Oh. What was your name again?'

'Newby. The reason I came, you see, we were just walking past and I thought how nice it would be to meet Dr Kenning again. You wouldn't have an address for him, would you? Phone number perhaps?'

'I could check. It might take a few minutes, though.'

While they were waiting Bob and Emily wandered around the entrance hall, looking at the pictures of smiling teenagers canoeing down rapids, climbing mountains, and brandishing exam results. It looked like a thriving, energetic place.

'Here we are.' The woman returned to the window with a folder she had pulled from a filing cabinet. 'He's moved to Harrogate, it seems.'

'Cath! Cath, you can't do that!' The first woman hurried to the window beside her colleague. 'We can't just hand out addresses, they're confidential.' Lowering her voice, she hissed. 'Remember, the police were here last week! They asked for Dr Kenning too!'

'What? Oh, yes – did they?'

'It was probably your day off.' She snatched the file from Cath's hands, and turned to Bob with a bright, insincere smile.

'I'm sorry, sir, we can't help you. Data protection laws, very strict. I can pass on a message though, if you like. Then Dr Kenning can contact you, if ...' Her voice trailed off, she shrugged.

'No, that's all right.' Bob turned to go.

'I'll tell him you called,' said the older woman Cath. 'Mr, er ...?'

'Thanks for your help.' Embarrassed, Bob almost ran to the door. With a cheery wave, Emily followed him. Halfway to the school gate Bob realised his hands were shaking. 'That was awful,' he muttered. 'We should never have come.'

'At least we know he lives in Harrogate, Dad.'

'Yes, and the police have been to see him already.' Safely outside the school gates he drew several deep breaths, to compose himself. 'Ah well. She was right, of course.'

'Who?'

'The young one. If that older woman, Cath, had given out the address she'd have been sacked. She would have in my school. So at least we've prevented one crime.'

And nearly caused another, he thought ruefully. *A few simple questions and I'm acting like a criminal.*

24. New Client

'MRS NEWBY?'

'Yes?'

'Solicitor on the phone for you. Lucy Parsons.'

'Oh, great. Put her through.' Sarah leaned back gratefully in her office chair, pushing away the bundle of evidence she had been studying. It was a detailed description of a man who had systematically claimed disability benefits for the past year, while simultaneously moonlighting as a bouncer outside a strip club and defaulting on paternity payments to his partner. Prosecuting him would be a pleasure, she thought. But scarcely a challenge. It was a long way from the high profile, complex cases that she really enjoyed.

'Lucy. What can I do for you?'

'More what I can do for you, lovey, I think. Remember what you said to me a while ago, Sarah?'

'I've said lots to you, Lucy love. Told you my whole life story, nearly, several times over. To which of my pearls of wisdom do you refer?'

'The one about murder, it was.'

'Sorry?'

'A good murder trial. That's what I need to pay the mortgage, you said. Keep me off the streets.'

'Ah. Yes, quite.' A little electric jolt of excitement tingled along Sarah's spine. 'Why, have you got one?'

'I have, yes. If you're interested? Not too busy with commercial fraud?'

'I could probably find a space. When is the trial scheduled?'

'Beginning of January. Shall I send the brief over?'

'Why not? Who's the client?'
'Young man called Adrian Norton. Nice lad. He's in Hull.'

* * *

The visit to Hull prison brought back many memories for Sarah, all of them painful. The visits to her son Simon, when he was charged with murder. She remembered the exquisite pain of watching him scream at Bob across the grimy metal table in the public visiting room, to the unconcealed delight of other prisoners' families. That was the moment when her marriage began to unravel, never to be healed again. She'd had to choose, and had chosen her son.

But it hadn't been easy. She remembered – how could she ever forget – the terrible times when she and Lucy Parsons had sat in a grim interview room with Simon, listening as he apparently damned himself out of his own mouth. And then later – against her own better judgement – agreeing to defend him herself in court.

In those moments of madness her heart had felt raw. So often in Sarah's life it had been her mind, her reason which defined her, but not then; she'd been consumed by a cocktail of rage, love, maternal fury – when she looked back it was impossible to define the emotional chemistry which had driven her at that time.

Nor did she wish to. Those days were long gone. Simon was safe, a free man, soon to be a father. And the client she had come to see today had no such pull on her heartstrings.

And yet when Adrian Norton was ushered into the interview room, there was more than a little resemblance. This young man was strong, too; perhaps shorter and less powerful than her son but still broad in the chest, slim-hipped with muscular biceps. Easily strong enough to drown a woman on his own, Sarah thought grimly. Not only that, but to drag her dead body from a hot tub, lift it into the boot of a car, and later, throw it in the river. No easy tasks, but this boy could surely manage them.

But it was the look on his face that really took her mind back. Skin pale and unshaven, the eyes wide and anxious, the lips surly, the brows drawn together in a defiant scowl as though the whole world was against him. Like a dog surrounded by wolves, scared, defiant, ready to bite but longing to run.

She'd seen that look many times before, on young men trapped on remand or in the dock from which there was no escape, nowhere to run. It had depressed her when she'd seen it on Simon; it depressed her now. More often than not, it was the face of guilt.

Nonetheless, it was her duty to defend this young man. As Lucy Parsons introduced her Sarah held out her hand, a brisk friendly smile on her face. It's even the same room, Sarah thought as they sat down. Not just me and Lucy and this young man facing each other across this battered graffiti-scarred table, but the same narrow view through filthy cobweb-strewn glass over rooftops to the wind-blown clouds that meant freedom. She saw Adrian's eyes drawn to it.

'So, Adrian, I've been hired to present your defence in court,' she began. 'Your solicitor Mrs Parsons has told me about your case and I've read all the statements, but I'd like to go through it all with you in person before the trial begins.'

'When is that, exactly?' He dragged his eyes back from the window.

'Three months from now. In January. Plenty of time to check everything thoroughly to make sure there are no surprises. You still intend to plead not guilty?'

'Of course. Why do you ask that?'

'I have to. It's your decision, but you need to know all the options.'

'Which are?'

This is where he starts to hate me, Sarah thought, noting the sullen anger behind the question. But I need to tell him, even though a guilty plea will cut my fee. And I do need this trial, heaven knows. She thought of the horrible bank statement on the dining room table in her lovely flat.

'As I'm sure Mrs Parsons has told you, a guilty plea at this stage would reduce your sentence quite substantially – by one third. If you leave it until the day of the trial, when all the preparatory legal work has been done, and then plead guilty, you would still qualify for a reduction, but much less, about 10%. And if you plead not guilty, go through a full trial, and then lose, there's no reduction at all.'

He thought about this. 'It's a gamble, you mean?'

'You could say that, yes. It's a way for the prosecution to put pressure on you to save themselves time and money. I know it seems harsh, but you need to think about it.'

His eyes met hers. Fear, indecision, resentment, a cry for help. 'You mean, you think I might lose?'

'That's always possible, yes. The Crown Prosecution Service have a reasonable case; they wouldn't be going for trial otherwise. But there are several weaknesses in it; areas which I can work on if you want me to. All we have to do is to create reasonable doubt in the minds of the jury and they should find you not guilty.'

'Reasonable doubt? Is that what they call it?' Adrian said cynically. He tossed his hair back. 'Can't you do better than that?'

'We don't *need* to do better than that, Adrian,' Sarah said softly. 'This is how it works. The prosecution have to prove your guilt *beyond reasonable doubt*. If they can't do that, you're not guilty. Simple as that.'

'Obviously.' The young man leant forward, resting his elbows on the table, his hands under his chin, staring at her. 'Aren't you going to ask?'

'Ask what?' Sarah met his eyes coolly. She guessed what was coming.

'Did I kill Vicky Weston? I thought you might want to know.'

Was this a challenge? Some criminals enjoyed teasing their lawyers, gaining a thrill from it, a sense of power. Watching him, Sarah thought, there's a trace of that here, but not much. He's too young, too fresh-faced, too innocent. Even the stubble on his cheeks is soft. He's a student of English literature after all. A nice middle-class boy.

But even they can have hidden depths.

Choosing her words carefully, she said: 'I'm not the police, it's not my job to interrogate you. I'm your defence, I'm on your side. If you decide to plead not guilty, that's enough for me.'

'So you don't want to know, is that what you're saying?'

Sitting beside Sarah, Lucy Parsons spoke for the first time. 'We've been through this before, Adrian, you know we have ..'

'I know, I've got a degree, I've read all that stuff. But it's different, sitting here now. You say you're my defence, on my side in one of the most important, scary situations in my life, and yet you don't actually want to *know*, do you, whether I'm a murderer? You're afraid to ask!'

Sudden tears flooded his eyes, and he tore his gaze away, staring through the grimy window at the scurrying distant clouds.

'You're happy to present my defence, take money for it, even though you think I might be guilty!'

That's how it works, Sarah thought, a trifle wearily. If I only defended clients I was sure were innocent, I'd be out of a job. She'd explained this to her husband, her friends, her children many more times than she cared to remember. *It's all a game, a game of proof.*

But that, clearly, was not what this young man wanted to hear. For him it was all too raw, too real.

'That's not what I think, Adrian,' she said carefully. 'I didn't say that.'

'Well, what *do* you think, then?' He dragged his gaze back from the window, bored into her with his eyes.

'I think you want me to ask you, isn't that right, Adrian?' Sarah felt Lucy's foot nudging hers in warning under the table, and ignored it. 'You want me to ask you if you killed Vicky Weston, don't you? That's what I think.'

Adrian swallowed, surprised. 'Yeah, that's right.' He drew a deep breath. 'Well, go on then. Ask.'

'Adrian Norton, did you kill Victoria Weston?'

'No. No, I didn't.'

'Do you know how she died? Were you there when it happened?'

'No, I wasn't.' Relief flooded his face.

'Right then.' Sarah smiled faintly. 'In that case, we'd better start working on your defence statement, don't you think? Now, why exactly did you lie to the police?'

* * *

'So, did you believe him?' Lucy asked, as they drove back over the Yorkshire Wolds towards York, taking the scenic route to avoid the M62.

'It's not our job to believe him, Luce, you know that.'

'Which is why we never ask, lovey. But this time you did. So ..?'

'What I think,' Sarah said after a pause. 'Is that either he's in denial, and has buried the memory of his guilt deep inside because the grisly truth is too terrible to face up to – or alternatively, he believes he's innocent because he really is.'

Lucy laughed. 'Wonderful! So what you're saying is, you don't know.'

'Exactly.' Sarah smiled wryly. 'Who are we, to open windows into men's souls?' She slowed down, changing lanes and watching the traffic carefully as she negotiated a roundabout. 'Maybe I should use that line in my summing up. What do you think? Too poetic?'

'Not if it makes you happy.' Lucy smiled at her friend. 'You're very cheerful, Sarah, considering.'

'Considering what?' They headed west, out of the market town of Beverley toward the racecourse, where cattle grazed freely beside the unfenced road. Sarah slowed as they drove past a string of racehorses walking back from the gallops, their work riders perched on tiny saddles on their backs, chatting cheerfully to each other.

'Well, Bob, I suppose.'

'Ah yes, Bob.' Sarah sighed. 'Don't remind me. I gave a statement to that wretched man Starkey, for what it's worth. How's his case going?'

'Not particularly well. I keep pestering Starkey on the phone, but you've met him, you can imagine. It's like getting blood out of a stone. He's very determined. Says he has a lot of support from higher up. *Operation Hazel*, they're calling it.'

'Sounds like a gardening program. What evidence have they got?'

'Just these two witness statements, so far as I know. But of course we're not allowed to talk to the complainants – or victims, as he insists on calling them. Meanwhile he's looking for corroboration – hoping for someone else to come out of the woodwork, no doubt. More recent accusations to establish a pattern of criminal behaviour. That's the point of all the publicity.'

'There isn't a pattern,' Sarah said firmly. 'I don't believe it. Bob isn't that much of a fool.'

'Well, you know him better than I do, lovey. But yes, I'm inclined to believe you.' Lucy gazed out of the window as they passed through a village, small brick houses with cottage gardens, post office, farm shop. 'It's not doing much for his relationship with Sonya, of course.'

'My heart bleeds for the poor woman.'

'You wouldn't think of taking him back, then?'

'Who, Bob?' A bitter smile crossed Sarah's face. 'No chance. What's broken, is broken. He didn't ask you to suggest that, did he?'

'No, not exactly. But I got the impression that if the possibility did ever cross your mind ...'

'Well it won't and it hasn't. I told him when he came to see me. Anyway, I told you, I've got a new man.'

'Yes. How's that going? Come on, lovey, don't blush! You know I keep secrets – I'm all agog.'

'Well ... it's certainly helping.'

'Helping? How exactly?'

'My recovery.' And so as she drove on towards York Sarah described how she felt. It was pleasant to have a friend like Lucy who was also a sort of confessor. She was still uncertain about her new relationship with Terry, she said, but for the moment at least it felt like part of the healing process. She found herself explaining, not for the first time, how emotionally frozen she had felt in those months after her former lover, Michael, had been murdered in front of her. By a client whom she and Lucy, ironically, had successfully released from prison.

'It's not something you get over quickly,' she said, pulling out to overtake a tractor. 'Even though I know the bastard's back in prison for life, I still see him sometimes in my dreams, coming towards me swinging that spanner in his hands, murder in his eyes. And I can't move, so ...'

She paused, glancing briefly at her friend in the passenger seat beside her. *After all Lucy's not just my friend and confessor, she's also the person who sends me most work, and if she thinks I'm not up to it ...*

'And this affair with Terry is helping you get over that, lovey, is it?'

'Well, yes, I think so. It feels like that anyway and ...' a long wistful sigh '... I just wish we could spend a whole night together. But he's got two daughters and I ... well, I just can't just march into his house and announce that I'm here to stay. Even if he'd want me, which he probably wouldn't. It's ... probably just a passing thing, Luce, but for now, it feels good.'

'Well, I'm truly glad for you, Sarah. And ...'

Just at that moment Sarah's mobile rang. Holding up a hand of apology to her friend she pressed the button on the handsfree set to take the call. Lucy watched as a look of astonishment crossed her friend's face.

'Simon? No, when? Half an hour ago ... but, is she ... are they both ok? But Simon, that's fantastic! Where are you exactly? When ... can I come?' When Sarah ended the call her face was radiant. 'That was Simon, my son. He's in the hospital. His girlfriend, partner, Lorraine – she's just had a baby boy!'

25. Family Fortunes

It was the first time Sarah had seen the baby and she couldn't get over it.

'He's got your eyes,' she told the young mother, Lorraine. 'All babies have blue eyes of course but there's definitely something about them. He's got Simon's mouth and chin but the eyes take after you, definitely. Aaaah, look, he heard that! See him wrinkling his forehead! He's trying to work out what we're saying!'

'Filling his nappy, more like.' Lorraine giggled shyly. 'That's his look when he poos.'

'Ah well. I'm sure his dad will take care of that for you.' Sarah smiled teasing her son. 'Start as you mean to go on, eh, Simon?'

'Happen. It's a bit fiddly, like.' A wary frown creased the young father's forehead as he considered this unwelcome, challenging idea. Sarah recognized masculine evasiveness when she saw it.

'Get on. A handy man like you? All the dads do it these days.'

'Yeah, well. I've had a go,' Simon admitted reluctantly. 'It's all runny and yellow, like. Not that bad really.'

'That's because he's drinking milk.' Sarah Newby smiled at her handsome, brawny young son, thinking that's a first then, if he really has used those strong, calloused hands to clean his baby son's bottom. It was a strange picture to imagine. 'Gentle' or 'soft' were not the first words his appearance brought to mind. Over six feet tall, Simon had always been strong, and in the past year he had filled out and developed quite noticeably. But it was his character, Sarah thought, that had developed the most. Three years ago he had been lost, an angry young man arrested by the police and charged with the rape and murder of his former girlfriend, Jasmine. Simon had only been rescued from a life sentence in prison by the determined, almost obsessive efforts of herself, Lucy Parsons, and Terry Bateson.

Who would have thought then, that a day like this would ever come? She watched him now, his powerful body sprawled and hunched slightly awkwardly in the chair beside the hospital bed, beaming contentedly at the sight of this little boy – *her grandson!* – opening his tiny mouth eagerly as his young mother, Lorraine, gently squeezed her breast to express the first drops of milk, and then guided his tiny lips around the nipple. Sarah watched entranced as the little hands – *five fingers on each, but so small* – instinctively clutched and pressed his mother's breast as he sucked.

For a while Lorraine smiled down at him, the archetypal madonna and child. Then she looked up and, noticing her audience, shyly drew across a shawl to cover herself.

'Don't mind us,' Sarah said. 'He's feeding well.'

'Yes. He's a tough little beggar. Like his dad.' Smiling, Lorraine reached out for Simon's hand across the blankets. Sarah's eyes filled with involuntary tears.

How wonderful! she thought. *I wish – did that ever happen to me?* She delved in her memory and came up with an answer that filled her with comfort and fear, both at once.

Yes, it did. Just like this.

Sarah had been just sixteen when Simon – this giant beside the bed – had been born. She'd still been a child herself, *three years younger* than this teenage girl in front of her, Lorraine. And just like Lorraine, she too had sat in the maternity ward, proudly beaming down at the tiny boy she had so miraculously, scandalously produced, against all the wise advice of her parents and social workers who – she shuddered to think of it now – had so wisely and cautiously invited her to consider abortion.

If I'd listened, Simon would never have been born.

Sarah had defied them all, because Kevin, Simon's father, had defiantly stuck by her. He had been a whole year older than her and *proud* of what he'd done, damn him, delighted to be the first cocky young lad on the street to get a girl pregnant. And so he'd sat beside her bed in a plastic hospital chair, just like Simon was sitting now, and defiantly held her hand when her frowning parents and the social worker and the nurses came to look. It had been a game the two of them shared.

Look at us – we're not kids, we can manage.

Only they couldn't. A year later, Kevin had gone, leaving Sarah with a black eye, a broken heart, and a baby.

Fine promises don't always last, Sarah thought sadly. *So will it be better this time, for these young parents?* Through a blur of happy tears she watched her son lean over the bed, his left hand caressing Lorraine's hair while he slipped a thick, calloused finger of his right hand into the tiny baby's grasp.

'Why are you frowning, mum?' Simon asked.

'Oh. No reason. Just thinking – remembering when you were that small.'

'I was never that small, was I?'

'Of course you were.' She smiled at the young couple. 'Have you thought of a name yet?'

'Well, we were thinking ...' Simon began, but Lorraine put her hand on his arm and to Sarah's surprise, he stopped. Lorraine smiled at him and turned to Sarah shyly, with a touch of defiance as though she was uncertain of her reception.

'We thought Daniel. Daniel Craig.'

'Oh.'

It's nice but it's the name of an actor, Sarah thought. The actor in the James Bond films. *You can't name your child after an actor; that's what people on council estates do.* Oh don't be so snobbish woman, it's a good manly name and he's a totally handsome actor, *for Christ's sake don't snub the girl now*, anyway what the hell's wrong with it? Nothing.

'That's lovely,' Sarah said swiftly.

The last thing she wanted was to offend this young woman, and it would be so easy to do. She had only met Lorraine a handful of times, and whenever they did meet the girl seemed in awe of her. It was hardly surprising: Sarah was a criminal barrister, whereas Lorraine worked on a checkout in Tesco.

'We like it,' Lorraine said, smiling up at Simon. 'It was my idea.'

Good for you, Sarah thought. *After all you bore him.* 'It's a great name, ' she said more firmly. 'One to be proud of. Daniel Craig Newby.'

'Well, yes, if ... ' Lorraine hesitated, and Sarah realized that they hadn't decided on the child's surname. They weren't married after all and Lorraine's surname was – what was it? – Scott. And Bob Newby wasn't even Simon's father.

'How is Bob anyway?' Simon asked. 'Have you seen him at all recently?'

'Yes,' Sarah said cautiously. 'I met him a few weeks ago. He's ... under a lot of strain. You know Lucy Parsons is his solicitor?'

'Oh, right. So, is it true what they say about him? That he's a child molester?' Her son's face hardened, and he made a slight unconscious movement closer to Lorraine, as though to protect her and her baby.

'The allegations relate to having sex with underage girls,' Sarah said judiciously. 'And he's not charged with anything yet, it's just a police investigation. Anyway I don't believe it. It must be a mistake.'

Simon shuddered. 'I never did like him, Mum, you know that.'

'I know, Simon.' Sarah bit her lip, thinking what to say. The last thing she wanted was a quarrel here now, on such a happy day as this.

'Nevertheless,' she said carefully. 'He's the only father figure you have, Simon. And he was very good to you when you were a little boy. Remember all those games of football, when I was busy studying?'

'Yes, I know, mum. Nobody's perfect. But when it really mattered and I needed his support, he didn't believe in me, did he? He thought I was a killer.'

This was true. When Simon had been charged with the murder of his former girlfriend, his stepfather had been convinced by the weight of evidence against him. Sarah remembered their bitter confrontation in the visiting room in Hull prison, that same room where she had recently met Adrian Norton. It had been one of the most painful moments of her life; her own son and husband screaming at each other in a public prison.

'He was convinced by the evidence against you, Simon. But then the police did have a good story, or thought they had. Even I had one or two doubts. Remember how hard it was.'

'Do you think I'll ever forget it?' The rough edge of anger in his tone was frightening; Lorraine looked across at them anxiously

'Of course not,' Sarah said, touching his arm gently. 'Neither will I; memories like that leave scars. But there is a strange irony here, Simon, don't you see? You resent Bob, quite naturally, for believing the allegations against you when you were innocent. Now the boot's on the other foot.'

Simon drew a deep breath, making a conscious effort to keep calm. He smiled reassuringly at Lorraine, and held out a finger for the baby to grasp in its tiny hand. 'I didn't say I believed he was guilty, Mum. What do I know about it? But if there is any truth in these allegations it ... makes it harder to like him. It must be hard for you too.'

'Of course it is, it's very painful. That's what's so horrible about situations like this. The story gains a life of its own. It can do tremendous harm, whether it's true or not. He's suspended from his job, he may never get it back.'

'That's harsh.' Simon smiled at the baby, who clung tightly to his finger as he moved it gently up and down. 'Teaching, that's his life, isn't it? Still, he's got a good lawyer, at least. Will you defend him, Mum?'

'I can't, Simon. I'm a witness.' She repeated the explanation she had given to Emily, before she went back to Cambridge. 'Your sister's fighting for him, anyway. She went over to see him last week.'

'Aye? Well, good for her. They were always close, them two.'

'Yes.' *Don't let this split my children,* Sarah thought. *Not now, in this time of hope.* An idea came to her. 'Have you told Emily yet? She'll be here again this weekend, staying with me. I'll bring her to see Daniel, shall I?'

'Aye. Why not?' Simon grinned. 'Happen it'll make her broody, too.'

'Maybe it will.' Sarah doubted that, but it was possible, she supposed. Just so long as they don't quarrel, that's all. Maybe this child will be a peacemaker.

For a while they sat watching the baby in silence. Mother and child, the perfect madonna scene. It's a high point in my life, Sarah thought. And even more so for Lorraine and Simon. This baby will change their lives forever. Part of her envied them: what would it be like, to start all over again? To live in hope and optimism, knowing nothing of the trials and disasters the future would inevitably bring?

I'm growing old, she told herself. She smiled at Lorraine.

'Have you bathed him yet?'

'Yes, the midwives showed me. He's a bit slippery, though, like a fish. I enjoyed it, though, it was nice.'

'I could come and help too, some days – if you'll have me,' Sarah said, impulsively. 'On days when I'm not busy in court.'

She suddenly realized that she longed to do exactly that. Hold this little boy, Daniel Craig, care for him, help with bath-time and feeding; things that had always been a chore before, something to get through and get out of the way so that she could get on with her studies, but now ... *this is my first grandchild.*

'Of course,' Lorraine said. 'Sometimes. If you're not busy. But I'll manage.' She smiled at Simon. 'We'll have to, won't we?'

Outside the ward, as she was leaving, Sarah said to Simon: 'I'll tell Bob, shall I? He'll be delighted, I'm sure. After all, whatever else he is, he's a grandfather now. Step-grandfather, anyway.'

'Yeah.' Simon hugged his mother, thinking about it. 'Well, I hope he's delighted, he should be. Bring Emily, by all means, and tell Bob ...'

'Yes?'

'Tell him ... it's okay to get in touch, if he wants to. I won't chase him away.'

26. Gooseberry

'Yes, why not? Bring her along.'

'You're sure? It does mean that ... well, you know.'

'I can't make mad passionate love to you on the table? Yes, I was aware of that.'

'Or afterwards, Terry. She's staying in my spare room. I'm sorry but ...'

'Sarah, it's fine, okay? I'd love to meet your daughter again. Wait till I tell my girls. They'll be quizzing me for hours afterwards.'

'You could always bring them along too.'

Terry considered the idea briefly before rejecting it. 'No. They've got school tomorrow, eight o'clock's too late. Besides, if they come it'll be all about them, and if Emily wants to talk about anything serious ...'

'Well, she might, I suppose. But she'll probably want to talk about her little nephew. I'm a grandmother now, Terry, it's official – and she's an aunt! We've just visited the baby together!'

'Congratulations. All well?'

'Yes, mother and baby are fine. Both home now. I'll bring a photo – you can show your girls.'

'Great. See you this evening, then. With Emily.'

As he put the phone down Terry wondered at the excitement in Sarah's voice. He'd known vaguely that her son's girlfriend was pregnant, but hadn't given it much thought. Now it sounded as though it was the highlight of Sarah's life. He felt uncomfortable twinges of jealousy. He had no connection to this mystery child, it was no part of his family.

He had clearer memories of Sarah's daughter Emily. She was a bright, attractive young woman whom his own daughters adored. Once, as a teenager, she had caused her parents great anguish by running away with her boyfriend – an earnest youth with long hair, Terry recalled, an environmental protester – but now she was a student at Cambridge. A role model for Jessica and Esther, he thought, if our two families come closer together.

And that's what I want, isn't it?

Terry sighed. Yes, probably. Though the presence of Emily, to say nothing of this new baby, made things complicated. He'd originally imagined this evening as a romantic, intimate occasion in an expensive restaurant where he'd gaze across the candle lit table into the sparkling eyes of his new ... what should he call her? Mistress? Lover? Sexual partner? And then afterwards they would stroll hand in hand back to her flat where crisp fresh sheets would be turned down on her queen-sized bed and ...

Trude would take care of the girls. He'd told her not to expect him back until the early hours of the morning. Now? Well, it would all be different.

Sarah arrived looking smart but not, perhaps, as ravishing as she might had she come alone. She wore a simple sleeveless black sheath dress which clung to her figure elegantly, but the high neck was respectable rather than raunchy. Emily looked slightly self-conscious in a figure-hugging black mini-dress with three-quarter length filigree sleeves which her mother had bought her on a shopping expedition that afternoon, to celebrate the new baby's arrival. Terry greeted the girl with a formal handshake and her mother with a kiss.

'So how long are you in York this time?' he asked when they had ordered. Emily looked more boyish than her mother, he thought, skinny, athletic and an inch or two taller. Her frizzy hair hung loosely around her face; Terry was not sure if this was a deliberate style, or an accident. Sarah, by contrast, looked trim, neatly groomed, professional – and oddly maternal.

'Just a couple of days. I've got a tutorial on Friday but then I'll be back.' Emily faced him with wide blue eyes. 'I'm here to help Dad, really. I came before.'

'Yes, your father. I've heard a little about his trouble ...'

'It's all rubbish! He's been framed. The police are idiots!'

'Emily!' Sarah touched her daughter's arm. 'Remember what I told you. You can't blame Terry; this has nothing to do with him.'

'Yes, yes. I'm sorry, Mr Bateson, I'm not blaming you. It's some crazy unit in Harrogate – *Operation Hazel*, they call themselves, stupid name. But it's so unfair! They're just keeping Dad on bail, they don't even have the guts to charge him so he can defend himself properly. He can't teach, thinks he'll never work again ...'

'So how are you planning to help?' Terry asked, interrupting the flow. 'He's got a lawyer, hasn't he?'

'Lucy Parsons,' Sarah said, giving Terry an apologetic look. 'She knows what she's doing.'

'Yes, Mum, I'm sure she's ok, but she hasn't got time like I have. I mean how many cases has she got on her books – ten, twenty, a hundred? And every time she sees him it costs two hundred pounds, minimum, even for a phone call ...'

'That's not expensive, darling, honestly. Solicitors have to make a living. What do you think I charge?'

'Yes, Mum, I know, but ... my point is that I don't cost anything, I've got bags of time and I care! And the woman accusing him is a criminal! So anything I can do I will. Look, I'm sorry, Mr Bateson, I shouldn't bore you with this, but you did ask.'

'That's all right,' Terry said. 'You can tell me if you like, I'm not involved. After all your dad did a lot for you, I suppose, as well as your mum. So it's only natural – admirable in fact – that you should try to help him when he's in trouble. I hope my daughters would do the same for me.'

'I'm sure they would.' Emily relaxed, a brilliant smile lighting up her face. 'How are they anyway? Jessica and Esther. I'd love to see them.'

For the next quarter of an hour the conversation shifted to the safer ground of Terry's daughters, their exploits at school, their friends and parties and the recent acquisition of a giant cage for their pet hamster. And that subject, naturally, led on to talk of her brother Simon's baby. They both showed him photos which Terry dutifully admired, and promised to show his daughters if Emily sent them on to his phone.

'Good news at last,' he said smiling. 'They'll appreciate that, after last time.'

'What? Sorry – last time? What do you mean?' Emily asked, confused.

'Last time they met your mother, I mean.' And so, as the food arrived, Terry found himself telling a sanitized version of his discovery of a body in the river, and the nightmares it had given his girls for a week afterwards. Emily, to his surprise, had heard nothing of this. She looked at her mother curiously.

'You were actually on the boat with him, Mum? Why haven't you told me?'

Sarah flushed, embarrassed. 'It just never came up. And I wasn't involved with the body, after all. I was in hospital helping to deliver a baby. Not little Daniel. Another one.'

'What?' Emily spluttered into her wine, amazed. 'What are you talking about now? For heaven's sake – Mum?'

And so Sarah told the tale of how Savendra's wife, Belinda, almost gave birth on the boat, which was the reason Terry and his daughters had been left to steer it downstream in the first place.

Flushed with the wine, Emily giggled. 'So much going on in York, which I knew nothing about! And now you two, as well ...'

A small silence. Emily glanced from her mother to Terry and back again, amused. 'Oh come on! You think I don't know?'

'Know what?' Terry asked, gently. How much has this girl had to drink, he wondered.

'That you and Mum are, you know ... having sex!'

It was unfortunate that the background music in the restaurant was being changed at that moment, so the words dropped into a lull in the surrounding conversation. Several heads turned to stare before the music resumed.

Terry met Sarah's eyes, wondering how to respond. This is a test, he realised suddenly. My answer matters now.

'I'm very fond of your mother,' he said carefully. 'I think – I hope – she's fond of me too. And so naturally ...'

'It's true. Isn't it? You are!'

'Yes, we are.' Terry suddenly felt absurdly happy and pleased that it was out in the open. Maybe it had been a good idea to invite this girl after all. 'Is that all right with you?'

'With me?' A surprised, thoughtful look crossed Emily's face. 'If it makes my Mum happy, then yes, of course, it makes me happy too.' She glanced at Sarah. 'You are happy, aren't you, Mum?'

Sarah, too, realised this was an unexpected test. I didn't come here to make a commitment, she thought. It's just meant to be a pleasant evening out. But Terry had risen to the challenge, so ...

'If I was unhappy about it I wouldn't do it.' She reached across the table for Terry's hand, grasped his fingers. 'Terry and I are ... good friends. So I hope you like him too.'

'Of course.' The solemnity of the moment had taken Emily by surprise, even though she had precipitated it herself. Watching her mother and this man gaze into each other's eyes she suddenly felt awkward, a gooseberry. She raised her wineglass. 'Then I propose a toast. To you both!'

'To us both.' Sarah and Terry clinked their glasses with Emily's and drank. Then they all looked at each other and burst out laughing.

'Well, that was a surprise,' Sarah said. 'Whatever next? Does that mean we have your blessing?'

'Absolutely!' Emily raised her hands like a priest. 'Go forth, my children, and multiply.'

'Oh no.' Sarah shook her head firmly. 'I'm much too old for that. I'm a grandmother, remember? And you're an aunt.'

Which led them back to the safer subject of whether Emily's brother would be any good at changing nappies, and how often Sarah would visit mother and baby. Terry smiled politely, thinking so far the evening had turned out a surprising success. But when Emily left them for a moment to visit the ladies' room, Sarah returned to the subject that interested him more. She didn't look entirely happy with it.

'So, we're officially a couple,' she murmured. 'In Emily's eyes anyway.'

'If you want us to be. I'd like that.'

Sarah raised an eyebrow, a wary smile crossing her face. 'If only it were so easy. There could be complications, you know.'

'Such as what?'

'Well, Bob, for one thing. Emily's dead set on saving him, as you see. He's her father, she's sure he's innocent.'

'Do you believe that?'

'I want to believe it, Terry. I'm almost sure, 98%, but ...'

'There's a tiny doubt?'

'Only the smallest. I despise myself for it, too. After all with Simon ...'

'You believed in Simon's innocence, didn't you, when no one else did? And you were right. You defended him in court; you were magnificent.'

'Was I? Well, thanks. But even so I had my doubts, at times. The difference was, I loved him.'

'And you don't love his father?'

'Not any more, no. Not since Simon's trial, in fact.' She smiled ruefully, meeting Terry's eyes. 'It's hard to talk of love, at our age.'

'Is it? I'm not so sure. Sarah ...' He felt the need to say something, but she raised a hand to stop him.

'Terry, wait.'

'What is it? Don't you want ...?'

'There's another problem we should talk about. A bigger complication, potentially.'

'Which is?'

'That body you pulled out of the river, Victoria Weston. A young man called Adrian Norton has been charged with her murder. His trial starts in January.'

'Yes. So?'

'I'm his brief.'

'Ah.' A sinking feeling in Terry's stomach. 'And you think ...?'

'There could be a conflict of interest. Terry, how closely are you involved?'

'I'm not the officer in the case. Jane Carter is.'

'I know, I saw that in the proof of evidence. But you did find the body, and do some of the preliminary work. If you're called as a witness ...' She bit her lip, pulled an agonised face. '... I might have to withdraw. And I need this case, Terry, there's not so much legal aid work around these days.'

'Well, will I be called as a witness? There's just my statement about finding the body, that's not controversial. And a couple of early interviews, but Jane was present too, at most of them.'

'Not all. My client says you interviewed him twice on your own. And he got the impression you believed him. Did you?'

'I may have done, at first. But he lied, didn't he? Got his girlfriend to give him a false alibi.'

'Yes, I know, silly bugger. That's a massive hole in his case. But he's adamant that he didn't do it, so it's my job – my duty – to explore every avenue to get him off. And that could involve calling you. See the problem?'

'Yes, but ... all I can say is what he told me. It's in the statements – you've read them.'

'No, Terry, it's not all. If I follow his instructions I may have to ask what you think. You're not the officer in the case anymore – why is that? Did you disagree with the decision to charge him?'

'He lied to me, Sarah. He has a broken alibi. But ...'

'But what, Terry?'

'Look, all the evidence points to him. If it had been left to me I might have waited a little longer, but ...'

'So it wasn't your decision? It was your boss Will Churchill, he took you off the case, is that what you're saying? Terry?'

'I ... you can't ask me that, Sarah. We shouldn't even be discussing this.'

'I know. But in court I may have to – if there's the slightest suspicion you think he's innocent. Do you?'

'Look, it's not my case anymore, Sarah. I don't know. All I can tell you is what's in my notes. You've got the second interview on tape, for heaven's sake.'

'Yes. I listened to that this afternoon. I wish I hadn't, really.'

'Why?'

'Because it's ruining our evening. I'm sorry, Terry, I didn't ask for this. But when I listened to that tape I got the impression first, that you're a kind, generous man – which I knew already, of course – and secondly that you liked my wretched client and wanted to believe him. Did appear to believe him.'

'Up until the moment when his lies were exposed, yes. And his alibi broke down.'

'Exactly. That tape's probably going to be played in court; the prosecution will insist on it – I would. And if so it'll be my job to make it look less bad. In which case I might need to call you as a witness. That's the problem ...'

'Sarah, stop. Why bring this up now?'

'Why do you think? Forewarned is forearmed.' Sarah ploughed on, concerned but determined. 'Look, Terry, this is awkward. I'm sorry, I hate it. But I need this case – my career's in a rut, I'm nearly bankrupt. And so far as anyone else knows, we're just friends – except Emily, of course, bless her. There's no problem if we just meet socially; that's understandable; detectives and barristers are bound to meet from time to time. A conflict of interest only arises when there's something more than a casual involvement – either financial or sexual, usually. See what I mean?'

'A casual involvement. Is that how you see me?' Terry was becoming more and more irritated. This was a side of Sarah's character which he remembered from old. Not the most pleasant one. And certainly not romantic.

'Terry!' She reached out, took his hands in hers, looking earnestly into his eyes. 'Of course not, no! This hurts me too, but don't you see? Just until this trial is over, it would be wise to be careful, make sure that's all it looks like. After all, no one knows we're anything but friends. Do they?'

'I haven't told anyone, no.'

'Well, then. It's our secret. But ...'

A camera flashed, lighting up the room. Emily laughed, sitting down between them. 'Don't jump, you two! No need to look so guilty! Look, here you are!' She held out her phone.

'Isn't that sweet! Two lovers holding hands across the table, gazing into each other's eyes. I've sent it to Larry on Snapchat.'

27. Heartache

FOR TERRY, the evening had been a disaster. He felt both hurt and furiously angry. Part of it – the most immediate part, perhaps – was sexual frustration. His original idea had been that he and Sarah would share a romantic, seductive evening over good food and wine in an expensive restaurant – chosen and paid for by him – followed by a pleasant stroll arm-in-arm back across the river to her apartment building where they would mount the stairs to her flat and tumble, laughing and kissing, through the door to her bedroom, strip off their clothes and ....

Well, not any more.

The inclusion of her daughter Emily had burst the bubble of that delicious fantasy, but he'd accepted that with the best grace he could muster: he liked the girl and she was part of Sarah's life; he could hardly refuse. But then there'd been all that talk about the baby which delighted both women and made him feel obscurely excluded. He'd never liked babies; to him they were just human caterpillars, yet to spread their wings. Even his own daughters had bored him until they could walk and talk.

But what had really upset him was not the talk of babies but Sarah's idea of postponing their sexual relationship until after Adrian Norton's trial in January, three months away. Did she really mean to suggest that they should stay apart, keep chaste, all that time? With Emily there it had been impossible to discuss that, of course. They had talked politely for a while longer, about a university drama production Emily was in, and the judo classes she had been attending; then he'd paid for the meal, escorted them home, kissed Sarah chastely on the doorstep, smiled politely, and left.

But as he recrossed the bridge his anger and disappointment surged within him, as strongly as the river below his feet. It was typical of Sarah, he thought – the flaw in her character that was also her greatest strength. There were two things that mattered to her more than anything else – her work, and her family. And very often it was in that order.

Her family, he'd thought, was broken – her husband, at least, had left her, and was now accused of child abuse. But as soon as he, Terry, dreamt of replacing that man – not just as lover but husband – what happened? Her work got in the way. Given a choice between building a relationship with himself and defending Adrian Norton, she had chosen Adrian.

Well, great! He saw a plastic bottle lying in his way and kicked it angrily across the street. He remembered a day, years ago, when he had been called to her house because her daughter – a teenage Emily – had been missing all night, possibly kidnapped or murdered. Her husband Bob had been distraught, white-faced, sleepless, pacing up and down hysterically, shouting at the police to *do something,* anything, just *find her!* What had Sarah done? Got on her motorbike, there in front of them all, and coolly ridden off to court to defend her client, a nasty thug accused of rape. In the middle of a family crisis she'd gone to *work!*

He'd been flabbergasted then and he was furious now. Perhaps that was why her husband Bob had left her. Not because he was a wimp or a child abuser but because he had a wife whose career mattered more than her family. More than her husband's feelings, anyway.

And now he, Terry, was in a similar position.

His chest heaved as he strode faster along Broadway towards the university and his small detached house near the university, on Field Lane. He was being unfair, he knew he was. That same strength, her commitment to work, had saved her son Simon from prison. Back then family and work had combined. She'd been a tiger in court, savaging his boss, Will Churchill, in a way the man had neither forgotten nor forgiven. She'd savaged him, too, Terry recalled with a shudder – she fought like a tiger for all her clients, whether defending or, occasionally, prosecuting on behalf of the CPS. It was an admirable quality, for a barrister.

Only ...

Only she's a very beautiful, sexy woman. And until tonight I thought .... What did I think?

Nearing his home Terry saw the light on downstairs in the living room where his young Norwegian nanny, Trude, was probably watching TV. No light upstairs – his daughters were probably asleep. Trude wouldn't expect him for hours yet – she knew he was out with Sarah. The thought of the surprise and concern on her pretty young face made him curse and stride on past the house, walking faster than before. Perhaps the exercise would calm him. He'd suffered more than his fair share of ribald jokes from colleagues envious of the fact that he shared his home with a nubile young Scandinavian girl. If I go home in this mood, Terry thought, I might just be tempted to try something unforgiveable, career-ending, stupid ...

Is that what I've been doing with Sarah Newby?

No. Surely not. We're adults, mature, unattached. Consenting too, until tonight, when she put me on hold. Just for a few months, so she's free to concentrate on defending a handsome young student who lied to me, cheated his girlfriend and – very probably – murdered his mistress.

Great. Terry strode on, across the Hull Road towards the village of Osbaldwick. Trying to exorcise the vision which rose before him in the darkness, of Sarah lying naked beneath him, breasts rising as she arched her back, dark hair strewn across the pillow, hazel eyes smiling up at him while she gasped his name in what he'd thought, erroneously, might be love.

***

Sarah thought the evening had gone well, on the whole. She had expected Terry to be a little disappointed by the news that they would have to cool their relationship until after the trial, but he had taken it like a gentleman, as she had hoped. After all, they had only slept together twice so far – it was hardly a permanent arrangement. And the reason she had given – the risk of having to withdraw from Adrian's case because of a conflict of interest – was genuinely important to her. Sex with Terry had been fun – exciting, enjoyable, therapeutic – but she could easily live without it. Her career, by contrast, was a fundamental, absolute necessity.

Part of the reason for this – a huge part – was economic. As a self-employed criminal barrister, she was entirely dependent on fees, mostly from the legal aid fund. Out of these fees – constantly cut by the government and often months overdue – she had to pay her share of the clerks' salaries and her chambers rent, as well as the cost of travelling to courts scattered across the north of England. The mortgage repayments on her riverside flat were like an open wound, draining her bank account. The prospect of an extended murder trial was her first chance in months to stem this financial haemorrhage.

But it was more than that for Sarah. Now that she was divorced, she was beginning to enjoy her independence. She wanted to be self-reliant, pay her own way. She liked men, but no longer trusted them. Her teenage husband, Kevin, had beaten and divorced her. After twenty years of marriage, her second husband, Bob, had left her for another woman and been arrested for child abuse. Her most recent lover, Michael, a criminal himself, had been murdered in front of her. So now, how far could she trust – or rely on – Terry Bateson?

He was a decent man, she knew that, a kind father, good in bed, but – this was the scary bit – she had begun to suspect he was in love with her. Earlier this evening he had been hinting at a declaration. And something in Sarah had shrunk away. She was a grandmother now, not a sex kitten. She thought fondly of the moment she had held baby Daniel in her arms. That had given her as much pleasure, she thought, as her moments with Terry.

Was it wrong to think like that? Were the two things comparable, or mutually exclusive? She wasn't sure. But Terry's polite boredom when they'd talked of the baby had diminished him a little in her eyes. Is that all men think of, sex?

'He's a nice man,' Emily said, brushing her teeth before bed. 'Why didn't you invite him in, Mum? I wouldn't mind.'

'What, with you here?' Sarah smiled. 'Don't be silly. I'd have been embarrassed.'

'No need.' Emily smiled. 'I could shut my door. Put my earplugs in.'

'Very thoughtful,' Sarah said. 'But I don't think so, somehow. Anyway, we're not quite as – involved – as you seem to think. Even if he has, as you say, slept here once or twice. That doesn't mean ...'

'Aren't you going to marry him, Mum?' Emily came out of the bathroom and sat on her mother's bed. 'You could do worse, you know.'

'Thank you, but no.' Emily's question was casual but Sarah's answer, she realised as she made it, was not. It brought into the open the thing she had been resolving in her mind. *I wanted him – needed him – before, when I was still recovering from the trauma of Michael's death. But now ... maybe he's healed me. Perhaps the sex was therapy; I don't need it any more. Or not so often, anyhow. Not now there's little Daniel to think about.*

'I don't think I want a husband, not just now.'

'What? Really? But Mum, you're still young.'

'Well, thank you for those kind words, young lady.' Sarah came and sat beside her daughter, realising as she did so that this tousle-haired, vibrant young woman was slightly taller than her and probably a lot stronger and fitter.

'But that doesn't mean I need a husband, does it? If I'm so young, there's still time to play the field.'

'Mother!' Emily looked shocked. 'That poor man's in love with you, can't you tell?'

'Well, maybe he thinks he is, but life's not always that simple, for us old folk. When you were out, I was explaining a problem to him ...' She described the difficulty she foresaw in maintaining a relationship with Terry while defending Adrian Norton. 'We'll be on opposite sides, you see, and that's not very ethical. So I hope that photo you took doesn't find its way onto the internet.'

'Oh. No, don't worry Mum, I only sent it to Larry on *Snapchat*. It will disappear in thirty seconds anyway unless he takes a screenshot, and ... why would he? Anyway, who'd be interested? It's just a romantic picture.'

'All the same, ask him to be careful, would you? As I said I'm fond of Terry but I'm not sure I want to take it any further and become a stepmother to his daughters, for example, nice though they are. I'd be rubbish at that.'

'Mum, you'd be fine! You're a good enough mother to me, aren't you?'

'I hope so. You haven't always said that.'

'You've got your career, Mum, I've always known that. But you're the only mother I've got, so I'll have to put up with it.' She smiled, and gave Sarah a hug. 'And now you're a granny too. Old lady.'

'Yes. Second chance.' Sarah smiled. 'I mean to make the best of that, at least. After work.'

* * *

Striding on into the night, Terry crossed the Hull Road and continued down a street of semi-detached houses on the edge of Osbaldwick. He wasn't thinking where he was going; it was just the speed, the movement which was calming him. He would have got more exercise from running; but in a suit and leather shoes it was inappropriate. Instead he stretched his long legs, swung his arms loosely, and breathed the cold night air.

You're a fool, he told himself. The trouble is, the bloody woman's right, as usual. If it became public knowledge that we were having an affair while on opposite sides in a trial, it wouldn't just be a problem for her; I'd be in the shit as well. He could imagine how Will Churchill would relish the opportunity for revenge. Terry was a little uncertain exactly what regulation he would be breaking, but he was sure Churchill would dig one up. And if he could ruin both their careers in one go, so much the better.

Well, there's no chance of that now. All I have to do is lie in my chaste bed for the next three months, caring for Jessica and Esther like a good father and never laying a hand on the nubile nanny in the spare room, and everything will be fine.

Christ, Terry, get a grip! Why are you thinking like this, all of a sudden? For years, since Mary's death, thoughts of sex had scarcely troubled him. That part of his emotional life had been frozen, loyal to his wife's memory and traumatized by her death. Now these two sexual encounters with Sarah had opened the floodgates, filling his mind with images and memories of what he had been missing.

And she called it a *casual involvement*. Two brief hours in bed which could be enjoyed and then forgotten, switched off like a tap. That's Sarah Newby for you. Shit!

At the end of the road he turned left into the village of Osbaldwick proper. A few scattered streetlights lit the scene. A little stream ran along beside the road, crossed here and there by small bridges giving access to gardens. The houses were varied and pretty, set back from the road with lawns and flowerbeds of individual shapes and sizes. He strode on, breathing deeply, past a village hall, closed now, which housed a children's playgroup in the daytime. As he rounded a corner he saw the pub, *The Derwent Arms,* on the right. On impulse Terry turned to go inside. He ordered a pint of John Smith's and took it outside. A group of men and women were talking noisily at one picnic table but another was empty. As he sat down another man, who was strolling up and down talking on his phone, suddenly took the phone away from his ear, tapped the screen, and said: 'Hold on, I'll ring you back in a few minutes.' Then he tapped the screen again and resumed talking, apparently to someone else.

Terry took a long draught of his pint, and stared moodily at nothing in particular. This was the pub outside which Adrian Norton was caught on CCTV, proving he'd lied. Silly young fool. He'd continued lying right up until the moment we showed him the video. Would he have got away with it without that?

Maybe. But then his girlfriend, Michaela, changed her story, breaking his alibi. That made me look a fool, Terry thought, for not challenging the girl in the first place, breaking her heart by telling her what really happened in her fiancé's literature tutorials. I'm getting soft, he told himself angrily, remembering the smirk on Will Churchill's face as he handed control of the case to Jane Carter. He's got her eating out of his hand now, another follower onside, hoping for promotion. All my own fault.

He finished his pint and walked on. Round the bend was the farm track leading down to Straw House Barn, where Victoria Weston had lived and died. He hesitated; the track was lit for a few yards by light from a window in the house of Mrs Bishop, the witness who lived on the corner; after that it was a tunnel of darkness, high hedges on either side blocking out the streetlights. Should he go down? Terry had no torch and no business here. Just the light in his mobile phone in his pocket if needed. But he knew where it led; he'd driven down here before. And there was still something in his mind about this case that was unsatisfactory, just as Sarah had hinted in the restaurant. The case against Adrian was strong; he'd recognized that and tried to put it behind him after Churchill had passed it to Jane. But he'd never liked or trusted Vicky Weston's husband; if her death had been suicide as it first appeared, he'd have been sure Tom had driven her to it. So what about now, when it was murder? Well, the man's first wife had died too, in mysterious circumstances. This time he had an alibi, but all the same ...

He took his first step into the dark lane, thinking: this is the way Adrian must have come that night, if he killed her, as all the evidence suggests he did. And if not? Well ... Terry smiled to himself grimly. If I could stop this trial by proving young Adrian wasn't the killer after all, what would that do?

Jane Carter would be devastated, Will Churchill apoplectic, and as for Sarah Newby ... there might not be a conflict of interest after all.

Stepping carefully to avoid the potholes, Terry walked down the lane. For about twenty yards he was in darkness, but there was a light at the end of the tunnel, probably from a window in Straw House Barn. Reaching the gate he stood beside one of the pillars, staring in at the statue of the mermaid in the fishpond. Water from the fountain trickled down her thighs, which were covered in green algae. Light came from within the glass doors behind her, where the chandelier in the shape of a wagon wheel hung in the stone-flagged hall. A dark green Range Rover was parked on the gravel.

Terry wondered bitterly how an editor in a small educational publishing house could afford such a place. But then the man's first wife, Christine, had been wealthy, Terry had established that much, and perhaps Victoria had brought money too. Two dead wives; it seemed careless; yet the first death had been ruled accidental and the second – well, it had looked like suicide at first, hadn't it?

Yet young Adrian's alibi had been broken while Tom Weston's remained strong.

Terry walked a little further down the track, to where a small wooden gate gave access to an extensive back garden. There was a large lawn, scattered with a number of small trees and shrubs, half-hidden in the darkness. Nearer the house was a patio with a gazebo, its roof covering the hot tub where poor Vicky had been drowned. He saw the cover on the tub and a light on the wall of the small garden room behind. It was here the SOCO team had found the bags of Dead Sea Salt used to salinate the hot tub. It had contained nothing else of value or interest – just an old sofa, a few wilting plants and garden chairs in a room which still had the key in the door. A few yards beyond it was the garage where, presumably, Vicky's car had been parked.

On impulse he stepped quietly through the gate into the garden. He had no plan in mind, just a sudden surge of curiosity. There's something we missed, a little imp in his mind insisted. Just find that, and everything here will change. He walked cautiously across the lawn, his feet in the soft grass. He was five or six yards from the house, moving towards the gazebo, when a light went on in one of the bedrooms to his right. For a second he thought he saw the pale outline of a face in the window; then it was gone. Terry stepped back further into the darkness and tripped, his ankle snagged in a rose bush. Cursing under his breath, he got to his feet, his hands covered in soft soil, and then ...

... a security light snapped on, flooding the lawn with light. Appalled, Terry froze, then ducked out of sight, seeking the only cover he could find, the dark shadow behind the gazebo, where the light didn't reach. But what now? He couldn't stay here, and his route back across the lawn was cut off by the glare of a thousand watts. He heard a window open and a male voice call out: 'Hey? Who's there?' and then a woman's voice asked: 'Did you see anyone?'

'Not sure,' the man's voice answered. 'Could be a fox. You stay there.'

This is absurd, Terry thought. I should come out and explain but that'll be awkward. I'm off this case; I have no right to be here. And that sod Tom Weston will make all the trouble he can. He glanced to his left and saw a small gate in the hedge. It was on the far side of the house from the lane, hidden from the glare of the security light by the garage. He ran towards it, opened it, and found himself in what seemed to be a grassy field, with the faint trace of a footpath leading diagonally across it. Quickly, he ran along the path, the field getting darker around him as he got further from the house. Twice he stumbled and fell, but the light and voices behind him grew fainter and soon he was through into a second field. At the far side he saw buildings in front of him, a fence, and the lights from the pub. Coming closer, he crossed the fence by a stile and found himself back in the pub car park, where the last drinkers were beginning to leave. He brushed the mud from the knees of his trousers and strode out into the village street.

Well, what did that achieve, he asked himself grimly. Nothing at all. No new evidence, just an embarrassment avoided. At least I hope it's avoided; I'm on a public road now. He turned left, picking up speed, resuming that long rangy stride which he hoped would calm his mind. After a few minutes he turned right, heading back down the road of semi-detached houses towards the Hull Road and home.

That was the moment when the thought came to him, quite suddenly, crystal clear. An epiphany in the darkness. Of course, he thought – that's what happened, that's what we missed! I'll check it when I get to work tomorrow and then, if I'm right, the whole case will change! It was there all along but I just didn't see!

The excitement put a spring in his step. He strode briskly on through the housing estate and then, when he reached the Hull Road, a second idea came to him. He fished in his pocket, glanced at his mobile, and grinned. He could test this out now, if the shop was still open. Instead of crossing the dual carriageway, he turned left, towards the *Inner Space Service Station*. Three cars and a van were parked at the pumps on the forecourt, and the neon signs above the brightly lit shop beamed their cheery message to passing drivers: *LAST STOP BEFORE MARS. OPEN 24 HOURS*. Three giant Daleks adorned the roof, and the shop *Entry Zone* was guarded by a twenty foot high humanoid transformer made of assorted car parts.

As Terry loped towards it, he became aware of an argument near a grey Mercedes parked by a pump a few yards to his left. The passenger door was open and a teenage girl was tussling with a man who was holding her arm, apparently trying to drag her back inside. The girl, a child of about twelve or thirteen in fashionably torn jeans and a grubby white teeshirt, was beating at the man with her fists and screaming, trying to pull away. As Terry watched, she aimed a kick at his thigh which caught him in the crotch, doubling him over so that he let go her arm. But as she turned to run he made a wild snatch which caught a strand of her long dark hair, jerking her head back so smartly that her feet ran from under her and she fell flat on her back on the concrete.

'Hey! Stop that!' Amazed, Terry turned towards the struggling pair, but only the man seemed to notice.

'Stay out of this pal, it's none of your business,' he said, trying to drag the girl to her feet by one arm.

'Police! That's an assault! Let the girl go!'

'What?' Stunned by the word *police*, the man hesitated long enough for the girl to whip round and bite the hand that had just held her. 'Ow! Christ, you little bitch. Come here!'

But the girl had gone. Dodging between the pumps, she sprinted towards the road, where cars and lorries whished by on the dual carriageway.

'Now look what you've done! Stupid fucker!' Waving his bloody wrist in Terry's face, the man turned to follow, but Terry grabbed him by the shirt, pushing him back against the side of the van.

'Leave it, all right! You've done enough damage already.'

'What's it to do with you?'

'You can't treat a child like that. Is she your daughter?'

'Yeah, sort of.'

'What's the argument all about, anyway?'

The man scowled, shaking his head as if searching for an answer. 'She wants an ice cream. I said no.'

'And for that you assault her?'

'You don't understand. She's a bitch. She bit me; you saw that.'

'Right. Well I'm a police officer. One more move and I'll arrest you for assaulting a child. Now get back in the car, stay there and try to calm down, okay? I'll find your daughter, bring her back and see if we can sort this out. What's her name, anyway?'

'Mary.'

Mary. Great, it would have to be. Gritting his teeth, Terry strode away across the forecourt. Glancing back, he saw the man had sullenly seated himself in the driver's seat. This is just what I need, he thought; a domestic when I'm off duty. Now what? If I really have to arrest the bastard I'll be up all night.

The girl, he saw with relief, was still in sight on the pavement just outside the service station, hovering up and down as though uncertain where to go. A skinny girl about the age of his own daughter, Jessica, with waist length long dark hair which her father had grabbed to yank her to the floor. She was shivering, just a thin grubby teeshirt in the cold night air, her arms folded across her chest to keep herself warm. Just the faintest hint of breasts; still a child.

'Mary,' he called out in the most reassuring voice he could manage. 'It's all right, I'm a policeman.'

There was no sign that she heard him. A bus and two cars swished past behind her, the sound of their engines masking his voice. Coming closer, Terry tried again.

'Mary, love. I want to talk to you. Is that okay? You're not in any trouble. I can help.'

It shouldn't have mattered that she had the same name as his wife but it did. His wife Mary had been killed in a car crash and this kid looked so vulnerable with these vehicles thundering past. A huge truck rumbled by and when the sound had faded Terry was only a few feet away from the girl. He smiled and held out his hand.

'Mary? I'm a friend. I want to help you, love.'

She noticed him for the first time. Up until then he'd been no one, just a random figure in a world full of strangers, vehicles, a garage with Daleks on the roof. She'd been searching the darkness for which way to go. Now suddenly a man, holding out his hand, smiling, coming closer ...

She panicked, turned to run, sprint away across the road. Looking *left*, Terry saw in despair, the way the traffic had gone, not where it was coming from. Like a child, a toddler with no sense. As she ran, hair flying, he ran too, grabbed her arm, pulled her back ...

'No! Look out!'

But he was too late. The driver of the forty ton wagon, hitting the air horn and brakes both at once, never felt the impact at all. He just saw the two soft bodies tossed up into the air, to land on the grass beside the road like crumpled broken rag dolls.

28. Headmaster

'So HOW did you find the address, Dad?' Emily asked, pulling a sheet of blue headed notepaper out of the envelope.

A faint flicker of triumph lit up Bob's strained, anxious face. 'I went to the library, of course. To look at one of the few things that's not available on the internet. But it's there in print for anyone to consult if they want to. The Electoral Register.'

'What's the point of it?'

'So that everyone, including political parties, can know who's registered to vote. You're registered in Cambridge, I guess?'

'Who knows? No idea.'

'Emily! For heaven's sake, this is a democracy! If you're not on the register, you can't vote. *Did* you vote, in the last election?'

'Er, no, actually. I was going to vote for the Greens, but then ... you're right, I wasn't sure how. If it was online ...'

'There'd be masses of fraud. Anyway, look, I found this man's address, and I wrote to him. Here's his reply.'

The handwriting was spidery, a little shaky, but clear.

Dear Mr Newby,

I do remember you, of course, even though you were at the school for a year and a half, a long time ago. Even if I had forgotten, I would have been reminded by the unwelcome visit of two plain clothes policemen a week ago. They had a number of rather surprising and unpleasant questions about you, and asked me to make a formal statement, which I did, rather reluctantly. I must say I found the whole business quite distressing, but they were very insistent.

Since I received your letter I have had several sleepless nights, pondering my course of action. I wish I had never heard of the business, but since I have told the police what I recall, it seems only fair that you should know it too.

If you wish to meet me, please ring to make an appointment.

Yours sincerely,
Nigel Kenning.

'So we're going?'

'Yes, this morning. I rang yesterday and he's happy for you to come too. I told him you were studying natural sciences at Cambridge and he liked that. He was at St John's.'

'Environmental science, Dad. Get it right.'

'It's all the same. Come on. That'll be the taxi now.'

Her father, Emily thought, was looking better than he had for a while. His cheeks freshly shaved, his beard trimmed, his dyed hair neatly cut, his skin smooth, the worry lines less marked. He wore a clean shirt, shiny shoes, and smart suit and tie. If they had met in a large primary school and he'd introduced himself as the head teacher, she would have believed him. This is how my Dad ought to look, she thought.

The taxi pulled up outside a large, detached house in Wheatlands Road, Harrogate. After Bob rang the doorbell there was a pause, so long that they feared no one was at home, but eventually the door opened to reveal a tall, stooped elderly man leaning on a walking stick. Even hunched, he was a foot taller than Bob. He wore baggy shapeless flannel trousers, a checked woollen shirt and grey cardigan. He peered at them over his reading glasses, which were kept safe by a string around his neck.

'Mr Newby, is it?'

'Yes, that's right. I rang to make an appointment. This is my daughter Emily.'

A piercing scrutiny of Emily was followed by a wintry smile. 'Charming. You'd better come in.'

They followed him into a long open-plan living room with a deep blue patterned carpet, a sofa and several reclining armchairs, a coffee table, a huge flat screen television, two wall-to-ceiling bookcases and a writing desk in the corner. Through the far wall, which was entirely made of glass, they could see an elderly woman in anorak and wellingtons pushing a wheelbarrow towards a greenhouse.

'Please sit down,' he said, indicating the sofa. 'I suppose I should offer you tea or coffee, but as you see my wife is otherwise occupied.' He waved towards the window. 'She does love her garden. Oh dear...' He caught Emily's grin and responded with one of his own. 'I see what you're thinking, young woman, that's not quite politically – what d'you call it – politically feminist, is that it?'

'Politically correct, sir,' Emily smiled.

'Quite. Well I could always make the tea myself, but much better to wait for the expert. Now, what can I do for you?'

Bob swallowed nervously. 'You've read my letter, sir, about these allegations made against me by these two women who were pupils back in 1991.'

'Yes indeed, nasty business. The police were here asking about that, as I told you. Made me sign a statement.'

Emily put her phone on the table. 'Would it be okay if we recorded this, Dr Kenning?'

'What? Yes, of course. I've got nothing to hide. Where's your equipment?'

'Just there. It's recording now.'

'What, that little thing? Dear me. What a world you youngsters live in! Magical gismos everywhere. Now when I was young ...'

'Back in 1991, sir,' Bob interrupted smoothly. 'You'd only been headmaster for a year or so, hadn't you?'

'I was appointed in 1989. Head of science before.'

'I joined the school in September 1990, to teach English,' Bob said. 'You appointed me.'

'Yes. Didn't stay long, did you? Ran off to pastures new.'

'I left at Christmas 1991, to teach in primary school. That's what I've been doing ever since, until now.'

'Too bad. Our loss was their gain, I suppose.' He winked at Emily. 'Recording ok, miss?'

'Yes, I think so.'

Bob frowned, annoyed by the flippant exchange. 'Would it be possible for you to tell me, Dr Kenning, what you remember about these two girls, Clare Fanshawe and Eleanor Wisbech? They're the ones who've made the allegations against me.'

He passed across two photographs which DS Starkey had grudgingly forwarded to Lucy Parsons from *Operation Hazel.* The old man picked them up in his long leathery fingers and examined each one carefully.

'Pretty girls, aren't they? Jailbait, I call 'em. You're a fool if you got involved with them, Newby. Should have seen them coming a mile off.'

'What?' A cold, familiar douche of fear flooded through Bob's brain. 'I swear I had nothing to do with them. Not like that. I just taught them English, for heaven's sake. I didn't do anything else.'

'Well, I hope not, young man, because look at all the trouble they've got you in now. You weren't the first, you know.'

'Sorry? *What* did you say?'

'You weren't the first, that's what I said. So whether you touched them or not I can't say, though I doubt it. What I do know is that these two little minxes came to me complaining about someone else, another young man who'd had his finger in their fannies – pardon my French, miss – and I sent them away with a flea in their ears. Would have caned 'em too, if they'd been boys. Things were better back then, more discipline.' He winked again at Emily, whose mouth had dropped open.

Bob looked shocked for a different reason. 'But who? When was this? Did you tell the police?'

'Not back then, no. Perhaps I should have, but I didn't believe them, at first. Then, when I thought there might be some truth in it after all, I called the young man in and gave him the option. Leave now or else. So he did.'

'But ... is there a record of this?'

'Only in here.' The old man tapped his head. 'I didn't write anything down, didn't see the point. For one thing, I couldn't be sure who was telling the truth. As I say, they were jailbait, it was probably six of one and half a dozen of the other. If I had called the police, what would have happened? There'd have been massive publicity, the school's name dragged through the mud, and for what? Young man's career ruined, and two schoolgirls branded as tarts. So I sent him packing, and told the girls not to be so damn stupid ever again.'

Silence fell in the room. They heard a door open, and the sound of someone moving around in the kitchen. Bob's thoughts were whirring, Emily's face flushed with shock. The elderly teacher glanced at them both in turn, an odd smile on his lips.

'Times were different then ...' he began, but before he could continue a woman's face appeared through a serving hatch in the wall.

'Hello! You must be Nigel's guests. I'm sorry I didn't greet you but I had something urgent to do with the azaleas. Tea?'

* * *

There was an awkward pause while Mrs Kenning carried in a tray. A blue and white china teapot with matching milk jug, sugar bowl, cups and saucers, silver teaspoons and a plate of crumbly shortbread biscuits. She beamed at Bob and Emily as she laid it out on the table in front of them.

'So seldom we get visitors these days. I like to do things properly. Were you a pupil at the school, dear?'

'Er, no.' Emily winced, still reeling from the image conjured up by *fingers in their fannies*. Was such behaviour so common in the old man's school that he hadn't even bothered to call the police? She watched, mesmerised, as his long lizard-like fingers selected a shortbread and dunked it in his tea. 'I went to school in York. I'm a student now. In Cambridge.'

'Cambridge? Oh, well done. Which college?'

And so, for a few minutes, they exchanged polite, meaningless conversation over the teacups. Then, when Mrs Kenning had withdrawn, Bob resumed, his voice low, intense, urgent: 'Who was this man, sir? Do you remember?'

'Ah. I thought you'd ask that. The police wanted to know too.'

'And?'

'Well, it seems to have slipped my mind, somehow.' Another wink, this time directed at Bob. 'When you reach my age, you know, names of things and places slide away. It's there on the tip of your tongue, but you can't – what's that ugly word young folk use nowadays? *Access* it, that's the thing. I can't access it. It's in here locked away!' He tapped the side of his head.

'But you *must* know! I need it for my defence, don't you see?'

'*Must* and *need* are strong words, mister. You should be careful.' The old headmaster's voice snapped harshly. 'Before you start to lecture me, young Newby, let me tell you something which will make you grateful. Should do, anyhow. I told those policemen I had nothing against you, nothing at all. Perfectly good teacher, in my opinion. No scandal whatsoever about you leaving early.'

'Well, thank you. I appreciate that.' Bob hesitated. 'What do you mean, no scandal about my leaving early?'

'What? Well, you did, didn't you? Just told me yourself; left at Christmas. But it wasn't the same reason, whatever the silly girls said. Once bitten, twice shy. That's my view, anyway. Hope to God I did right.'

'Sorry, I don't follow. What do you mean, *whatever the silly girls said?*'

'What I say, young man. Keep up.' Dr Kenning scowled, as if reproving an inattentive pupil. 'The girls, they accused you, didn't they? That's what all this is about.'

'Yes, but not back then.' Bob frowned, confused. 'They've only just come up with this now. Twenty-five years later.'

'You don't remember then?'

'Remember what?'

'Didn't I tell you at the time?' The old man looked thoughtful, slightly uncertain. 'Maybe not. Least said, soonest mended. Anyway I put the fear of God into them. That should have been an end of it. Thought it was too, till last week.'

'Let me get this straight.' Bob glanced at Emily's phone, hoping it was still recording. 'Are you saying these two girls made an accusation against *me* back then, as well as against this other chap? The one you dismissed?'

'Exactly, got it in one. Which made me think it was all in their minds, a fantasy. Which is what I told these detective fellows.' He dunked another biscuit in his tea, and munched it carefully.

'But you never told me. This is the first I've heard of it.'

'Well, maybe. If you say so.'

'I *do* say so!' Bob flushed indignantly. '*Why* didn't you tell me? I had a right to know, damn it! They were accusing me of a crime!'

'Which I didn't believe, not for a minute. Especially not the second time, with a different man.' Dr Kenning sipped his tea, frowning. 'Don't lecture me on rights, young Newby. There you were, a young teacher, accused of a nasty crime by a pair of young girls who, well ...' he glanced cautiously at Emily, '... were no better than they should be, let's say. Jailbait, miss; know what that means? Not nicely brought up like you. Now then, Newby, think for a moment, put yourself in my position. There you are, a good teacher so far as I know. Leaving school for another job. About to get married too, I seem to recall. Did you really want to hear some nasty lies spread about you? Best let sleeping dogs lie. That's what I thought, anyway.'

For a moment no one said anything. A radio chattered quietly to Mrs Kenning in the kitchen.

'But ...' Emily's voice intruded hesitantly into the silence. ' ... what about this other man? You believed the girls' story about him. Enough to dismiss him, you said.'

'Yes, well ...' The old man gazed at her thoughtfully. 'He was a different character. Looked a bit like your father but ... something about him not quite right, I thought. It was only a hunch, but it made their tale more believable.

Until they made this second accusation, that is. Then I began to wonder. Maybe I'd done him an injustice, been a bit hasty.'

Or maybe you did the girls an injustice, you old chauvinist, Emily thought, hating the idea as soon as it entered her mind.

But what would that say about Dad?

'What was his name?' Bob asked.

'I told you, I can't remember.'

'Really? Did you tell the police?'

'No, not then.' A stubborn look settled on the old man's features. 'I told you, Newby, I tried to help you.'

'What about this new lot of police? The ones who came to visit you recently?'

'I told them I thought you were innocent, too.'

'But you told them of the accusations. Against me?'

'Yes. Had to say that.'

'And against the other fellow? Whose name you can't remember?'

'Yes.'

'Were they interested? In him, I mean?'

'Hard to say. It was you they were asking about mostly.'

'Jesus.' Bob shook his head slowly. 'This gets worse, not better.'

'This other man,' Emily broke in. 'He looked like my Dad, you say?'

'A little bit, yes. I thought so.'

'Did he have a beard?'

'I think he did, yes.'

The ancient eyes twinkled. *If he winks at me again I'll scream,* Emily thought. *Dirty old man.* She pushed a photo across the table. It was the one of the whole school in 1991. The headmaster, a much younger version of Dr Kenning, sat proudly in the front row.

'Is it him? That man there?' Emily put her finger under a tall, bearded young man in the second row. The old headmaster studied the photo for a while, then looked up, licked his lips, and winked at her.

'It could be him, yes.'

Emily closed her eyes, counting slowly to ten. One hundred, two hundred, three hundred ... *This old lizard is Dad's best witness, don't antagonise him now!*

She opened her eyes and wrenched her face into a beaming smile. 'Thank you, Dr Kenning, that's very helpful. So if we look here ...' She lifted the picture and unfolded the index which had been hidden behind it. ' ... we see the bearded man in the second row is called ... Thomas Weston.'

29. Memory

'JUST A few minutes now. He's very sleepy.'

The nurse showed them into a room where a body lay in a hospital bed. The bed was surrounded by machines which bleeped and racks holding up plastic bottles and tubes, all connected to the body. The body itself had a head swathed in bandages, an arm encased in plaster, and a face which vaguely resembled their father's.

'Dad,' Jessica whispered softly. 'It's us.'

The body's eyes focussed slowly on the three figures hovering anxiously at the end of the bed. Two school age girls and a young woman, none in white coats or uniform, probably not nurses or doctors then, so *who?* ... a frown crossed the man's face followed by a smile, like sunlight emerging from a cloud.

'Jess. Esther. Come here.' Terry raised his left arm, the good one, and winced with the effort of shifting the other. His daughters came round either side of the bed, Trude, their nanny, hovering behind them.

'Daddy, how are you?'

'We brought flowers.' Esther, determined not to be left out, thrust a bouquet towards him.

'That's nice.' Terry tried to take it but his fingers slipped on the cellophane wrapping and the flowers slid towards the floor. Trude retrieved them smoothly and looked round for a vase.

'Daddy, what happened? How are you?'

'I'm ... a bit better. I had an accident, that's all. They say ... traffic accident.' A hint of confusion crossed his face, as though the details of the tale eluded him.

'They say you were run over,' Jessica said.

'By a lorry,' Esther added importantly. 'They had to call an ambulance.'

'Probably, yes,' Terry agreed. 'Blue lights flashing.'

'Daddy, what's wrong with your arm?' Esther asked.

'It's broken.' Terry moved the injured arm cautiously. 'Better soon.' He wiggled the fingers sticking out of the end of the plaster. 'Hand still works, see? Sort of.'

'And your head?'

'I must have banged it when I fell.' He smiled. 'Should have been wearing a helmet, shouldn't I?'

'Dad, don't be silly, you weren't riding a bike.' Jessica, the older girl, frowned. 'The police woman said you were just walking. Across the road.'

'Yes. If she says so that's probably true.'

'Don't you remember?'

'Why didn't you look?'

'What are all these wire and tube thingies?'

'I ... sorry, what?' Terry shook his head, bemused by the quick-fire stereo questions from opposite sides of his bed.

Trude intervened. 'One at a time, please. Remember what the nurse said.'

'Sorry, Trude. Esther, it's *my* turn, just wait.' An expression of immense concern and concentration spread across Jessica's face – a childish reflection of a look that, Terry remembered with a sharp stab of pain, he had once loved on her mother's face, ages long ago. 'Dad, you're not going to die, are you?'

'Die? No, love. Not if I can help it.'

Tears started in his daughter's eyes. 'Only Mum was in a car crash too and she ...'

'No.' Terry reached out with his left arm and drew Jessica to him. Esther clutched his fingers on the other side of the bed. 'Look at all these machines here and the doctors and nurses. They won't let me die, I promise. I'll be coming home soon and then you can look after me too.'

'Now then.' A nurse came in, holding the door open. 'That's enough for today, girls. Your father needs his sleep. You can come back again tomorrow.'

* * *

'You see, I'm not totally helpless,' Bob said, carefully slicing an onion in his small kitchenette.

'I never thought you were, Dad,' Emily said, with a determined, encouraging smile, banishing the gloom which this flat always induced in her.

Her father, scurrying busily round the mini supermarket on the corner, had collected the ingredients for what, he promised, would be a meal to remember. Spaghetti bolognaise, as refined and improved by Jamie Oliver. Now, wearing an apron decorated with exotic herbs, Bob chopped onions, mushrooms and tomatoes, heating olive oil into a pan to fry them when they were ready. Emily had offered to help him but he'd waved her away. There was no room anyway; the kitchen was no bigger than a cupboard, everything within reach without moving.

The food, when it came, was surprisingly good.

'Neither your mother nor I were great cooks,' Bob said, carrying the plates to the rickety scarred pine table crammed against the wall beside the front door. 'But now I'm single, it's time I learned.'

'You won't go back to Sonya then?'

'She doesn't want me,' Bob sighed. 'Maybe she's right. Even if I clear my name, there'll be a stain.'

'Dad?' Emily paused, her fork in the air. 'That old headmaster we saw today. He was gruesome, wasn't he?'

'Gruesome? What do you mean?'

'His attitude to those young girls. *Jailbait*, he called them. That's disgusting. And the way he covered the whole thing up. If he'd called in the police back then, everything would have been different.'

'I'd have been arrested, you mean?'

'Not *you*, Dad. That other man. Thomas Weston.'

'They'd have arrested me too, Emily, if there really was a complaint against me. I'm not sure I believe him even now.'

Emily twirled her fork in the spaghetti thoughtfully, listening to the popping sounds from the gas fire. 'Are you sure, Dad? It seems so strange that he could say something like that, and you know nothing about it.'

Bob lifted his wineglass, sipped, and put it down. After a long silence he said: 'Well, there may have been something.'

Fear froze Emily's stomach. *No,* a voice screamed in her head. *Please don't confess, I can't bear it! My father a paedophile?*

But she had to know.

'What do you mean, Dad, exactly?'

'Well ...' Bob ran a finger slowly round the rim of his wineglass. 'It's all so long ago, it's hard to remember. And I've been so angry, Emily, you've probably noticed that ...'

'Yes. Dad, what is it?'

'Well, talking to that man today ... you're right, Emily, his attitude is wrong, quite unacceptable today, but it was another era ... and he did help me, after all. I mean, I was just about to marry your mother, so if he had called in the police, who knows what would have happened. She might have called it all off; you might never have been born.'

'Dad, what is it? What do you remember?'

'It may be ... thinking about it, I guess he's jogged my memory ...' His finger circled the wineglass, making a resonant hum '... I could just be imagining it, but perhaps ...'

'You can't just *imagine* having sex with a schoolgirl, Dad! Either you did or you didn't!'

'*What?*' Bob took his finger from the wineglass, and stared at his daughter, appalled. 'No, *of course* I don't mean that, Emily! For heaven's sake!'

'But you said you remembered something. Dad? What are you talking about?'

'Not what you think. Not what they say. *God!*' He leaned forward, both elbows on the table, running his hands through his hair. 'But I do have this hazy memory – I was young then, Emily, you saw me in the photo. Not exactly handsome, but ...'

'Dad, you looked fine. A bearded weirdo, but still ... *what do you remember?*'

'A girl ... one of those girls who made the allegations perhaps – who knows? ... meeting me in the street and asking something ... questions about her homework maybe, books I was teaching then. I had a book which I thought might help her, critical stuff probably, she seemed interested ... so I went up to my flat to get it and she followed me ...'

Don't say this, Dad, Emily thought. *Don't let it be true.*

' ... and on my doorstep or in the flat maybe, there was a sort of argument ... I can see her face now, in my mind ...' He closed his eyes, to concentrate. ' ... she is crying, or that's how I remember it. Angry too, flouncing away down the stairs. And after that ...' He shook his head. 'That's all, really.'

'And that's all?' Emily asked. 'What do you think it means?'

Bob shook his head, frowning. He looked flushed, embarrassed.

'Who's to say? But I didn't rape her, Emily, I promise you that. If I had I wouldn't forget it, how could I? I'd have been scared for my job, crippled with guilt for weeks. Anyway, it doesn't feel like that, in this memory. If it is a memory, and not a dream. It's as if she's angry, as if she feels rejected.'

Silence. The gas fire popping. A police siren in the streets outside.

'I'm sorry,' Bob said at last. 'I shouldn't have told you. It doesn't get us anywhere, does it?'

'Dad, your mind's probably just playing tricks on you. It's a whole lifetime away, after all – my life. What we need are facts.'

'What facts?'

'Well, the other thing we found out today was the name of this other teacher. Thomas Weston. Look at him, here.' Emily rummaged for the yellowing school photo in her rucksack, and smoothed it out on the table between their plates. 'What do you remember about him?'

Bob peered at it gloomily. 'Him? Almost nothing.'

'Are you sure? He looks very like you, Dad. Bit taller perhaps, same full beard. Cool tweed jacket.'

'You like it? I've still got that somewhere. In storage.'

'Well, it's okay – a bit retro, but everything was then. What I mean though, with those beards covering your faces, you could be almost twins. You look like a couple of Muslims.'

Bob laughed. 'Spitting image. We didn't have many Muslims back then.'

Emily pulled out her phone. 'I'm going to Google him, Dad. See what I find. He looks a nice guy. You never know, he just might help.'

30. Flood Tide

SARAH DIDN'T learn about the accident until the evening when she bought a local paper. She glanced casually at an article about a dispute between the City Council and local shopkeepers about who would pay for the Christmas lights, and saw it at the foot of the first page.

Police Inspector in Crash with Mystery Girl

A detective inspector and a teenage girl were seriously injured in a road traffic accident last night. Detective Inspector Terry Bateson and the unnamed girl were hit by an articulated lorry outside the Inner Space Service Station on the Hull Road. Both victims are in intensive care at York Hospital. Eye witnesses report that after an altercation on the garage forecourt, the young girl appeared to run out into the road, pursued by the detective inspector, when ...

Sarah stared at the paper in horror. Terry? Serious injuries? Mystery girl? What on earth could have happened? Instinctively she searched for his number on her mobile before realising no, that won't work, not if he's in intensive care. My God - what if he dies? Quickly she scanned the article, trying to see how serious these injuries were, but there was no further information.

What to do? She had just come back from court in Scarborough and had been hoping to prepare a meal for Emily but that could wait. This was urgent. She had to find out.

She took a taxi from the station to the hospital. In the busy, crowded central hall she persuaded a receptionist to find his name on the computer and tell her his ward. The man frowned.

'That's intensive care, love. There may not be visitors.'

'Doesn't matter. I'll go there and ask. Which way?'

She followed his instructions down two long corridors and up a lift to a double door leading to small quiet ward where a nurse and a young male doctor were conferring over some notes in front of a computer. The nurse looked up when she arrived.

'Yes? Can I help you?'

'Terry Bateson. Is he here?'

'Bateson? Oh, yes. That's the policeman.' A frown crossed her face, not an expression that Sarah found encouraging. 'Are you a relative?'

'No, not exactly ... a close friend.'

'Well, I'm not sure.' She glanced doubtfully at the doctor. 'He's very ill. He saw his family this morning and that tired him out. He needs a lot of rest.'

'Please, I have to know. How bad is he?'

The doctor faced her for the first time. A young man, about twenty five – *Christ, how long have you been out of school?* White coat, blue tie, stethoscope round his neck. Practised compassionate frown. *If I'm not family who do they think I am?*

'He has a number of serious injuries, but he's stable now. Out of immediate danger.'

'Thank God for that. What injuries?'

He consulted a clipboard. 'Depressed fracture of skull, concussion, compound fracture of the right forearm, four broken ribs, punctured left lung. There was some internal bleeding but that seems to have stabilised.'

'My God. Is he conscious?'

'Intermittently.'

'Well then. Perhaps I could see him, just for a minute?'

The answer was clear on their faces, even as she asked. 'He is still very weak and under sedation. But if you leave your name we'll tell him you called. And maybe tomorrow, or in a day or two ...'

* * *

After the meal, Emily caught the train back to York. Outside York station, she turned right in Queen Street, walking beside the city walls to Micklegate Bar and then on down Nunnery Lane until the walls curved east towards Skeldergate Bridge. Crossing the road here, she turned down beside the bridge to the riverside path in front of her mother's flats, and stopped dead, surprised at the sight that met her eyes.

In the darkness beyond the path, the ancient Victorian streetlights on the bridge illuminated something strange. Below the bridge, a huge black serpent was twisting, writhing and flexing its muscles. The river had swollen since she left that morning; it seemed almost twice its size. The black shining water rushing downstream had almost reached the top of the arches under the bridge; little wavelets lapped over the edges of the bank along the path where she had to walk. The path wasn't flooded yet, but the grass beside it had vanished, swallowed up by the shiny, dark water which flickered with reflected light from the windows of the flats to her right.

Gingerly, she made her way around the back to the main entrance, and climbed with relief to her mother's front door. Entering, she saw Sarah sitting in a pool of light from a lamp at her kitchen table, a dirty plate, half-empty glass of wine, and a pile of papers in front of her. She looked up as Emily came in.

'Hi! The wanderer returns! Did you get my message?'

'About Terry Bateson? Yes. What happened?'

'Run over by a lorry. Look, read that.' She held out the *Press*, the local paper with the drawing of York Minster in the headline. Emily shrugged off her coat and dropped it carelessly over the back of a sofa, still reading.

'Mum, that's terrible. Is he okay?'

'I don't think he'll die, if that's what you mean. I went to ask in the hospital.'

'How was he?'

'They wouldn't let me see him, but he's stable, whatever that means. In intensive care. He's seen his kids, apparently. Only family allowed.' She grimaced, still bitter about the young doctor's refusal to let her in.

'Well, maybe that means he can talk, do you think? I mean, they wouldn't let his girls in if he was really bad, about to die? Or would they?'

'No. Yes. Maybe, I'm not sure.' Sarah smiled, flustered by her own incoherence. 'You're probably right, Emily, that's a nice thought. But the truth is, I don't know.'

'Anyway, how did it happen?' Emily studied the paper again, a frown creasing her forehead. 'What's all this about a mystery girl? A teenager?'

'Who knows? Perhaps he was trying to help her.'

'Yes, but why? Surely he knows how to cross the road!'

'Obviously.'

They looked at each other. An unwelcome suspicion was trying to burrow into Emily's brain. She shook her head defiantly.

'Mum, not him, too.'

'Of course not. Don't be absurd. The main thing is he's still alive. I'll try to see him tomorrow. Or the next day. Whenever they'll let me. Now, come on in. Tell me what you've been up to. I meant to make a meal but ...' She shrugged.

'It's okay. I'm not hungry.'

'Glass of wine then? I've got that at least.'

'Yes, thanks.' While Sarah was in the kitchen Emily wandered towards the balcony window.

'Mum, what's happened to the river?'

'Oh, that? It's come up a bit, hasn't it?' Sarah returned with two glasses of wine.

'Up? It's climbing the walls. It chased me up the stairs.'

'Really?' Sarah laughed. 'Don't worry, darling, these flats are flood proof, or so the agent assured me when I bought it. But it is a bit dramatic, isn't it? Let's take a look.'

She put down the wine glasses and opened the door to the balcony, letting in a gust of cold night air which fluttered the papers and curtains in the room. Following her mother outside, Emily looked down on the river from this new vantage point. It seemed to have spread into a small lake.

'Look,' Sarah pointed upstream, to their left. Beyond Skeldergate Bridge lights flickered on the water by Ouse Bridge, the one in the city centre. 'The *King's Arms* will be flooded again.'

The *King's Arms*, a popular pub on the quay beside Ouse Bridge, was regularly flooded every year. The floors and walls were all stone, long ago stripped of carpets or electric sockets, and a marker on the wall lovingly recorded the height of the floods every year.

'But why has it come up so quickly?' Emily asked. 'It wasn't so full this morning. It's not even raining here.'

'Heavy rain in the hills last week, I expect,' Sarah said. 'It happens every winter, you know that.'

'I suppose I did. But we never lived on top of it before.' They watched for a while in silence. A tree branch shot through the arch of the bridge and whirled away downstream, glimpsed and gone in an instant. 'Mum, are you sure we're safe here?'

Sarah laughed. 'What, on the third floor? If the floods rise this high, we'll see Noah's Ark going past the window!' She put an arm round her daughter's waist. 'Let's go in, I'm freezing. Are you sure you're not hungry?'

'Yes, honestly, I'm fine. Dad made spaghetti bolognaise. It was good.'

'Really? That's a first! Come on, sit down and tell me all about it. How is your dad?'

'A bit better in some ways, less good in others.' Emily sat on her mother's sofa, sipped her wine, and began hesitantly to tell the story of her day. 'He's still angry and upset, flaring up for no reason ...'

'Anyone would be, in his situation. It's understandable.'

'... but he's making an effort, trying to be positive. And we made a bit of progress today, in a way. It was a bit weird though.' Emily began to tell the story of the visit to the headmaster, finding the words come easier as the level of wine in her glass fell. She was worried at first – was she betraying a confidence? But her mother knew all about the allegations, after all, she told herself, and said she didn't believe them. But there was one thing that was troubling her. It took a second glass of wine for her to find the courage to mention it.

'Mum, there is one thing Dad said. Later, when we were in his flat. It worried me a bit.'

'Yes? What is it?'

'Well, it was because of this flat he's renting – it's really grotty, you know, it's a dump – and I think that reminded him of the flat he lived in before I was born, you know, when he worked at that school ...'

'Yes? I remember it. So?'

'You went there, didn't you?'

'Yes.'

'Oh. Okay, then ...' Emily chewed her lip, thinking. 'That may make a difference, even help perhaps. What was it like?'

'His flat? Very nice, really. Not luxurious, of course, it was very cheap. But he'd made the best of it, for a man.' A soft, reminiscent smile lit Sarah's face. 'It was up a narrow flight of stairs, I remember, with a landing at the top. Shared bathroom one side of the landing, bedsit and kitchen the other. That made it a bit awkward if you needed the loo in the middle of the night. You never knew who you might meet!'

'What? Mum, you mean you slept there?'

'Once or twice, darling, yes. I did marry your father, you know.'

'Yes, but ... I thought that after you divorced Simon's dad, Kevin, you went back to living with Granny.'

'Yes, I did. That's why I only stayed with your father there once or twice, before we married. Granny – my mum – didn't approve. In fact she was furious.'

'Well, you were only – what? – seventeen.'

'True. And I left baby Simon at home with her on those nights, too. No wonder she was cross.' Sarah smiled ruefully, taking Emily's free hand and patting it gently. 'I'm so glad you were a sensible teenager, not like me.'

'Well, I did run away and live in a treehouse,' Emily said. 'You thought I was dead.'

'Apart from that.' Their eyes met, each remembering, from a different perspective, those terrible days when a teenage girl's body had been found and Sarah had thought it was Emily. 'Well, maybe you weren't perfect either. But about this flat. What is it you want to know?'

'Apart from the bathroom, what was the rest of it like?'

'Very pleasant. A single large bedroom with a sort of dressing room off it, which was made into a small kitchen. Enough for a young man to make beans on toast, that sort of thing – there were no microwaves back in those days. But anyway I didn't go there to cook. It had a gas fire, two comfy armchairs, nice soft carpet – dark blue, I remember – and a very hard narrow single bed.' Sarah smiled. 'That was another reason I only stayed a couple of nights.'

Emily winced. *Too much information*, she thought. But then the question she wanted to ask was much more embarrassing than the knowledge that her parents had shared a single bed together.

'There was also an old glass-fronted book case,' Sarah continued, still reminiscing. 'He'd picked it up in an auction somewhere. Your father had a lot of books in those days. Still does.'

'Yes, well it was that I wanted to ask about,' Emily said. 'You see, when I was talking to him this afternoon, he had a sort of flashback. You know this woman Clare Fanshawe who claims he had sex with her in his flat? Well, he denies that but he did say he sort of remembered that she might have come to the flat all the same ...'

'To borrow a book?' Sarah prompted, when Emily hesitated.

'Yes. But according to Dad, he never let her in. He turned her away, and he remembers her crying. As if he'd rejected her.'

'Mm. He said something like that to me too.' Sarah shook her head sadly. 'God help him if he goes into court with a story like that.'

'Why, Mum? I mean, if it's true?'

'Darling, I do this for a living, remember? If any man stood up in court with a story like that, I'd tear him to shreds.' Sarah smiled cynically. 'I mean, why would any male teacher invite a fifteen year old girl to his flat, alone? To lend her a book? Please. And then, according to his own story, she leaves in floods of tears? What is a jury going to make of that?'

'But ... in Cambridge I have tutorials with a male academic. Usually there's two of us, but if someone's ill, it's just me. And nothing bad has ever happened.'

'That's different. It's a university and you're not fifteen years old.'

'So what do you think of this memory of Dad's,' Emily asked. 'Is it true, or what?'

'That ...' Sarah sighed. 'Is the million dollar question. If we could answer it, we'd be close to understanding the whole thing. But even if we could get inside your father's mind, it might not help.'

'Why not?'

'Well, apart from the fact that he's a man, and they're different ... memory's a funny thing, Emily. Think about it. This happened twenty five years ago, before you were even born. And we're talking about a visit to his flat by a young girl. Your father may genuinely not remember anything about it, if it was just a brief visit and nothing else happened. Even if they had sex he may have blotted it out.'

'Yes, but he didn't, Mum, did he?'

'No ...' Sarah's response was slower, more hesitant than Emily would have liked. But it was clear enough when it came. 'He says he didn't and I believe him, mainly because it's so out of character. Your father may be all kinds of idiot but he's not a rapist, darling, I don't believe that.'

'Well, good. But it might not have been rape, exactly, if she, you know, consented.'

'At fifteen years old it's still statutory rape. Whatever the girl agreed to.'

'But it's so terrible! After all these years – it's ruining his career! She must be lying, this woman, mustn't she? She's got to be stopped!'

The earnestness of Emily's appeal troubled Sarah. She put down her drink, and took her daughter's hand in both of hers. 'Look, darling, I'm proud of you for taking such an interest, but it's not your fight, really. He's got a good solicitor, Lucy Parsons – let her deal with this.'

'But I want to help – he's my dad! Mum, really, I'm not a child. I just wish I knew what really happened, that's all. And when Dad came up with this story, you know, saying she might have visited his flat after all, where does that come from? When before he said it was all lies.'

'Well, memory can play tricks on us, like I said. I've met several witnesses in court who remembered things that didn't actually happen. Think about it. Your father's been interrogated for hours by the police and has spent days worrying about it ever since, so he searches through the cupboards of his memory to see if he can find something – anything – that's vaguely similar to the allegation. Then he puts two and two together and makes five. In the process sounding even more guilty.'

'But what about this woman, Clare Fanshawe, who's accusing him? If his memory's so unreliable, Mum, what about hers?'

'Good point. She may be either telling the truth, imagining it, deceiving herself, or even deliberately lying. Any one of those.'

'So how can we know what's true?'

Sarah sighed. 'After twenty five years, when it's her word against his? Almost impossible, I'd say. What we need is real, objective evidence. And that's exactly what we haven't got.'

31. Hospital Visitors

'So WHAT do we have so far?' Will Churchill asked.

He was sitting in a conference room with a dozen officers, mostly in uniform. It was, on the face of it, a road traffic accident, but any injury to a police officer had to be treated with the utmost seriousness. Even if the victim was Terry Bateson, his least favourite colleague.

'Well, the CCTV first of all.' David Mattesson, a sergeant in the traffic division, pressed a remote control to activate the ceiling projector. A video came up on the wide screen at the end of the room. 'You can see it quite clearly here. Two cars and a van parked at the pumps in the service station. If you watch this one, the grey Merc, you can see the driver gets out, fills the tank, and goes in to the shop to pay. While he's away the girl gets out – watch.'

He used a pointer to highlight the figure of a skinny long-haired girl in jeans and white teeshirt. She got out of the back seat of the car and glanced nervously towards the shop before leaning back into the car again.

'What's she doing there?' Will Churchill asked.

'She seems to be arguing with someone else inside the car. It's hard to see clearly but we catch a few glimpses now and again. We've had the images blown up and we think it's another girl, about the same age. But she never gets out.'

'Is she trying to persuade her, perhaps?' Mike Candor asked. 'Asking her friend to run off with her?'

'Could be, who knows? Anyway, if we let this run on, here, we see the driver coming out of the shop after paying. When he's halfway to the car she sees him and starts to sneak away but he's too quick. He sprints over, grabs the girl by the arm and it all kicks off. Not a happy family.'

The room watched entranced as the driver – a burly six footer in his mid thirties, with tattooed arms and neck, remonstrated with the skinny teenage girl. He seemed to be trying to force her back into the Mercedes, but the kid gave as good as she got, wriggling and battering him with her fists.

'Witnesses say she was screaming as well, but we can't hear that,' Sergeant Matteson said. 'Anyhow, here's where we get the first sight of DI Bateson. Top left, there – see.'

The tall rangy figure of DI Terry Bateson appeared, striding purposefully across the forecourt towards the shop. He was still some distance from the scene beside the Mercedes, which he had not yet noticed.

'Very well dressed for a knight errant,' Will Churchill commented. 'Ten o'clock at night and still in a suit and tie. What's he after – a Mars Bar?'

No one responded to this. On the screen Terry stopped, noticing the argument for the first time. The skinny girl kicked the man in the balls and tried to run, but he grabbed her by the hair and pulled her to the ground. Terry watched for a moment, then appeared to shout something, strode across to the Mercedes, and after a few words seized the driver by the collar and pinned him against the side of his car. While this was happening the teenage girl slunk away, heading across the forecourt towards the dual carriageway on the Hull Road.

After a few more words with the driver, Terry turned to follow her. The cameras showed him weaving his way past the pumps towards the road. He was walking, not running, and twice he held his hand out in a gesture of friendship, perhaps. The camera was set to cover the forecourt, not the road, and sometimes only the girl's legs were visible at the top of the screen, walking up and down uncertainly on the pavement.

'Where's she going?' Will Churchill asked.

'Hard to say, sir. It look like she's lost, doesn't it? Looking for a bus stop, maybe. Or wondering whether to cross the road.'

If that was what the girl was wondering, Terry's approach seemed to make up her mind. He was within a couple of yards now, holding out his hand for the second time. She stopped pacing, stared directly at him, and then darted out into the road. Terry sprang after her. Both of them vanished off the top of the screen for a second, and then the lower half of Terry's legs reappeared, making small urgent steps back towards the forecourt. The girl's legs too, as though he was pulling her. And then, a fraction of a second later, two bodies, flying through the air to land on the ground beside the road in the top left hand corner of the screen.

'Bloody hell,' someone murmured. The room fell silent as they watched, entranced, hoping perhaps for the bodies to move. But they didn't. Sergeant Matteson let the video run on while a car, apparently oblivious to the drama, moved away from the petrol pump towards the exit. Just before it reached the bodies it stopped and the driver got out. Then a woman emerged from the shop. She ran up to the bodies, bent over them, then appeared to say something to the driver who pulled out a mobile phone.

More time elapsed – half a minute perhaps – then a third figure, a man, ran in from the road. He looked distraught, clutching his head and waving his arms towards the road and the motionless bodies. The car driver and the woman appeared to be shouting at him.

'That's the truck driver,' Sergeant Mattesson said. 'Poor bugger, what could he do?'

'Stop, perhaps?' Will Churchill suggested. 'Slam on his brakes?'

Mattesson sighed. 'We've timed it,' he said patiently. 'He had two seconds, max, between the girl running into the road and the moment of impact. You try stopping a forty ton wagon in two seconds – no chance. Even if he was speeding which there's no sign he was. But there's more – watch this. Not the crash scene – behind.'

He ran the video on further and they all saw what he meant. A van driver got out of his vehicle beside the pumps and made his way hesitantly towards the bodies, but behind him, the driver of the grey Mercedes did the opposite. Having stood by his car and watched the accident from a distance, he opened the driver's door, got in, and reversed away from the pumps so that he could turn the car and leave the forecourt by the entrance, near the roundabout.

'The bastard,' Mike Candor said. 'Where's he going?'

'You tell me,' Sergeant Matteson murmured. 'You're the detective.'

'But you've traced him, haven't you?' DC Candor insisted. 'You've got the car number on CCTV.'

'That's just it,' Matteson answered, a tight smile playing around his lips. 'The Merc had false number plates.'

* * *

Sleep, for Terry, seemed no different from waking. Or if there was a difference, he couldn't quite put his finger on it, not yet. His dreams, induced by the morphine, were so vivid and kaleidoscopic that the moments when he imagined his eyes were open seemed grey and disappointing by comparison. Had his daughters really been here, in this room, with Trude? He thought so, but why they had brought balloons and Esther had walked on the ceiling he couldn't quite understand. Sometimes the dreams were fun but they could change in a moment. Once Mary, his wife, stood beside him at the altar in a church. She was wearing a wedding dress and smiling happily, like the photo by his bedside at home. But then he took her hand and led her out across a road where she shrank to the size of a child and then carried on getting smaller and smaller until she vanished down a drain and he wept. *Mary*, he pleaded with the nurse in the middle of the night. *Mary, come back.*

But it was Jane Carter, not Mary, who sat beside his bed in one of his waking moments. Detective Sergeant Plain Jane, with a uniformed traffic policeman by her side taking notes.

'What can you remember, sir?' Jane asked, her voice sympathetic but firm.

'Remember ... about what?'

'The accident. We need to know as much as possible.'

It was then, when Terry tried to put his mind to it for the first time, that he realized there was a complete blank. He remembered a lot about the dreams but exactly how he got injured, how he arrived here in this hospital – nothing.

'Take it slowly. What's your last memory before being here in this hospital? Think back.'

Walking. Striding along in the darkness past my own house. Lights on downstairs but children asleep. Why didn't I go in? I was angry about something – what? Oh God, Sarah Newby. Pretty woman, not like this one, Plain Jane the detective. Can't tell her that. Why?

'I was out for a walk.'

'Where were you going?'

'Nowhere special. Out for some air.'

'Do you remember which direction you were walking?'

'Towards ... Osbaldwick, I think. Hull Road.'

'Why Osbaldwick?'

'No reason. Just needed the walk.'

'Ten o'clock at night?'

Terry met Jane's eyes. That's *her* case, he remembered, Osbaldwick. The woman who was murdered. Vicky something – Wilson, Weston, whatever. A fuzzy memory of that came back, at least. I thought it was her husband who killed her but it wasn't. Why? Alibi, Scotland, that's it. He's got an alibi and I wanted to break it. Why? Can't remember. Something, perhaps. But that's why she's annoyed. Understandable. She thinks I was trying to interfere.

'It's a nice place to walk, that's all. Pretty village.'

Jane sighed, frowning. She didn't entirely believe him but he was still very weak and she only had a few minutes left. The doctor had been very strict about that.

'Do you remember going to the service station? The *Inner Space Station* on Hull Road?'

Terry shook his head slowly. 'No. I was walking, wasn't I? I didn't have a car. So why would I go there?'

'That's where the accident happened. Just outside the service station.'

'Oh.' Terry searched his mind again. Still nothing. Just darkness. It scared him. 'I'm sorry, but ...'

Jane could see the nurse talking to someone just outside the door. About to come in. 'What about this girl?'

'What girl?'

'The one who had the accident with you. You were talking to her, holding out your hand.'

'Was I? I'm sorry, I don't ... What was her name?'

'Mary.'

* * *

Outside in the corridor Jane saw a woman standing by the nursing station. A slender woman, early forties, professional looking, dark hair combed back, a look of concern on her face. Jane would have taken her for a doctor, consultant, perhaps, if she hadn't been carrying a shoulder bag and wearing a bright blue duffle coat and knee-high leather boots with heels. A visitor, clearly. Then she recognised her.

'Hello. Mrs Newby, isn't it?'

'Yes.' Sarah looked surprised. 'And you are?'

'DS Carter, CID. We've met once or twice, in court.'

'Oh yes.' Sarah shook her head apologetically. 'Sorry, forgive me. Are you here for DI Bateson?'

'I've just been talking to him, yes.'

'How is he?'

It was the earnestness of the question that struck Jane, when she reflected on it afterwards. What little she knew of Sarah Newby had led her to expect someone hard, cynical, emotionally controlled. But there was an appeal behind the question that spoke of something more – the anxiety, the need to know that usually came from a close relative; a wife, sister perhaps.

Or lover.

'He's ... very sleepy. Sedated, I think. You'd better ask the medics.'

'Is he talking? Did he recognise you?'

'Yes. Only for a few minutes though.' Jane glanced towards the nurse, who was attending a patient in an adjoining room. 'He's very tired.'

'Do you know what happened?'

'A road traffic accident. We're investigating. I can't discuss that.'

'Really? There was a girl involved too, wasn't there? A child. How is she?'

'As I say, you must ask the medical staff. Now if you'll excuse me.' Jane made her way to the door. Then, thinking that her response had been a bit harsh, she turned, relenting. 'They tell me he'll survive. He'll probably be off sick for a fair while but the good news is, he'll live at least. Good news for his family, don't you think? He loves those kids.'

'Yes, of course.'

Bitch, Sarah thought as the door closed behind the detective. She knew exactly what she was saying. *One day I'll have you on the witness stand; then you'll answer my questions.*

She turned to the nurse who was just emerging from the other room. 'Hello. I'm a friend of Terry Bateson. My name's Sarah Newby. I was here yesterday. Could I see him? Just for a minute or two.'

'I'm sorry.' It was a different nurse from yesterday, but the same response. 'Only close family at the moment, I'm afraid. And police. Maybe tomorrow.'

'You did give him my name? I left it with the nurse last night. To say I called.'

The nurse searched on the computer and the papers on the desk. 'I'm not sure ... yes, here it is, Sarah Newby?'

'That's me.'

A practised, professional look of sympathy on her face. 'I'm sorry, love. He's not really well enough yet. Maybe tomorrow. I'll tell him you called again, all right?'

* * *

'So, what about this girl?' Will Churchill asked. 'What do we know about her?'

'Almost nothing, so far,' Sergeant Matteson replied. 'Serious head injuries, broken limbs, internal bleeding. She's lucky to be alive. If she still is alive, that is.'

'Who is she?'

'No idea. She can't talk; they've put her in an induced coma. We've got a female officer by her bed but ...' Matteson shrugged. 'It's a waste of time, really.'

'No ID? Phone, surely? All kids have phones, don't they? Permanently grafted onto their hands.'

'Not this one. Not on her anyhow. Maybe she left it in the car.'

'What about her clothes? Don't they tell us anything?'

Matteson smiled. 'Jeans, teeshirt, trainers. That's hardly unusual, is it? The only thing that's odd is that she wasn't wearing anything else. No coat, nothing to keep her warm. It's not exactly midsummer, is it? Oh, and then there's this.' He pulled a plastic evidence bag from his pocket. Inside it was a small round coin. He passed it across the table. 'We found it in the back pocket of her jeans.'

Churchill picked up the coin and looked at it. On the front was a large number 1, with the word *EURO* boldly written across a map of western Europe, including the UK. 'A one euro coin. Not a wealthy girl, then?'

'Hardly. It was jammed into the stitching as though she'd forgotten it. But look at the other side.'

Churchill turned the coin over. On the reverse was an image he hadn't seen before. A sort of cross took up most of the centre of the coin. It was like the usual Christian cross but with two arms, an upper and lower. The cross appeared to be standing on a small mound, one of three, probably the hills of Golgotha. All around the rim of the coin were the familiar stars of the European Union. Between the cross and the rim of stars were the words *SLOVENSKO 2009.*

'Slovensko? What's that?'

'Slovakia, sir,' Matteson replied. 'It's a euro made in Slovakia.'

32. La–La Land

'So, HOW are you?'

It was an obvious, trite question, and Sarah felt foolish asking it. Yet however banal it was, what else could she say? As soon as she entered the room she saw how pale and weak he was, propped up in the hospital bed with the tubes going into his arm and the monitors flashing quietly behind him. He had a three day beard, she noticed; perhaps he didn't like the nurses shaving him. The darkness of the stubble emphasized the pallor of his skin.

For answer he smiled. Not a flashing, exuberant smile; just a crinkling of the eyes and a brief gleam of teeth below the incipient moustache. Quite fetching, she thought; like a wounded soldier in a film. But the query in his voice worried her.

'Sarah?'

'Terry. You do remember me?'

'Um ... yes, of course.' But the slight hesitation was a surprise, a wound to her pride. And – much worse than that – a fear for him. She knew he'd suffered concussion but if he didn't recognise her after a week what did that mean? Either she wasn't very significant in his life or, much more scarily, he might not recover.

It was a shock. After all he'd seen his children each day and that detective, Jane Carter, at least twice. His sister too, had come over from Leeds, and been allowed in before her. Sarah knew all this because she'd either rung or visited each day and it was only now, six days after the accident, that she was finally allowed in to see him. And only for five minutes, the nurse had insisted with a mixture of reproach and compassion. Ten at the outside.

It was an unusual position for Sarah who was used to having control of situations. But not here, in the kingdom of the medics. Police and family had rights, but not friends, or whatever she was. She'd toyed with the words *girlfriend* or *partner*, wondering if perhaps they'd gain her faster access, but she'd not dared to use them. They didn't seem right, somehow; she wasn't sure they were true. After all, she'd sent in her name each day. If he'd wanted to see her he only had to ask.

'I brought you some grapes. Food for invalids.'

'Thanks.' Terry indicated the locker beside his bed, where there was already a bowl of grapes beside the flowers. 'Kind of you.' Again, the briefest of smiles.

'Well, it's the thought that counts.'

She deposited the grapes and sat down in the plastic chair beside his bed. It was so low she had to look up at him. She smiled encouragingly.

'Your girls have been to see you then?'

'Yes. Every day.'

'Terry, you know I've been here too, don't you? They did tell you that?'

He frowned, as if chasing an elusive memory. 'Yes. I think ... probably.'

'Well, I'm here now.' She reached out for his hand. 'I've been worried about you, Terry, of course I have. I'm sorry if ...'

'What?'

'Last time we met. You remember – in the restaurant, with Emily. My daughter Emily?'

'Yes. Tall girl. Messy hair.'

'That's the one.' A laugh rose in her throat like a sob. *He wouldn't normally say that, surely?*

'Well anyway, we had a nice meal together, the three of us, but then afterwards I said – I feel bad about this now, but at the time – I suggested we should cool our relationship until after the trial. You remember, the trial that's coming up? Adrian Norton?'

Again the frown, the pause for thought, followed by a smile – of relief, as light dawned. 'Yes, yes. You're defending. Against Jane.'

'Jane?'

'Plain Jane the Brain Drain.' He threw his head back and laughed, beating the side of the bed with his good arm. 'That's funny, isn't it? Plain Jane No Brain. You're bound to win. Pretty woman like you.'

Oh my God. It's worse than I thought! It's like Alzheimers, inhibitions gone. Sarah smiled painfully. It was good to see him happy. And it was funny too. In a way.

She waited until he had stopped chuckling.

'Yes, well. I hope I do win, of course. But the thing is, that evening after the meal, I wondered if maybe I'd upset you, you see. More than I realised at the time. And it was soon after that you got run over. It wasn't ... because of me, in any way?'

'Because of you? *Sarah?* You're not Mary, are you?'

'What? Mary? Terry, I don't understand.'

Again the frown, an earnest attempt to remember, to communicate. 'You weren't there, were you? You were at home with Emily. Tall girl, frizzy, good fun.'

'Yes, that's right.'

'Well then, it couldn't be you. Not if you were at home, how could it be?' Terry grinned. 'Sarah Newby the Alibi Girl. Not guilty. But there *was* a girl there, that's what they tell me. I can't remember, you see, it's all blank, but she was called Mary. Mary, like my wife. You never met her, though, did you?' He looked pained now, anxious.

'No, Terry, I didn't. I'm sorry.'

'Not your fault, don't apologise. It was boys killed her, not you.'

A tear trickled down his face. He ignored it, pursuing his thought earnestly. One moment he stared into her eyes, then away out of the window somewhere.

'Anyway, there was this girl, you see, Mary. Not my wife Mary, but another one, younger. That's what they tell me. A child, teenager, like Jess. And she was there too, with me, at the accident. That's what they say. Run over, nearly killed. Poor kid, knocked down by a lorry. Juggernaut, massive. Not Jess, you understand, she's okay, she comes to see me, with Esther, thank God. Not Jess, but Mary.'

He gripped her hand, looking straight into her eyes now.

'And it may be my fault, you see.'

* * *

'The girl,' Will Churchill said. 'She's come out of the coma, but she doesn't speak English. Only a few words, anyway, and the main one is fuck. So because of this coin, we think she's Slovakian. East European, anyway. We're getting an interpreter up from the Embassy tomorrow: no one at the university speaks Slovak, it seems. Anyway, given her age and the state of her, I'd like you to be there, Dave. With a female officer, of course.'

'You think she's been trafficked?' DS Starkey asked.

'More than likely, in the circumstances,' Churchill agreed. He recited the details: the argument, the driver, the false number plates, the possibility of a second teenage girl inside the Mercedes. 'Looks just up your street, doesn't it?'

'As if we hadn't got enough cases already,' Starkey muttered. 'Still, I'll give it a go. What about this officer, the one who was injured? What does he say about her?'

'Nothing, so far. Concussion, can't remember a thing, so he claims. Keeps babbling on about her being his wife.'

'His *wife?*'

'Yes. She was called Mary, apparently. Died a few years ago.'

'And this kid's called Mary too, is she?'

'According to one of the witnesses, yes. He was filling up his car and heard a bit of the argument, with the driver yelling at the kid. Says he heard the name Mary. The doctors have tried it on her at the hospital but she just looks blank. And since they don't speak Slovak ...' Churchill shrugged.

'What about the driver? Did he speak Slovak too?'

'The other witness, the woman at the checkout, thought he sounded Scottish. Could be bilingual, of course.'

'What about this officer, DI Bateson? What was he doing there?'

Churchill looked at his colleague thoughtfully. There was a long, significant pause before he said: 'Coincidence, it seems. He was just out for a walk.'

'Ten o'clock at night? At a service station?'

Churchill shrugged. 'That's what he says. And the rest he can't remember.'

'If she *was* being trafficked, you don't think he went there for a rendezvous, and the argument was about payment? He took her hand, tried to drag her across the road, you say?'

'Rescue her, is what it looks like.' Again the meeting of eyes, the unspoken thoughts, the thoughtful silence. 'But if there is a crime, whoever it's committed by, I want it solved, Dave, that's what I'm saying. No cover-ups in this force, just follow the evidence wherever it leads you. Without fear or favour. Understand?'

* * *

'Of course it's not your fault, Terry,' Sarah said. 'How could it be?'

'Well, I don't know. I can't remember. It's hell, this not remembering, but it's all blank. Nothing there. I was walking past my house, girls asleep, Trude downstairs watching telly, so I thought, I'll go for a walk – and next thing, here I am in this room. Nothing in between. So when Jane says there was a girl, Mary, at the service station ...' Terry shook his head wearily. 'I wish she wasn't called, that, Sarah. This girl I never met.'

'Mary?'

He nodded. 'My wife's name. And I was holding her hand. That's what she says. Plain Jane the Total Pain. I wish she hadn't told me. It's the dreams, you see. I get confused. I have so many dreams.'

'You poor man. It will get easier, Terry, I'm sure.'

'Will it? I hope so. You come and see me, Sarah. You're pretty, not like her. We should have sex.'

Oh my God. Sarah closed her eyes and drew a deep breath. She gripped his hand firmly, making sure it stayed where it was, on the side of the bed. *Don't you dare make a move now, not with all these tubes and machines, that would be ridiculous.* Keeping a light smile on her face – after all it was funny, as well as sad – she said: 'That's nice, Terry, and we will, when you're better. But for now ...'

A nurse opened the door. 'Time's up, I'm afraid.'

Saved by the bell. Sarah stood up. 'I'll come and see you again, Terry. If you'd like me to?'

'Yes. Help me get better.' He winked.

Walking away down the long hospital corridors, Sarah wondered whether to laugh or cry.

33. No News Is Bad News

'IT'S BEEN over two months now, Mr Starkey,' Lucy said. 'My client has been suspended from his job and seen his reputation trashed in the media. He has a right to know what evidence you have against him.'

'He already knows the details of the allegations, Mrs Parsons. We showed them to him on day one, when he was arrested.'

'Those are just allegations,' Lucy said patiently. 'What I'd like to know is whether you have any evidence to back them up.'

'We are proceeding with our enquiries, madam. We have interviewed a number of witnesses and there are more in the pipeline. This is a complex investigation and as always with historic child abuse, it takes time. Mr Newby will just have to be patient.'

Detective Sergeant Starkey's telephone manner reminded Lucy of a robot; one of those wretched machines programmed to say *Your call is important to us. Please hold the line.* Any second now, she thought, I'll be cut off and the phone will start to play Vivaldi.

Gritting her teeth, she said: 'You do realise, don't you, that according to Dr Kenning, the retired headmaster, these girls made similar accusations against another male teacher who was dismissed? Have you started proceedings against him as well?'

'Dr Kenning's an old man, Mrs Parsons. There are several inconsistencies in his evidence. Ms Fanshawe doesn't remember this other teacher ...'

'Thomas Weston?'

'Is that the name? Yes. As I say she doesn't remember him and hasn't lodged a complaint against him. Her only complaint is against your client, no one else.'

'So you'd rather believe her than Dr Kenning?'

'As I said, Mrs Parsons, there are inconsistencies ...'

'You are aware, Mr Starkey, that Clare Fanshawe has a criminal record? Theft, drug abuse, shoplifting, benefit fraud – it goes on and on.'

'All of which could have been triggered by your client, though, couldn't it? A vulnerable teenager abused by an older man in a position of authority. Enough to send anyone off the rails, wouldn't you say?'

'Perhaps. Or she might just be a sick fantasist with a history of mental illness. That's not going to look too good on the witness stand, is it?'

'Which is why we're looking for evidence to corroborate her story, Mrs Parsons. As we are obliged to do.'

'Or disprove it.'

'What?'

'You are also obliged, Detective Sergeant, to look for evidence that might disprove this allegation, isn't that right? Or do you believe everything a witness says nowadays, in sex abuse cases like this?'

The pause after her question gave Lucy her answer. In recent years, ever since the horrific revelations about the TV personality Jimmy Savile, and the scandal about the way that for decades the police and public authorities like the NHS and BBC had ignored the complaints of his victims, the pendulum had swung the other way. The most notorious recent example had been that of a senior police inspector who stated on national TV not that he was *investigating* an allegation, but that he definitely *believed* the allegation to be true, just as Lucy had suggested now.

Starkey, clearly, was aware of this trap. 'If we find any evidence that exonerates your client, that will of course be disclosed to you in the fullness of time, Mrs Parsons. But I would have thought that you, as a woman, would understand how difficult it is for victims to come forward in cases like this, and how important it is for them to be treated sensitively.'

'If they are genuine victims, yes,' Lucy said drily. 'But you, as an experienced police officer, will have met liars and fantasists before.'

'A few. But I don't think that's the case here.'

'Really? Not everyone tells the truth all the time.'

'Indeed.' Starkey laughed. 'Tell that to your client, Mrs Parsons, why don't you?'

For heaven's sake, Lucy thought. *When did Bob lie?* Trying another tack, she asked: 'How's your fishing expedition going?'

'What?' Starkey sounded confused, as though she'd developed some strange interest in his holiday arrangements.

'You know, your advertising. Making your investigation public in the hope of attracting further allegations against my client. Any luck so far?'

'A few minor complaints,' he conceded. 'Mostly from parents who thought their kid didn't deserve to be punished, or should have got higher grades. Nothing recent, no.'

'Well, halleluja! So Mr Newby really is a model headmaster, just as he seems to be, then?'

'I have no evidence to the contrary. At present.'

'That's something at least. Look, Mr Starkey, I'm not just ringing you to score points. We both agree that child abuse is a serious crime; but there's a matter of justice here too. My client is suffering from this delay. He can't work, he's been forced to leave home, his reputation is ruined ...'

'My heart bleeds for him.'

The cool sarcasm stopped Lucy in her tracks. She'd imagined she was making progress towards some sort of reasonable human negotiation. Apparently not. She drew a deep breath.

'I'm not asking for sympathy, sergeant. I'm asking for fairness. If you think my client is guilty, when are you going to charge him?'

'When I'm good and ready. Not before.'

'His police bail ends next Thursday. November 10th. Are you going to charge him then?'

'Maybe. If we're ready. Otherwise we'll just extend it for another two months.'

'That's what I mean. Justice delayed is justice denied. If you've got enough evidence to support these allegations, bring him in, charge him and show us what you've got. If not, let him go.'

'All in good time, Mrs Parsons. Now, if you'll excuse me, I've got an investigation to run.'

The call ended. Lucy Parsons put the phone down and stared out of her office window, slowly shaking her head.

* * *

'So he's not interested in what Dr Kenning said?' Bob asked. He was in Lucy's office in Leeds and had been listening on the speakerphone.

'Apparently not. You heard what he said.'

'All that effort. Emily even recorded it.'

'I know. But Dr Kenning's evidence wasn't entirely in your favour, was it? He did confirm he'd received a complaint against you, even though he'd dismissed it.'

'He dismissed it because he knew the girls were lying,' Bob insisted. 'Which they obviously were! *Jailbait,* he called them.'

'Not a phrase which we'd want him to repeat in front of a jury,' Lucy pointed out. 'If it ever comes to that, which I hope it won't.'

'Do you?' Bob asked bitterly. 'I think a proper trial would clear the air. At least it would be better than all this – delay, deception, limbo. If we met these women in court you could cross-examine them, couldn't you? You or a QC – someone nasty and forensic like Sarah. Show them up for the liars and fantasists they are!'

'Be careful what you wish for,' Lucy said cautiously. 'A trial is like a battle; it doesn't always go the way you want. You're in the hands of a jury you can't control, and their decision is final. If both women tell the same story, you could be in trouble.'

'I'm in trouble already, in case you hadn't noticed,' Bob snapped waspishly. 'No job, no reputation. Why is my name all over the media, while these two lying cows are anonymous? Isn't the law supposed to be about justice – you know, innocent until proven guilty, that sort of thing? Whatever happened to that?'

'There is a constant debate about the rights of anonymity in cases of sexual abuse,' Lucy said, realising as the words left her mouth that she was wasting her breath. 'But try to look on the bright side ...'

'The bright side? You've got to be kidding!'

' ... you're not on remand, so you haven't been charged with anything and you're free to go wherever you want. If they felt they had a cast iron case they'd have charged you and set a date for trial by now. Which means they still have doubts.'

'Then I should get the benefit of them!'

'Maybe you will. You've made some progress with Dr Kenning, at least. Can you find anyone else who would give you a decent reference?'

'Well, I can try, I suppose. It's not as though I've got much else to do. But Lucy ...'

'What?' She didn't entirely like Bob using her first name, now that he was a client. She hadn't even known him that well before; he'd been Sarah's husband, that's all. But to insist on *Mrs Parsons* now would be a slap in the face.

'Look, we know the names of these two women; you could find out where they live easily enough. Why don't we just go round and have it out with them?

You could make an appointment, do it formally, come along with me to make sure there was a proper record, tape record it even. That way we could clear all this up ...'

'*No,* Bob!' Lucy held up a hand, horrified. 'It was just about all right talking to Dr Kenning, but not the victims. You *mustn't* do that! You could be arrested, charged with interfering with the course of justice, harassing witnesses, assault ...'

'I wouldn't assault them. Just talk ...'

'You don't need to actually touch someone to commit an assault. Just putting them in fear, verbal harassment ...'

'I'm not going to shout! Just ask them *WHY? FOR HEAVEN'S SAKE!*'

He stopped, as he realised he was shouting. He was on the edge of his seat, his hands trembling with rage. Lucy watched him, smiling sadly.

'You see? Bob, that's what would happen. You might not mean to, but you'd terrify these women, make everything worse.'

'How can it be worse? I've been arrested already.'

'But you're not in prison, are you? Look, Bob, I know this is difficult, but you've got to do it my way. By all means contact colleagues, anyone who can give you a good reference, but stay away from these two women, please! Promise me, Bob! Otherwise our next conference will be in prison and you really don't want that!'

'No.' He shook his head grimly, meeting her eyes. 'All right, I promise, I'll play by the rules. But that's where all this is leading, isn't it? Prison? If all this goes wrong.'

* * *

The next time Sarah visited Terry she took Emily. It seemed odd, to be taking her own daughter as a sort of chaperone, but Emily was home for a couple of days and knew Terry so why not? She was almost as concerned as Sarah was.

As it was it turned out well. A wide smile lit up Terry's face when they entered the room, though to Sarah's chagrin it seemed to be prompted more by the sight of Emily than her. He was sitting in a hospital armchair beside the bed, and looked slightly more alert than last time, less pale.

'Welcome. No more grapes?'

'Not this time, Terry, no – anyway, you haven't finished those yet.' She indicated the bowl of grapes on his locker, together with a vase of flowers and a selection of *Get Well Soon* cards, including two large home-made ones from his daughters. 'But I brought Emily instead.'

'Yes, I see. Two for the price of one. Good to see you, miss. Sorry about the furniture; maybe a nurse ...'

'It's okay, Mr Bateson.' Emily perched on the bed while Sarah took the only other plastic chair. It had the comic effect of placing Emily - a tall girl anyway - in a position where she looked down on the two adults, like a schoolteacher supervising her charges. 'So how are you, anyway?'

'Everyone asks that. Getting better, is what I'm supposed to say. This arm itches like fury though. You didn't bring any knitting needles, did you? To help me scratch?'

'Sorry, no. But I've got a pen.' Emily pulled a biro out of her bag. 'I'll sign it too, if you like. Did your daughters draw those?'

'Mostly, yes.' Terry held out the pot on his arm, proudly. It was decorated with colourful drawings of dragons, horses and smiling faces. 'Nurses too. I never fancied having a tattoo but I'm beginning to come round to the idea.'

'Don't you dare!' Sarah said, a little more earnestly than she had intended. Terry and Emily stared at her in surprise.

'Why not? A death's head with handcuffs and a police badge underneath? Tasteful, don't you think?'

'No,' said Sarah firmly. 'It would be a turn-off.'

'Ah well.' Their eyes met, Emily watching curiously.

'So,' Sarah continued briskly. 'You must be a bit better if you're out of bed. How long before you're allowed home?'

'Next week, they tell me. They've got to do a few more scans and tests first.'

'Not too long then. How about the memory?'

Terry shook his head. 'No change. I still can't remember anything about the accident itself. In fact it hurts when I try – gives me headaches, like migraines. Not nice at all.'

'Oh. But they'll pass, won't they?'

'Hope so, in time. The psycho gives me magic pills.' He frowned, as if going away from them into his mind for a moment; then brightened. 'Still, the rest of my mind feels clearer. I can do puzzles, logical stuff, talk better.' He looked at Sarah thoughtfully. 'I probably seemed a bit strange to you last time you came, didn't I?'

'A little, yes. Uninhibited.'

She smiled, and their eyes met again. Emily sat watching from above, like an audience at a play. Terry grinned.

'Well, I'm more inhibited now. All my naughty thoughts locked away in here.' He tapped his forehead. 'With those memories I still have.'

'Good. Keep them there.' This is better, Sarah thought. Much more hopeful. Terry, remembering their audience, turned politely to Emily.

'So, young lady, have you come all this way just to see me? Or is it your father you're most worried about?'

'Both of you, of course,' said Emily. 'Dad hasn't been run over, but he's still pretty depressed, unfortunately.'

'Oh? Why is that? Tell me ...'

34. Quite Contrary

'TERENCE. GOOD of you to come in. How are you, old son?'

All the worse for seeing you, Terry thought. He'd answered this summons to come and make a witness statement about his accident, but hoped it would be dealt with by the traffic police. No such luck, it seemed. As soon as he'd arrived Will Churchill had advanced on him, held out his hand with a pleasant beam on his face, and ushered Terry into his office. Which would have been fine if they were colleagues with a good working relationship, but, as everyone knew, they were not. They were just oil and water, chalk and cheese.

There was another man in the room; a slightly built man, about Churchill's age, with dark hair and a seamed, narrow, intense face which reminded Terry of a ferret.

'You haven't met my old chum, Dave Starkey, have you? Dave, this is Terence Bateson, our oldest and most respected DI. And before his unfortunate accident, the most senior member of my team.'

Terry felt the sting of the words *oldest*, *senior*, and *before his accident*. He thought: the man can't help himself. He's like a scorpion; he scuttles round and jabs his poison in just for the fun of it.

'Pleased to meet you,' said Starkey, holding out his hand. Terry took it awkwardly with his left hand, noting the sharp curious eyes, and an accent similar to Churchill's. 'I hope you're recovering?'

'Slowly but surely,' Terry said.

'Good. Because I need to ask you a few questions about the events of that night, I'm afraid. If you feel you're up to it, that is.'

'Dave and I were at school together, believe it or not,' Churchill informed

Terry cheerfully. 'We worked together as coppers down in Essex. Now here he is, exiled to a northern wilderness like me, in charge of *Operation Hazel.*'

'Oh yes. What's that?'

'Haven't you heard?' Churchill beamed, delighted by his subordinate's ignorance. '*Operation Hazel* is our drive to respond to the rise in cases of historic child abuse.'

Of course, Terry thought, cursing the way his mind worked so slowly since the accident. This is the investigation which has arrested Sarah's ex. That's why her daughter Emily keeps going to Harrogate to visit her dad. To try and help him – against these two, presumably. Good luck with that.

'*Operation Hazel* was set up on my initiative,' Will Churchill continued. 'The Chief Constable asked me to oversee it. But that's hardly necessary with a competent sergeant like Dave here, now is it?'

Sergeant, Terry thought. Churchill couldn't resist a sly dig about his old chum's rank. I wonder how that feels.

'So what's that got to do with me?'

'Probably nothing,' Dave Starkey said. 'Not the historic part anyway. But since your accident we've been trying to find out about the girl. You know, the one who was injured with you.'

'Yes. How is she?'

'Two broken legs. Head injuries. But she's young, she'll live. She's learning to walk again.'

'I'm glad to hear it.'

'Yes.' Starkey leaned forward, his bright, ferret-like eyes focussed on Terry intently. 'How well do you know this girl?'

'What? I don't know her at all.'

'So why were you holding out your hand to her?'

'Was I? Who says that?'

'We've got it on CCTV. We'll show you later.'

Terry tried hard to concentrate, feeling – as so often since his accident – that the situation was getting away from him. 'This is the girl called Mary, is it?'

'That's right. So you *do* know her name.'

'DS Carter told me. In the hospital. It was my wife's name too. But she died.'

'Sorry to hear that, sir,' Starkey said, subtly reminding Terry of their relative status. 'That must be distressing. And ... you'd never met this girl before?'

'No. Of course not. Who is she?'

'Ever been to Slovakia?'

'Sorry, where?'

'It's a country, Terence,' Churchill informed him. 'In Eastern Europe. One of our so-called partners in the European Union.'

'Yes, I've heard of it. Why? Is that where this girl comes from?'

'Got it in one,' said Starkey. 'Trafficked, we think. Thirteen years old.'

'Poor kid.'

'Yeah.' Starkey's eyes had still not left Terry's. 'You've got kids too, haven't you?'

'Yes. Two daughters.'

'Me too. Left them down in Essex till I'm sure this move is permanent.' Starkey picked up a sheet of paper from a folder beside him. 'So ... temporary amnesia, according to your medical report. What's the last thing you remember before the accident?'

'Walking past my home,' Terry said. 'I told the psychiatrist. And DS Carter, as I'm sure you know.'

'So the events in the service station are a complete blank to you, are they?'

'Yes. Apart from what I've been told.'

'Well, we'd better show you the video then. Maybe it will refresh your memory.' Starkey pressed a key on the laptop on Churchill's desk. Terry stared intently as the recording of the incident played on the screen. It was compulsive viewing, like a dream which has somehow been downloaded. The tall, loose-limbed hero of the drama seemed like a hologram, a pirated version of himself with which he had no actual connection

'Bring back memories?' Starkey asked curiously.

'No, sorry.'

'All right, let's watch it again.' Starkey ran the film back to the section where Terry was arguing with the driver of the grey Mercedes. 'What's he saying to you?'

'No idea. Abuse, by the look of it.'

'Why abuse?'

'Well, he was beating the girl, wasn't he? I was probably trying to stop him.'

'Look again.' Starkey rewound the video. 'Seems like *she's* assaulting *him*, at first. He's just trying to restrain her, till she kicks him in the balls. Then he loses it.'

'So? She's just a kid.'

'Granted. Whatever he wants her to do, she's resisting. Then you come along.' He wound the tape forward a few frames. 'You grab him by the throat, pin him against the car. What's that about?'

'I guess I was angry.'

'Not correct procedure though, is it Terence?' Churchill chipped in. 'If he saw this, he could sue you for assault.'

'Has he seen it?'

'Not yet. We haven't found him.'

Thank God for that. Tiny bubbles of rage were seething in Terry's mind, like a pot coming to the boil. He clenched the fist of his left hand, driving the nails into his palm to control himself.

'You weren't arguing about a price for the girl?' Starkey continued.

'What? No, of course I wasn't!'

'How do you know, if you can't remember?'

'Because ... don't be ridiculous.' Terry half rose from his chair, thinking *I may be an invalid but this pot on my right arm will crack your skull if I swing it.*

And end your career for good, the voice of reason whispered. As well as re-breaking your arm. Slowly, he sat down.

Starkey, who had been watching him intently, gave a thin smile. 'I realise that these questions are painful, DI Bateson, but I do have to ask them, I'm afraid.'

'Why?'

'I'll explain that in a minute. First, watch this.' He wound the video forward to the section where Terry, at the top of the screen, could be seen approaching the girl, his arm held out. 'What are you saying to her there?'

'I can't remember. You know that.'

'All right.' He ran the video on and froze it at the point where the girl turned to run into the road. 'Does it look as though she's pleased to see you?'

'Obviously not. I must have scared her.'

'That's what she says too.' Starkey sat back in his chair as though the video had served its purpose. 'You were a punter, according to her.'

'What?'

Starkey picked up a folder and began to leaf through it. 'She's Slovakian, as you know. Doesn't speak much English so we had to get an interpreter from the Embassy. Maria Slavik, she's called – Slavik means nightingale, apparently. Pretty name – Mary Nightingale, 13 years old, from Bratislava. Snatched off the street and trafficked to a brothel somewhere in Holland, she thinks, where she learned all kinds of sex acts and serviced ten men a day for ...' he flicked over the page. ' ... four months. Then she and another girl were sold to a Scotsman called Angus – that's probably your driver – who claimed he felt sorry for them and would send them to school in Scotland if they worked in his cafe three evenings a week, serving food. They didn't really believe him but thought it had to be better than the place where they were so they went along with it until something happened along the way – he asked for a blow job and while she was doing it he was on the phone telling a mate what was happening and, she thought, negotiating a price for her to do the same for him and telling him where they could meet. So at the next service station she got out and decided to run, but her friend was too scared to go with her. Angus came back and tried to stop her, and then this other guy turned up and the two men started arguing – about the price, she assumed. She's sure he was a punter because he came after her and started calling out her name, Mary, and saying that he loved her. Which is what some of her customers used to say, apparently, especially the British ones.'

Starkey closed the folder and looked up. 'Did you call her Mary, or love?'

Terry shook his head, appalled. 'How could I even know her name? I'd never seen her before.'

'Exactly.' Starkey was watching him carefully. 'Maybe this Angus told you. The driver.'

'I might have heard him shout it at her. When he was dragging her to the ground by her hair.'

'Of course you might.' Starkey glanced at Will Churchill. His tone softened slightly. 'Look, Terence – okay if I call you that ..?'

'No.' If Starkey was trying to be friendly he had chosen the wrong tactic. 'I'd rather you didn't.'

'Okay then. DI Bateson sir, if you insist. Look, you've had a terrible accident and you're signed off sick, I appreciate that. But since you have no memory of this incident yourself I'm duty bound to take this girl's story seriously. The interpreter's convinced she's telling the truth as she sees it and I've got the Slovak Embassy breathing down my neck, threatening to apply for a European Arrest Warrant. Which could mean you taking your holidays overseas for a while courtesy of the Slovak government, and God knows what sort of legal system they have over there. So for the moment ...' he hesitated, glancing at Churchill for support.

'For the moment, Terence, you're formally suspended on full pay until this investigation is complete,' Will Churchill said. 'And since you're already on sick leave, I suggest you take up gardening for a while. They say it's very therapeutic, when the spring comes.'

Part Four

Trial and Terror

35. Campus East

As THE date of Adrian Norton's trial approached, Sarah and Lucy spent long hours poring over the prosecution evidence. Even though this was a relatively straightforward case, there were six lever-arch files of it – witness statements, photographs, post-mortem report, mobile phone and computer evidence, and extensive detailed forensic analysis of the victim's home, garden, car, and clothing.

Only two of the six files contained evidence which the prosecution intended to rely on in court. The other four contained 'unused material' – evidence which the police had collected but did not intend to use because in their opinion it was not particularly helpful, either in establishing the guilt of the accused or his innocence. Nonetheless the pre-trial process of discovery obliged them to supply it to the defence, in case they saw things differently.

All of this was time-consuming but useful in the interests of justice. A slightly less useful detail to Sarah, was that the defence also had to submit an outline of their case. This document, called a Defence Statement, had given Sarah and Lucy several headaches. It was perfectly reasonable in law to say that Adrian didn't kill her, and leave it at that; but the jury, being ordinary lay people and not lawyers, were bound to ask themselves the obvious question: okay, if Adrian didn't kill her, how *did* she die then?

If I can't present them with at least some alternative answer to that, Sarah thought, then my client is doomed.

'So, which way do we go?' Lucy asked. It was a late afternoon in November. Sarah stood at the window of her chambers in Tower Street, gazing out at the trees in the riverside park, which stood bare and stark against a grey evening sky. Beyond them, the river, full after another week of rain, lapped against the quayside and surged beneath the arches of Skeldergate Bridge. Anyone falling in today would have no chance, she thought. Even in August, everyone assumed Vicky Weston had drowned in the river.

'I wonder,' Sarah murmured softly. 'Are we really sure this is murder? An awful lot depends on very little.'

'The salt in her lungs, you mean? And the traces of blood in the boot of her car?'

'I know, that's their case,' Sarah said. 'But there's no reason why we shouldn't contest it. Drowning is drowning to most people. Linda Miles may be a good pathologist but even she can make mistakes.'

'You're not going to challenge her, are you?'

'Of course, that's my job!' Sarah grinned. 'Make the jurors wonder about suicide. If I can manage that, the prosecution case falls away.'

'You can't surely?'

'I can always try. That's why I'm paid, to spread confusion and doubt.'

'But if the Crown do convince them it's murder, you know what the jury are going to ask, don't you? If Adrian Norton didn't kill her, who did?'

'That, Dr Watson, is what everyone would like to know. Even though I will carefully explain to the jury that they are not meant to act like amateur detectives, still ...'

'It's only human nature to ask the question, isn't it?'

'Quite. Well, her husband had a motive, but no opportunity, sadly. You've checked his alibi again, have you?'

'Twice. He left for Scotland on Friday, returning on Monday. So if his wife was killed on Sunday evening, he wasn't there, Sarah. And no, he hasn't got a private helicopter.'

'Poor man. It's amazing how some people manage. Well, luckily, it's not our job to prove who did it. Just to show who didn't. And question whether it was murder at all.'

'So you're going to send in a defence statement with two strands, are you? We don't believe it was murder and someone else killed her?'

'Exactly. That should make them laugh,' Sarah said wryly. 'What else are we here for, but to amuse the CPS?'

* * *

While Sarah was feeling cheerful, the men in her life were in despair. Bob, as

Lucy expected, had had his police bail extended for a second time, with no apparent progress in his case, either towards acquittal or charge. And Terry was suspended on full pay, while convalescing at home on extended sick leave, with the possibility that he might never be fit enough to return to work.

Sarah tried to maintain her distance from both. She had visited Terry several more times with Emily, which proved a surprising success. To her amusement and relief, the pair seemed to get on very well. As Terry's mind gradually recovered, he seemed eager for new ideas and impressions to take his mind away from the confusion of guilt and rage that oppressed him in the aftermath of the accident; and Emily's bright young mind inspired him. She copied him in on some of the amusing texts and tweets which she and her friends exchanged each day, and she rang him sometimes when she was on the train or stuck with a boring essay.

Emily found Terry's new slightly vulnerable persona both intriguing and amusing, his predicament not dissimilar to her father's. She loved talking to his daughters on her visits, making his house ring with cheerful girlish laughter. Watching her, Terry thought this is the sort of young woman my Jessica and Esther will grow into in a few years' time; and perhaps, if we keep this friendship up, she will help show them the way.

In December, when her university term was over, Emily came to stay with her mother for the Christmas holidays. She spent a lot of time with her father in Harrogate, but visited Terry too. One afternoon, while Trude was fetching the girls from school, they went for a walk round the new York university campus east. It was a crisp sunny afternoon, with a blue sky and a keen icy north-east wind. Terry walked slowly, in a dark blue overcoat buttoned awkwardly over his right arm, which was still in plaster and too thick to get through the sleeve. Emily wore a red anorak and patterned woolly hat with a pompom and long braided flaps hanging over her ears. She walked slowly to accommodate Terry's invalid pace.

'They say Cambridge in winter is the coldest place on earth,' she said, watching the wind send tiny wavelets zipping across a small lake. 'But this must come close.'

'Doesn't matter,' said Terry grimly. 'I need the exercise. Good for me.'

'Any news about when you'll go back to work?'

'No. They're still investigating, stupid bastards. Let them get on with it. Enjoying my freedom. Anyway ...' He turned his back to the wind as a particularly vicious gust nearly lifted them off their feet. '... best I stay out of the way until your mother's finished her murder trial.'

'Why is that?'

'Didn't she tell you?' Terry grinned. 'I'm an embarrassment to her.'

'What do you mean?' Emily stepped smartly to one side as two student cyclists, the wind at their backs, whizzed past on their way to the huge, east European style college buildings.

Terry limped onward. 'Thought she'd told you. See, that evening before my accident. I remember it now, clearly.' He tapped his forehead with his gloved left hand. 'Memory coming back at last, thank God. Bits of it anyway. You remember that evening, don't you, miss?'

'I think so, yes.'

'Well, you took a picture with your phone, didn't you, and told the whole restaurant we were having sex, your mother and I? Remember that?'

'So?' Emily laughed. 'It's true, isn't it?'

'Not any more, unfortunately. Crippled old fool. I think I embarrass her. Anyway ...'

He held up a hand to forestall any protest. 'The point is that same evening she told me we can't any more. Not for the moment ...'

'Have sex, you mean?'

'Or any relationship, whatever you call it, because of this wretched trial. You see, she's defending, and I could be called as a witness for the prosecution. Less likely now since I'm under investigation. But there could be a conflict of interest. Understand?'

'Yes, well, sort of.'

The ends of Terry's scarf blew out horizontally in the wind. He fumbled with his left hand, trying to wrap it tighter round his neck. 'There's a café down here, I think. Let's get in out of the cold.'

They made their way down a wind tunnel between two buildings to an artificial lake, where a few ducks paddled through icy wavelets, their feathers ruffled by the wind. An automatic glass door in the university building behind them opened the way into a vast airy hall, three storeys high, with staircases and lifts at the side and a cafeteria on the far wall. The sudden warmth was welcome. Terry paid for two coffees and slices of carrot cake and Emily carried their tray to an empty table.

'So what you mean, is that you think that man is guilty, do you? The man that Mum is defending?'

'Well no, actually. I'm not sure he is.'

'So why don't you say so?'

'Because it's not my case. And most of the evidence says he *is* guilty, anyway.'

'I don't get it.' Emily dragged off her woolly hat and dumped it on the table, shaking her head to free her unruly mop of frizzy hair. 'If you think he isn't guilty, why don't you stand up in court and say so?'

'Because it might get your mother in trouble. She's not supposed to have a close relationship with any of the witnesses. Anyway, imagine what my colleagues would think. DS Jane Carter for example. She's spent hours and hours getting the evidence together for the CPS – it's probably her biggest case yet – and then I stand up and say she's got it all wrong. How do you think that would go down?'

'Yes, but if she *is* wrong, you'll have to, won't you? Otherwise an innocent man might go to prison.'

Terry smiled. The innocence of youth. 'I never said I *knew* she's wrong. I don't. I just have my doubts, that's all.'

'Even so, it's important. I mean, if you think this man didn't do it, you must think someone else did, right?'

Terry smiled. 'I thought your mother was the lawyer.'

But Emily was in no mood to be patronised. 'So who? Come on, you must know!'

'Must I? Why?'

'Because you're a policeman, a detective.'

'That doesn't make me a magician, does it? Or a – what do you call it? Clairvoyant.' He tapped his forehead again. 'There you go. Another fancy word. It's good for me, talking to you.'

'Don't you have any suspicions?'

Terry glanced around, to make sure they were not overheard. The only person near them was a Chinese student, peering intently at his laptop. 'Look, you shouldn't gossip about this, all right? As I say, it's not my case any more. But there's the victim's husband. He had a motive, but no opportunity.'

'Why not?'

'Alibi. He was in Scotland on the day she was killed.'

'Oh. That's no good then. Why do you say he had a motive?'

'They had a history of quarrels. He admitted that. He benefitted from her death: if she'd lived long enough to divorce him she'd have got half his wealth. This way he inherits it all. And ... something very similar happened to his first wife too.'

'What? You're kidding! He killed his first wife too?'

'Whoa! Ssssh!' Terry glanced anxiously at the Chinese student, who continued typing, oblivious to the world around him. 'Hold on, young lady!

There's no evidence that he killed her, all right. It's just that she drowned, in a sailing accident in Devon. And he inherited the house her parents had bought them. The inquest verdict was accidental death.'

'Yes, but ... two wives drowned!' Emily's eyes shone with excitement. She pulled her phone from her pocket. 'I see what you mean. What's his name, this careless husband? I must check him out on the internet.'

'It's Tom. Tom Weston.'

* * *

Emily dropped her phone on the table and stared at him.

'Did you say Tom Weston?'

'Yes. So?'

'Thomas Weston? A man in his mid fifties? Tall, thin? He wouldn't be a former schoolteacher, would he?'

'Possibly, yes. He works in educational publishing.'

'Oh my God.' She picked up her phone and started scrolling through it. When she'd found what she wanted she swiped her finger and thumb to enlarge the picture and held it out, stretching her arm across the carrot cake. 'There. Could that be him?'

Terry peered at the small screen. He saw a fuzzy black and white image of a thin bearded man in a tweed jacket, standing in a row of uniformed secondary school children. He looked about twenty-five.

'Well, it could be, I suppose. Why, where did you find this?'

'It's a photo of my dad's school. Back in 1991 when Dad was accused of this awful child molesting thing. This man's called Tom or Thomas Weston too. He was another teacher there at the time. He looks a bit like my dad at that age, don't you think? Look!' She took the phone back, scrolled and enlarged another section. 'See? That's my dad!'

'They look very similar, I agree. But ... why is this important?'

'It could be hugely important, don't you see!' Emily's words came tumbling over each other. 'My dad, he's accused of this awful thing which he says he didn't do, just like you, only worse, and I don't believe it not for a moment, of course he couldn't, but anyway ... I've been helping him, you see, trying to find out what happened, and we went to this school where he worked and then to his headmaster who said ...'

The words poured out and Terry listened intently, trying hard to get his fuzzy brain to follow. Another part of his mind was thinking: this is either arrant nonsense or a colossal coincidence – but which? And even if it *is* the same man what does it prove? As he struggled to make sense of it he leaned forward, his elbows on the table, his head in his hands.

Emily faltered. 'Terry? Mr Bateson? Are you all right?'

At first Terry didn't answer. He had his eyes shut, concentrating on the vision – memory – what was it?

'Do you need help? Shall I call a doctor?'

'No. No, I'm fine, I think.' Terry opened his eyes and sat up, resting his right arm in its plaster on the table in front of him. 'It's just ... I had a memory. Sometimes this happens. It's a good thing, the psychologist says. Synapses reconnecting.'

'What did you remember?'

'A pub. In Osbaldwick. It's not very clear.' He closed his eyes again, concentrating. 'I think ... it must be before the accident, that night. I walked past my house ... I always remember that ... but then ... I think I went on. I was in this pub, sitting outside at a picnic table, having a drink, then ... that's it ... I must have walked from my house, across the Hull Road, down through Osbaldwick to the pub. So I didn't go straight to the service station, as they say.' He opened his eyes and smiled at Emily. 'That's progress, at least.'

'Yes. What happened then?'

'Well, that ...' Terry closed his eyes again, rubbing his forehead ferociously with his left hand '... that's still blank, I'm afraid. But there is one thing ... something else there, it's important ...'

'What is?'

'I don't know. It was when you were talking about this man, Tom Weston. He lives there, just past the pub, down a track, and when I was there I was thinking ... I was thinking about him, I must have been, and I knew ... *something*.'

'You don't remember what it was?'

He shook his head, smiling ruefully at Emily.

'No. Sorry. Maybe it'll come.'

'Wow!' Emily's eyes widened in amazement. 'So this man Tom Weston is not only connected to the historical accusations against my father, but also to the murder of his wife – two wives, maybe, if your theory is correct, and here are you too, also suspended because ...'

'Stop ... please!' Terry waved a hand distractedly in her direction, then fumbled in the pockets of his coat. 'Sorry, headache. It always comes after ...' He dragged a packet of pills from his coat, snapped a couple out of the foil, and gulped them down with cold coffee. He was pale, Emily saw, hand shaking slightly.

'Will you be all right?'

'In a minute. Sorry. Just ... talk amongst yourselves.' Terry smiled weakly. 'Joke. It's just my eyes, like a migraine. I know there's only one of you really.'

He closed his eyes again. Emily sat watching and sipping her coffee anxiously for a few minutes, wondering whether to call for help. All around them was the clatter of the cafeteria and the bustle of students and lecturers wandering back and forth. There was a porter at a sort of reception desk, like in a hotel. Should she ask him? She was about to get up when Terry drew a deep breath. 'Better now. Sorry.'

'That's okay. What do the doctors say about it?'

'Bloody quacks. If this doesn't stop soon I'll be looking for another job. Even without all this crap at work with Will Churchill and his chum.' Terry got his feet. 'Look, there's a student bus outside this building, it's free. Maybe we should take that back, if you don't mind.'

Following him to the door, Emily thought: first my father, now him. What is it with middle-aged men?

36. First Day

THE FIRST day of a new trial always made Sarah nervous. Even though she'd done the preparation, there were plenty of things that could go wrong. She'd heard actors say they felt nervous before every performance, and her job was a little like going on stage, with the added anxiety that you only knew part of the script.

In the robing room she put on her white bands and gown, smoothed her hair back, clipped it into a short ponytail, and took her wig out of its tin. It was an old friend now, no longer white and new as it had once been when she was a novice. She settled it carefully on her head, and peered into the mirror to check her make-up – her war-paint, as she liked to call it. Nothing much wrong there – a quick retouch of her lipstick and a scowl: *see, I can look fierce if I want to!* The wig made her look severe – professional, she hoped. And perhaps the face was a little more mature than it had been once – tiny wrinkles around the edges of her eyes and lips, the lines from her nose to the side of her mouth deeper than they used to be. Ah well, so much the better; I want the judge and the jury to take me seriously today. Anyway I'm a grandmother! She wrinkled her nose at the mirror, her hazel eyes sparkling with fun. Grannies are meant to look old!

Not too old, though, if you want to win your lover back. After the trial.

She grinned, blew herself a kiss, and marched smartly downstairs to meet her client.

Adrian, she was pleased to see, had also taken pains with his appearance. His dark suit was a little worn but quite acceptable, and he wore a white shirt and blue tie. His hair was cut brutally short at the sides and long on top, a fashion popular with young footballers today. His face, however, was pale and his manner nervous; in the cramped cell he could hardly sit still.

'What's going to happen? What should I do?'

Sarah sat beside him, her hand on his arm. 'Nothing much is going to happen today; just the opening speech from the prosecution and the first witnesses. All you have to do is answer loud and clear when the clerk asks you how you plead, and then sit quietly and look respectable. Don't fidget or call out, even if you don't like what the other side say. Remember, the jury are watching and trying to make up their minds about you.'

'Yeah, well that's just it. What if they hate me?'

'This is the first time they see you, Adrian; there's no reason why they should hate you. Just try to look what you are, a respectable intelligent young man, who couldn't possibly commit a murder like this. That'll sow the first seeds of doubt in their minds.'

'You believe me then?'

Sarah smiled, as warmly as she could, remembering how mature and *grandmotherly* she'd looked in the mirror. She must seem ancient to this boy. 'We've been through that. You've told me you didn't do it and I accept that. It's not a matter of belief now; it's all about testing the evidence. And that's what we're here to do.'

Upstairs in the courtroom she met her opponent for the first time. Alexander Corder QC was a bluff, grey-haired man in his late sixties, nineteen stone and probably circular like a huge fleshy beachball when he was undressed, Sarah thought wickedly. He grunted genially and hauled himself to his feet as she approached.

'Alex Corder, pleased to meet you. So you're the young lady who's been landed with this defence, are you? Not much hope, I'm afraid.'

'I'm sorry to hear it,' Sarah smiled sympathetically. 'Still, I'm sure you'll try your best.' She was used to the pre-trial jousting. Once she'd felt intimidated by put-downs from senior counsel; now they were just water off a duck's back. She nodded appreciatively at his junior, a slim handsome youth who was introduced as Jasper Grey, and then turned to check that Lucy Parsons was behind her. As she did so she saw Adrian entering the dock from the steps leading up from the cells. A security guard showed him where to sit.

'All stand!' the clerk of the court called out, as the judge, the Honourable Mrs Justice Catherine Eckersley, entered and took her seat beneath the royal coat of arms, the prancing unicorn and lion. It was the first time Sarah had conducted a trial before a female High Court judge. She wondered if it would be an advantage.

While everyone else resumed their seats, the clerk told Adrian to stand.

'Would you give the court your name, please.'

'Ad ... sorry.' He coughed and started again. 'Adrian Norton.'

'Adrian Norton, you are charged that on or about the date of Sunday 28th August, you did murder Victoria Ann Weston, contrary to common law and the Homicide Act 1957. How do you plead: guilty, or not guilty?'

'I, er ... not guilty.'

After the initial stumble the words were loud and clear, just as Sarah had instructed.

'Very well. Sit down.'

The next half hour was taken up with the process of empanelling a jury – a casual business, Sarah thought, compared to the days or even weeks which she had heard the same procedure could take in the United States. Twenty jurors were led into the room and twelve of their names were picked out of a hat. English law required jurors to be selected at random, so neither side could question the prospective jury members. The judge would only exclude them if they turned out to be related to the accused or any member of the court, or if they proved unable or unwilling to take the oath. In theory Alexander Corder had the right to exclude an individual juror if he had been informed they were a threat on the grounds of terrorism or national security, but that clearly did not apply today. The defence had no comparable right to challenge; it had been abolished in 1988.

So seven women and five men were duly empanelled and filed dutifully into the jury box, two rows of six sitting one behind the other.

Alexander Corder hauled himself to his feet, placed his notes on a little lectern he had brought with him, and began his opening address.

'Members of the jury, you have been called upon to perform a most important public duty, perhaps the most important of your lives. We are here today to try a case of murder. In this trial I represent the Crown, so it is my duty to put the case on behalf of her Majesty the Queen. My learned colleague on my right, Mrs Newby, represents the accused, the man in the dock, Adrian Norton. It is your duty to listen carefully to the evidence we will lay before you, and then decide, at the end of the trial, whether Mr Norton is guilty as charged, or not.'

He then proceeded to explain who Victoria Weston was, and describe how the police had first suspected something was wrong when her car, a powder blue Mercedes, had been found abandoned beside the river on 29th August while her husband was away at a conference in Edinburgh, and how her body had been found a week later.

'At first the circumstances led the police to think that she had committed suicide. Her husband told them that she had been unhappy in recent weeks. She was wearing a coat whose pockets had been filled with stones, to make her sink. He received a text from her phone, which appeared to be a suicide note.

'However, further investigation proved this to be an elaborate deception. You will hear evidence from the pathologist, that scientific examination of the water in Dr Weston's lungs contained salt, of a type commonly found in a hot tub or jacuzzi. Clearly this salt could not have come from river water. She must have drowned somewhere else, in a place where such salts are commonly used. And you will hear from forensic scientists that salts with a very similar chemical composition to those found in her lungs were present in the hot tub in her garden at home.

'It therefore became clear that this was murder, and that the murderer had cleverly disguised his wicked crime to make it look like suicide. The police believe that Victoria Weston was drowned in her own hot tub in her garden at home, and then, in the dead of night, was transported in the boot of her own car to the river at Landing Lane. The killer then lifted her body from the car boot, carried or dragged her to the river, and threw her in. He probably then stood there watching her sink under water, which would have happened quickly because he had dressed her in a coat and filled the pockets of that coat with stones.'

Sarah sat quietly a few feet away, listening as Corder outlined his case. He was doing a good job, she thought. He had a slightly high-pitched, squeaky voice, and he paused often for breath, but he told the story well enough. The jury watched with rapt attention.

'A dreadful crime, members of the jury. But who was the killer? How can you be sure that Adrian Norton, the man accused here today, is the murderer? Well, there are a number of reasons, which I will lay before you. Firstly, the forensic evidence. His fingerprints, and his DNA, were found in her car, both on the dashboard, the passenger seat, and on the car boot, where her body was hidden. One of his fingerprints was also found in the gazebo sheltering the hot tub, where the police say she was killed.

'But why would he do such a thing, you may be asking yourselves? What possible reason could he have for such a terrible crime? Well, the answer is very clear. Adrian Norton was a student at the university and his supervisor – his teacher – was Dr Victoria Weston. So he knew her and met with her often. She was a good teacher, all her colleagues say. She cared about her students and her work. He was studying for a doctorate in English literature, and much of the teaching on this sort of course is individual, just the teacher and the student together in a room, discussing books and poetry. All very well, you may think, but in this case it went further than that. Their relationship became sexual as well as educational. They did not just discuss literature, members of the jury, they had sexual intercourse – sometimes in her office, sometimes in her bedroom at home, while her husband was away at work.

'Well, such things happen in life. Sometimes no great harm is done, sometimes it leads to tragedy. This case, it seems, was one of the latter. Things came to a head when Adrian Norton took a summer job in Prague in the Czech Republic. While he was there he met and fell in love with a young Czech woman, Michaela Konvalinka. She came back to England with him and the pair planned to get married. She was pregnant with his child. But this, of course, made Adrian's life more complicated. He was still having sex with his supervisor, but his fiancée knew nothing about this. He decided he would have to do something. But what, exactly? How did this result in Victoria Weston's murder?

'The story Mr Norton told the police was that he visited Victoria Weston's house on Thursday 25 August, while her husband was at work, and had sex with her, as he had done before. But after the sex – this is his story, not mine – he climbed out of bed, and told her flatly that this was the last time. He was engaged to be married, he said; they couldn't do this anymore.

'Not very gentlemanly behaviour, you may think. Naturally, the lady was upset and angry. She shouted at him, and he shouted back. But according to Adrian, that was all that happened. After the argument, he rode away on his bicycle. He didn't kill her, he told the police, she was still alive when he left, and he never saw her again.

'Well, this was on the Thursday. The police believe she was killed, drowned in the hot tub in her garden, on the following Sunday, probably in the evening. So, you will hear, the police asked young Adrian Norton to account for his movements on that Sunday. Where was he, they asked. And this is where the lies start.

'He told them he had an alibi. He was with his girlfriend, this Czech girl, Michaela Konvalinka, the young woman he had promised to marry. They spent all day together, he said – first in York, then at home in his flat. If the police didn't believe him, they could ask his girlfriend, Michaela.

'Well, the police did exactly that, and the young lady confirmed the story. She made a statement saying that they went shopping and visited the *Jorvik Viking Centre* in York that day and spent all evening together in his flat. They went to bed early, she said, it was natural, they were in love.

'Unfortunately, members of the jury, this story turned out to be untrue. You will hear two pieces of evidence which contradict it – in fact they destroy Adrian's alibi completely. The first is from a CCTV camera in the main street in Osbaldwick. The film was recorded at 8.22 on the evening of Sunday 28 August. The camera is less than half a mile from the house where Victoria Weston was murdered. On that video you will see a young man on a bicycle. It is a good quality camera and we say that it is quite clear that this young man is Adrian Norton. We will show you the video so that you see it for yourselves.

'But the second piece of evidence is equally devastating. When this young woman, Michaela Konvalinka, confirmed her fiancé's alibi, she had no idea about his sexual relationship with the murdered woman, Victoria Weston. Adrian hadn't told her; it was his guilty secret. So when the police came calling – we must not be too harsh; remember this is a young woman in love, recently arrived in a strange country where she knows nothing about the police – she decided to lie to protect him. It was wrong, of course, but it is understandable.

'But then the police interviewed her a second time. They showed her the CCTV images, and told her about Adrian's secret sexual relationship with his supervisor. A painful interview for the young lady, no doubt. But as a result of it the truth came out. Adrian hadn't been with her all evening that Sunday, she admitted. He had gone out about 7.30 and hadn't returned until much later, after 11 o'clock, when she was asleep in bed. Which, of course, gave him plenty of time to commit the murder, just as the police say.

'So there you have it, members of the jury. A terrible heartless murder disguised as a suicide. All the evidence points to Adrian Norton as the killer. His fingerprints, his DNA in Victoria's house and car. His motive, an attempt to hide his secret sexual relationship from his fiancée. The lies he told when interviewed by the police. And his alibi, destroyed by the CCTV and the evidence of his own girlfriend, whom he deceived.

'That is the case I shall put before you.'

37. Pathologist

THE FIRST witness for the prosecution was the pathologist, Linda Miles. When she had taken the oath, Alex Corder asked her for her qualifications.

'Certainly. My first degree was a BSc in Neuroscience from Edinburgh University. I also have a Bachelor of Medicine and Surgery and a Diploma in Medical Jurisprudence from the University of Leeds. I have been a registered pathologist since 2008 and became a Fellow of the Royal College of Pathologists in 2012.'

As she recited this impressive list she glanced around the court confidently. She doesn't look an easy nut to crack, Sarah thought gloomily. Why bother?

'I believe you performed an autopsy on the body of Victoria Weston,' Alex Corder said. 'Could you tell the court what you found, please.'

'Yes. I examined the body of a white female, 170 cm tall, slender build, weight 51 kgs. The body had been dead for some time and was considerably bloated by the effects of gases produced by bacteria in the early stages of decomposition. The right eye and part of the lower lip were missing, presumably nibbled away by fish or small aquatic crustacea.'

Hearing a smothered groan, Sarah glanced to her right and saw a female juror bend forward, her hand over her mouth.

'Were you able to ascertain the cause of death, Dr Miles?'

'Yes. It was clear she had drowned. Her lungs were full of a mixture of blood and water.'

'I see. Were there any other signs of injury that might have contributed to her death?'

'Nothing significant that I could find. There were a number of places on her hands and face where the skin had been scratched or torn, but this seemed most likely to have been caused by collisions with tree roots, rocks and other underwater objects in the river where she was found. None were likely to have contributed to her death.'

'Only on her hands and face? Why was that?'

'The rest of her body was clothed. She was wearing a long jacket like a chignon or house coat, tied at the waist with a belt. Under that she wore a blouse, slacks, bra and pants, all from Marks & Spencers.'

'Nothing on her feet?'

'No. No socks either. The skin on both feet was also torn in several places, and her right ankle was bruised.'

'Thank you. Did you find anything in the pockets of this coat?'

'Yes. Both pockets contained stones – large shiny round pebbles. There were six in the right pocket and four in the left; ten altogether. I presume they had been placed there in order to weigh the body down.'

'Can you tell us anything more about these stones?'

'Yes. They looked unusual so I send them to be examined by a geologist. His report established that the stones were made of quartzite, of a type most common in pebble beds which form the beach at Budleigh Salterton, part of the Jurassic Coast in South Devon. They are attractive pebbles typically of a smooth round or oval shape which shows that they once formed part of a prehistoric river, which began in central France and flowed northwards across the Channel, which was land at the time, towards what now is south-western England.'

The judge turned to the witness with an appreciative smile as she absorbed this nugget of geographical information. Alexander Corder nodded.

'Indeed. I have been there myself on holiday. Would you describe these pebbles as ornamental, perhaps?'

'Yes, I think so. They were quite colourful and attractive.'

'Very well. But we must return to your own area of expertise. Were there any other significant facts you noticed about the body which would help to determine how and why she died?'

'Yes. Two points in particular. The fingernails first. They were unusually clean.'

'Why is that significant, doctor?'

'Well, in any case of suspicious death it is normal practice to look beneath the victim's fingernails and in a case like this, of drowning where the body was found in a river, I would expect to find traces of mud, small sticks and leaves and so on, detritus which came from the river. Especially if the person has drowned by accident, and been clutching at tree roots, the riverbank, grass, whatever, in a desperate attempt to survive. But I found very little of such detritus here. Just a few scraps, that's all.'

'What did you deduce from that?'

'Well, it made me wonder if Victoria Weston was either already dead, or at least unconscious when she entered the water. In which case her hands would have just drifted, not clutched at anything.'

'I see. And did you find anything else which supported that hypothesis?'

'Yes indeed. One very important thing.'

Here we go, Sarah thought, sitting at her table in the well of the court, watching the witness attentively. The first key point in the trial. *Cast doubt on this, and young Adrian is a step nearer freedom.*

But the pathologist was in full flow, looking supremely confident.

'As I said, the victim had drowned, a fact which I was able to confirm by opening up the chest cavity to examine her lungs. But when I did so, I noticed several things which appeared to be unusual. Or perhaps I should say, not entirely consistent with what one would expect from someone who had drowned in the river Ouse, where her body was found.'

'What were these differences?'

'Well, when I made my first incision into the lungs, I was surprised by the copious amounts of bloody fluid which flooded out.'

'Isn't that what you would expect?'

'Not such large amounts, no. I would have expected less fluid, a whitish froth perhaps.'

'I see. And did you notice anything else unusual?'

'Yes. When I lifted out the lungs to weigh them they were unusually heavy, for a woman of her size and condition. And they felt slippery, jelly-like in my hands, when I would have expected a more doughy consistency.'

Sarah, listening intently, glanced up from her notes to see how the woman in the front row of the jury box was taking this information. There were no more groans, but her face, like that of several other jurors, was pale, set in a grimace of mingled disgust and fascination. If there was a sofa here that woman would be hiding behind it, she thought wryly.

'I see. And what else did you notice about the lungs?'

'The lining. It was a pinkish colour. Normally, the lungs of a person who has drowned in a river, particularly one who had apparently been submerged for over a week as I believe was the case here, would be grey.'

'So, Dr Miles, what did you conclude from these observations?'

'Well, as I say, it seemed strange to me, so I made some further tests. Firstly, I made a chemical analysis of the liquid which I found in the lungs. To my surprise it contained quite high levels of potassium, which is a substance normally found in the blood, but not in river water. After that I tested the victim's blood, and found a surprisingly high count of red blood cells.'

'Could you explain the significance of all those observations – in simple terms for the court to understand, if that is possible.'

'I'll try.' Linda Miles turned to face the jury, an encouraging smile on her face, like a motherly school teacher. 'The key point is that there is a difference between fresh water and salt water, as everyone knows, if they've been to the sea. It's a vital difference; the cells of our bodies can easily absorb fresh water, but not salt water. So if a person's lungs are filled with fresh water, that water quickly passes through the lining of the lungs to enter the bloodstream, where it causes your red blood cells to swell and burst, so they can't supply oxygen to your brain and heart. As these cells burst they release significant amounts of potassium into the bloodstream.

'But if a person's lungs are filled with salt water, the opposite happens. Instead of the water passing through the lining of the lungs into the bloodstream, it draws the blood out of the veins and into your lungs. So your lungs fill up with a mixture of blood and water, and you basically drown in your own fluids.

'This is what appeared to have happened to Victoria Weston. When I opened her lungs I was surprised by the copious amounts of bloody fluid which flooded out, more than I expected. If she'd been drowned in the river, I would have expected less fluid, because a lot of the water would have been absorbed into her bloodstream. And the consistency of the lungs would have been different; the reason the lungs felt slippery and jelly-like was because the alveoli, the cells which form the lining of the lungs, had been altered and made slimy by the salts in the water. The pinkish colour of the lungs was also significant; the lining had been stained by the plasma being drawn through it, out of the bloodstream into the lungs.

'All of these observations led me to suspect that even though the body had been found in the river, it was not the river water which had killed her. She must have been drowned elsewhere, either in the sea, or in a pool or bath of some kind full of salty water.'

Sarah, who had known this was coming, looked to her right to see what effect this key piece of evidence was having on the jury. Several raised their eyebrows or gazed at the witness, their eyes wide with astonishment. One elderly gentleman in the back row even let his jaw drop open for a second, closing his mouth quickly when he saw Sarah watching. Three others, heads down, were scribbling furiously on notepads. It's going to be hard to challenge this, she thought gloomily.

'I have a few more questions, Dr Miles,' Alex Corder continued. 'Could you explain the significance of the analysis you performed on this fluid you found in the victim's lungs?'

'Yes, certainly. I found quite high levels of potassium, sodium chloride, and magnesium, much higher than I would have expected to find in fresh water. I took several samples from the river Ouse, near where the body was found, and analysed them to make comparisons. In each case, the chemical level found in the sample from the lungs was much higher than that found in the river.'

'And did you then make other comparisons?'

'I did. A week later, the police brought me a sample of water from a hot tub they had found in Mrs Weston's garden, together with a container of Dead Sea Salt which had been used to salinate the water. When I analysed that I found traces of all three minerals. The levels were not identical but were broadly similar to the levels found in Mrs Weston's lungs.'

'And from that, what do you conclude?'

'That it is entirely possible that she was drowned in the hot tub where this sample came from.'

'Thank you, Dr Miles. Please wait there, in case Mrs Newby has any questions.' Lowering his bulky body into his seat, Alex Corder emitted a sigh like a punctured balloon, and beamed genially at Sarah, as if to say 'There you are young woman. See what you can do about that.'

38. Hypertonic Millimoles?

SARAH NEWBY had passed many exams but she hadn't studied biology since GCSE. Over the past week she had been frantically researching the pathology of drowning, a subject totally new to her. But as a barrister she was used to mastering briefs quickly, using her mind like a scalpel to cut through irrelevant detail to what really mattered.

As she got her feet to cross-examine a highly qualified pathologist, she felt a physical reaction which was not new to her at all. A horde of butterflies were fluttering in her stomach, their wing-beats sending waves of nervous energy thrilling through all her veins. She was nervous, as she always was at important moments in court; and she had learned long ago to live with those butterflies and love them, as if the tremors in her body sent nectar to her brain.

'Good morning, Dr Miles.' She respected this pathologist and had no intention of antagonising her; if she got into a detailed medical argument she would be certain to lose. Nonetheless, if she could weaken this plank in the prosecution's case, it would go a long way towards sowing reasonable doubts in the jurors' minds. And that was what she was here for.

'Good morning.' Linda Miles smiled pleasantly back.

'Your conclusion, you told my learned colleague just now, is that it is entirely possible that Victoria Weston was drowned in the hot tub where this sample came from.'

'That's right, yes.'

'*Entirely possible* is not the same as *certain*. That means there is an element of doubt about this finding, does it?'

The pathologist thought carefully before answering. 'I am a scientist, I go by the evidence. Having examined that evidence, I think it is highly *unlikely* that Victoria Weston was drowned in the river where she was found, and highly *likely* that she was drowned in a bath of salty water.'

'Highly likely, you say. But not 100% certain?'

'I would say ... 95%, 98% certain, maybe.'

That's too high, Sarah thought. *Silly question, I walked into that.* 'But as a scientist, you admit there's a small element of doubt?'

'A very small element, yes.'

'Very well. This bloody fluid which you found in the drowned woman's lungs. Copious amounts, you said. If her body was moved after death, as the prosecution suggest, would you expect some of it to leak out from her mouth and nose?'

'Quite possibly, yes. If she was moved some of it would almost certainly leak out.'

'I see. So if the body was lifted into a car boot – a difficult, awkward task – you would expect to find traces of that fluid there?'

'I would, yes.'

'Quite noticeable amounts of it?'

'Probably, yes.'

'So would it surprise you, Dr Miles, to hear that almost no traces of a similar fluid were found in the boot of Dr Weston's car? Only a tiny stain, scarcely visible to the naked eye?'

The pathologist shrugged. 'I only examined the body, not the car.'

'Nonetheless it would surprise you, to learn that no more fluid was found?'

'It ... does surprise me a little. But there may be an explanation that I am unaware of. You would have to ask the forensic scientist.'

'Indeed I will.' Sarah smiled. *So far so good.* 'What about the water in the hot tub? You were sent a sample of it, I believe. Did you find any traces of blood in that sample?'

'No.'

'*No*? I see.' Sarah raised a quizzical eyebrow. 'Didn't that surprise you too? Given that the prosecution allege that Dr Weston was drowned in the hot tub, wouldn't you have expected some of her blood – these copious amounts of bloody fluid which you mention – to have leaked out into the water where she was drowned?'

'Possibly ...' Dr Miles thought for a moment, frowning. 'But that would depend on a number of factors. How long she was in the water, for one thing. If the body was removed quickly after death there would be less chance of contamination – leakage – to occur. And anyway, if this tub is as large as I suppose it is, small amounts of blood would become extremely dilute, very hard to detect.'

'But it would be possible to detect traces of such blood in the water, would it? If it was there?'

'Possible, but difficult, for the reasons I've given. If the body was left there for a considerable time, that would be different.'

'So on a level of 1 to 10, how surprised are you that no such traces were found anywhere in the water from the hot tub? Just as you found no blood in the sample you were sent?'

Linda Miles smiled, amused by the simplistic question. 'Level one or two, perhaps. It's not very surprising, given the different factors involved. You'd be better off asking the forensic scientist.'

'I will, Dr Miles.' Sarah smiled gratefully, and took a sip of water. 'All right, let's move on to some of the other details of your findings, shall we? You described a number of minor injuries on the body – to her hands, feet and face, I believe?'

'Yes, there were a number of abrasions in these areas which were probably caused by collisions with underwater objects. And her right eye and lower lip had been eaten.'

'Anything else of that nature?'

'No. Not that I observed.'

'What was her skin like?'

'It was pale, swollen in places by the internal action of bacteria during decomposition. Puffy and wrinkled by prolonged immersion in water. Covered by algae in several places.'

'And her hair?'

'That also had algae growing on it. There were small sticks, leaves and other underwater debris entangled in it.'

'Did you find any cuts, bruises, or other injuries not attributable to prolonged immersion in the river?'

'After such a time in the water it's hard to be certain. There was diffuse haemorrhaging all over the scalp, which I attributed to lividity – the way blood collects in certain places when it is no longer being circulated by the heart – and subsequent putrefaction. This could have masked any earlier cuts or bruising which may originally have been there; certainly I could not detect any.'

'You understand why I am asking, I hope, doctor? If, as you allege, this poor lady was murdered, that would take some force, wouldn't it? Her head would have been held underwater against her will, for four or five minutes. There would have been a struggle as she fought for her life. You would expect a few bruises, grip marks perhaps, where she had been held down. Yet you say you found none?'

'As I say, any such injuries could have been masked by lividity and subsequent putrefaction. To say nothing of the puffiness of the skin caused by prolonged immersion in water, and the algae which had begun to grow on her skin.'

'Did you find any injuries on the arms or legs?'

'None that I could see, no. But they would have been covered by clothing in the river.'

'Her skeleton was intact? No broken bones?'

'Yes.'

'Did that surprise you, doctor?'

'Not really, no. Why should it?'

'Well, if, as the prosecution allege, this lady did not commit suicide but was drowned at home in her own hot tub, then the murderer somehow had to lift this dead woman out of the hot tub, dress her – a difficult, awkward task with a dead person – then drag or carry her from the hot tub to the boot of her car, lift her in and close the boot without trapping any of her fingers or toes in the lid. Then, having driven the car to the riverbank, he would have to go through the whole process in reverse – lift or drag her inert, heavy body out of the car, carry her to the riverbank, and throw her in. Quite a challenging task, wouldn't you think? She would have been, quite literally, a dead weight. Floppy, uncooperative, hard to move.'

The judge leaned forward from her throne. 'Is this a question, Mrs Newby? It's beginning to sound like a speech.'

'I'm sorry, My Lady, I was just setting the scene. My question is: do you agree that is quite likely, in that sequence of events, that she would have sustained a number of minor injuries? Bruises perhaps, a broken bone caused by rough handling?'

'I see what you mean.' The pathologist smiled, rather patronisingly, Sarah thought. 'But such bruises would not have shown up. Once a person is dead, the blood ceases to flow, so even if you bang a dead person's arm hard against a door, for example, the bruise wouldn't come out. As for broken bones, the dead body – assuming that rigor mortis hadn't yet set in – would have been completely relaxed, which makes such injuries less likely. Anyway, I found none.'

'So you found no injuries at all to this woman, other than the fact she was drowned. Is that right?'

'Put simply, yes, that's right.'

'Very well. I put it to you, doctor, that there could be a very simple reason why you found no such injuries. Which is that she was not murdered at all. She simply walked into the river of her own free will, wearing a coat full of stones to help her sink, and let herself drown.'

'Well, yes, but ...' The pathologist looked surprised and shocked. 'I've already explained why that cannot be true. The symptoms of salt water drowning.'

'To be precise, doctor, you said it was *highly likely* that she was drowned in salt water. You did admit a small element of doubt.'

'A very small element, yes. But the symptoms ...'

'Forgive me, I'll come to the symptoms in a moment. But first, please answer this question. Do you agree that apart from the symptoms you found in her lungs, you found no other evidence to suggest that that this woman did not commit suicide. No other evidence whatsoever.'

'She had clean fingernails,' Dr Miles said. 'That was unusual.'

Damn, Sarah thought. *I forgot that.* Thinking quickly, she said: 'Would those fingernails, *on their own*, be sufficient to make you think this was not suicide?'

'On their own, probably not. They raised a question, that's all.'

'All right. So if today you found a body identical to this, but with no symptoms of salt water drowning, suicide would be a possible conclusion?'

The pathologist shrugged. 'In that hypothetical situation, yes.'

'Thank you, doctor.' *That's as far I can go with that argument,* Sarah thought, looking down at her notes. *Now for the really difficult part.* She looked up, attempting a confident, friendly, totally insincere smile. 'I'd like to move on, if we may, to the subject of potassium.'

'Very well. What would you like to know?' The smile that met hers expressed considerably more professional confidence, and rather less friendliness.

'Potassium is found in all human blood, is that right?'

'Yes.'

'Both in the red blood cells and in the blood plasma – the liquid in which the red cells float?'

'Yes.'

'Very well. Now you told us that when a person drowns in fresh water, the fresh water, which is hypotonic, passes easily through the alveolar layer in the lining of the lungs and into the bloodstream. Is that correct?'

'Yes. Whereas if a person drowns in salt water, which is hypertonic to humans, this does not happen.'

'Quite.' These two infuriatingly similar words – **hypo**tonic and **hyper**tonic – had been buzzing around in Sarah's brain all night, as she tried to get the difference clear to avoid making a fool of herself on the day. She hoped, however, that her use of them might simultaneously impress and confuse some jurors, thus helping to sow doubt.

'So if I understand this correctly, doctor, it is freshwater drowning, not saltwater drowning, which increases the amount of potassium in the blood. Is that correct?'

'It is, yes.'

'This happens because the water causes the red blood cells to burst, releasing further potassium into the blood plasma?'

'Yes.'

'What would you say is the normal level of potassium in the blood plasma of a healthy adult?'

'Somewhere between 3 and 5 millimoles per litre, I think.'

'Yet you found much higher levels of potassium – 7 millimoles per litre – in Victoria Weston's blood. Doesn't that suggest she was drowned in fresh water, not salt?'

Dr Miles drew a deep breath, controlling her impatience with difficulty. 'If you look at page 7, you will see that I measured exceptionally high levels of potassium not just in her blood, but in the fluid from her lungs. It was chiefly the potassium in the lung fluid which convinced me that she drowned in water which contained more dissolved salts than fresh river water. That, and the physical condition of the lungs. Because salt water, being hypertonic as I described earlier, draws blood from the body into the lungs, filling them with bloody fluid and making them slippery and jelly-like. That is what I observed here.'

Sarah glanced surreptitiously at the jury, seeing a number of glazed expressions. That didn't matter too much; all she was trying to do was cause uncertainty and doubt.

'So why did the potassium in the blood remain so high, if it was leaking into the lungs as you say? This shouldn't happen, should it – if she was drowned in salt water?'

The pathologist sighed. 'It is ... not quite as simple as that; these things rarely are. You have to remember that the water in the hot tub had been salinized with Dead Sea Salt, which itself contains a high level of potassium. So some of the potassium in the lungs – and possibly the blood – may have come from there. And Dead Sea Salt contains a relatively low concentration of other salts, such as sodium chloride. The salinity level of the water from the hot tub was about 3%, which made it brackish, like the water from a river estuary. More salty than fresh water, but much less salty than sea water. It is that which makes this diagnosis so difficult and the symptoms less clear.'

'Less clear. Thank you, doctor. So the symptoms of salt water drowning you observed were much less clear, less certain than if Dr Weston had drowned in the sea. Is that right?'

'Yes. But they were also significantly different from those I would expect to find in someone who had drowned in fresh water, like the river Ouse.'

'And that is why you accept some uncertainty?'

'A very small level, yes.'

Stop now, Sarah told herself firmly. *The best you can hope for here is a score draw. I'll never win this argument, but I may have awakened a few doubts.*

'So Dr Miles, to sum up. Your conclusion that she was not drowned in the river is based solely on a diagnosis which you have just described as *difficult* and *less clear.*'

'I think it's clear enough,' Linda Miles insisted irritably. 'Difficult, but not impossible.'

'Yet no trace of blood from her lungs was found in the sample of water from the hot tub?'

'No.'

'And you found no evidence whatsoever to suggest that Vicky Weston had been involved in a violent struggle, forcibly held under water or dragged from one place to another.'

'Yes, that's true.'

'Thank you, Dr Miles. That's all I have.' Sarah closed her pad of questions, and sat down. She glanced at the jury on her right, wondering if she had done enough to cast doubt in their minds, or simply confused them thoroughly.

39. Secrets and Lies

'SO IF we're really lucky, the jury may decide this is a suicide after all,' Sarah said. 'In which case you're clearly not guilty.'

'Legally perhaps, but not morally,' said Adrian gloomily.

Sarah gazed at him in surprise. Her cross-examination of the pathologist had gone moderately well, she thought. She was still pumped up with the rush of adrenalin from today's events in court. It was a familiar, addictive sensation – these were the challenges she lived for. After she sat down, Alexander Corder had lumbered to his feet, trying to restore the impression of scientific certainty which she had chipped away at; but Sarah hoped some damage had been done.

Both the judge and the pathologist had been annoyed, she knew, but that didn't matter; her duty was solely to her client.

To her disappointment, he seemed unimpressed. He sat slumped in the cell below court, waiting to be transported back to prison in Hull. His tie was loosened, his hair rumpled, the expression on his pale face miserable.

'What do you mean, Adrian?' she asked. 'How could you be morally guilty?'

'If she did kill herself, it was my fault for letting her down. That's what I told the copper months ago, when he first came to see me. I dumped her and she did it.'

'Adrian, you mustn't think that.' Sarah sighed, more exasperated than sympathetic. She'd never found it easy to warm to this client. Did this vain youth – a boy really rather than a man – really think a mature woman, a doctor of philosophy, a university lecturer – would kill herself out of unrequited love for him? She might have enjoyed taking him to bed, but more as a toyboy surely, than a serious lover. He wasn't even that handsome really – especially not now, after all this time on remand. His skin had that dough-like prison pallor that came of months without sunlight, and his hair was more ragged than it had been this morning. But it was his eyes that really troubled her – alternately blank and staring, unfocussed. She had commissioned a psychiatric report to open the possibility of a plea of manslaughter via diminished responsibility, but it had not been helpful. Yes, the psychiatrist had agreed, he was clinically depressed, but that was a *result* of the situation he found himself in – locked up for months on end with young thugs and tearaways, with a possible life sentence ahead of him. He showed symptoms of paranoia too, but the world really was out to get him. There was no evidence that he had been depressed or paranoid *before* Vicky Weston died, or that either condition had somehow *caused* her death.

'Look,' Sarah said. 'All I'm trying to do is convince the jury that we don't know what happened to her. If you didn't kill her, then you don't know either. If she did commit suicide, it probably isn't your fault.'

'I should have told someone. Listened. Tried to find out.'

'I don't understand. Told someone what?' There were noises outside in the corridor; cell doors opening and closing, loud cheerful laughter. The prison van must have arrived to take him away.

'I don't know, do I?' he said enigmatically. 'She just hinted once, that's all.'

Sarah looked at Lucy, puzzled. Was this another of those delusions, part of the paranoia which the psychiatrist had diagnosed? Despite the trick cyclist's unhelpful report, Sarah wondered if Adrian had ever enjoyed robust mental health. Adrian had often seemed awkward, self-pitying, confused; in their interviews it had often been difficult to get him to focus.

'You're talking about Vicky, right? What did she hint at, Adrian?'

'I don't know. Something about her husband. She'd suspected it for years, she said. Then she clammed up.'

'Did he beat her, perhaps? Abuse her in some way?'

Adrian looked up, bleakly. 'Could be. Who knows? I never saw any bruises. Though I had a good look, mind. Everywhere.' His grin met no answering smile from his lawyers. 'Sorry, that was tasteless. She was fit, though. Strong enough to fight back. I don't think she meant he beat her, no.'

'What then?' The voices in the corridor outside sounded closer.

'If I knew I'd have told you. I did mention it once to the police but they weren't interested. Not after, you know – Michaela.'

Michaela, exactly, Sarah thought. Adrian's former fiancée was due to give evidence in a couple of days. She would be Sarah's next big challenge. Everything would depend on how the girl came across in court. If the jury believed both her and the pathologist, Adrian was doomed. Unless they found some other evidence that no one was aware of.

'Adrian, if Vicky told you something that might be significant, I need to know about it. When did this happen?'

'On that last day. When I went there to, you know, break up with her.'

'Time, ladies and gents please. Your taxi is waiting, young man. Free, gratis and paid for by Her Majesty the Queen.' The cell door opened to reveal a burly prison guard, grinning cheerfully and dangling a pair of handcuffs. 'So if you'll excuse us, ladies. We'd like to miss the rush hour if we can.'

As Adrian was cuffed and led from the cell, Sarah said urgently: 'If you do remember any more of what she said, just write it down, Adrian, will you? It could be important, you never know.'

When Adrian had been led away, Sarah and Lucy made their way upstairs and out into the daylight. It was a grey, windy afternoon; York's medieval castle, Clifford's Tower, stood out bleakly in the twilight. The two lawyers, one dark and slender, one genial and plump, stood together on the wide stone balustrade outside the court. High on the roof above them, the blindfold statue of Justice sailed unseeing through the darkening sky.

'So, what do you think?' Lucy asked, as the prison van drove away below them, carrying their client back to HMP Hull behind its tiny darkened windows. 'Will he come up with anything useful?'

'I doubt it,' said Sarah, shivering in the thin cotton of her gown. 'New day, new story. He seems to have a new memory every hour, that lad. Damn that psychiatrist! Couldn't he recognise a boy with mental health problems when he saw one?'

She turned left, striding briskly towards her chambers in Tower Street.

* * *

Terry Bateson hadn't visited the city library for years, and he was surprised how warm and welcoming it was. Brightly displayed books at every turn, helpful assistants ready to renew his York Card, and a busy reference library upstairs. This must be what it's like being a pensioner, he thought, emerging with a bag of books into the evening rush hour. Well, that could be my future, if the medics won't sign me back on. Or if Churchill and Starkey get their way.

He turned right, towards the bus station across the river. His ribs were healing and his energy was returning, but he didn't like driving with his arm in plaster, so he had caught a bus.

As he crossed Lendal Bridge, the northernmost of York's three great Victorian bridges, a cold wind blew in his face. The river below was full, surging dark and brown through the arches, small wavelets lapping against the stone-built embankments. A seagull swooped overhead, probably driven inland by a storm on the North Sea. Crowds of shoppers and commuters, hunched into their winter coats and hoods, hurried past him to some warmer destination.

'Mr Bateson, hi!'

A tall young woman, in jeans, trainers and an army surplus anorak, stood grinning before him, frizzy hair blowing in the breeze. 'Oh, Emily. Hello.'

'What are you doing here?'

Terry held up his plastic bag sheepishly. 'I've been to the library. New experience for me.'

'Really? I've been in one too. With Dad, in Harrogate.'

'Ah. How is your father?'

Emily grimaced. 'Well ... could be better. He hates being suspended.'

'Tell me about it. He should take up reading.'

'He has. Loads of books. Time for a coffee?'

'Well, I ... ok, why not?'

A few minutes later, in Starbucks, Terry found himself listening with fascination and concern to Emily's recital of the latest details in her father's battle to prove his innocence.

'We found out a bit more about his second accuser, Eleanor Wisbech. She lives in Bournemouth now, apparently, on the south coast. And she has a history of mental health problems. That might help, don't you think?'

'Why?' Terry sipped his latte, studying her flushed, enthusiastic young face.

'Well, obviously, if she's a nutter, that should help, shouldn't it? She probably made it up. Or got it all wrong. She's just mad!'

'You can't say *mad* and *nutter*, Emily,' Terry teased. 'It's not politically correct. Or kind.'

'Well, mentally ill, then.' Emily grinned. 'I don't care. If she's saying my dad raped her she must be clinically bonkers.'

'Is she still receiving treatment?'

'Don't think so, no. This was several years ago. She was in the nuthouse – mental hospital, sorry – for depression and anxiety disorders, apparently.'

'Poor woman. How did you find this out?'

'Internet.' Emily touched the side of her nose significantly. In a fake German accent she said: 'I haff my vays.'

'There are laws about data protection, you know. You can't just hack into someone's medical records and use it against them.'

'I know,' Emily sighed. 'That's what dad's solicitor said too. She was quite cross.'

'Yes, well, she has a point. You don't want to get yourself arrested too.'

'No, but it's so unfair! I mean ...' Emily's eyes widened suddenly. 'You're not saying *you* would arrest me, are you?'

'Of course not. I'm suspended, remember?' Terry smiled ruefully. 'Off duty for the foreseeable future.'

'Well, good ...'

'It is most definitely *not* good, young lady!' Terry spluttered indignantly. 'It's a fucking insult!'

'Mr Bateson, language, please!' Emily held up a finger primly. 'Ladies present!'

Terry burst out laughing. His anger dissolved in a second. This scruffy young student was hardly a lady in the traditional sense of the word, but she was certainly fun to talk to. Was she flirting with him? Hardly. But no one else teased him like this – except Jessica and Esther, of course. That's what this was like – a sort of father daughter relationship, with someone he wasn't actually related to.

'My humble apologies,' he said. 'And no, I can't arrest you while I'm suspended, so I guess it's good in that way. All the same, Emily, you should be careful. You can't just go snooping around people's private details without permission.'

'Isn't that what detectives do?'

'Well yes, but we need a warrant. Anyway,' he went on in a serious tone. 'If this woman does have a history of mental illness, it might work against you, don't you see? She could claim that what your father did to her as a schoolgirl ...'

'Which he didn't!'

' ... unsettled her mind, you see? The abuse – ok, *alleged* abuse – could have caused her mental breakdown.'

Emily groaned, tapping her fist softly on the table. 'I know, I've thought of that already. But it could be the other way too, couldn't it? She lied because she's a ... delusional person. She's been in contact with the other woman, too.'

'How do you know that?'

A sly grin crossed Emily's face. 'There's a private Facebook page, for old school friends. I just joined it.'

'You what?'

Emily's grin broadened. 'You're suspended, aren't you? You just said so. Well, I got hold of a list of Dad's old students, and er ... impersonated one.'

'Now that,' Terry said with admiration, 'is both clever *and* illegal. What did you find out?'

'Well, there's a lot of chat about stuff that's no use, of course. How many kids they've had, what sort of jobs they do, who's married and divorced and who isn't; but then there's other stuff – who had a crush on whom, what were the teachers like, who got expelled for shagging the gardener, and there it is!'

'What? The gardener?'

'No. The accusations against Dad. The first woman, Clare Fanshawe, she brought it up, and she writes directly to Eleanor Wisbech, who says yes, it's true.'

'That's not good.'

'Ah, but wait. There are others in the group who disagree. Quite violently, in fact. They use all sorts of words that would shock you, Mr Bateson, like *slag, whore, bitch, tart, bike...*' Emily deliberately raised her voice so that the two middle-aged women and the young couple sitting at the nearest adjoining tables lifted their heads in surprise. '... and quite a few posts have been deleted. Some people have left the group altogether. They're the ones, unfortunately, who seem to disagree. I'm trying to get in touch with them.'

'Any luck so far?'

'Not yet, but I'm still trying. The main one I want to talk to, though, is this Clare Fanshawe. If I could prove that she's lying, somehow ...'

'How are you going to do that?'

'I wish I knew.' Emily sipped her coffee thoughtfully. 'It's so difficult, doing all this. Interesting, though. More fun than writing essays on the environment.'

'You don't enjoy your studies?'

Emily shrugged. 'It's okay. The more I learn, the more depressing it gets. I think humanity is doomed.'

'Don't say that. You're still young.'

'I know.'

'So what are you going to do when you graduate? You could become a detective, maybe?'

'Join the police? Too much discipline for me. I'd like a job where I could be my own boss, set my own hours. None of this nine to five stuff.'

'Detective work isn't all nine to five.'

'No, but you have to wear a uniform first, don't you? Obey orders. I wouldn't like that.'

'What about being a journalist, then? They seem to get a lot of free time. Detective work without the responsibilities.'

'Hm.' Emily nibbled the biscuit which came with the coffee. As she did so, her eyes lit up. 'Maybe. Thanks. Now that *is* an idea...'

40. Blood and Salt

As THE jurors filed into court next morning, Sarah watched them curiously, wondering how many doubts her cross-examination of the pathologist had raised in their minds. The signs were not encouraging. Few of them looked her way and none of them smiled. Their response to the judge, who welcomed them politely, and Alex Corder, who rose to his feet to call the next witness, was very different. Several smiled and nodded back as though greeting old friends, and one or two produced notebooks and pens, as though preparing for a useful, interesting lecture.

Did they do that yesterday? Sarah wondered. She didn't remember it. But then she had been so keyed up, firstly to listen carefully to the pathologist's evidence and then to challenge it, that she had scarcely looked at the jury.

The fact remained, however, that today they were not looking at her. That's what comes of trying to cast doubt on a scientist, she thought. To suggest this isn't murder is like denying global warming.

Oh well. She didn't entirely believe it herself.

Alex Corder's re-examination of Linda Miles had, he hoped, demolished Sarah's challenge and persuaded the jury of the principal fact in the case: that Vicky Weston had not committed suicide but been murdered, drowned in the salt water of her own hot tub. To demonstrate exactly how that had happened, he called a forensic scientist, Adam Parry. Dr Parry presented the evidence collected by the two SOCO teams which had examined Vicky Weston's house and car.

Adrian's fingerprints, he said, were everywhere – in the victim's bedroom, kitchen, living room, and bathroom. The most significant was a single thumb print on one of the pillars supporting the gazebo over the hot tub. Alex Corder spent several questions on this, using a printed diagram in the evidence bundle to show the jury exactly where it had been found.

'This is from the left thumb, Dr Parry, is it?'

'Yes.'

'About four feet from the ground. What does that suggest to you?'

'That the defendant, Adrian Norton, was standing inside the gazebo, facing the hot tub, grasping the pillar with his left hand.'

'So a person standing in that position, two feet from the tub, would in fact be looking directly down at anyone who happened to be inside it, would they?'

'Yes, most probably.'

'And this is a very clear, detailed thumbprint, you said. Showing pretty much every line and whorl of the defendant's thumb?'

'Yes, it's an excellent example. We don't often get prints as detailed as that.'

'So the defendant would have had to have been holding the post pretty firmly, would he?'

'It might suggest that, yes.'

Instead of objecting to these leading questions Sarah let out an audible sigh, just loud enough for Alex Corder to glance sideways at her before moving on. Over the years she had picked up a repertoire of these tricks, most of which senior barristers had tried on her.

Corder waved a hand irritably, as though swishing away a fly. 'Now, Dr Parry, did you examine the water in the hot tub?'

'We did, yes.' The scientist explained in some detail the different minerals and salts found in the water, which were consistent with Dead Sea Salts.

'Did you find any traces of blood in that water?'

'We did not, no.'

'Very well.' Corder glanced sideways at Sarah, an amused twinkle in his eyes. 'I fear that my learned friend may wish to make much of this point, so to speed things up a little, do you have any explanation for why you found no such traces?'

'Well ...' The faint, conspiratorial smile on Dr Parry's face suggested that he had been forewarned of this question. 'For two reasons, really. Firstly, when she was drowned, the water went into her body rather than out of it, so if the body was then removed quickly, only the very smallest, almost undetectable traces of bloody fluid would have leaked out into the water. If the body had been left there for longer, perhaps ... but unfortunately, in any case, we understood from the husband, Mr Weston, that the tub had been drained and refilled in the week before we examined it. So ...'

'The water you examined was probably not that in which the victim had been drowned?'

'Exactly.'

Corder glanced again to Sarah, a smug grin on his face. *Checkmate – end of that line of enquiry*, his look seemed to say. Sarah, however, wasn't so sure. She was scribbling urgently on a notepad. *Why drain it then?* she wrote. *Did he know? Adrian couldn't do it, surely – no time. Then who?*

Corder, disappointed by her reaction, moved on to the car, which was more promising, from his point of view. Here too Dr Parry had found Adrian's fingerprints, on the dashboard, the passenger seat, and a very clear handprint on the car boot, about a foot to the right of the handle. Further detailed examination of the car had found a small pinkish stain on the damp carpet inside the car boot.

'Were you able to examine this stain?' Corder asked.

'Yes. The pinkish stain was caused by a mixture of blood and water. DNA analysis of the blood showed a clear match with the deceased, Victoria Weston. Further analysis of the stain showed a relatively high presence of salts, particularly potassium.'

'What did you deduce from that?'

'The salts were entirely consistent with the container of Dead Sea salts which was found in the garden room near the hot tub, and which we believe was used to salinate it. And the blood in this stain seemed likely to have come from fluid leaking from the victim's lungs, after she had drowned.'

This, Sarah knew, was a potentially devastating blow to her stubborn suggestion that this was suicide. If she was unable to cast doubt upon it, that first strand of Adrian's defence would collapse.

'Did you find traces of blood anywhere else on this carpet?'

'I did, yes. I found ten fibres from a blue bath towel, three of which were stained with a mixture of salty fluid and Victoria Weston's blood.'

'What do you conclude from that?'

'It is possible that this blue towel was between the body and the carpet, and absorbed some of the fluids leaking from the body.'

'But you never saw this towel?'

'No. I asked the police but they hadn't found it. They suggested that the murderer must have seen that it was stained and removed it.'

'I see. So to be quite clear, Dr Parry, what you are saying is that the most likely way this carpet stain could have occurred, was that after Mrs Weston had been drowned, her body was placed in the boot of her own car, possibly on top of a blue bath towel. Is that right?'

'Yes, precisely.'

'An act which must have been performed by the killer, clearly. So let return to the handprint on the outside of the car boot, Dr Parry. A very clear handprint, I understand, showing four fingers and the thumb, all belonging to Adrian Norton.'

'That's right, yes.'

'If you look at the diagram of where this handprint was found – page 73 in the bundle, members of the jury – what does the position of those prints suggest to you?'

'That the defendant rested his hand quite firmly on the car boot.'

'Yes, thank you.' This was not quite the answer Alex Corder was hoping for, so he tried again. 'What I'm wondering is, could those prints have been caused by the defendant pushing down on the car boot, in order to close it? After, perhaps, putting something inside the boot?'

'They could have been caused by that, yes, certainly.'

'Thank you, Dr Parry. Wait there, please. In case my learned colleague has some questions.' Alex Corder lowered himself into his seat, beaming smugly at Sarah as he did so.

Sarah stood up smartly, resting a pad of questions on the lectern in front of her. *If you're in trouble, look as confident as you can.* 'Is that the only way those prints could have been caused, Dr Parry?'

'Well no, I didn't say that. It's one way, that's all.'

'So these prints could simply have been caused by the defendant leaning on the car, for example; or just touching it as he walked by?'

'Possibly, yes. I can't say for certain how they were caused. Just that they were there.'

'And you can't say *when* they were made either, can you?'

'No, that's not possible.'

'So they could have been made a day before you saw them, a week before, or six months earlier, couldn't they?'

'In theory, yes. But the car looked quite clean, so I would imagine it was washed regularly.'

Wrong answer. Sarah winced. 'All right. Let's turn to the other fingerprints, shall we? The ones you found inside the car. See the diagram on page 71.' She waited while the jury flicked through the pages of their bundles, causing a rustle in the still air of the court room. 'You found three partial prints on the dashboard and one on the passenger seat near the headrest. And several on a book of poetry which was found inside the glove compartment. Is that right?'

'Yes.'

'All of the partial prints on the dashboard are near the glove compartment, on the passenger side, where the book was found. What does that suggest to you, Dr Parry?'

Dr Parry shrugged. 'That Mr Norton was a passenger in the car. And read this book.'

'Quite.' Sarah smiled. 'He is a student of poetry after all. He admits being a passenger in the car. Dr Weston drove him to the airport, when he flew to the Czech Republic for his summer job. What about the steering wheel? Did you find any of Mr Norton's prints on that?'

'No.'

'Or the gear lever? Were there any of his prints on that?'

'No.'

'The door handle? Any of the door handles?'

'We didn't find any of his prints there, either.'

'I see. Well, that's fairly clear. It suggests that Mr Norton didn't drive the car then, doesn't it?'

'Not necessarily.' Dr Parry frowned. 'He may have worn gloves when he drove the car. Or cleaned the steering wheel afterwards.'

'Oh come, Dr Parry. That's stretching things a bit, isn't it? You've found five prints on the passenger side of the car, which show clearly that Mr Norton didn't wear gloves when he sat on the passenger side. You have no evidence that he ever sat in the driver's seat at all, have you? Wearing gloves or not?'

'No. All I can tell you is where we did find prints. As you see on the diagram.'

'Exactly, thank you. But these aren't the only fingerprints you found in the car, are they? Could you tell us about the others?'

'Well, yes, there were fingerprints belonging to the car's owner, Victoria Weston. Naturally we eliminated those, and those of her husband, Tom Weston. Then ...'

'Just a minute. Wait there.' Sarah held up a hand. 'You say you found prints belonging to Tom Weston?'

'Yes.'

'What do you mean, you eliminated them?'

'I mean, we eliminated him from our enquiries. I understand he is not a suspect.'

'Really. Nonetheless you found his fingerprints in the car. Including one on the outside of the window in the driver's door and another on the glass of the speedometer display.'

'Yes. It looked to me as though perhaps her husband had been adjusting the digital display.'

'You don't think she could do it herself?' Sarah, an accomplished motorcyclist before her accident, reacted to this chauvinist suggestion with withering contempt.

The scientist shrugged. 'Honestly, I have no idea.'

'No idea. Thank you. Now, the prosecution theory is that Dr Weston was drowned in the hot tub and then her body was somehow lifted out and dragged or carried to her car, where it was lifted into the boot. A difficult task. No doubt you examined the area around the tub, particularly the area between the tub and the garage, to see if you could find traces of this action. Did you find any?'

'Unfortunately not. The tub is on a stone patio which extends all the way to the garage. The stones of the patio were very clean, there was nothing useful there.'

'You found no traces of any kind to suggest that a body had been dragged from the tub to the car?'

'No. She was a small woman. Perhaps she was carried?' Dr Parry's glance strayed towards Adrian in the dock. Several jurors looked the same way, no doubt assessing his strength.

'All right,' Sarah said briskly. 'So the only evidence you have that the dead woman was there at all is this pinkish stain which you found on the carpet of the car boot. Was it saturated with blood?'

Dr Parry thought for a moment. 'I wouldn't say saturated, no. But there were significant traces of blood. Enough to obtain a DNA sample which proved it came from the victim – Dr Victoria Weston.'

'And the blood appeared to have been diluted with this salty water, is that correct? The stain was pinkish rather than red?'

'That's correct.'

'How large was this stain?'

'Four or five centimetres in diameter, approximately.'

'I see. Less than the palm of my hand, then?' Sarah opened her palm for the jurors and witness to see.

Dr Parry nodded. 'About that, yes.'

'Very well. A faint pinkish stain a few centimetres in width. Did you analyse other areas of the carpet? Parts that were not stained?'

'I did, yes.'

'What did you find there?'

'I tested several areas of the carpet, and found traces of salt, consistent with the Dead Sea salts which were used in the hot tub. And several fibres from a blue bath towel.'

'Are these the areas shown in the photograph on page 26 of your report?'

'They are, yes.' Judge and jurors turned to the photo in their folders which showed little red arrows illustrating the relevant areas on the lemon yellow carpet, with the faint pinkish stain to the left.

'Would you agree, Dr Parry, that the area where you found traces of salt but no blood is much larger than the small pinkish stain? Twenty or thirty times bigger, perhaps?'

'Something like that, yes.'

'And the bloodstain is very faint? Hard to detect with the naked eye?'

'Yes. It's clear with good lighting and magnification, though.'

'All right. But the fact that the stain is pinkish rather than bright red, leads you to think that the blood was in a fairly dilute solution, doesn't it? Just a few drops in – what? A small glass of water perhaps? Could that have made this mark?'

Dr Parry frowned doubtfully. 'Um ... a very small glass of water. A dozen drops in a teacup full of water, perhaps. Something like that order of dilution.'

'Thank you.' Sarah smiled gratefully. His attempt to amend her estimate was actually helpful. 'Nonetheless, a relatively small amount. A dozen drops of blood, in a teacup full of water. The amount that would come from a small cut to a finger, perhaps? An injury that you would hardly notice?'

'Well, yes, I suppose so, but ...'

'Have you read the pathologist's report, Dr Parry?'

'I have ... looked at it, yes.' The slight hesitation meant, she guessed, that he had skimmed it at speed. He was a busy man, not one to waste time.

'So you will be aware, then, that the pathologist was surprised by the copious amounts of blood she found in the dead woman's lungs. This was part of the reason she concluded she was drowned in salt water.'

'I read that, yes.'

'Copious amounts of blood in the lungs, Dr Parry. You would expect, would you not, that if the dead woman was lifted – bundled – into the boot of her car by an assailant, some of this bloody fluid would come out of her mouth and nostrils and stain the carpet?'

'Yes. Well, that's what I think did happen.' Dr Parry nodded, glad that she had understood him at last. Sarah frowned, her schoolmistress face.

'My question, Dr Parry, is not about the *existence* of the blood on the carpet, but about the *amount*. I put it to you that there is a discrepancy – no, a contradiction might be a better word – between the pathologist's report and yours. She describes copious amounts of bloody fluid in the lungs which, surely, would have leaked out and stained large areas of the carpet, whereas what you actually found was a very small stain. Three or four drops of blood, no more. How do you account for the difference?'

This was the key point – the only real point – which Sarah had to make about this otherwise damning piece of evidence. She waited for a response.

Dr Parry shook his head, bemused. 'I can't, for certain. But the most likely possibility is that the majority of the bloody fluid was absorbed by the blue towel which the killer placed on the carpet, before he lifted the dead woman's body in. Three of the fibres from that towel were found to be soaked in blood.'

'Yes, but forgive me, Dr Parry, this is conjecture, not fact. You haven't actually found that towel, have you? No one has?'

'No, but I did discover fibres from it. On the carpet in the boot of the car.'

'So you say. Do those fibres tell you *when* the towel was put there?'

'Not for certain, no.'

'Or who put it there?'

'No.'

'So all you can say is that once upon a time a blue towel was in the car boot, and shed ten of its fibres – correct?'

'Yes, but all of those fibres had traces of salt water, and three of them were stained with blood – Victoria Weston's blood.'

'I understand that, Dr Parry. But I put it to you that this still does not prove your theory that the towel was actually there when – if – Ms Weston's body was in the car boot. All the existence of these fibres proves is that a blue towel was in the boot *at some point* – it could have been days, weeks before, during a trip to the beach or the swimming pool, perhaps, and the fibres could have fallen off it then. And it could easily have been removed, long *before* Mrs Weston's death. In which case, on Sunday 28th August, the day when the prosecution allege Ms Weston's body was lifted into the car boot, *there was no towel at all between her and the carpet*. Just ten towel fibres, that's all. Logically, that is equally possible, is it not?'

Dr Parry sighed. A faint, contemptuous smile crossed his face, as if he was at once disgusted and impressed by Sarah's ingenuity. 'It's a theoretical possibility, I suppose. But I would hardly call it the most likely interpretation.'

'But you agree it *is* possible? It could actually have happened like that?'

'In theory, yes.'

'Thank you. So I return to my previous question. In the absence of this mythical towel – which no one has ever seen or found – how do you account for the gross discrepancy between the large amounts of bloody fluid which the pathologist found in the dead woman's lungs, and the tiny amounts which you found on the carpet?'

'I can't,' Dr Parry admitted. But then with a rush of enthusiasm he saw – or thought he saw – the answer. 'But that's just it, don't you see? The towel explains the discrepancy! If there were indeed large amounts of fluid leaking from the body, the towel *must* have been there to soak it up and protect the carpet. That's probably why the killer put it there, and disposed of it afterwards.'

'A towel which no one has seen or found,' Sarah repeated drily. 'It's a clever theory, isn't it, Dr Parry? It all depends on a missing towel, which may not have been there at all.'

'It *must* have been there. I found the fibres,' Dr Parry insisted, expecting to continue the argument.

But it was the best Sarah could do. She had already sat down.

41. Cars and Bicycles

THE FORENSIC evidence had been damaging, Sarah thought, as she arrived in court next morning. Alex Corder, in his re-examination, had done a competent job of repairing the holes she had tried to pick in it. She had tossed and turned in her sleep, disturbed by dreams of Vicky Weston's body, dumped floppy and helpless in the boot of her car, bloody fluid leaking from her mouth and nose onto a blue bath towel which slid mysteriously away ...

And if that image that kept *me* awake at three in the morning, Sarah thought glumly as she watched the jury come into court, it probably gave them nightmares too. So much for my defence of suicide. Several jurors looked distinctly the worse for wear, and scowled at Adrian resentfully.

This morning's evidence, though, promised to be better for her client, awkward for the prosecution. Mrs Arabella Bishop made her way nervously to the witness stand. In a bright blue two-piece suit, with matching pillbox hat, she had clearly dressed for the occasion, as if she was going to a wedding or a day at the races.

She took the card from the usher's hand and read it through diamond-encrusted spectacles, which hung on a silver chain round her neck. Then she handed the card back, removed her reading glasses, and peered anxiously around the room, surprised, as most witnesses were, to find herself raised above everyone else but the judge, and the focus of many curious eyes.

Alex Corder hauled himself to his feet, wheezing slightly with the strain. 'Good morning, madam. Could you give the court your full name and address, please.'

'Arabella Bishop. Lobelia Cottage, Main Street, Osbaldwick.'

'Thank you. It's right to say that your cottage is the nearest house to Straw House Barn, the home of Dr and Mr Weston, isn't it?'

'Yes. We live at the end of their drive, about fifty yards away.'

For the next fifteen minutes Alex Corder fed her a number of easy questions to establish exactly where she lived, how long she had lived there, and how well she had known her neighbour, Victoria Weston. As she spoke, Sarah studied the printed map from the evidence bundle. It showed Lobelia Cottage on the bend of a road going through Osbaldwick village. A farm track, leading past Straw House Barn, joined the road just beside the cottage. A cycle track, leading towards the city centre, branched off the farm track just before the Westons' house.

'How well did you know Dr Victoria Weston?'

'Quite well. She'd lived there for a couple of years, maybe more.'

'So you were neighbours. Did you know her well enough to speak to?'

'Yes, of course, we had a chat from time to time. When she was passing or out for a walk. We waved more often than spoke – she used to drive past, you know, on her way to the university. Or cycle sometimes, on a sunny day.'

'Yes. So you knew her as a neighbour, rather than a friend, is that fair?'

'Yes, I suppose so.'

'You knew what she looked like, but you didn't talk to her on a daily basis?'

'Well, no.'

Tricky, Sarah thought, a faint smile on her lips. She leaned forward with her elbows on the table, her fingers folded under her chin. The prosecution had to call this witness – her evidence was vital for the timing of the murder – and yet they didn't entirely like what she had to say. Sarah imagined there had been long frowning discussions between the police and the CPS. They might even have felt the temptation – if Will Churchill had had anything to with it – to persuade the witness to change her mind. But she looked fairly confident so far; a wrinkled, apple faced lady in her mid sixties, well dressed, used to being treated with respect.

'Very well, Mrs Bishop. Now, we see from the map that the drive leading to Straw House Barn goes right past your house. Is that correct?'

'Yes, that's right.'

'In fact some of your windows look straight out onto the drive, is that right?'

'Yes, the kitchen window does. And our spare bedroom upstairs.'

'So, without suggesting for a moment that there is anything wrong with this, Mrs Bishop, it would be fair to say that you notice people going up and down the drive?'

'Well, yes, I couldn't avoid it really. If I was standing at the kitchen sink, for example; that's what I look out on.'

'Quite. Perfectly understandable. So, if you cast your mind back to the months before August – beginning in May, say, and carrying on through the summer – were there any visitors that you noticed paying regular visits to Straw House Barn?'

The witness frowned. 'Well, there weren't that many actually. Delivery vans, of course, quite a few of those. Postmen and bin men. A few others – I think some friends came to stay over the summer, with their teenage kids. Also his sister, I spoke to her once, nice lady. And then there were her students. At least that's what I thought they were.'

Come on, she knows what he's driving at, Sarah thought. *It's right there in her statement!*

'Was there one visitor in particular?'

'Yes. A young man used to come on a bicycle. He came quite often in May, June time. He seemed to get on well with Victoria – Dr Weston. Very well in fact; I saw them kissing once.'

'Really. What did you think when you saw that?'

Mrs Bishop shrugged. 'Well, what anyone would think, I suppose. I thought they must be lovers.'

'You saw this young man quite often, did you?'

'Yes. Until perhaps the end of June. Then he stopped coming; at least I didn't see him again until August. And then only once, I think.'

'Do you remember the date when you saw him last?'

'Yes. It was Thursday 25th August. Late morning it was; about 11.30, 12 maybe. I was getting my car out to drive to the supermarket; we had family coming that weekend. I met him coming into the drive on his bike.'

'Did you speak to him?'

'No, I didn't know him to speak to. Just gave him a friendly wave and smile, that's all.'

'He was cycling towards the house, you say. Did you see when he left?'

'No. After the supermarket I went to visit a friend of mine. I didn't get back until five, six o'clock. I didn't see him again.'

'All right, Mrs Bishop. I want to take you forward a few days, to Sunday 28th August, if I may. I believe you had visitors that day, is that correct?'

'Yes. My daughter came over from Manchester with her husband and our grandchildren. They came for lunch and we ate it in the garden. It was lovely; we both enjoy playing with the children.' She smiled at the memory.

'I'm sure. And what time did your daughter and her family leave?'

'About eight o'clock. We were all tired. The grandchildren sleep in the car on the way back but my husband and I, we just collapsed into armchairs and closed our eyes for a nap. We're not as young as we were.'

'It comes to us all, Mrs Bishop, I assure you,' Alex Corder wheezed, clinging onto his lectern as though taking his last breath. 'So, how long would you say and your husband were asleep that evening? After your grandchildren had left?'

'About an hour, perhaps more. I think I woke up at about half past nine.'

'So if anyone had gone past your house down the drive at that time, either going towards Straw House Barn or coming from it, you wouldn't have noticed them, would you?'

'No.'

'But you did notice someone later that evening, I believe. Could you tell us about that?'

'Yes, well after my nap I got up to start clearing away, you know. There were toys all over the place and plates and cups still out in the garden where we had eaten. So I went outside to start clearing up – not before time, either, because I could see there was a storm coming. The sky was black and the first big drops of rain were falling. And that was when I saw her.'

A slight sigh of exasperation escaped the elderly barrister, like a tyre being gently deflated. *This is what he didn't want her to say,* Sarah thought, a faint smile playing around her lips.

'What did you see, exactly?'

'I saw Dr Weston – Vicky – driving her car out of the drive.'

'What time was that?'

'It was just before ten o'clock. About five to ten, I think.'

'How can you be so precise?'

'Because just after I waved to her the BBC news came on. And I remember the forecaster had said earlier it would be a fine night with a few scattered showers, and I thought silly buggers, they've got it wrong again, here comes a thunderstorm – and it did! By the time the news started the rain was pelting down.'

'I see. But you saw the car clearly, did you?'

'Yes. It was Vicky's car, the light blue Mercedes. I'd know it anywhere.'

'All right. So you're sure about the car. But it was raining, you say, and ten o'clock at night, so well after sunset, even in August. Could you be sure about the driver?'

'Yes, it was Vicky. I waved to her, and she smiled.'

Another sigh from Alex Corder. Polite, but exasperated. Sarah was grinning broadly. Since Arabella Bishop was his own witness, called by the prosecution, Corder could only lead her. He couldn't challenge her or cross-examine her unless the judge gave him permission to treat her as a hostile witness, and to treat Arabella Bishop as hostile would be absurd; she had no interest in the case, she wasn't hiding anything. She was simply telling the truth as she saw it.

'You're quite sure about that, are you?'

'Perfectly sure, yes.'

'Hm. How fast was the car going, would you say?'

'Fairly fast. She always drove quickly.'

'Fairly fast, you say. So, in terms of seconds, how long would you say you were looking at the driver of the car?'

'Oh ... two, three, four seconds maybe. I know it was her.'

'Very well. Mrs Bishop, forgive me if this sounds insensitive, but I see you use glasses. Is that because you are short-sighted, perhaps?'

'No it is not!' Mrs Bishop glared at him, clearly affronted. She raised the spectacles which hung round her neck. 'These are my reading glasses. I use them for looking at things close to, that's all. I can see you perfectly well without them!'

'Yes, I see. Well, thank you, Mrs Bishop. Stay there, if you please.'

Alex Corder sighed, lowering himself onto his bench, which creaked in protest. Sarah rose to her feet and smiled politely at the witness.

'Good morning, Mrs Bishop. I have a few questions on behalf of the defendant, Adrian Norton, the young man in the dock behind me. Now he has seen your statement and he accepts that he is the young man on the bicycle whom you saw on the morning of Thursday August 25th. Do you recognise him?'

The old practice of prosecution barristers asking a witness to identify a prisoner in the dock had been abandoned years ago, as being obviously prejudicial; but if Sarah, for the defence, chose to concede it, there was no objection. Mrs Bishop met Adrian's eyes, and smiled nervously. 'Yes, that's him.'

'You have no difficulty recognizing him without your glasses, then?'

'No, of course not.'

'This is a young man you've seen dozens of times?'
'Yes.'
'You've seen him alone, and with Victoria Weston?'
'Yes.'
'Does he look like Victoria Weston to you?'
'No, of course not. Nothing like her.'
'All right. So, just before ten o'clock on the evening of Sunday 28th August, who did you see driving past your house?'
'Victoria Weston.'
'You're sure of that, are you?'
'Quite sure, yes. I waved to her and she smiled.'
'All right. Now Mr Corder didn't seem quite happy with that answer. He pointed out that it was a rainy night and dark, after sunset. He thinks you must be mistaken. He thinks that it wasn't Victoria Weston driving that car at all. You know what Adrian Norton looks like. Could it have been him you saw driving that car?'
'No!' She laughed. 'Of course it wasn't him!'
'Was there anyone else in the car?'
'Not that I saw, no.'
Sarah beamed at the witness. 'Thank you, Mrs Bishop. You've been very helpful.' Glancing smugly at Alex Corder, she sat down.

* * *

Unfortunately for Sarah, Alex Corder had anticipated her mini victory. Rising to his feet, he said: 'My Lady, I call Detective Sergeant Jane Carter.'

Sighing, Sarah watched DS Carter take the stand. This was the officer in charge of the case; the woman whom Terry had been so rude about when he was recovering in hospital. *Plain Jane the Brain Drain.* It was unkind, Sarah thought. The detective who now faced the court was certainly no beauty, but she had a quiet confidence which commanded respect. Tall, five foot ten at least, she looked strong and fit, easily able to deal with a man resisting arrest. Not that Adrian Norton had offered any physical resistance; his trouble lay in the mind, and his slippery relation to the truth.

Alex Corder took Jane Carter through the details of the investigation: the discovery of Vicky Weston's car by the river, the initial suspicion of suicide after interviewing her husband, the discovery and identification of her body. Much of this was uncontroversial, accepted by the defence. Corder moved on to Adrian's first interview with the police, when the young man had suggested her suicide might be somehow his fault, and then, when he was told it was murder, he had changed his story and attempted to create an alibi.

It was the final part of the police evidence that was most crucial for both sides: the CCTV. Alex Corder had clearly chosen to introduce it now in order to nullify what he saw as Mrs Bishop's mis-identification of the driver of the car. Having established from Jane Carter that Adrian had quite clearly stated that the last time he saw Victoria Weston was on Thursday 25th August, and that he'd been with his fiancée Michaela all day on Sunday 28th, Corder asked his junior, Jasper Grey, to show the CCTV recording. The jury watched entranced as a young man on a bicycle cycled past the pub in Osbaldwick. The young barrister deftly paused the video at the exact point when the cyclist's face was turned directly towards the camera. The time at the bottom left of the screen read 20.22, 28 August 2016.

He's been practising, Sarah thought. I bet he's watched this scene twenty times.

'Did you show this video to the defendant?' Alex Corder asked.

'We did, yes,' Jane Carter replied.

'What was his response?'

'He said it wasn't him. He said it must be someone else.'

'And did he later change his mind?'

'He did, yes.'

'How did that come about?'

'He changed his mind when he was confronted with the second statement from his girlfriend, Michaela. In her first statement she had confirmed his story that they were together that evening, but she later changed her story and admitted that was untrue.'

'How did the defendant react when you told him that?'

As she remembered her moment of triumph, a grim smile crossed Jane Carter's face. 'He looked very shocked and distressed. Then he admitted that the cyclist on the video was him. His earlier statement had been a lie.'

'A lie.'

Alex Corder stood quite still for as long as he could, letting the word settle quietly into the pool of silence around the court. Nearly fifteen long seconds passed before the judge raised an eyebrow and Corder, reluctantly, came back to life. 'I see. And what did he say happened next? After he had cycled past the pub?'

'He said he cycled past Dr Weston's house.'

'Past the victim's house, you say. That would involve turning right just after the pub?'

'Just round the bend, yes. And down the track.'

'Did you ask him what happened when he got to her house?'

'We did, yes. He said he stopped and looked into the garden. He admitted that he saw Victoria Weston.'

'He saw her, he said?'

'Yes.'

'What was she doing when he saw her? Did he say?'

'No. Detective Inspector Bateson asked him whether she was in her house or in the hot tub in the garden, but he refused to answer. Instead he asked for a lawyer.'

'Did he get access to a lawyer?'

'He did, yes. He spent an hour with a solicitor and after that he refused to answer any more questions. He simply said no comment.'

'No comment?'

'Yes. Whatever we asked, the answer was the same.'

'I see. Well, well, well ...' Once again Alex Corder stood for a good fifteen seconds, as though deep in sorrowful contemplation of the wickedness of the world. At last he said: 'Thank you, detective sergeant. Wait there, please.' With a slow sigh of satisfaction, he eased himself down onto the bench.

There were moments in some trials when Sarah wished she wasn't there. This was one of them. It was the high point of the prosecution case. She felt conspicuous and alone. The judge peered down at her over her reading glasses, a thin smile of curiosity twitching her lips. Out of the corner of her eye Sarah saw the nearest juror, a middle-aged man at the end of the bench, sit back and fold his arms, gazing at her with contempt. Jane Carter stood quietly, waiting. Was there a flicker of scorn in her eyes, Sarah wondered? *She knows about me and Terry. She was rude to me in the hospital. Well, now's my chance.*

'Detective sergeant, I only have a few questions,' Sarah began. *Your client lied,* a voice whispered in her mind. *You're on a certain loser here.*

Still, there were some details, perhaps, that she could pick away at.

'When you discovered this CCTV recording, did you watch the entire tape?'

Jane Carter nodded confidently. 'We watched the next two hours, yes.'

'From 8.22 till about 10.22, then?'

'About that, yes.'

'Did you see Vicky Weston's car on that tape? Mrs Bishop told us it drove past her house just before ten.'

'No, we didn't. The car must have turned right at the end of the drive, and gone the other way.'

'I see. So you have no video evidence to confirm the fact that Vicky Weston was driving it?'

'No.'

'No other CCTV cameras picked up the car?'

'No.'

'That's a pity. Well, did you see Adrian Norton cycle away from the house?'

'No, we didn't.' A grim smile crossed Jane's face. 'That's probably because he was driving her car down to the river. With her body in the boot.'

'Really?'

It had been an incautious, slightly arrogant answer. The detective clearly thought, like Alex Corder, that the prosecution were in a strong position. They were. Nonetheless ...

'It's also possible, isn't it, that after seeing Vicky Weston in her house, Mr Norton cycled back another way? The same way the car went, perhaps?'

Jane Carter shrugged. 'It's possible, I suppose.'

'You can't prove it's wrong – you have no other CCTV of the bike, or the car.'

'No, we don't.'

'I see. When you arrested Mr Norton, I presume you looked him up on the National Police Computer. Was he there?'

'No, he wasn't.'

'So he is a person with no criminal record. No previous convictions of any kind?'

'That's correct, yes.'

'Does he have a driving licence?'

'I believe not, no.'

'So how do you suppose he drove Vicky Weston's car?'

'Well, a lot of young men know how to drive cars, but just don't bother to get a licence.'

'No doubt you've met many such petty criminals in your career. But Mr Norton is a well educated university student studying for a doctorate. A person with no criminal record whatsoever. He's hardly your typical teenage car thief, is he?'

'Perhaps not.'

'No. He's a world away from that sort of character. A graduate student of literature, a person who spends much of his time in libraries, cycles everywhere and has no driving licence. And yet you think he murdered this woman and drove her car to the river, with her body in the car boot?'

'The evidence suggests that, yes.'

'Does it? Very well.' Sarah turned a page of her notes. 'When you arrested Mr Norton, where did you find his bike?'

A faint look of surprise crossed Jane Carter's face. 'Er ... in his flat, I think. In a corridor near the back yard.'

'The same bicycle as we saw on the video?'

'I believe it was the same, yes.'

'But you didn't check?'

'I ... think someone checked, yes.'

'But you're not completely sure?'

A slight rosy flush coloured Jane Carter's cheeks. This was her first murder case and she was a perfectionist. This apparently trivial point was embarrassing. The barrister was beginning to annoy her. 'It was in his flat. I'm sure it was his.'

Sarah was beginning to enjoy herself. 'You don't think he stole it, then? He's not that sort of young man?'

The detective, it seemed, could think of no suitable answer. It was a trivial point, a tiny victory. More to come, perhaps?

In her sweetest, most charmingly reasonable voice, Sarah said: 'We've heard a great deal about a few small traces of blood which were found in the boot of Dr Weston's car. Was anything else found there?'

'There was a pink plastic umbrella, I believe, and a reusable shopping bag from Morrisons.'

'Was anything significant found on those?'

'Only a few traces of salty crystals. Nothing else.'

'I see. And the car was generally very clean, was it? Well looked after?'

'It was, yes.'

'Did you find any traces of bicycle oil in it? Any mud, dirt, rubber tyre marks – anything to suggest that a bicycle had been carried in the car, either in the boot or on the back seat?'

'No.' Jane frowned, beginning to see the significance of the question.

'None at all? So help me if you can, detective sergeant. If Adrian Norton drove Vicky Weston's car to the river, as you say, passing Mrs Bishop's house at ten o'clock and being back in his fiancée's bed soon after eleven, possibly earlier – what happened to his bicycle?'

Jane Carter glared at her. Then, turning to the judge for support, she said: 'I'm not sure I follow the question, My Lady.'

Judge Eckersley peered down at the witness, her reading glasses balanced precariously on the end of her nose. 'I think what counsel is asking, detective sergeant, is how is it possible for the defendant to have arrived at the victim's house on his bicycle, and then left in her car – without the bicycle – and yet somehow retrieved it before returning home an hour later?'

Sarah smiled. Not such a bad judge after all, then. She waited for the answer.

'I can't be sure about that, My Lady. But ...' Jane hesitated, then rallied as a solution came to her. '... there's no way of proving for certain what he did with the bicycle. He could have driven the car to the river, walked home and retrieved the bike from Dr Weston's house next morning.'

'Before her husband came home, then?' Sarah asked. 'Was the bike there when he returned from Scotland?'

'I ... can't say.'

'No, of course you can't. This is a vital piece of evidence which seems to have gone missing, doesn't it? It doesn't fit in with your chain of events.'

There being no obvious answer to this, Jane wisely chose to remain silent. But an ugly red flush had appeared on her neck.

Quit while you're ahead. Like Alex Corder before her, Sarah stood silently for a long moment, letting the implications of her unanswered questions sink into the jurors' minds. Jane Carter was watching her hungrily, like a hawk whose prey, for the present, has escaped.

Sarah smiled, and sat down.

Not quite such a watertight case then, after all.

42. Private Eye

'NATURALLY WE'D keep your name confidential,' Emily promised. 'I don't think we'd be allowed to publish it, anyway, without your permission. Not even when the case comes to trial.'

'Yeah, well that's important,' the woman on the phone said. 'I'm a victim, I have a right to anonymity.'

Unlike my father, whose name your accusation has plastered all over the media, Emily thought bitterly.

'Of course,' she said in a concerned, reassuring voice. 'I do understand that, really. We'd give you a pseudonym – a different name – and write everything in very general terms, so that no one could possibly indentify you from reading the article. Like the one in the *Yorkshire Post*.'

'Yes, well that didn't say much. It was all about him, not me.'

'Well, quite. But your story's important, isn't it? That's what our readers are interested in. We want to know how sexual abuse affects a woman – or young girl as you were then – so that they can understand the impact this sort of crime has, and the effect it has on your life as you grow older. I can write about that without giving any specific names or details. It would be like a public service – a way of helping other victims of child abuse. It's a really hot topic nowadays, you know; it's happening all over the place.'

'I don't know.' Emily could hear the reluctance in the woman's voice. She clutched her phone tighter, feeling the opportunity slipping away. 'Would there be money involved?'

'Um ... well ... we're just a small newspaper, you understand, we don't have a lot of funds. But if it's a good article, our main feature, we might perhaps stretch to ... a hundred pounds.' As she named the sum Emily bit her lip, thinking *that's never going to work, that's chickenfeed surely*. But it was a lot of money for her, as a student. Her father would be able to afford more, of course, but she hadn't even told him her plan – and what would he think about paying money to the woman whose allegations had ruined his life? There was no guarantee that this scheme would help him, even if she managed to bring it off. It might even make matters worse. If Clare Fanshawe did agree to talk, she might be so convincing that Emily would actually believe her.

And then what would I do? Emily's heart was beating so loud that she held the phone away from her ear, afraid that the woman on the other end might hear it.

'Make that two hundred.'

'What?'

'I said ... make that two hundred – and fifty – pounds, and I might be interested. You can afford that, surely?'

'I ... I don't know. I'd have to ask my editor. We're only a student newspaper, you know.'

'Yes, well, students are rich, aren't they, with all these loans? Which university did you say?'

'Cambridge.'

'Well, exactly. Two hundred and fifty quid, in cash, and I'll think about it. As you say, there's a public interest. I could get thousands from the *Daily Mail*.'

'Yes, probably. But sometimes,' Emily improvised rashly, 'an article in a small paper like ours is picked up by one of the nationals, in which case you might be in line for more. Quite a lot more.'

'All right, love. Well, you check with your editor, see what she says. Two fifty in cash, mind. Then if she agrees, get back to me and we'll work out somewhere to meet. No names or photographs, though.'

'Okay, I promise. Complete victim anonymity. Thanks, Ms Fanshawe. Bye.'

As she switched her phone off Emily felt the sweat break out all over her body. She was huddled in jeans and anorak, sitting on the grassy banks of the river Cam in Cambridge. On the far side of the river the winter sunlight illuminated the magnificent fourteenth century Gothic architecture of King's College Chapel. A few yards in front of her a young man was slowly poling a punt full of warmly wrapped German tourists downstream, while a swan drifted superciliously out of their way. The contrast between this setting and the grubby, devious conversation she had just ended struck her forcefully. This is what surrealism means in the age of the internet, she thought; you can be in two places at once and neither is more real than the other.

Certainly the plan she was hatching had elements of unreality. She had submitted a couple of articles to the university newspaper, *Varsity*, but had never met the features editor and thought it highly unlikely that he or she would sanction any such wildcap scheme, let alone agree to pay the interviewee. Emily did not have a press card and in any case had realised that an attempt to approach Clare Fanshawe under her own name, Emily Newby, would be bound to fail. Instead, for a joining fee of 127 euros plus a further 22, she had applied for and obtained an International Press Pass in the name of Helen Beasley from a site she had found online called *GNSPress*. She doubted it would convince many serious journalists but she hoped it would impress Clare Fanshawe.

She had got Clare Fanshawe's name from her father, but she had not told the woman that. Instead she had explained that the article in the *Yorkshire Post* (which had so enraged her father) had given the name of Wellborough Comprehensive School, where the alleged abuse had occurred in 1991, and that she had met a former pupil who had believed the complainant might be her. She had found her landline number in the online phone book. It was a thin story but, to Emily's delight, Clare had swallowed it.

So now what? Lucy Parsons, the solicitor, had issued very firm and explicit warnings to her father against making any contact with the victims who had made the damaging allegations against him. It was a serious offence, she had said, to put pressure on a witness to change their evidence. Any contact with Clare Fanshawe could be construed as harassment, however polite the questions asked. And if Bob met her, as Lucy had pointed out, there was no way the contact would be polite. Her father's rage, always bubbling just below the surface, would be certain to result in a spectacular outburst of fury which would do his search for justice nothing but harm.

But these warnings had not been issued directly to Emily. She, too, was furious with the woman, but she thought – hoped – she would be able to keep her temper. After all, if they did meet, she would be using a false name, and the discipline of impersonating the fictitious journalist Helen Beasley should help. And also, beneath the nervous anticipation, there was an aspect of genuine curiosity. What would this woman be like? Why had she made these allegations – especially now, so many years later? And – most worryingly of all for Emily – were they really as false as her father maintained, or was there a tiny grain of truth in them?

Emily hoped not, but she had to admit the possibility.

* * *

They met in a café in a park in Harrogate. It was a sunny day, so they sat at a picnic table outside. The cafe was a few yards from an adventure playground, and the only other customers were a group of young women – probably nannies rather than young mothers – who leapt up periodically to supervise a toddler on a slide, before returning to gossip eagerly in some Eastern European language. The air was pierced by the shouts and screams of pre-school children.

The woman in front of her, Emily realised, was just two years younger than her mother. Born in 1976, she had been 15 when the alleged offences had happened. It was an odd thought; Emily felt like a historian, an archaeologist even. To her, this past was another country. People behaved differently there. Her own mother had been pregnant at 15, married at 16, and divorced a year later. In 1991, when she met Dad, Emily thought, my Mum was just 17 years old. She married him on her eighteenth birthday.

Both Mum and this woman were Dad's pupils. He married one and this other claims he abused her. What really happened back then?

She thought of the photographs in her bag – the image of her lanky youthful father, full-bearded and impossibly thin in his quaint tweed sports jacket. He had a gauche, appealing smile, quite attractive in its way – had that been the problem, perhaps? The thing that had attracted her teenage mother and this woman too?

Or was there some connection with that other bearded young teacher, a few rows back – Thomas Weston? Why had he lost his wife?

The Clare Fanshawe sitting in front of her today looked quite different to the other photo in Emily's bag, the one of her as a schoolgirl. In that image she was young, pretty, with silky dark shoulder-length hair, which she had exploited with naive artfulness in the pose where she had turned sideways to the camera, her chin lowered towards her breasts, the kohl darkened eyes glancing up provocatively. *Jailbait,* Dr Kenning had scornfully called her, and Emily, while seething at the sexist remark, saw truth in it all the same. She'd tried poses like that at school – most teenage girls had, she imagined – but not in the official school photograph; she wouldn't have dared.

To Emily this adult Clare looked old – much older than my mother, she thought with surprise. Her dark hair, flecked with grey in places, flowed loosely below her shoulders, down to her breast – inappropriately, Emily thought, for the face which it framed. Her skin, so smooth and clear as a teenager, had thickened, grown lines and become somehow coarser – the effect perhaps of the cigarette which she lit with a sigh of relief, as though it was as essential as breathing. She was still slim for her age though, and the black anorak, tight jeans and calf-length boots gave the impression of a woman still confident of her fading attractions.

'Bit young for a journalist, aren't you dear?' she said, tossing her hair back as she blew smoke past Emily's ear. Her voice was deep, throaty, no doubt affected by tobacco and possibly alcohol too. The voice of a knowing older woman, Emily thought with a shudder; one who has seen and tasted everything – including my father, perhaps, God help him! – and yet knows the value of nothing.

'I'm twenty-three,' she said firmly. 'I'm a third year student and I write for *Varsity* in my spare time.'

'Sweet.' Clare smiled, showing a gold filling in one of her nicotine-stained teeth. 'So remind me. Why do posh students want to read about me?'

'It's human interest,' Emily said earnestly. 'Anything to do with sexual exploitation is newsworthy nowadays. Especially if it concerns young girls. Our readers are not long out of school themselves, and female students, well ...' She shook her head with an attempt at weary cynicism. ' ... you can imagine.'

'Not sure I can, love. Tell me.'

'Well, I just meant that, you know ... male students, they make passes all the time, you get used to it. They even have sex education classes now, in freshers' week, to teach boys to show respect.' She shrugged. 'Not that it works, so far I can see.'

'Men just think with their dicks. Always have, always will.' Clare took a long drag on her cigarette, blowing the smoke out through her nostrils. 'Have you brought the money?'

'Yes, £250.' Emily looked round nervously to check they were alone, and patted her bag. 'In cash. But first, we should get started.' She put her phone on the table. 'All right if I record this?'

'Remember, no names,' Clare said. 'I've got a kid, you know. I don't want her dragged into this.'

'No, of course not.' Emily touched a button on the screen, hoping that the screams of the children in the playground wouldn't mask the recording. 'How old is she?'

'Sharon. She's five. Just started school.' Clare's face softened slightly. 'Light of my life.'

'I'm sure. So ...' Emily unfolded a sheet of prepared questions from her pocket, and smoothed it out on the table in front of her. It was a long list. The problem had not been in coming up with the questions, but in deciding which were most important, and guessing how many Clare would be ready to answer. She took a pad and pencil from her bag too, hoping to look professional.

'This must be very difficult for you,' she began thoughtfully. 'I think ... maybe it would be best if you told me what happened, in your own words.'

A frown deepened the lines on Clare Fanshawe's leathery skin. She pursed her lips, her eyes focussed on Emily's phone as though it were a sort of snake, slithering across the table to bite her.

'No,' she muttered, her husky voice suddenly shy, quieter than before. 'Not like that. You just ask what you want and I'll answer. Better that way.'

'All right.' Emily drew a deep breath. 'Well, I understand that when you were fifteen you had a sexual relationship with a teacher at your school. Is that right?'

'Yeah. Relationship. You can call it that if you like.'

Not abuse, then? She didn't jump to that word straight away, Emily thought with relief.

'Who was this teacher?'

'Mr Robert Newby,' she said venomously.

'I see. And ... how did it happen, exactly? It was his idea, was it – not yours?'

'Mine?' The woman took a long drag on her cigarette and blew the smoke past Emily's face. 'Well of course not, I was just a kid. He was the man, the teacher, the one in authority. Of course it was his idea.'

Careful, Emily thought, noting the hostile look in the woman's eyes. *Antagonise her and this interview's over.*

'So did this happen at school or somewhere else?'

'A couple of times in the school, in the classroom, and then later, in his flat.'

Emily made a brief, unnecessary note. 'How did it begin?'

'Well, he was my teacher, you know, taught us English. And he was quite young for a teacher back then, probably his first job, I don't know. Quite friendly, good looking in a hippyish sort of way, with a beard, longish hair. Several of us girls quite fancied him. So when he asked us to stay behind, go through our essays, we thought that was great, at first. Then one afternoon when it was just me, it started.'

'What started, exactly?'

'What do you think? He was sitting very close then he puts his arm round my shoulder, and starts kissing me. Tells me how beautiful I am and how he loves my hair ...' She flicked her greying locks back over her shoulder as though to remind herself that it was an attraction she still had, even now. ' ... and then, fondling my tits, you know, sex ...' She exhaled a long cloud of smoke and studied Emily curiously. 'You do know about sex, I suppose, young lady – don't need me to describe it for you?'

'Not if you don't want to,' Emily responded cautiously, trying to imagine the scene. 'You mean you had sex, full-on, in the classroom?'

'Not that first time. Just kissing, you know, and fondling – his hand in my knickers. Then I got his dick out and tossed him off.'

'Gosh!' Even as the word escaped her Emily realised how silly it sounded, as if she had just escaped from a book by Enid Blyton. Nothing like this had ever happened at her school, so far as she knew. 'Weren't you afraid someone might come in and see you?'

'Yeah. 'Course, that was part of the fun.' Emily's prim astonishment seemed to amuse the older woman; a mocking smile crossed her face. 'It only lasted a few seconds; he was bursting, poor bugger. And I didn't know any better back then. But sure, we cleaned up the mess pretty quick.'

'Did it happen again?'

'A couple of times, yeah, in the classroom. But then we went back to his flat. He had a bed there, and condoms. So we could do it proper.'

'You were a virgin, of course.'

'Ye ... yeah.' To Emily's surprise, Clare hesitated slightly, then hurried to explain. ''Course I'd done things with a few older boys, his wasn't the first cock I'd seen. But I was a virgin, yeah, there was blood.'

Is this true? My dad with this woman, in his flat? Emily closed her eyes for a second, then asked: 'What was it like?'

'Like? Come on dear, you must know, surely ...'

'Sorry. I mean the flat, not the sex.'

'The flat?' The woman frowned, surprised by the question. 'Well, it was just a bedsit, in an old Victorian house near the school. You went down some steps behind railings; it was a converted cellar, I guess. Nice though; you could lie in bed and see the legs of people passing by on the pavement above. We had a laugh about that, I remember.'

A converted cellar! A pulse began to throb in Emily's throat. She found it hard to get the next question out.

'He lived there alone, did he?'

'What? Yeah, no girlfriend, not that I saw. No make-up in the bathroom, nothing like that.'

'Did you go there often?'

'Couple of times. Then it ended.'

'How did that happen?'

The older woman paused, dropping her cigarette stub and grinding it beneath her foot. She tapped a new one out of the packet and lit it. 'Dunno. Bastard got scared, I think. Thought everyone would find out so next time I came to his flat he slammed the door in my face. Either that of he was tired of me. Found someone *better.*' She spat the word viciously. 'Older, maybe. I was just a kid, after all. A schoolgirl, a plaything, good for a laugh.'

'He rejected you, then? Took your virginity and cast you aside?' Emily pretended to take notes.

Clare Fanshawe laughed; a deep throaty laugh that ended in a nasty coughing fit from somewhere deep in her chest. 'You can call it that for your posh student gels if you like, Ms Beasley. Yeah – he shagged me and dumped me, the shit.'

'But didn't you tell anyone? The other teachers, the police? I mean, he could have lost his job, couldn't he? Even back then?'

Another laugh; more cynical this time. 'I tried. I told the headmaster, Dr Kenning. Know what he said? Keep your knickers on and your mouth shut. Tell any more lies and you'll end in the gutter. Which is where he thought I'd come from in the first place. Toffee-nosed git.'

'Did any of the other girls know? About you and this teacher, Mr Newby?'

'One or two, probably yes. You know what girls are; it wasn't exactly a secret.'

'So why didn't they support you?'

'Jealous, probably – I don't know. Anyway he left the school soon after. So what was the point?'

'So he got clean away, did he? You never saw this man again?'

'Yeah. Good riddance, I thought; but I was fond of him too. You know; it was abuse, of course, but he was the first. I thought maybe he still liked me and would come back some day. So I used to think of him, wonder where he was. He went abroad, I think. I saw his photo once, a few years later, in some article about bringing aid to third world countries. There he was, in shorts and sandals, grinning all over his face with little Asian kids gazing up at him. I recognised him at once – tall, skinny, full beard.' She shook her head, absorbed in the memory.

'What did you think when you saw that?'

'Well, it turned me over, you know. I wondered if the same thing happened to one of those little Asian girls as did to me. More than one, maybe. It happens a lot over there, so they say – with white men.'

'This is the same Mr Newby you're talking about? You saw him teaching kids in Asia?'

'Yes. His name wasn't there but I recognised him at once – tall, skinny, full beard. Same man.'

'Did you tell the police about this?'

'Hm. No, don't think so. They didn't ask. Why?'

Careful, Emily warned herself, noticing the suspicious glance. *Show some sympathy. This isn't an interrogation.*

'No reason. I just wondered how all this affected you, in the years after school.'

'Well, that's just it. I won't say it ruined my life, but it's something you never forget. It's always there, in the background. I mean this was rape, wasn't it? I was only fifteen; if that headmaster had told the police like he should have, the bugger would have been locked up, wouldn't he? Instead of being free to teach in other schools, go round the world like he has done. You know where he ended up, don't you?'

'No, I don't think so. Where?' Emily frowned, carefully maintaining her pretence of ignorance. It wasn't so difficult; she was already confused by the previous revelation.

'As a head teacher in Harrogate! Or he was, until I shopped him to the police.'

'Oh yes, of course. I read about that in the *Yorkshire Post. St Asaph's Primary School,* wasn't it?'

'That's the one.'

'How did you find out he worked there?'

The older woman laughed, without coughing this time. She lit a second cigarette from the stub of the first before replying. 'Because of Sharon, bless her.'

'Sorry, who?'

'Sharon, my little girl.' A scowl like a sudden storm blotted out the sunny smile evoked by her daughter's name. 'I took her along to the school, didn't I, to enrol her. It's not our nearest school, but there's this thing called parental choice, or supposed to be. And *St Asaph's* got a good OFSTED report, I checked online. So who do I see when I knock on the head teacher's door? Robert fucking Newby, that's who! And he turns my kid down!'

'He turned your daughter down?'

'Yeah, exactly. No help, no kindness, not even a sodding cup of tea. School's full, he says. You live outside the catchment area, no siblings here, we've already got our quota of kids with special needs so you haven't got a hope, sod off back to where you came from.'

'He said that?'

'His words exactly. In posh teacher speak.'

'But ...' Emily shook her head shocked. *Had her father really been so callous?* This tale of casual cruelty hurt her almost as much as the sexual allegations, which she was increasingly coming to doubt.

'Didn't he recognise you?'

'No. I stared him straight in the eye and there wasn't a flicker, not a dicky bird, nothing. So I thought you pompous self-satisfied git, here you are surrounded by all these happy middle-class kids and their mums and we're just dirt to you, we don't belong here. You don't want me nor my Sharon neither. You've made it and I haven't and you don't even remember how I had your dick in my hand in your classroom once, or how I worshipped you like a god. And then when you'd had what you wanted you just slammed the door in my face just like you're slamming it in Sharon's now. God, that man made me angry! I was screaming inside, all the way home.'

'But you didn't say anything at the time?'

'No, not to him. But revenge is best served cold, don't they say? So I told the police instead, and that worked a proper treat. That's why you're here now, isn't it, miss, helping me tell the world? While he's on his way to chokey. Guess how they'll treat him there.'

'Yes.' Emily shivered. The mixture of venom and triumph in the woman's voice was terrifying. She glanced at her phone on the table, praying it was still recording. 'So, just to be clear, you had no idea he was the head of that school before you went there?'

'No.'

'And then, when he turned your daughter down without even recognizing you, that reminded you of the time when he turned you away from his flat, and when the headmaster, Dr Kenning, refused to listen to your story. It brought back all those memories?'

'Exactly.' The bitter scowl faded, the seamed tobacco raddled face lit up in a smile which must once, have been pretty. 'That's a good story for your readers, isn't it, Ms Beasley?'

43. Duck with Orange Sauce

A TAXI drew up outside York Crown Court, and the driver hurried round to open the rear passenger door for Alexander Corder QC to climb out. Such deference, Sarah thought, watching from the main entrance. They never do that for me. But then, as the elderly barrister began the laborious task of heaving his bulky body up the court steps towards her, she understood the driver's concern. The old gentleman could collapse at any minute, she thought. Abandon the unequal struggle and roll back down like Humpty Dumpty. The driver, a skinny youth, followed him anxiously, handing over the barrister's heavy briefcase at the door.

'Thank you, my boy.' Corder fumbled in his waistcoat and passed the man a tip. He beamed at Sarah, wheezing slightly from his exertions.

'So, ready for the fray, young woman? I fancy you won't be so happy with today's witness.'

'That remains to be seen,' said Sarah politely. But she had little doubt that he was right. Today's witness, Michaela Konvalinka, was likely to be a nightmare for her client. A strong performance from her could send him to prison for life.

Sarah had not seen Michaela before but the moment she took the stand, she realized the nightmare had just got worse. The girl was quite stunningly beautiful. Tall, about five foot ten, with auburn hair which flowed beneath her shoulders in elaborate luxuriant curls in an effect which had probably taken hours in front of the mirror. She had a bronzed slightly coppery skin, a wide sensual mouth, and greenish eyes which reminded Sarah of a cat or a tiger. She wore a simple apple green woollen dress, with short sleeves and a high neck which no one could have considered provocative had it not been for the narrow black band, like a very high waist, which circled the dress like a shadow just under her breasts. The effect, Sarah thought, glancing at the jury who were watching with rapt attention as she read the oath from the card, might well be to mesmerise the male jurors for the entire period of her evidence.

No wonder Adrian fell in love with her, she thought, as Alexander Corder heaved himself to his feet.

'Good morning,' Corder said, smiling politely. 'Would you give the court your full name please.'

'My name?' She tossed her hair back imperiously. 'Michaela Konvalinka.' Her voice, Sarah noted, was low, clear, penetrating.

'And your nationality?'

'I am from Czech Republic. European Union.'

'Thank you. Do you know the accused, Adrian Norton?'

'Know him?' Her eyes flicked contemptuously towards Sarah's client in the dock. 'Yes, of course. Unfortunately.'

'What is your relationship to him exactly?'

'He is father of my child. Nothing more.'

Of course, Sarah thought, she's six months pregnant. That explains the bloom on her skin, the striking fullness of those breasts, so artfully emphasized by the black line on the dress. Perfect. The most deadly witness possible. A woman scorned; a young mother betrayed.

'Now, Ms Konvalinka, in your statement you say that you met Adrian Norton last summer when he was visiting Prague. And as a result of this relationship you later became pregnant with the child you are carrying at the moment?'

'Yes. I did that.'

'Now, as you know, Mr Weston is charged with the murder of Victoria Weston. So I would like you to cast your mind back to the time when Dr Weston's body was found in the river Ouse. Where were you living at that time?'

'With him – Adrian. In his flat in Heslington. I thought ... good days. All good days back then, that's my thinking. Love's young dream, that's what you say in English, isn't it? Big fool me.'

'You were living with Adrian Norton, is that right, and you were very happy together? Before Victoria Weston's death?'

'I *was* happy, yes. I think so. I think he was happy too – he should be! I'm sorry, my English ... he *should have been* happy. Bastard.'

'I see. Did you know Victoria Weston at that time?'

'Know her? When?'

'Before she died.'

'I met her, yes. Once only, I think. She was his teacher – he meets her to discuss poetry, English literature, Shakespeare, Virginia Woolf, all this. So of course we meet, in library. We talk a little about Czech writers – Vaclav Havel, Milan Kundera – nice clever lady, I think then. *Thought*, I mean.'

'You thought she was a nice lady.'

'Before she drop her knickers, screw my boyfriend, yes.'

'Quite. When did you discover this, that she had er ... screwed your boyfriend, as you put it?'

'Never, when she was alive. They keep it all big secret, the two of them, bloody liars. He is going to discuss literature at the university in the day, writing his bloody thesis on Virginia Woolf, then back to see me at night. I have no idea – stupid Czech girl keeping the house clean and tidy, cooking meals, learning English, getting pregnant, and all for what? So he can talk about Virginia Woolf with no clothes on in her study! Fine British education that is! Cunt.'

'So, to be quite clear, you are saying that you had no idea that your boyfriend Adrian was having a sexual relationship with Victoria Weston, until after she had died. Is that right?'

'Dead right, yes. That's when – the police told me.'

'What did the police tell you, exactly?'

'No, I'm sorry, not tell – *ask*. First the police came to ask questions, where was Adrian on that day she died. And I said – stupid me – I told them he was home with me all that evening. At first I said that. I'm sorry, I know is wrong, but ...'

'Was that true, that he was at home with you all that evening?'

'No, was a lie. I'm sorry, I told lie to protect him. *Because I loved him.* Then.'

'So in your first statement you told a lie to protect your boyfriend, is that what you are saying? But in your second statement you told the truth?'

'Yes. The whole truth and nothing but the truth, so help me God. That's it.'

'Why did you change your mind, and decide to tell the truth after all?'

'Because I see how serious it is. This woman is dead, maybe Adrian killed her. I cannot lie about that.'

'So, as clearly as you can, please tell this court what exactly happened on Sunday 28th August.'

'Yes, all right. It was good day at first, that one. In the morning we go into town, shopping, see sights, you know – all fine until Adrian say let's visit *Jorvik Centre*, historic site, Viking remains. Well, quite interesting but dreadful stink, made me sick – you know, because of the baby, pregnant pains. So then we come back, Adrian fed up with me, I lie down while he sit at table studying, we was both at home together until six thirty, seven maybe. But not so good atmosphere, not friendly and loving, I can see something is worry him, bad temper. So then he says 'what about food' and I say 'beans or pasta, you want cook it yourself?' and we argue a while, not very nice. So to make peace I suggest why not Chinese, I'll go out fetch if you like. So then I go – *went* – out to Chinese restaurant.'

'What time was this?'

'Soon after seven. I know that because local TV news on, *Look North*, I watch Paul the weather man, cute guy, then we argue and I went out. So about seven fifteen maybe, seven twenty.'

'So you went to a Chinese restaurant to buy some food, is that right? And then brought it home. How long did that take?'

'Twenty minutes, half an hour maybe. I was not counting.'

'When you returned with the food, where was Adrian?'

'Where he was? You tell me. Not bloody home, is all I know. Here I am, stupid pregnant Czech girl bringing his favourite duck with orange sauce and special fried rice, and he is gone. Missing.'

'Did you try to contact him?'

'Sure. I ring his phone. Switched off, no answer. Please leave voice mail. So I did. *Food ready, come now.*'

'What did you do after that?'

'Put his food in oven. Eat my own. Wait.'

'Answer this next question very carefully, if you please. To the best of your recollection, when did you next see your lover, Adrian Norton?'

'My lover? Huh. Next morning.'

That's not what she says in her statement, Sarah thought. *She's going off message.* Alex Corder frowned.

'Really? You didn't see him until the following morning? Is that what you're saying – he was out all night?'

'Out all night? No.'

'But you said ...'

'You asked when I next *see* him, right? Next morning, I tell you truth. But he is home long before that, of course. Lover boy, you call him – dead right. He crept into my bed at night, when it's dark, lights out. Guess what he wants then? I give, ok? But I not *see* him.'

One of the younger male jurors snorted with suppressed laughter, which he attempted to disguise from the judge's cold glare by fishing in his pocket for a tissue.

'Ah. So you are saying he came home some time after dark, when you were already in bed. Is that right?'

'Yes.'

'What time was that?'

'Eleven. Eleven thirty maybe. I don't know exact.'

'So between the time of quarter or twenty past seven, when you went out to buy the Chinese food, and eleven or eleven thirty at night, you had no idea where Adrian Norton was. Is that right?'

'Yes.'

'Did you try to call him again, on his mobile phone?'

'I tried. Sent text too. *Where are you? Food in oven.* Nothing.'

'Was this normal behaviour? Had this happened before?'

'A couple times, yes. After arguments, quarrelling. So I thought maybe he is still angry, punishing me, gone out for a drink with some mates. That happened before.'

'How did he seem next morning? What was his behaviour like then?'

'Quiet. Not speaking much. Not especial strange.'

'Did you ask him where he had been last night?'

'No. Silly me, I should have. But I was angry – pissed with him, you say. I thought okay, you want sulk, go ahead. I have dignity.'

'Did he go out that morning? To the university perhaps?'

'Yes, I think so. Probably.'

'You just think so, or are you sure?'

'I am sure. Was bad atmosphere. I not want him there. Good riddance.'

'All right. When he went out, did he take his bike with him, or did he walk?'

'Bike, walk – why this matters?'

'It does matter, Ms Konvalinka, I assure you. Think carefully – do you remember?'

'Yes, okay. He take his bike, as usual. Why not?'

'You're sure of that, are you? He didn't say he'd left his bike somewhere, and was going to fetch it, did he?'

This was a leading question, but Sarah didn't care. She was watching Alex

Corder in astonishment. He had just broken one of the barrister's main rules – *never ask a question unless you know the answer already* – and it had backfired on him spectacularly.

'Left somewhere? No, I see. Mud from wheels on carpet, I remember. More shouting. I have to clean.'

'All right.' Corder hesitated, apparently wondering whether to pursue this subject further. *If you're in a hole, stop digging*, Sarah thought gleefully, and after moment's agonised reflection, Corder moved on.

'So when the police came, what happened then?'

'First time was just me. Adrian out. I was surprised – frightened, of course. Two detectives, man and woman. They ask questions. 'Adrian says he was with you all evening that day 28th August, is this true?' And I think, Oh my God, I must lie, to save him from police. So I did that.'

'You told the police he was home with you all Sunday evening?'

'Yes. Look, if I can explain. In my country, you know, Czech Republic, the police – we are afraid of them, even now. Not so long ago we were Communist. My parents have many stories – one of my uncles was arrested one day, no one knows why, he disappeared. Sent to prison for ten years. When he came out, he was not the same, my father says – he was old man when I know him, white hairs, very quiet. His hands – when he lifts a cup his hands are shaking. So when the police come for Adrian, asking questions, to me it is natural at first, to protect him. I lied. I know it was wrong now, but not then.'

'I understand. So this account you have given to the court today, that is the true one, is it?'

'Yes.'

'Thank you, Ms Konvalinka. Wait there, please. Mrs Newby may have some questions for you.'

Too right I have, Sarah thought.

* * *

'Good afternoon, Miss Konvalinka.'

'Hello.' The young woman's eyes focussed on Sarah scornfully, as though she were an irrelevance. *I've already told my story*, her body language suggested. *What's the point of you?*

'You gave two statements to the police, you say,' Sarah began coolly. 'Would you turn to the first statement, please. It's page 84 in the bundle in front of you.'

'The what?'

'The bundle – the file of papers.' The court usher crossed to the witness stand and opened the file at the relevant page. 'Can you see that now?'

'Yes, I see it.' Michaela read the first few lines of the statement, and then looked up angrily. 'But is wrong, is the old statement.'

'This statement is full of lies, isn't it?'

'Yes, but I explain to him just now, that fat man there. I tell – *told* – these lies to help Adrian – to protect him. Later I told truth – in this other statement, where is it?' Her fingers searched through the file. 'Further on.'

'Yes, we'll come to that in a minute, Ms Konvalinka. But I want to ask you about this first statement. Look at the top of the first page, please, where it gives your name, address and age. Read out what it says underneath that.'

Reluctantly, Michaela stopped searching for her second statement and returned to the first. Slowly, she read: *'This statement (consisting of 4 pages each signed by me) is true to the best of my knowledge and belief and I make it knowing that, if it is tendered in evidence, I shall be liable to prosecution if I have wilfully stated in it anything which I know to be false or do not believe to be true.'*

She looked up, green eyes blazing, her voice sharp, angry. 'Yes, but I explain all that later – I give new statement, true one! Let me show you.' She resumed her search through the file.

'In a moment, Ms Konvalinka. Go back to your first statement for now, if you don't mind. At the bottom of your statement there is a signature, beside your own. Could you read out what it says, please?'

'DI – what is that? T. Bateson.'

'Detective Inspector Terry Bateson. Were you frightened of him?'

'Well, of course, he is police man. Is natural to be scared.'

'But he didn't shout at you or hit you in any way, did he? He didn't force you to make this statement?'

'No. He was polite man. Is my own words.'

'All right. Now let's turn to your second statement, shall we – the one you've been looking for. Page 104 of the bundle.' Sarah waited while the young woman found the correct page. 'Is there a signature on that too?'

'DS Jane Carter.'

'Detective Sergeant Jane Carter. Do you remember that policewoman? What was she like?'

'What like? A big woman, ugly. Very – what you say? Aggressive. Not polite.'

'You didn't like her, you mean. Were you afraid of her?'

'Afraid? Yes, of course. She come with lots of police, arrest me and Adrian, both. Early in morning, lots of shouting, handcuffs, locked us in van, very scary. She was angry woman. She tell me – *told me* – that I was liar, I could go to prison for my first statement, it was perjury, she said, new word for me. Of course I was afraid.'

'Did she say anything else?'

'She tell me Adrian is bloody liar, has been screwing his supervisor, unfaithful. Police knew before but never tell me. All the time when he was saying, *'You are beautiful, I love you, come to England, marry me, have my baby'* he is fucking his teacher in secret. Lying bastard!'

Michaela glared over Sarah's head at Adrian in the dock. A tear trickled down her cheek and she brushed it away furiously.

'How did that make you feel?'

'Angry. Weeping. What you think?'

'And this was the first time you knew about this, was it? When Detective Sergeant Carter told you?'

'Yes.'

'What else did she say, when she had told you this?'

'Don't lie for him, Michaela, she says. Tell the truth now, then maybe you will be ok. First statement was perjury but I'll forget it, if you get everything right this time. Otherwise big trouble. So I did that.'

'She told you to be careful to get everything right, this second time?'

'Yes.'

'All right. So when did you make this second statement, exactly? Was it soon after DS Carter had told you that Adrian had lied to you about his teacher, Victoria Weston? That he had been having sex with her, while he said he was in love with you?'

'Soon after? Yes – same morning. Same day.'

'So how did you feel about Adrian, at the time you were making this statement?'

'About him? Angry. Betrayed. Lying bastard!' Michaela glared at Adrian once again. *Serves him right,* Sarah thought, remembering the pain when her own husband had announced he was leaving, because he'd found *someone better than you.*

But however much sympathy she felt for this young woman, it was her job today to cast doubt on the truth of her evidence. She made her voice kind, understanding.

'So you wrote this statement when you felt angry and betrayed. Is that right?'

'Yes, of course. What you think?'

'Is it fair to say, then, that this second statement is a sort of vengeance?'

'Vengeance? What's that?'

'A sort of punishment for Adrian. You told this second story in order to punish him for the way he had treated you.'

'If you like, yes. Is his own fault.'

'Exactly. He treated you badly and now you are punishing him.'

'Yes. But is true what I say, this time. No more lies.'

'No more lies, you say. So you admit you lied the first time, do you?'

Tell one lie in a court of law, and everything else you say comes into question.

'Yes. I told you. And him.' She glanced at Alex Corder, wheezing quietly on the bench a few feet to Sarah's left.

'Yet now you ask this court to accept that everything in your second statement – the one you wrote when you were angry and weeping – is the whole truth and nothing but the truth. Which you've sworn to tell on the Bible. Is that right?'

'I think so. Yes.'

There was a hint of nervousness now, as Sarah had expected. 'Well, which is it? You *think* it's true, or you're *sure* it's true?'

'I'm sure. Is truth.'

'All right. Let's look at some of the details of that second statement, shall we? You say you went out to buy a Chinese meal. What dishes did you buy?'

'Dishes? No, was just take-away. You know, in plastic cartons, you bring home in plastic bag.'

'No, I mean what items did you choose from the menu? Like sweet and sour pork, prawn fried rice, chicken curry, things like that.'

'Oh, sorry. Well, for Adrian was his favourite, duck with orange sauce and special fried rice. And for me, I think ... er ... sweet and sour king prawn, I think.'

'Very well. So what did you do, when you came home with the food, and found Adrian was not there?'

'What I do? Ring him – no answer, phone switched off. Send text. *Where are you? Food in oven*. Then eat my food. Wait.'

'All right. And then when Adrian still didn't come did you tried to phone him again?'

'Yes. Is in my statement.'

'And when he still didn't come you read a book for a while and then went to bed. Is that right?'

'That's it.'

'Before you went to bed, did you turn the oven off?'

An odd high-pitched sigh – presumably of protest – emanated from Alex Corder. But, perhaps because of the effort involved in rising, he stayed in his seat.

'Um ... yes, I suppose. Probably.'

'*Probably,* you say. You're not sure?'

'No. Well, I suppose I must ... it was not on next morning, I think. No, it was cold. So yes, I turn it off.'

'Are you sure? It's not in your statement.'

'No, well, the policewoman ... she didn't ask.'

'And now you can't remember? Because it's not in your statement, you can't remember, is that what you're saying?'

'Like I say, it was cold next morning. What would you do, lady, when you go to bed? Leave the oven on? I don't think so. You switch it off.'

'Mrs Newby?' Judge Eckersley seemed amused. 'She has a point there, wouldn't you say?'

'Indeed, my lady. The reason I ask, Ms Konvalinka, is that your boyfriend, Adrian, is going to tell this court that when he came home that night he found the oven still on with a dish of Chinese food keeping warm inside it. He ate the food and switched it off himself. Is that possible?'

'Look, why this matters? I come here to tell the truth, all right, the whole truth and nothing else. I don't remember so much about food and ovens. I am not perjuring.'

'That's all right, Ms Konvalinka. It's the truth we're after here, and you're helping us to find it. So what you're saying is, it's perfectly possible that after you went to bed, Adrian came home, found the food warm in the oven, and sat down to eat it. Is that right?'

'Possible, yes. I don't know what he did.'

'Because you were asleep?'

'Yes.'

'And the food wasn't there next morning, and the oven was switched off, so this must be what happened?'

'I suppose, yes.'

'What time did you fall asleep?''

'I ... after ten, sometime. Ten thirty, maybe. I was tired.'

'Did you look at a clock before you went to bed?'

'No. Why should I?'

'Well, you were angry, and worried perhaps. Adrian hadn't come home. You might have wanted to know what time it was.'

'Yes, well it was after ten. I remember thinking, why is he so late? I sent him text, calls, but he didn't answer.'

'We have the times of those texts. The last text was at 10.03. Do you remember sending that?'

'Yes. I sat on the bed to make it, I remember. I was angry and tired.'

'Then you fell asleep? Soon after ten?'

'Yes.'

'All right, let's go back to your statement. Look at paragraph 26. Would you read it out, please?'

'I went to bed and fell asleep. Adrian came home between 11 and 11.30 and woke me up. He wanted sex. We had sexual intercourse and then I went back to sleep.'

'Thank you. *Adrian came home between 11 and 11.30,* you say. How do you know that?'

'What?'

'How do you know what time it was?'

'Well, I ... I looked at my phone.'

'You don't have a clock in your bedroom then? Or a watch?'

'No, I use my phone. Mobile.'

'I see. Adrian came in and got into bed beside you, wanting sex, and the first thing you did was to check the time on your mobile phone, is that it?'

'Not, then. After.'

'After the sex?'

'Yes.'

'I see. You remember this clearly, do you? All these months afterwards?'

'Ye..es.'

'You don't sound very sure. Are you sure?'

'I am sure about the time, yes. It's written in my statement.'

'What about the mobile phone? Why isn't that in your statement too?'

'The policewoman didn't ask me.'

'But that was the only way you knew about the time, wasn't it? By looking at your mobile phone. Yet you didn't mention it to the police officer and it isn't here in your statement.'

'Maybe I mention it, I don't remember. She wrote the statement, not me.'

'Ah.' Sarah glanced meaningfully at the jury, hoping they would see the significance. 'So this statement isn't really your words at all, it's something written down by the police woman.'

This, as all the lawyers in the court knew, was a standard defence tactic. Police officers frequently assumed witnesses were incapable of writing clear coherent statements, and so did it for them. No doubt this had happened here. Michaela Konvalinka was clearly not illiterate – as many witnesses (and some police officers) were – but she was a non-native speaker of English, so Jane Carter had composed her statement for her. There was nothing illegal about this, but it could easily look suspicious to a jury.

'Yes,' Michaela confirmed. 'She wrote it. But I read, after, before I sign. Is truth.'

'Yes. But it isn't the whole truth, Michaela, is it? It doesn't say anything about the mobile phone, which you're relying on now.'

'Well, no, but ...'

Sarah waited for her to finish, but no more came.

'So how do we know that this time is accurate, Ms Konvalinka? You see, the police officer wrote this statement, not you. So isn't it possible that *she* suggested the time that Adrian returned, 11 to 11.30, and you simply agreed with her suggestion? Since there's no clock or watch in your bedroom.'

'No. Look, why this matters? He came late, that's the truth. Ten o'clock, eleven, twelve, who cares?'

'It matters, Ms Konvalinka, because of the time the police say Victoria Weston was killed. Look, I put it to you that Adrian Norton's evidence is that he returned soon after ten, when you had fallen asleep. He found the duck with orange sauce still warm in the oven, and sat down to eat it. After that, according to him, he watched television for a while with the sound down. Then he came to bed, woke you up, and made love, as you say. How long would you say this love-making lasted?'

'How long? I was not counting.'

'Well, make an estimate. Five minutes? Ten? Fifteen?'

'Not long. Was quickie. Just sex.'

'Did you talk to him before, or afterwards? Ask him where he'd been?'

'Not really, no. Was angry.'

Be careful, a voice whispered in Sarah's mind. *In a moment you'll have her claiming it was rape, and how will that help?*

'And then afterwards, you looked at your mobile phone?'

'Yes.'

I've come as far as I can with this, Sarah thought. She sighed. 'All right, Ms Konvalinka. Let me put this to you one more time. You went to bed soon after ten, you say. Leaving the oven still on with Adrian's food in the warmer. He must have eaten that food before he came to bed, because it wasn't there in the morning. So if you were asleep soon after ten, it's quite possible he was home before ten thirty, isn't it?'

'Maybe.' She shrugged. 'Who knows?'

'Exactly. You couldn't know, because you were asleep. So when you say in your statement he came home after 11 that's not true, is it?'

'Yes ...'

'Wait, let me finish the question. You can't know if he was home or not because you were asleep. What your statement should say is not that he *came home* after 11, but that he came *to bed* sometime after 11, you see? When he woke you up.'

'Well, yes, okay ...'

'But even then, it's hard to be certain of the time, because you didn't actually write your own statement at all, did you? It was written for you, by the police officer.'

Michaela Konvalinka stood very silent for a moment, thinking. It was clear she was very angry. For a moment Sarah wondered if she would speak at all. Then, with impressive dignity, she said clearly: 'It is not me that is lying, lady. It is him. That bastard there.'

Well done, Sarah thought, applauding her opponent silently.

'No more questions, My Lady,' she said, and sat down.

44. Revelations

'So IF you hadn't turned her away from your school, this might never have happened!' Emily insisted excitedly. 'Don't you see, Dad? This is all a colossal coincidence!'

'But I hardly spoke to the woman,' Bob said. 'Only five minutes, ten at most. I hardly remember anything about it.'

'And yet she remembers everything. Christ, Dad, what did you say?'

'I just told her that the school was full. We'd been oversubscribed for months, she lived outside our catchment area, and her child didn't qualify for any of the special exemptions. If she wanted a place she'd have to appeal to the Council. Should have done that months ago, anyway, stupid woman.'

'So you just brushed her off, just like that?'

'Must have done, I suppose.'

'Oh Dad, Dad. I love you dearly, but you can be a bit ... brusque, sometimes. It meant a lot to her, this woman.'

'I'm sure I was perfectly polite, Emily. I always am. But even if I wasn't that's no justification for ... *this!*' Bob Newby flung his arms around dramatically, indicating the grubby woodchip wallpaper, the battered pine table, the gas fire, the faded armchairs, the tiny kitchen that made up his present home. 'She's ruined my life with her lies, that woman!'

'Yes, well now at last we have proof that she's lying!' Emily brandished her phone triumphantly. 'You're quite sure your flat wasn't in a converted cellar, are you?'

'Sure? Of course I'm sure. It was up two flights of stairs. I showed you. Ask your mother. She'll remember.'

'I will. And there's the other thing. Even better really. You never taught in a third world country, did you?'

'No, of course not.'

'Then we've got her! She's lying! She's confused you with someone else. All we have to do now is show this to your solicitor and the police will drop the case. They're bound to, aren't they?'

Bob wasn't so sure. And later that day, when he phoned Lucy Parsons' office, the old familiar feeling of desperate anxiety returned. Mrs Parsons was in court all day, he was told. Involved in a murder trial. Perhaps next week?

When Bob angrily persisted, Lucy's secretary phoned back to say if he could get himself to Leeds by 4.30 she would give him half an hour, traffic permitting. But even then, when Lucy turned up, things did not go smoothly.

'You did *what?*' Lucy asked, when Emily had completed her initial, breathless explanation. 'Impersonated a journalist?'

'Well yes, sort of, but it was the only way I could think of to get her to talk, and it worked! Wait till you hear what she says, I'll play it to you now!'

Emily held up her phone, but Lucy wasn't quite ready to listen. 'Let me get this straight. How exactly did you do this?'

'I phoned her, told her I was writing an article about the long-term effects of sex abuse, and offered her £250 for her story. At least, that's the price we agreed in the end.'

'*Are* you a journalist? In any shape or form?'

'Well, I've had a couple of articles in *Varsity* – the university newspaper. Nothing like this though.'

Lucy breathed a sigh of relief. 'Well, that's something, at least. Did you tell her your name?'

'Well, no, obviously – that would have given the game away. I showed her my press card, though.' Emily passed it over.

'Helen Beasley.' Lucy examined the card curiously, as Emily told her how she had got it and what it had cost.

'I spent a lot of money on this. But it's worth it, anyway, because ...'

'Let me think about this,' Lucy said, frowning and pressing her hands together under her chin. 'I gave your father strict instructions not to make any attempt to contact the complainants – victims, as the police insist on calling them. Did you know about this, Bob?'

'Not until Emily told me, no. She did it on her own initiative.' Bob glanced at his daughter gratefully.

'Well, that's some relief, at least. But the fact remains you are family,

Emily, even if you're not a party to the case, so ... well, that's arguable, either way. But then you obtained this information under false pretences.'

'Not all that false,' Emily said. 'The money was real. It was a lot for me.'

'I'll pay you back,' Bob said. 'Every penny ...'

'*No!*' Lucy broke in. 'You will definitely *not* do that. That would instantly make you a party to this, which could be construed as harassing the witness. Exactly what I warned you against!'

'I didn't harass her,' Emily protested indignantly. 'I made her an offer, she accepted, and I paid her price. What's wrong with that? All I got from her in return was information, which she expects to appear in an article. I may actually write it – why not?'

'Saying what, exactly?' Lucy asked. 'That your father was a sex abuser?'

'Well, no ...'

'That's what she told you, isn't it?'

'Yes, but my article will say, if I write it, that she's got the wrong end of the stick. Confused him with someone else. Either maliciously or because she's stark staring bonkers.'

'There's a law of libel, too,' Lucy responded faintly. 'And contempt of court. Show the article to me first, whatever you do.'

'Yeah, okay, of course.' Emily grinned, sweeping her frizzy hair back defiantly. 'But that's plan B really. I mean I only know one editor, and he may not be interested. Still it would make a good threat, wouldn't it, if she doesn't withdraw her whatsit – allegation?'

'What's your plan A then?' Lucy asked.

'Show it to you, obviously, so you can use it with the police. That's why we're here.'

'I was afraid it would be that.' Lucy glanced from Emily's triumphant, cheerful, excited face to Bob's more anxious, desperate, needy expression. 'Well, Mr Newby, I congratulate you on your daughter's initiative. I think she's just about within the law, though I'll have to check.'

'You *can* use it though, can't you?' asked Bob. 'Tell the police. Their witness is simply wrong.'

'I'll certainly try. Though exactly how *much* I tell them, and in what way, will need a certain amount of thought. You don't want them knocking on your door at four in the morning, do you, Emily?'

'No way. No.'

'So it was probably wise that you called yourself Helen Beasley, wasn't it? She'll have your phone number though, won't she – this Clare Fanshawe?'

'Yes.'

'So if she passes that on to the police they may ring you. For heaven's sake don't answer with your name. Maybe think about getting a new phone. New number anyway.'

The grin vanished from Emily's face. 'That would be just *so* much hassle. All my friends, my contacts ...'

'It'll be even more hassle to have DS Starkey knocking on your door, accusing you of fraudulently contacting and harassing a witness. Believe me, that man is not easy. Look at all the grief he's given your father. I think he actually enjoys it.'

'Yes, but ...' Emily frowned. 'What are you going to say to him, exactly?'

'I'll have a good long think about that when I've listened to this recording.' The initial signs of shock and disapproval were fading from Lucy's expression. She smiled reassuringly. 'Come on, let's hear it. Don't worry, love, I am on your side. If it can help your father, we'll use it. But let's stick to plan A for now, shall we?'

* * *

In York's Fulford police station, Detective Sergeant Dave Starkey was talking to DI Terry Bateson. Terry, who had not been looking forward to the interview, was relieved that Will Churchill was not present. Without his old school chum, Starkey appeared more friendly.

'Tea? Coffee? Only from the machine, I'm afraid.'

'Thanks, I'll pass.' Terry grimaced. 'One of the few joys of being home on sick leave. Real coffee.' He took a seat in the conference room. A bare table, half a dozen chairs. Starkey sat opposite, a blue folder in front of him.

'So, how's the arm?'

'Plaster comes off this week, thank God.'

'You'll miss the artwork.' By now every inch of Terry's plaster was covered with Get Well messages, signatures, jokes, and multi-coloured children's drawings.

'Yes. I'm thinking of having it framed.'

'Do that. Send it to Sothebys.' A thin smile lit up Starkey's seamed face. He opened the folder in front of him. 'The reason I asked you in, sir – thank you for coming – is that we've found out a bit more about Mary.'

Not my wife. 'The girl who was injured, you mean?'

'Yes. She's gone home to her family in Bratislava. But before she left we had more interviews with her via the Slovak interpreter, and she gave us some details which helped to identify the brothel in The Hague where she worked for four months. The Dutch police raided it last week and – here's the good news – they've given us a trace on Angus.'

'Angus?'

'The Scotsman, the driver of the Mercedes, remember?' A look of impatient concern crossed Starkey's face. 'The man you argued with at the service station.'

'Yes, of course. I'd forgotten the name for a minute.' Terry shook his head, annoyed with himself.

'Sure you're ok?' Starkey studied him curiously.

'Fine. Carry on.' *For Christ's sake don't let him think you're confused. That's the high road to medical retirement.*

'Right. Well, he left a phone number, landline, with one of the other girls. He'd made the same offer to her, too, apparently – work as a waitress three days a week, and he'd send her to school like a normal kid. But she didn't believe him. So this number's been traced to a town in Scotland – it really is in a café apparently – and two days ago the Scottish police raided it. Here. Recognise him?'

He pulled a photo out of the folder and slid it across the table. Terry studied it carefully. A bald-headed man with a long nose, dark frowning eyebrows and a narrow, thin-lipped mouth stared up at him resentfully. *Do I remember him?* Terry felt his mind straining hard, as though little electric shocks were trying to connect across broken wires in his brain. He closed his eyes, rubbed his scalp, and looked again. The face was haunting, threatening. Something about it made him close his fists, ready to fight. But ...

'It's hard to say. I couldn't swear to it, no ...'

'Pity.' Starkey took the photograph back. 'If you did recognise him it would help, of course. But we've probably got enough, without that. His real name's Alastair MacFarlane, but he calls himself Angus to hide his record. He's on the PNC – history of petty crime, including attempted rape. It turns out the police in this town – Melrose, in the Borders – had been watching this café for a while, but it seemed above board and as I say he wasn't using his real name. And there is a sort of school, too – clever bastard this – which gets state funding to care for difficult kids and refugees. There are actual teachers and care workers there. Only guess what – some of these kids are escaping at night – helped out no doubt by friend Angus and his mates – and pimped out to paying customers. Quite a little earner, it seems – he gets paid to house, educate and prostitute them, all at once. Slimeball.'

'Quite a hit for you, then.'

'Oh yes. The Scots are doing most of it but *Operation Hazel* will be credited with an assist, I hope. Feather in our caps. Thanks to you, in an odd sort of way.'

Again a thin smile lit the seamed, worn face of the younger detective. Friendly, almost. Terry felt some of the tension ease from his body. This was not what he had anticipated.

'Why thanks to me?'

'Well, if you hadn't picked a fight with this Angus, and nearly got yourself killed trying to rescue the girl, we wouldn't have known anything about it, would we? He was just crossing our territory.'

'So ... there's no actual connection to York?'

'Not so far as we know.' Starkey hesitated. The smile mutated into a thoughtful grimace. 'But there is that first statement of the girl, Mary. She says she thought he had a customer here who he was talking to on the phone. That's why she tried to run in the first place, and when you came after her she thought, yeah, right, this is him. Hence your near death experience with a passing truck. But in the first place she doesn't speak English – or Scottish, for that matter – so she may have got the wrong end of the stick, and even if she was right ...' Starkey shrugged apologetically. ' ... it can't have been you.'

'No? Why not? You seemed to think it was, last time.'

'Yeah, I know. Sorry.' The awkward grimace took on another strange shape. 'Look, it was the first time we'd met, okay? Since then I've been making enquiries, asking around – it's what detectives do, right? And what I've found is that you're as far away from the profile of the average John who screws teenage girls as it gets. I've been wrong before, of course ...' He faced Terry with a cold stare, then relented. '... but not this time, I don't think so. All your colleagues say the same – decent straight bloke, no vices. Even DCI Churchill who, clearly, is not your best mate.' He saw the look of surprise on Terry's face and laughed. 'Look, just because he and I went to school together doesn't make us best buddies. I know what he's like, better than most. He's a Marmite policeman: some love him, others loathe his guts. Same story everywhere he's been. Added to that he's got a sort of smartass smarmy quality which somehow rockets him to the top, where he can piss down on ordinary mortals like you and me. Sir.'

'I see.' Terry wondered how to respond. Was this being secretly recorded perhaps, to tempt him into some indiscretion which would lead to a disciplinary offence? No, surely not. The man seemed genuinely friendly. 'So does this mean my suspension is being lifted?'

'If it were up to me, yes, right now. But I need to exclude you completely, and there's a simple way to do that, which should just take a couple of days. Since this Angus – Alastair MacFarlane – has been arrested, we'll check his mobile phone records and if your number doesn't show up, hey presto! You're in the clear. Also, if the girl Mary's right and he really was phoning someone in Yorkshire, there may be an bonus. We'll pay that person a visit too.'

Starkey grinned. 'Nothing I like better than nicking paedophiles, let me tell you. Especially those disguised as care workers or school teachers. It makes this job worth doing.'

45. Not me Guv

'Do I have to give evidence?' Adrian asked. He sat hunched on a bench in his cell, a tray with a half-eaten sandwich beside him. He looked small, shrunken, terrified; a shadow of the cocky young man he had once been. 'I'll say something wrong, I know I will.'

Sarah sighed, glancing at Lucy beside her.

'Legally, no, you don't have to,' she said patiently. 'But we've been through this before, you know we have. Most of the evidence against you is circumstantial, and I've cast as much doubt on it as I can. But the two really big things are these lies you told. That's what the prosecution are relying on, to portray you as a liar and a coward. If you don't take the stand, that gives them a free run. Even the judge will condemn you in his summing up.'

'A liar and a coward? Christ – is that how they see me?'

'They will if you hide away, yes.' Sarah's words stung; they were meant to. She had not warmed to her client in the course of this trial. He was handsome enough, despite the inevitable prison pallor; but the strain of the trial had diminished him. She had felt much more warmth towards his fiery girlfriend Michaela, and had silently cheered the girl's vengeful rejection of her deceitful former fiancé. Good for you, lass, she had thought; he's not worth it. Never was, probably.

Sarah suppressed the thought as soon as it had arisen. After all, she was his advocate, and his story *might* be true, for all she knew. Her task was to convince the jury of that.

'*You* hate me too, don't you?' Adrian looked up, a spark of anger in his eyes. Well, that's what I wanted, Sarah thought. A bit of life, a bit of courage.

'Of course I don't hate you, Adrian. I just want you to do your best. And the only way to do that is to take the stand and tell the truth. As clearly and honestly as you can.'

'Fake sincerity, you mean?'

'What?'

A sly smile crossed the young man's face; the sort of clever boyish grin that, in happier circumstances, must have entranced Michaela Konvalinka. And Vicky Weston, too, perhaps.

'That's what they say about politicians, isn't it? If you can fake sincerity, you've got it made.'

'For heaven's sake, Adrian. I'm not asking you fake anything. If you do, the jury will see right through you.'

'Will they? They don't look that bright to me. How are they chosen, anyway? From the unemployed?'

Sarah's glare unnerved him. He took it back.

'Okay, I'm sorry, it was just a wisecrack. Those jurors scare me, they look thick.'

'They're all human, Adrian. Just speak clearly, simply, and honestly. Remember, they'll be judging your character. They may not have higher degrees in literature but they know about life. And your life is in their hands; for the next twenty years, anyway.'

He closed his eyes. 'God. It's so scary. And it's all lies. All of it.'

'Good. Just take the stand, and tell them that.'

But later, as the lawyers climbed the cold stone staircase which led up from the cells to warmth, sunlight, and freedom, Lucy turned to Sarah quizzically. 'All lies. What did you understand by that, exactly?'

Sarah shrugged. 'That the prosecution are lying, of course. That's what I hope he meant, anyway.'

* * *

'My Lord, I call Adrian Norton.'

All eyes turned to the back of the court as the security guard opened the door of the dock and Adrian crossed the floor of the court to the witness stand, where he read the words of the oath from the laminated card which the usher gave him.

He glanced nervously at the jurors, a few feet to his left, then across the court to Sarah, who stood facing him.

'Adrian Norton, did you kill Victoria Weston?'

'No ... sorry.' He coughed, a frog in his throat. 'No, I did not. Absolutely not.'

'Do you know who killed her?'

'No, I don't.'

'Very well. Could you tell this court, please, a little about the circumstances in which you first met Victoria Weston?'

'Yes, well, I came to York about a year and half ago now, in September, to take a postgraduate course in English literature leading to a doctorate – a PhD. And Vicky – Dr Victoria Weston – was my supervisor on that course, so I met her then.'

'By supervisor, you mean she was your teacher?'

'Yes, that's right.'

'So how often did you see her?'

'At least once a week, sometimes more. We had regular weekly seminars as well as supervisions – tutorials – about once a fortnight. It was in the supervisions that I got to know her best.'

'Tell us about that. How did it work?'

'Well, I would meet her in her study on campus and we would discuss my ideas for a thesis which I had to write for the course. Sometimes I'd show her what I'd written so far and we would talk about that.'

'Was she a good teacher?'

'I thought so, yes.'

'And how did this relationship develop?'

Here we go, Sarah thought. She watched as the young man squared his shoulders and glanced nervously at the jury, a few feet away. Seven women, five men. The younger women, she noticed, were looking at him brightly, charmed perhaps by his handsome appearance and physical proximity. The faces of others, two older women and an elderly man in the back row, wore expressions of disapproval, disgust perhaps, at being so close to a boy accused of murder. Their frowns deepened as he developed his story: how Dr Weston, his academic supervisor, a professional married woman ten years older, somehow seduced this boy into first visiting her home, then sharing her bed, and occasionally even closing her office door and letting him screw her on her desk, while students and other academics passed a few feet away in the corridor outside.

'You are saying that she initiated this sexual relationship, are you?'

'Well, I think so, yes. I mean of course it was mutual, it was my idea too.

But nothing would have happened if she hadn't wanted it to. She was my supervisor, after all.'

'And how did you feel about this relationship?'

'Well, obviously, it was exciting. Flattering too. She was a very sexy woman.'

'How long did this go on for?'

'Four, five months maybe. Most of the spring and summer term.'

'Was there a time when it came to an end?'

'Well, yes.'

'How did that happen?'

Adrian explained how he had travelled to Prague for his summer job teaching English, where he had met Michaela. They had fallen in love and Michaela had agreed to come to England with him, where they planned to get married. Soon after their arrival in York she discovered she was pregnant.

'Did you tell Michaela about your relationship with Victoria Weston?'

'No.'

'Why not?'

'Well, I thought it would upset her. And anyway my feelings towards Vicky had changed. I had never really loved her, it was just ... something exciting, I suppose. But now, since I was going to marry Michaela, it was time to bring it to an end. I thought if I did that, if I told Vicky privately, then she would understand and Michaela need never know.'

'Did you explain this to Victoria?'

'Yes, I did.' Adrian drew a deep breath and began to launch into what, Sarah felt sure, was the most damaging part of his evidence. How, on Thursday 25th August, he had indeed gone to Victoria Weston's house, but instead of honestly telling her why he had come, he had instead gone to bed with her to have sex 'one last time' before telling her — afterwards — that he didn't want to see her any more. The disgust on the jurors' faces was now universal.

'And how did she respond when you told her this?'

'She was very angry. She screamed at me and tried to hit me. Then she started to cry.'

'Were you surprised by this reaction?'

'Not really. I knew she would be upset.'

Alex Corder let out an audible sigh, shaking his head in condemnation. The best way to deal with this evidence, Sarah thought, was to draw the sting of these distasteful admissions herself as gently as she could before her opponent had a chance to cross-examine.

'Now that you have had the chance to reflect, how do you feel about your own behaviour in this situation?'

'Well, it was difficult. She's not – was not – an easy woman to resist.'

Sarah sighed in her turn. 'Do you feel proud of what you did?'

'Proud? No. I was glad I'd managed to do it, stand up to her and tell her that I wanted to end the relationship. I felt relieved, I guess. But I'm not proud of the way I did it, no.'

'What would have been a better way?'

'To have .... just told her, I guess. Not gone to bed with her first, perhaps.'

'Quite.' Sarah agreed. 'So what happened next?'

'Well, I stayed there for a while. Five, ten minutes maybe. While she was shouting at me and crying. Then I left.'

'During this argument, did you hit her?'

'No.'

'Did she hit you?'

'Once or twice. She threw things, tried to slap me. I held her arms, to protect myself.'

'But you didn't hit her or injure her in any way?'

'No. Definitely not.'

'So when you left, she was alive and healthy?'

'Yes. She was still upset, but that's all.'

'What time did you leave?'

'About two. Two thirty, perhaps.'

'All right. Did you ever meet or hear from Victoria Weston again?'

'I never met her again, no. But the following day she sent me a text.'

'All right.' Sarah glanced at the judge. 'My Lady, there is no dispute about this text. I ask the witness to turn to page 37 in the bundle. Adrian, would you read out what it says there, please.'

Storm is over, sweet boy. For now, at least. Meet next week? We can be adults, look and not touch. If you insist on changing supervisor, I will accept, with fond regrets.' Adrian looked up. 'That's the text she sent me.'

'Did you reply?'

Yes.' Adrian read from the next page in the bundle. *'Cool. c u then. no regrets.'*

'And what did you understand by this exchange of texts?'

'That she had calmed down and accepted that our sexual affair was over.'

'Did her text make you feel angry with her?'

'No. Quite the opposite. I felt relieved. And a little sad, perhaps.'

'Sad? Why?'

'Because it meant that our affair – if that's the right word – was definitely over. She'd accepted that. So I was relieved but a little sad.'

'Very well. Let's move on then to the events of that Sunday evening, 28th August. Now in your first statement, Adrian, you told the police that you were with your fiancée Michaela Konvalinka all evening. Was that true?'

'No, I'm afraid it wasn't.'

'Why did you lie to the police?'

'It was stupid, I know, but I was afraid.'

'What were you afraid of? Had you done something wrong?'

'No. Well, yes, in a way. I don't mean I had done anything to Vicky, I was afraid of Michaela really. But when the police told me Vicky's car had been found by the river, I thought maybe despite that text message she was so upset that she'd killed herself. And if so it would be my fault. I really didn't want Michaela to know anything about me and Vicky, I even asked the police detective to keep quiet about it. So that's why. I know it sounds stupid.'

It did sound stupid, Sarah thought. But maybe the very fact of its stupidity was something she could use. After all, this murder – if it *was* murder – had been carefully planned. So for Adrian to lie in such a clumsy way might be proof that the murderer wasn't him.

'So you thought Vicky might have killed herself because she was upset at your ending the relationship?'

'Yes.'

'Had she ever given you any other reason to think she might take her own life?'

'Well, I knew she was unhappy with her husband.'

'Did she tell you what she was unhappy about?'

'She hinted at it. Once, in the summer term, she said there was some terrible secret that she'd found out that made her ashamed to be married to him. But when I asked what it was she wouldn't say.'

'What about the last time you met her? Did she mention it then?'

'No.' Adrian sighed, rather theatrically, Sarah thought. 'But looking back, just after we made love, she said there was something she wanted to tell me, but I said no, there's something I have to tell you first. So that was it, really. I never found out what it was.'

'But you thought it was something to do with this secret she knew about her husband?'

'It might have been, yes.'

Throughout this exchange Sarah had been aware of restless muttering to her left. Alex Corder's junior had passed him a note which caused Corder to nod his old grey wig incredulously. Before he could rise to voice an objection, Sarah moved on.

'All right, Adrian. So what did you really do on that evening, Sunday 28th August?'

'Well, I'd spent the day in the city with Michaela, like I said in my statement. It was a good day at first, we had fun. But then we came back to our flat and we were tired. Anyway we had an argument; nothing serious, I can't even remember what it was about. But it was upsetting. So when she went out to get some Chinese food, I thought I'd get on my bike and go for a ride.'

'Why did you do that?'

'Just to clear my head, I think, and perhaps to punish Michaela for this argument, whatever it was. I thought if I just rode around for a bit, spent some time on my own, I'd calm down and feel better.'

'Did you tell Michaela where you were going? Ring her perhaps or send her a text?'

'No. In fact I switched off my phone. I was upset. I just wanted to be alone, not pestered by her.'

'So where did you go?'

'Well, Osbaldwick, obviously. The police saw that, didn't they? On the CCTV?'

'You admit that it's you in the video, then?'

'Yes.'

'Why did you go there?'

'Well, partly out of habit, I suppose. But also because I was thinking of Vicky. I'd just had this quarrel with Michaela, and Vicky was nice, you know – she and I had got on well, until Michaela came. Look, I know it's not noble, but just for a moment I sort of ... wished I could have my cake and eat it.'

'You wanted to stay friends with both women?'

'In a way. But I knew it was nonsense, really. After all, I'd just broken up with Vicky – and promised to marry Michaela, God help me.'

'So ... *did* you go and see Vicky that night?'

'I nearly did, yes.'

For a moment the court went very quiet. Sixty pairs of eyes watched Adrian intently, like one enormous animal intent on its prey. Sarah's hands started to shake. *This isn't going to plan,* she thought, *he's changing his story again. The silly fool's going to confess now in the middle of the trial, when he's lost all chance of remission and we've been through all this expense and performance.*

'What do you mean, *you nearly did*?' she asked carefully.

'I meant to go and see her,' Adrian said at last. 'I actually cycled down that track towards her house, and I was thinking all the way, shall I go in or not? One last time, I thought, and then no, don't be stupid, that's crazy. She'll probably scream and throw me out, after what happened before. Or else we'll start again and never be able to stop, and sooner or later that'll ruin everything with Michaela.'

Stick to your statement, Adrian, please, Sarah thought. *You told the police you just cycled past the house, that's all.*

'So, to be absolutely clear, did you see Victoria or not?'

'I saw her in the hot tub.'

'What?'

Sarah failed to keep the surprise out of her voice. This was news to Sarah; neither she nor Lucy had heard him admit this before. She had the impression he was making it up as he went along.

'Yes. At least I think it was her. I could only see her head but then ... someone else came out of the house to join her.'

Oh come on, Sarah thought. *Why did you never mention this before?*

'You saw a person come out of the house? Was it a man or a woman?'

'I don't know, it was dark. I thought ... maybe it was her husband.'

'I see. But you didn't mention this in either of your statements to the police, did you?'

'No. Sorry. I forgot.'

Sarah heard a strange squeaking noise behind her to her left. She guessed it was Alex Corder, smothering delighted giggles. This is how I ruin my reputation, she thought. Interviewing idiots in public.

'All right. So there you are, on your bicycle, outside Straw House Barn, and you see Vicky in the hot tub, and someone comes out of the house to join her. What did you do next?'

'Nothing. As soon as I saw she wasn't alone I just left. I rode away.'

'You rode back to Osbaldwick?' *But he's not on the CCTV twice,* Sarah thought. *Only once.*

'No, I turned off along the cycle track. I rode all the way into York, and then down to the river and came back that way.'

'I see. What time did you get home?'

'Nine thirty. Ten perhaps. I can't remember.'

'Was Michaela awake?'

'No, she was in bed.'

'Did you wake her up?'

'Not at first, no. She'd left my Chinese in the oven, so I ate that in front of the TV. I watched a bit of the BBC news. Then I went to bed. I woke her up like she says, and we made love.'

'How long had you been home before that happened?'

'Half an hour, maybe more. Hard to say.'

'Didn't you wake her up when you switched the TV on?'

'I don't think so. I was being considerate, you see.' He smiled sarcastically. *Don't be a smart aleck, Adrian, it just makes you look worse.* But Sarah had reached the place she'd anticipated. Via the scenic route, to her surprise.

'Was your bicycle there next morning?'

'Yes, of course. I used it to cycle onto campus.'

'All right, Adrian. Let me ask you one more time. Did you enter Victoria Weston's house on the night of 28th August?'

'No. I cycled past. I just told you.'

'Did you murder her?'

'No, I did not.'

'All right. Wait there please. Mr Corder may have some questions.'

Quite a lot, I imagine. Deadly ones.

46. Facts and Fiction

FROM THE moment Adrian entered the witness stand, Sarah had been aware of movement to her left. Cushions creaked and papers rustled as Alex Corder shifted his huge bulk and turned to whisper to his junior in the bench behind him. These muttered conversations had continued sporadically throughout Adrian's evidence-in-chief, to the point where she had expected the judge to intervene. When she had not, Sarah herself had scowled at them, to be met with an apologetic wave which did nothing to obscure the grin of eager anticipation on her opponent's face.

She was not surprised. Adrian's evidence was the strongest part of the prosecution's case. If the boy had not lied, he might never be here in court at all. But he *had* lied, and here he was.

The trouble is, to tell the truth, you have to know what it is. And at times with this client, she wondered if he actually knew it himself.

Alex Corder hauled himself to his feet and peered across the court at Adrian, a wide smile on his face. Rather like a shark grinning at a herring, Sarah thought. His first question was unexpected.

'Mr Norton, you are a student of English literature, are you not?'

'I am, yes.'

'So you study novels, plays, poems – that sort of thing?'

'Yes, of course.' Adrian looked surprised, confused by this unexpected approach. 'I am halfway through a doctorate in modern feminist literature. Or I was, before all this happened.'

Sarah shook her head in disgust. *Don't boast, Adrian, please. No one likes it. Think of the jury.*

'Quite.' Corder's grin widened. 'So from your perspective as an academic student of literature, could I ask you to define the word *fiction* for this court, please?'

'Fiction?'

'Yes, what is it?'

'Well, it's a very broad term, commonly used to describe works of imagination, to put it simply.'

'Yes. And by works of imagination, you mean things that didn't actually happen, is that right?'

'Well yes, that might be a layman's definition, I suppose. It's a bit crude though. There is such a thing as artistic truth, after all.'

'Oh really? Could you give an example of that?'

'Well, let me think ...' Adrian looked surprised but also comfortable with the way this was beginning. His gaze swept across the jury, the lawyers, the press and spectators, as though they were an audience in a lecture theatre. *Walking straight into a trap*, Sarah thought.

'Take the episodes of *War and Peace,* Tolstoy's novel which has been on television in recent weeks. It's a work of fiction, because none of the characters in the novel – apart from Napoleon and the Russian General Kutosov – actually existed; but literary scholars might argue that it contains an artistic, imaginative truth which takes us closer to the real events of the war of 1812 than any factual history book could ever do.'

'Thank you so much.' Alex Corder bowed, as if enlightened. 'So what you are saying is that events which didn't actually happen are still true, in some way – imaginatively true, perhaps?'

'Well yes, in a way.' Adrian frowned, as the first doubt entered his mind about where this was leading.

'Very well.' Alex Corder turned to the clerk of the court, sitting directly below the judge. 'I wonder, could I trouble you to show the witness the card with the oath written on?'

The clerk, surprised, searched on her desk for the card, and summoned the usher who carried it across to Adrian.

'Would you read that out for us, please, Mr Norton?' Corder asked.

Still frowning, Adrian read: 'I do solemnly, sincerely and truly declare and affirm that the evidence I shall give shall be the truth, the whole truth and nothing but the truth.'

'Thank you. Is there anything on that card about fiction or imaginative truth?'

'No, of course not. But ...' Adrian shrugged. '... this is different. This isn't a novel.'

'Well quite. I was wondering if you understood that. This is indeed a court of law, where we deal in the truth. Simple facts. Things that actually happened in real life, not in novels or works of imaginative fiction.'

'Of course. I understand that.'

'Do you? I wonder.' The amiable grin had vanished from Corder's face. He shook his head sadly. 'Do you know the difference between a lie and the truth, Adrian?'

'Of course I do.'

'Tell us then.'

'A lie is ... well, it's not so simple.'

'Really? I should have thought it was extremely simple. I expect the jury think it's simple too. You see, the reason I ask is that you have sworn to tell the truth, and yet you have lied to this court again and again, haven't you?'

'Have I? When?'

'Well, let's take some examples. Look at your original statement to the police, page 59 in the bundle. Read out what it says, if you would.'

With a weary voice Adrian read: *'On Sunday 28th August I spent all day with my fiancée Michaela Konvalinka. We spent the morning and afternoon in York and the evening together in my flat.'*

'That's a lie, isn't it, Adrian? It's not even imaginatively true, is it?'

'No.'

'It's a simple lie.'

'Yes. I know. I'm sorry. It was a mistake. I told the truth later.'

'Did you? But first you persuaded your fiancée, Michaela, to tell lies to support you, didn't you? Why did you do that?'

'It was because I was afraid. The police said Vicky had been murdered. I was afraid they might think I'd done it.'

'And had you?'

'No. Of course not!'

'And yet your first reaction was to lie?'

'Well, yes. But I told the truth later.'

'Not until you were caught on CCTV. That's when you changed your story, isn't it? When you were caught out in a lie.'

'Yeah, okay.' Adrian mumbled his answer so quietly that it was difficult to hear. This is a massacre, Sarah thought.

'Let's look at another lie, shall we? Not such a big lie perhaps but a lie all the same. On that Sunday evening you sent Michaela out to buy Chinese food, didn't you?'

'Yes.'

'She expected you to be there when she came back, so that you could eat it together, yet when she came back you were gone. That's true, isn't it?'

'Yes.'

'And when she phoned you, you'd switched your phone off.'

'Yes.'

'So you were deceiving her, weren't you? You'd tricked her by sending her out to get food, knowing that you wouldn't be there to eat it. That's a sort of lie too, isn't it?'

'I was upset, that's all. I needed time by myself.'

'Oh really? Let's think of another lie, shall we? You told Michaela you loved her.'

'I did love her! I still do!'

'And yet you were having an affair with Vicky Weston.'

'I wanted to end it. I did end it.'

'Yes. By killing her!'

No! I've told you! I went to her house and told her it was all over.'

'But first you took her to bed. Isn't that another sort of lie, Adrian? A deception at least. You let your mistress think you were pleased to see her, and only after you had taken your satisfaction you got out of bed, put your trousers on, and dumped her. You're proud of that, are you?'

'I'm not proud. I understand it was a thoughtless way to behave. I'm ashamed of it now.'

'What about the lies you told Michaela, the girl you say you still love?'

'What lies?'

'Lies of omission. You could have told her about Victoria, right from the start. But you didn't, did you? You lied by not telling the truth.'

'Yes, but I was afraid. I thought she'd be upset if she knew.'

'So you decided to end the affair instead?'

'Yes, that's right.'

'But Victoria didn't want to end the affair, did she? She wanted to continue?'

'She did at first, yes. She was upset. But then she changed her mind. You saw that text she sent me. She'd accepted it.'

The text, Sarah thought, was the strongest piece of evidence in his favour. Not surprisingly, Alex Corder chose not to dwell on it.

'All right, let's move on to the evidence you've just given to your counsel. You were caught on CCTV outside the pub in Osbaldwick. Where did you go after that?'

'I cycled down the track past Vicky's house.'

'And when you got to the house you stopped, you said. You saw your mistress, Victoria Weston, in the hot tub, you say.'

'Yes. I thought it was Vicky, anyway.'

'And then a moment later you saw another person come out of the house and join her?'

'Yes.'

'Was that a man or a woman?'

'I don't know. It was dark. I couldn't see. Anyway I left soon after.'

'That's very interesting. Would you turn to page 85 in the bundle, please. Your second statement to the police. Have you got it?'

'Yes, I think so.'

'All right. Adrian, I'll give you a minute to read through that statement.'

While Adrian was reading Alex Corder glanced at the jury. Apparently satisfied with the expressions on their faces, he looked down at Sarah, his eyebrows slightly raised as though to ask: *enjoying this, are you?*

Adrian looked up, shaking his head in frustration. In his silkiest tones, Corder asked: 'Now that you've had time to look through it, Mr Norton, could you read out the sentence where you describe that moment, seeing Vicky in the hot tub and someone coming out to join her?'

'I can't. It's not there.'

'Really? Why not?'

'I ... didn't tell them at the time.'

'I see. So the police were asking you to tell the truth about your movements that day – a very important day when Victoria Weston was murdered – and yet you missed out a crucial piece of evidence, Adrian. Why? I don't understand.'

'I ... don't know. I just forgot. I've only just remembered it really.'

'You've only just remembered it now?'

'Yes.'

'And this is true, is it? *Really* true, not just an imaginative truth like we were talking about before? A piece of imaginative fiction?'

'No! It's true. I think so, anyway. I remember it clearly.'

'And yet you didn't remember it before, when you were talking to the police?'

'No.'

A look of concern crossed Alex Corder's face. *This is weird,* Sarah thought. *Genuinely concerning. This boy may be mentally ill.*

But Corder's job was to prosecute and he was going in for the kill. The witness's mental health was incidental.

'Maybe your memory *is* coming back to you, Adrian. It sometimes does, after traumatic events. Perhaps I can help. Let me tell you what I think happened, shall I? I think you may be telling the truth about sitting on your bike outside Victoria Weston's house. The truth, but not the whole truth. There's more to this story, isn't there?'

'No.' Adrian looked genuinely terrified now. 'That's it. That's all there is.'

'Is it, Adrian? I put it to you that there's more. A lot more, in fact. Things buried deep in your memory. You told the court a little while ago that you felt sad. Do you remember that? You'd had a quarrel with Michaela that evening, so you decided to leave her while she was out buying Chinese food, just like that. Why? Because you wanted to go back to Victoria, didn't you? You were having second thoughts. So you slipped away on your bike, and switched your phone off, so Michaela couldn't contact you. Then you cycled away to Vicky's house, because you wanted to see her one more time. Or even resume your relationship, apologise for what you had said before. All these thoughts were going through your head, weren't they?'

'Well, yes, something like that.'

'Yes, quite. But you were nervous too, weren't you? It's a difficult thing to approach a woman just after you've dumped her, isn't it? She might be angry, refuse to see you.'

'She didn't see me. I saw her.'

'Really? Well yes, you were very lucky, weren't you? You approach this woman's house in the twilight, when it's just getting dark, and there she is sitting in her hot tub. Naked, presumably?'

'I don't know. I only saw her head.'

'Only her head? Was she looking away, Adrian? Or towards you?'

'Away. Sort of side on. In profile.'

'Did she see you? Standing at the gate watching?'

'No. I don't think so. She looked relaxed. Asleep perhaps.'

'All right, so there you are, feeling lovesick and sad, standing at the garden gate while this woman, who you've made love to many times, is there a few yards away, naked in the hot tub. You've been in that hot tub too, haven't you, Adrian? Shared it with Vicky?'

'I did once, yes. In the summer term.' Adrian's voice was hoarse.

'Yes. In fact the police found one of your fingerprints on the gazebo, didn't they?'

'So they say.'

'So let us consider what happened next, shall we?'

'Her husband came out and I rode away.'

'Oh, this mysterious figure, it's her *husband* now, is it? You saw that?'

'I thought it was him, yes.'

'Really? That's interesting. A few minutes ago you told your counsel you'd couldn't be sure. It was dark, you said.'

'I think it was him. *He* killed her. Not me.'

'Oh really, is that what you think? Well, that's quite natural Adrian, isn't it? It has a sort of imaginative truth – it's what you'd expect to happen in a novel, perhaps. But unfortunately the police checked that out, you see. The facts of the matter. Mr Weston was two hundred miles away that night, in Edinburgh. He wasn't there.'

'Well, I thought it was him. It looked like him.'

'And yet you didn't tell the police. You've told no one, not even your own counsel, until today.'

'No.'

Corder shook his head sadly. 'It's no good, Adrian is it? This isn't true, it's just a story you're making up. A fiction, something you'd like to be true, a fairy story from your imagination. In plain English, a lie.'

'It's not a lie. I saw her. And him.'

'So what happened next, in this story, Adrian?'

'I don't know. As soon as I saw she wasn't alone, I rode away. I wish I hadn't now. I might have saved her.'

At this, Corder lost patience. Like a cat who was tired of playing with his mouse, he went in for the kill.

'Let me tell you what really happened, Adrian, shall I? Let me help you remember. You stood there at the gate, as you say, and saw Vicky, your mistress, lying naked in the hot tub. And so you did what any hot-blooded young man would do in that situation. You went into the garden and approached her. But unfortunately, she wasn't as pleased to see you as you'd hoped. After all you'd surprised her, she was probably afraid. And you'd dumped her three days before. So she shouted at you, she was angry. And a quarrel developed. And as a result of that quarrel you drowned her, in her hot tub. That's what happened, isn't it, Adrian? That's how your affair really ended.'

'No.' Adrian shook his head desperately. 'I don't think so. That's not right. I don't remember that.'

'Oh, I think you do, Adrian. I think that's exactly what happened.'

Then, without waiting for an answer, Alex Corder sat down.

47. Memory Lane

'I THINK we'll lose,' said Sarah miserably. 'After that performance we deserve to.'

The two lawyers stood on the wide stone balcony outside the court, watching Alex Corder manoeuvre his bulky personage into the back seat of a taxi at the foot of the steps. As he closed the door he looked up, saw them watching, and waved graciously like the Queen. Even from this distance the cheery grin on his face was quite clear.

'Well, there's always tomorrow,' said Lucy, hunching her collar up against the rain. 'Tom Weston on the stand.'

'I know, and I'm dreading it,' Sarah replied. 'Chances are it'll make things even worse. The judge despises me for calling him, and if the jury pick her attitude up we'll be sunk without trace. Most of them hate me already, I think.'

'Only because you make them think,' said Lucy. 'Most people aren't used to that; it hurts.'

'Yes, well it hurts being lied to as well. If that boy had told the truth from day one, he wouldn't be in this mess. Doesn't he know the difference between truth and fantasy? He's just a typical spoilt narcissistic professional student; universities are full of them. He should grow up and get a real job.'

'Hello, look who's here!' Lucy glanced behind them, where a young woman was just emerging from the main entrance. Following her gaze, Sarah gasped in surprise.

'Emily! Good lord, what are you doing here?'

'Hi Mum! Mrs Parsons.' Emily came over to join them. Her frizzy hair was pulled back and tied in a bow, and she was wearing trainers, jeans, and a matching blue woollen coat, Oxfam's best. 'I was in the public gallery, watching the trial.'

'Well! What did you think? No, on second thoughts, tell me later.' Sarah corrected herself swiftly, as several other members of the press and public emerged through the door. 'Walk back with me?'

'Yes, sure.' Emily turned to Lucy Parsons. 'No response from DS Starkey yet?'

'Nothing definite. He's looking into it, he says. Got a lot on his plate just now, apparently – haven't we all?'

'Dad hasn't,' Emily retorted defiantly. 'He's just got one thing. Stuck there in limbo, waiting.'

'I do understand, Emily, really,' Lucy said. 'But we've got to handle this carefully. Have you done what I said with your phone?'

'Not yet. It'll take ages. I'll start work on it tonight.'

'Well, see that you do. I've only told him in general terms, so far, but he's bound to follow up before long.'

'All right, Mrs Parsons.'

'Good. My car's just over there, thank heavens. This weather! It's miserable, driving back to Leeds. Enjoy your walk home, if it's still safe to cross the river.' She walked down the steps, and headed around the grassy circle called the Eye of York, towards the car park.

'Come on, share my umbrella,' said Sarah, unfolding it. 'That all sounds very mysterious. What were you and Lucy talking about?'

'Hasn't she told you, Mum? I thought she would. It's about Dad.'

'No. We just talk about this trial.' Linking arms under the umbrella, mother and daughter hurried along the stone balcony of the court house towards Clifford's Tower, from where a slope led down to Tower Street and the riverside park near the quay. 'My goodness!' Sarah exclaimed at the sight that met their eyes. 'Has all that come up since this morning?'

The park was under water. Only the tall silhouettes of the bare leafless trees, standing like dark sentinels against the grey evening sky, showed that the water in which they stood was not normally part of the river, which seemed to stretch from the bus stop right across to the distant warehouses on the far bank. Gangs of soldiers and Environment Agency workers in hi-viz jackets were building a wall of sandbags to prevent the flood spreading over the road itself.

'Can we get to the bridge?' Emily asked.

'Yes, I think so. Come on.'

Huddled against the rain, they hurried across Tower Street, dodging puddles as they went, and up onto Skeldergate Bridge. Traffic was still flowing here, but slowly, as drivers dawdled to gawp at the torrent of dark brown water streaming past a few feet below their vehicles. Peering over the parapet, Emily saw that that the flood had almost reached the top of the arches of the bridge.

'You don't think the bridge will go, do you?' she asked with a nervous laugh.

'It's been here over a hundred years. It must have seen worse than this.'

'Yes, but your flats haven't.'

'No.' Downstream to their left, they could see that the riverside footpath, outside the flats, was now six inches deep in water. 'Now I understand why the main entrance is at the back,' Sarah laughed. 'Don't worry. They're built for an ocean cruise. I think that's what the agent said, anyway.'

Home and dry at last, they left the umbrella to dry in the bathroom, shrugged off their coats, and gazed out of the window at the floodscape below them. St George's car park on the far side of the river was a lake, a few abandoned vehicles standing forlornly up to their wheel arches in water. Sarah put the kettle on for tea.

'So, what was this mysterious discussion you were having with Lucy?'

'Oh, that? Well, it was about Dad.' As Sarah made two mugs of tea Emily gave a brief explanation of her interview with Clare Fanshawe, and the discrepancies which proved the woman must be lying. Sarah listened, entranced.

'But of course your dad's flat was upstairs. I told you that ages ago.'

'Yes, I know. That's what made it clear she was lying. And then all this stuff about seeing him on TV, teaching in Thailand or whereever. It's obviously not Dad. She's mixed him up with someone else. She's got the wrong person.'

'Well, who could that be?'

'I know who it is. It's a man called Tom Weston.'

'What?' Sarah almost spilt her tea, clutching at the mug just in time to keep from scalding herself. '*Who* did you say?'

'Tom Weston. You know. The man whose wife was murdered. Or killed herself, whatever.'

'But ... why haven't you mentioned this before?'

'I thought you knew. I told Lucy.'

'When?'

'When we were discussing Dad's case. After Dad and I visited his old headmaster. You remember – you told me all that stuff about Dad's flat, before I was born. I told you then, didn't I? Ages ago.'

Sarah shook her head, bemused. 'Yes, we talked about his flat and his old headmaster, but not about Tom Weston. If you had ...'

'Mum, I *did*, I'm sure I did! The headmaster, Dr Kenning, he told us there was another teacher who'd been accused at the same time, and was dismissed. You must remember that!'

'I remember ... yes, but not that he was called Tom Weston! That's such a strange coincidence! I couldn't have forgotten it!'

'Why didn't Lucy tell you then? You work together, don't you?'

'Yes, but ... we don't discuss your father's case much, if at all. We make a point of trying to keep them separate. It would be unprofessional - she's *his* solicitor, not mine.'

'Well, now I've told you, what difference does it make?'

Sarah drew a deep breath. She laughed nervously. 'I don't know. I'll have to think about that. You do realise I'm putting him on the witness stand tomorrow, this Tom Weston?'

'Are you? Why?'

'Well, it's complicated really, and I don't feel particularly good about it. That's what I was talking to Lucy about outside court. It could be seriously unpleasant. The judge tried to stop me, and even though I insisted, she's still not happy. One false step and she'll slap me down in front of the jury. I can see it coming.'

'Why? Come on, Mum, explain. This sounds interesting.' Emily kicked off her shoes and drew her feet up onto the sofa, tucking them comfortably under her as though she was about to listen to a bedtime story. Sarah sat forward on the edge of her chair, holding her half-empty mug of tea between both hands.

'Well, you know it's this Tom Weston's wife who's died, right? And unusually, there are two strands to Adrian's defence – which, as you saw, wasn't going very well today. One strand is that he didn't do it, it wasn't him. That's what Adrian was claiming this afternoon. But the other strand is that she wasn't murdered at all, she may have committed suicide just as it appeared in the first place. Now ...'

'Don't they contradict each other?'

'Well yes, logically they do, which is part of the problem. She can't have been murdered *and* committed suicide, obviously. But remember, the defence doesn't have to prove anything, we just ask questions and – to put it crudely – try to muddle the issue. If the jury think it might be suicide, then clearly Adrian didn't kill her. But even if they accept she was murdered, someone else may have done it, not him. So this way he gets two shots at acquittal, not just one.'

'Clever! I knew you were good at this, Mum.'

'Thanks, darling – but it doesn't feel like that at the moment, I assure you. Firstly because Adrian lied and keeps changing his story, the little rat, but also because of what I've got to do tomorrow. I feel sick just thinking about it.'

'Why? What are you going to do?'

'Well look, this man Tom Weston's wife has died, right? Whether she was murdered or killed herself, either way that has to be a horrible, traumatic experience for him. Not one you want to answer public questions about. Now normally, the prosecution would have called him as a witness, but early on in the case, Lucy saw they weren't planning to, and when she asked why the CPS said they wanted to spare him the trauma. So we cited him as a witness ourselves. Given the nature of our defence, we had to.'

'So? What's the problem? I don't get it.'

'Come into court tomorrow and you'll see. Think about it. This couple – the Westons – were heading for divorce. Obviously they didn't like each other anymore. So if she did commit suicide, it could be his fault, couldn't it? Her husband drove her to it. So I've got to ask questions about that. But think how cruel it makes me look, if she really was murdered all along.'

'But what if *he* did it, though?' asked Emily eagerly. 'If Tom Weston and this whatshername – Vicky – didn't get on, and Adrian didn't murder her, then surely her husband's the next best suspect!'

'I wish, I wish.' Sarah gave a wry, wistful laugh. 'That would be great, wouldn't it? The brilliant barrister stands up in court and gets the wicked husband to confess! Don't think I haven't dreamt about it. But unfortunately, he was in Scotland, two hundred miles away at the time she was killed. The perfect alibi. The police couldn't break it, and neither can I.'

Sarah drained her mug of cold tea, and stood up. 'So, tomorrow I'll be the wicked witch, the jury will hate me, and Adrian will go to prison for life. And the fact that this man may be a child abuser, whom this woman has mistaken for your father, is ...' She shook her head slowly '... undoubtedly weird, but of no obvious relevance whatsoever, so far as I can see. What do you want to eat? Pasta okay?'

* * *

A few miles away across the river, Terry was arguing about mobile phones.

'Dad, it's just not fair!' Jessica was saying. 'Ava has got one, and Sophie! Even Carly, and she's only eleven!'

'You've both got an Ipad at home,' Terry said. 'The school's online – they've got better technology than I have at work. What do you need a smartphone for?'

'To play games, to send snaps, make friends. Everyone does it!'

'In class, you mean? In the playground?'

'Yes, why not? Dad, *please!*'

'If it's in class, you're supposed to be following the lesson. And in playtime, your friends are all there! Physically there in front of you!'

'Yes, but they've all got phones! Ava's is brilliant – Dad, you're so mean!'

It was a battle he knew he was destined to lose, but please God, not yet. There was so much in the world of today's tech-savvy kids that was magical; but also, to a parent who was also a policeman, terrifying. He longed to keep his daughters away from the world of online bullying, casual everyday pornography, sexting, and grooming by the sick sadistic swine which the internet, so marvellous in other ways, had seemingly multiplied by the hundred million. But however much he tried to protect his daughters, they were growing into teenagers, and soon – on a day still unimaginably far off but rushing towards them like an express train – they would be adults, eager to inherit the world. A new world, different from today's, and far, far different from the one he had grown up in.

For Terry, information technology was a constant frustration. No sooner had he mastered one marvel, than six new ones demanded attention. More than anything else, it gave him intimations of his increasing age. Only in his forties, but already the digital world was leaving him behind. He had only the vaguest comprehension of the games his girls played on their Ipads; if he tried to keep up, they mocked him for his slowness, like Einstein teaching a chimpanzee. Yet luckily, or so he fondly hoped, they had so far only discovered the beauty, the challenge, the good side.

When today's battle was over and the children were safely in bed, Terry decided to go out for a walk. Trude was watching a football match in which her boyfriend, Odd, was playing. Terry had no interest in football and feared the day when they would marry and she would leave. Odd had already pointed out that the paltry salary Terry paid her was less than he could earn in a day. So far she had decided to stay. But soon? Farewells, interviews, negotiations.

He shrugged on his coat and set out into the night. The rain had stopped, but the roads and pavement were still damp. The air was keen, with that sharp penetrating cold that a damp English winter brings, even when the temperature is above freezing. But Terry felt fit and in need of the exercise – already he was stronger than he'd been for weeks, thank goodness. His arm was still a nuisance – inside the coat while his right sleeve hung empty – but the plaster would come off tomorrow, thank God.

He thought back on the interview with Starkey. That had been a pleasant surprise; he'd been dreading it. Now, if the suspension was lifted as the man had promised, all he had to do was get fit and go back to work. That couldn't be long, surely.

He lengthened his stride, deliberately testing himself. He could breathe more easily now. His ribs had healed, and the sharp inhibiting pain that exercise had still provoked a week ago had gone. He remembered the sudden sharp cry that Sarah had let out when they were making love – her ribs had been sore back then, he'd had to be careful. Well, now the boot was on the other foot; perhaps soon, after this trial, she'd let him back into her bed. Go gently, he'd say; remember how I was with you.

Or had that been just a nine-day wonder, a flash in the pan? Well, we'll soon see.

He realised he was approaching the Hull road, unconsciously retracing the steps he had taken the night of his accident, so long ago it seemed now. He'd been angry that evening, he remembered – what had that been about?

Of course, it was Sarah! He'd taken her and Emily out for a meal – expensive, too – and all the reward he'd got was for Sarah to put their affair on hold. No more sex, till the trial was over.

Typical Sarah, work before pleasure! Well, the wretched trial would soon be over now. Terry hadn't followed it closely, but he gathered that the student – what was his name, Adrian – wasn't doing too well. Well, he shouldn't have lied. Soon he'll be locked away at Her Majesty's pleasure and then perhaps I'll phone Sarah, offer my commiserations, and say...

He was approaching the Hull Road. Following the path across a stretch of damp grass and trees, he saw the lights of the *Inner Space Service Station* beyond the roundabout. Daleks on the roof, giant robot transformer guarding the shop entrance. Pity *they* didn't protect me! Terry thought wryly. Images of the CCTV flashed before his mind, and the photo of that man Angus. But that was all he had. Nothing personal, no memory of how the accident had seemed to him. His brain hurt, it was frustrating. *Why can't I remember?* There may be something important there, something I need to know.

He crossed the dual carriageway, looking carefully right and left, and headed towards Osbaldwick. This is the way I came that night – a trip along memory lane. By the time he reached the village proper he was breathing steadily, feeling the benefits of the exercise. He passed the pub, where people were leaving – cars, a man talking on his phone. Round the next bend was the track leading to Straw House Barn – *don't go there, Terry, it's none of your business now.* He hesitated, then turned to go on.

Put it behind you, Terry, that case is all over now. And yet ....

What is it I can't remember?

48. Grieving Husband

SARAH PEERED into the ladies' room mirror, adjusting her eye-liner. Just a little touch here, maybe – how will that do? She sat back and surveyed the result. *Is my face getting thinner, perhaps? Deeper lines round the mouth, more crow's feet at the edge of my eyes? What's that – the effect of age or the strain of this trial?*

Ah well, it'll do for today. *Cruella de Vil*. She lifted her lip and snarled at her reflection; then slowly, let the snarl subside into a gaze cold and stony as death. *A Gorgon, perhaps, Medusa – all I need now is a head full of writhing snakes to help me shrivel the bastard to stone!* She lifted her wig carefully onto her head. *No snakes, exactly, but still ... this is why we wear it, a helmet, a disguise.*

I'm acting a role today. It won't be me, personally, wielding the knife. Trying to make a grieving husband feel guilty. It's justice. Adrian's right to a vigorous defence.

Inside she was trembling. *Butterflies before court she was used to, but not these black ones – moths of self-doubt. Come on, Sarah, you're growing soft. Just do your job – that's what young Adrian's hired you to do, the lying little toad. Just because you're a granny doesn't mean you can't act the witch as well. There are lots of fairy tales like that – must be.*

But none with happy endings. The witch gets the best part, and dies. Aaargh! She scowled, then relented, and beamed at the mirror instead. Her image beamed back at her, a wide, false, cheery smile.

I'm a nice person really, most people love me. Those who don't, deserve to die!

As she turned away from the mirror her phone rang. *Oh God, not now, what's this?* She fumbled in her bag, picked it up, and said:

'Terry! Hi! This isn't really a good time.'

'Sorry. Are you just about to go into court?'

'Yes. Ring me later, this evening.'

'That could be too late. Listen, Sarah, this is important. It's to do with your trial.'

'I can give you one minute, no more.'

'I spoke to Emily this morning, she says you've got Tom Weston on the stand today ...'

'Yes, that's right. So?'

'Last night I remembered something, you see. I went for a walk and my mind's coming back, at last. I'm going into work later. They're lifting my suspension.'

'Well, good for you, Terry, but ...'

'That night when I had the accident, I was thinking hard about the murder, and I had this idea. You know, I always had my doubts about young Adrian – well, perhaps you didn't know, but anyway, I did ...'

'Terry, get to the point, please.'

She opened the door to the corridor, and saw Alex Corder walking past with his junior, heading into court. Any moment the judge would come in too, and the last thing Sarah wanted to do was start her morning with a public apology for being late.

'... I always suspected Tom Weston, but he had an alibi, as you know. But last night, on the walk, I remembered something. It's important. Look, Sarah, this what you've got to ask him. Please.'

'I can't just change my questions now, with ten seconds to go! Terry, that's not how I work.' In every case, Sarah tried to have her line of questioning not just written down clearly on a pad in front of her, but also burnt into her memory as well – the main points at least. Only that way, with a clear framework in front of her, was she able occasionally to improvise – often with devastating results. So for Terry to suggest changing her plan now ...

'Look, Sarah it's very simple, on the surface anyway. Not controversial or aggressive or complicated. Just ask him one thing. With luck, he'll never even guess it's a problem. Then I can explain the significance later perhaps, at lunch time ...'

'Okay then, Terry,' Sarah sighed. 'Just tell me.'

'Right. All you've got to ask him is this ...'

* * *

It was the first time Sarah had seen Tom Weston, but there was something oddly familiar about his body language. As he took the oath, she saw a tall skinny man, clean shaven, about fifty years old, with receding sandy hair, a lined forehead, and short goatee beard beside which deep lines ran from his nose to his mouth. This man really does look a little like Bob, she thought, just as Emily said. He wore a dark blue suit and tie in keeping with his mourning but no wedding ring on his thin bony fingers, she noticed – why was that? Had he removed it the moment he became a widower – for the second time – or did he, like many men, regard wedding rings as a feminine affectation, a statement of attachment for wives, not husbands?

Bob had been like that, she remembered bitterly. She'd bought him a ring with the fee from her first big case, solid gold, twenty four carat, but he'd only worn it for a couple of years before hiding it somewhere. It gets stuck on my finger, he'd said, it feels claustrophobic.

So much easier to play away if you pretend to be single.

Shut up, Sarah. That's just the sort of callous comment that will get you into trouble with the judge. In an earlier meeting in chambers Judge Eckersley had made the limits to this cross-examination quite plain. 'This trial is to establish the guilt or innocence of your client, Mrs Newby, nothing more,' she had said sternly. 'Any gratuitous attempts to explore wider pastures will be firmly stamped on.'

And yet that was exactly what Sarah intended to do. She had made that clear in Adrian's defence statement. The defence refused to accept that the prosecution had proven – beyond all reasonable doubt – that Vicky Weston had definitely been murdered. The pathologist had admitted a small level of uncertainty – her diagnosis was difficult, she might be mistaken. The crystals of salt and diluted blood in the car boot might have innocent explanations. An eye witness, Mrs Bishop, had seen Vicky Weston driving her own car that Sunday evening – she might have been driving to the river to commit suicide. It was a long shot, but Sarah refused to give it up. Keep that awkward idea in the jury's minds, and they were halfway to an acquittal.

The trick today would be to focus the jury's suspicions on the bereaved husband, without making them dislike the barrister in the process. Not too much Cruella de Vil, she thought. Try to avoid that face if you can.

Sarah got her feet and stood silently for a moment, waiting for Tom Weston to focus on her.

'Good morning, Mr Weston. Victoria Weston was your wife, wasn't she? How long had you been married to her?'

'I think ... three years. Nearly four.'

'I see. She was your second wife, wasn't she?'

'Yes.'

Judge Eckersley cleared her throat, just loudly enough to attract Sarah's attention. The two women's eyes locked. The judge had made it crystal clear, in chambers, that there was to be no reference to the first Mrs Weston's untimely death, also by drowning. Sarah's suggestion that the jury might find this useful information had been dismissed with contempt.

'So when you met Victoria, you were divorced, were you?' Sarah asked casually, looking away from the judge.

'No. My first wife died, unfortunately.'

'Oh.' Sarah waited, hoping for more. In particular the words *she drowned at sea in a sailing accident* would have been very helpful. But they did not come.

'Mrs Newby?' the judge prompted pointedly, after a few moments.

'Yes, My Lady.' Sarah drew a line on her pad, turning to her second line of questions. 'In your statement to the police, Mr Weston, you say that you last saw your wife on the morning of Friday 26th August. Is that correct?'

'Yes, it is.'

'Tell us about that morning. What did you say to each other?'

'We ... excuse me.' Tom coughed, and took a sip of water. 'We argued, as I have already said. It was very unfortunate.'

'Yes. What did you argue about?'

Tom shrugged, as though irritated by the question. 'It was about a number of petty unimportant things, but chiefly about my wife's sexual behaviour. I believed she was having an affair with one of her students. Which, as we now know, turned out to be true. That man there.' He pointed to Adrian in the dock.

'This was quite a heated argument, I believe,' Sarah said. 'Plates were thrown, harsh words said.'

'That's true, yes. Unfortunately.'

'Did you throw the plates, or did she?'

'She threw them. Not me.'

'Was there any violence involved?'

'No. Just harsh words. Shouting.'

'This was about a text which she had sent to the defendant, was it? Which you happened to see on her phone?'

'It was, yes.'

'I see. Mr Weston, I wonder if you could help the court with this. It seems a little strange, if this was an argument in which you were accusing your wife of infidelity, that *she* was the one who threw the plates. Can you explain that?'

Tom Weston shrugged. 'She's a passionate woman. She was like that.'

'She wasn't accusing you of anything?'

The judge, who had been taking handwritten notes, put down her pen and leaned forward. 'Mrs Newby, is there a basis for this?'

'There is, My Lady. My client gave evidence that Mrs Weston told him that she was very disturbed by some of her husband's behaviour. She had discovered some secret which she was about to reveal. I wondered if Mr Weston could help us with that. And since the possibility of suicide has not been entirely ruled out ...'

'Very well. But be brief.'

'Thank you, My Lady.' Sarah glanced down at the pad of handwritten notes on the lectern in front of her, trying to find the key question in this sequence. And where she could fit in Terry's questions. *Why were they so important?* 'Mr Weston, what was the secret that your wife suspected you of concealing?'

Tom Weston shook his head, exasperated and slightly flustered. 'There was no secret. I don't know what you're talking about!' He glanced up at the judge, who sat with pen poised, considering whether to intervene.

'No secret, Mr Weston?'

'No. None.'

'All right. You had no secrets from your wife. That's clear then, thank you. Let me move on to something else. Do you remember the day when the police came to tell you your wife's car had been found by the river?'

'I remember it very clearly, yes.'

'They asked when you had last seen her, didn't they?'

'Yes.'

'You told them about the quarrel and your suspicions of your wife's infidelity, and that you had been away in Scotland. Then they asked if you had had any contact with your wife over that weekend and you said you spoke on the phone at about seven p.m. on Sunday 28th – is that right?'

'Ye ...yes.' The answer was a little uncertain, Sarah noticed, slightly more anxious than before.

'Did she phone you or did you phone her?' Sarah knew the answer; Vicky Weston's phone records were in the file.

'She phoned me.'

'What did you talk about?'

'Well ...' the man drew a deep breath, glancing briefly at the jury. 'It was just ordinary things. She asked how the conference was going when I'd be back and ... things like that.'

'Really?' Sarah consulted her notes. 'Is that all you said? It was quite a long phone call – nine and a half minutes. Didn't you talk about the argument you'd had before you left? The row when plates were thrown?'

'We ... did discuss that, yes. I tried to calm her down. I said if she really wanted a divorce I wouldn't stand in her way.'

'How did she respond to that?'

'She seemed quite calm, really. I think she was pleased. It was what she wanted, after all. To be with lover boy.' His gaze flickered to Adrian, behind Sarah in the dock.

'Pleased and calm, you say. So it was a reasonable conversation, that's what you're telling this court? She didn't seem upset or unhappy?'

'Not particularly, no.'

'All right, let's move on. Mr Weston, would you turn to page 43 of the first bundle, please. What do you find there?'

Tom Weston leafed through the file. 'It ... oh yes, this. It's a printout of a text message from my wife.'

'Indeed. Have you seen it before?'

'Yes. I showed it to the police that morning. When they came to tell me they had found her car.'

'All right. Would you read it out to us please?'

In a flat expressionless voice Tom read: *'Everything ends and this is how it is for me. Love turns to hatred, hope to despair. No understanding, no one cares. Let the river wash away the pain.'*

The court had fallen silent. No one, not even in the public gallery, coughed or muttered or fidgeted. Sarah paused for a while before continuing.

'When did you receive this message?'

'It was sent to me at 9.37 on Sunday evening. But I didn't read it until next morning.'

'Why was that?'

'I was busy. I'm not a teenager – I don't check my phone every five minutes. After all we'd spoken only two hours before. I wasn't expecting to hear from her again.'

'When you saw the message next morning, it must have come as a shock to you, then?'

'Well yes, a bit.'

'Is that all?'

'Look, Vicky often sent crazy messages. I didn't really take it seriously. I thought she must have been drinking, perhaps.'

'Did you send her an answer?'

'No.'

'*No?* Why not?'

'I ... couldn't really think of what to say.'

'Did you ring her, to see if she was all right?'

'I tried to ring, but I got no answer. Just a message that said *number unobtainable.*'

'Did you leave a voicemail?'

'No. I hate voicemail. Anyway I thought she would explain it to me when I got home. If she wanted to.'

'I see. And then when you did get home and she wasn't there, you showed this message to the police?'

'Yes.'

'Try to help the court, Mr Weston, if you would. What do you understand, exactly, by this message? What is your wife trying to tell you?'

'Well, it *appears* to be a suicide note.'

'Indeed. Your wife, with whom you admit you quarrelled, and whom you are thinking to divorce, sends you a suicide text. And yet here we are trying my client for murder. Can you explain that, Mr Weston?'

'Well, I don't believe it's genuine. I think it's a trick – it must have been composed and sent by her killer – that man over there!'

'And yet when you showed it to the police, Mr Weston, you thought it was genuine then. It reads like something your wife might have written, doesn't it?'

'Possibly, yes.'

'*Love turns to hatred, hope to despair. No understanding, no one cares.* It's quite poetic, isn't it? And your wife was a student of poetry.'

'Yes, but she didn't write this!' No longer dejected, Tom flashed out the words sharply, glaring at his tormentor. But his gaze slid over Sarah, seeking someone behind her. Adrian in the dock, she assumed.

'How do you know that?'

'Because she was murdered! The police say so, they've proved it! So this message is a fake. It was written by her killer!'

'That is one possibility Mr Weston, indeed. But I put it to you that there is another one. You say this reads like a message your wife might have written. Is it not possible that she might actually have written it? That this conversation you had at seven o'clock was not nearly so reasonable as you have said. That it was actually quite a nasty vicious quarrel lasting over nine minutes on the phone. And that it upset her so much that she decided to commit suicide as a result? And actually did so that same evening? While you ignored her last message?'

Alex Corder heaved himself to his feet. 'My Lady, please. This charade has gone on long enough. This witness cannot possibly answer that question. He has no way of knowing.'

'Quite.' The judge turned towards the witness. 'Please don't try to answer, Mr Weston. Mrs Newby, is that all?'

Almost, Sarah thought. She looked down at her pad. She had planned to end here, with a bang. *But what were those questions Terry said I should ask? Are they really so important? This is the dramatic moment, I should end here.*

She felt a tap on her shoulder. She turned, to see Lucy with a sheet of paper in her hand. For the past few minutes Sarah had been subliminally aware of movement behind her, rustling and the opening and closing of files, but had ignored it. Now she saw the urgent, eager look on her solicitor's face. Sarah turned back to the judge.

'My Lady, if I could just confer for a few moments?'

Judge Eckersley glanced benevolently at the jury. 'In that case, I am sure we could all do with a break. Fifteen minutes, Mrs Newby?'

'Thank you, My Lady.'

* * *

'So, Lucy, what is it?'

They huddled together, talking in urgent whispers, their backs to the prosecution team so that, with luck, they couldn't be overheard. Lucy had a ring-binder open in front of her – a blue one full of the unused material that they had ploughed through ages ago and forgotten, agreeing with the CPS that it was irrelevant. It was open at a page showing phone records.

'I've been on the phone to Terry Bateson. He's really psyched up about this – says his memory's coming back and he's remembered what worried him about this case. He was transferred to other duties before his accident – did you know?'

'Yes. So, what's he excited about?'

'Well, it's this ...' For the next fifteen minutes they conferred urgently together, Lucy flicking back and forth through the file while Sarah scribbled notes on her pad. Sarah chuckled softly.

'I start the morning suggesting he drove her to suicide and end by accusing him of murder. Brilliant, Luce – we should go on stage!'

'You *are* on stage,' Lucy hissed, as the jury filed back into court. The judge walked in. All the lawyers rose and bowed, but only Sarah stayed on her feet.

'Well, Mrs Newby,' Judge Eckersley asked. 'Do you have more, or can we adjourn for lunch?'

'A few more questions, My Lady.' She turned to the witness. *He really does look like Bob,* she thought suddenly. *It's quite eerie.*

'Mr Weston, the sudden death of your wife, however it was caused, was clearly a terrible shock for you.' She paused. No response, just an angry glare. Fair enough, she acknowledged – I've been trying to blame him for it all morning. 'When you realised your wife was missing, and had sent you this curious message, did you phone anyone for support?'

'Well, yes. Several people. Colleagues at work. My sister.'

'Your sister. That would be Mrs Audrey Adair, would it?'

'Yes, that's right.'

'You're quite close to her, are you?'

'Fairly close, yes.'

'How did she find out that your wife was missing, and that the police had called?'

'Well, I phoned her, I suppose.'

'You rang her, from your mobile phone?'

'I suppose so, yes.'

'Did you call her again, over the following days? Exchange texts, perhaps – communicate several times?'

'We may have done, perhaps, yeah.' A flicker, just the faintest sign of worry, crossed his brow.

'You may have done, or you did?' Sarah pressed smoothly.

'We did.'

'All right. In the week after your wife's disappearance, you called your sister and exchanged texts several times. Perfectly natural in the circumstances. Did your sister come to visit you too, during that week?'

'Yes. She was very helpful. Vicky had left the house in a mess; Audrey helped me clear it up. Hired a new cleaner, too – Vicky had quarrelled with the last one.'

'Very helpful, I'm sure.' Sarah leafed back through her pad to a note she had made on the evidence of the forensic scientist. 'Was that when you drained and refilled the hot tub?'

'About that time, yes.'

'Was that your idea, or hers?'

'Audrey's, probably, or the cleaner. It needs regular maintenance.'

'I see. And this was before the forensic scientists took samples?'

'I suppose it must have been.' The casual shrug which accompanied this answer was not, Sarah thought, entirely convincing. He was looking rattled.

'All right, let's return to these phone calls. When was the first time you rang your sister? After your return from Scotland, I mean?'

'I don't know. That same day, probably. When the police came to tell me they'd found Vicky's car. I rang after they'd gone.'

'To say Vicky was missing, and ask if your sister had seen her or knew where she was?'

'Something like that, yes.'

'But she didn't?'

'Didn't what?'

'Know where Vicky was?'

'Obviously not, no. She'd been away on holiday, anyway.'

'Oh, really?' Sarah hadn't known this. 'When did she get back?'

'Saturday night, I think. You'd have to ask her. She'd been in Ibiza.'

'I see. Were you in contact with her then, too? While she was on holiday?'

'We may have spoken once or twice. Why does it matter?'

Sarah shook her head. Terry had asked her to slip this in but she wasn't sure why. Neither, from the expression on her face, was the judge. Swiftly, she returned to the line of questions she had jotted down five minutes ago.

'I believe your sister was also present when the police first called to inform you that they were treating your wife's death as murder, is that right?'

'Yes, she was there then too.'

'And she subsequently made a statement to the police? As you did?'

'Yes.'

'On that occasion, did the police ask to see your mobile phone?'

'I think so, yes.'

'What kind of phone is it, Mr Weston? Do you have it on you, perhaps?'

'I ... what? No, no I don't. Sorry.' His right hand flew to his jacket pocket, then as swiftly away as though scalded. Quite suddenly, the man's face had paled, his dark eyes staring at Sarah in shock. *He's lying,* Sarah realised triumphantly. *He guesses where I'm going now, too. Terry must be right!*

'You don't carry a mobile phone?' Her voice so sweet, so innocently surprised.

'No, not always. I told you.'

'You're sure it's not in your pocket, right now?'

Once again Alex Corder lumbered to his feet. 'My Lady, I fail to see the relevance of this. My learned colleague is badgering the witness to no purpose.'

'Mrs Newby?' the judge asked, raising an eyebrow curiously.

'There is a firm basis, My Lady, which I will turn to now. Mr Weston, I invite you to look at bundle number 4, from the unused material. Page 97. If the clerk of the court could help the witness?'

Several minutes followed while the clerk helped the witness, jury, judge, and prosecution barristers to find the relevant ring binder. While this was going on around her, Sarah stood watching the witness coolly. Twice, when he thought no one was looking, his right hand fluttered towards his jacket pocket. Once he patted it gently, as if to reassure himself about what was inside.

When everyone was on the right page Sarah said: 'Mr Weston, this is a page from your mobile phone records, for the period from 26th August to 7th September. Could you show us, please, the calls and texts you made to your sister, Audrey Adair.'

Tom Weston ran his finger down the page. There was a pause, which lasted some time. At last he looked up.

'I'm sorry, I'm not sure. I don't remember her number.'

'Oh dear. Perhaps I can help you. It's 17948 776392.'

Another pause, nearly twenty seconds. 'I can't find it.'

'No. It's not there, Mr Weston, is it? Would you turn to page 105, please.'

More rustling and turning of pages. Sarah waited until she was quite sure everyone – especially the judge and jury – had found the correct page, and had a moment to guess about what might come next.

'This is the mobile phone record for the same period 26 August – 7 September – for your sister, Mrs Audrey Adair. Could you check please for calls and texts coming from your own phone to her, please, Mr Weston? You remember your own phone number, do you?'

'I'm not sure, I ...' His right hand fluttered away from the file, but he brought it back swiftly.

'You could check the phone in your pocket, if you like.'

'I ... no, it's okay.' An angry red flush was appearing on the neck below the pale, shocked face. He bent his head, running his finger furiously down the printed page. Sarah waited, staring intensely at the witness, her face cold and serious beneath her wig, like Medusa.

At last he looked up, speechless.

'It's not there, is it, Mr Weston?'

'No, I ... probably made a mistake. I used the landline.'

'Really? Shall we check those records too?' Sarah turned, hoping that Lucy, as agreed in their hurried whispered conference, had tracked the landline records down as well. Lucy shook her head. Not yet. *Shit.*

Sarah turned to the judge. 'My Lady, it may take some time to trace the landline records but I anticipate the result will be the same. Would this be a moment to adjourn for lunch?'

49. Phone a Friend

SARAH HAD no time for lunch. She was on the phone to Terry as soon as she had left the court. He was just leaving the hospital and about to drop in at his work, he said cheerfully. His arm was out of plaster and his suspension was about to be lifted.

'That's great, Terry. Now, I've asked your questions. Come on, explain.'

'Had he phoned his sister as he claims?' Terry asked.

'No. No record of it. Not a trace. Oh Christ, look at this.' In front of Sarah, the river had seeped through the barrier of sandbags and was halfway across Tower Street. The road was closed to traffic, Environment Agency workers and young squaddies everywhere. Sarah and Lucy picked their way along a line of duckboards through plastic barriers towards her chambers.

'What's up?' Terry asked.

'Just the floods. I need wellies, not court shoes. So, Terry, why does all this matter?'

'Did he show you his phone?'

'No. Claimed he'd left it at home. As if. His hand kept fluttering to his pocket.'

'You need to see it, Sarah.'

'I can't – I haven't got a search warrant. I can't arrest him. Why, anyway?'

'I'll bet you it's got two SIM cards.'

'What?' She was climbing the stairs to her office as she spoke, Lucy toiling behind her. Terry's voice was urgent in her ear.

'I saw it before. It was months ago, but it's all coming back now, my memory. Like a flood.'

'Don't talk to me about floods.' Sarah kicked open her door, walked to the window, and stared out. She might have been on a ship. The park had totally vanished, the arches of Skeldergate Bridge were only six inches above the swirling brown torrent of the river Ouse. Beyond it her apartment building was still standing. For now, at least.

'Yes, it feels great, it's like ... well, anyway. The thing is when I first asked him to show me his phone, months ago – it's just a little black Nokia, nothing fancy – he slipped out of the room to fetch it. He didn't have it on him then, either, or so he claimed. But I remember – I'm almost sure about this – when I looked at the screen it said something like *SIM card 1, SIM card 2*. Only *SIM card 2* was blank.'

'So, what does that tell you?'

'Well, nothing I thought at the time, but now ... you see later, that night before my accident, I saw a man on his phone outside a pub and there was something he said – I thought he had two SIM cards too – and that triggered this other memory, you see.'

'*You* may see, Terry, but *I* don't. Why does it matter?'

'Well look, he says he spoke to his sister but there's no record of it, right? You established that this morning. So if there is a second SIM card I'll bet he used that.'

'He had two phone numbers on the same phone, you mean?'

'Yes, exactly. And when I asked to see his phone he slipped out of the room to remove the second one, before he gave it to me.'

'The devious bastard,' Sarah murmured. 'But even if that's true, I still don't see ...'

'Well look, you know this was my case before Will Churchill passed it on to Jane Carter, don't you? And although your client, young Adrian, clearly lied and was in the area when we think the woman was killed, there were a number of things that didn't quite fit ...'

'Like the bicycle, you mean, and the fact he can't drive?'

'Yes, that, and the motive too. I interviewed him twice and it never rang true to me. Whereas Tom Weston, her husband – I never took to him, Sarah. You know his first wife died too, don't you? Drowned as well – in a sailing accident, apparently. He inherited the house which her parents had bought for them.'

'Yes, I know,' Sarah said. 'I tried to sneak that in but the judge wouldn't let me. Anyway, Terry, I still don't see how this helps. He may have driven Vicky to suicide – that's one line of my defence – but he couldn't have murdered her. He was in Scotland, remember? He has a cast iron alibi.'

'Yes, I know.' Terry sounded deflated. 'What about his sister?'

'*His sister?*' Lucy, sitting at Sarah's desk leafing through the files, looked up in surprise. 'You think *she* killed her? Why?'

'Well, there's that eye witness, Mrs Bishop, remember?' Terry said. 'She saw Vicky Weston's car being driven by a woman. Jane Carter tried to shake her but she was adamant.'

'I know. Mrs Bishop stuck to her story in court too. And she knew Vicky; she swore it was her. That's why I still say it could be suicide.'

'It's not suicide, it's murder, Sarah. Trust the pathologist.'

'Well ... look, let's not argue about that. If you're suggesting Tom's sister murdered Vicky Weston, what possible motive could she have?'

'Well, that ...' Terry hesitated. Even on the phone, Sarah could almost see him shrugging in exasperation. 'I don't know. Maybe she loves her brother. Did it for him.'

'Sounds a bit thin, Terry.'

'Maybe. But it's not so thin if, as I suspect, Tom Weston was on the phone to her all the time using *SIM card 2*, is it? A card he's deliberately hidden? Perhaps he was giving her instructions, knowing that he was safe in Scotland with his wretched alibi.'

'Terry, I don't know. This sounds like a fantasy ...'

'A fantasy based on facts, Sarah. A few facts, anyway. Look, all you've got to do is get his sister – Audrey something she's called – on the witness stand and take it from there.'

Sarah laughed. 'You want me to ask if her she's a murderer, do you? In open court? Fat chance. The judge will laugh in my face.'

'Well, look – you've got her statement and her phone records, haven't you? It'll be in there somewhere in the – what do you call it – unused material. Ask her how often she phoned her brother, and ... see how it develops.'

'Well, maybe.' Sarah sighed. 'I can give it a try. But I don't think this judge is entirely sympathetic to me. She hates my suggestions about suicide – and now this.'

'You want to win this case, don't you?'

'Sure.' Sarah didn't sound too convinced, even to herself. 'Obviously.'

'Well, go for it then. If you do win you can buy me a drink, or something. A victory celebration.'

'Oh yes?' Sarah smiled. 'Don't get your hopes up, cowboy.'

* * *

As Sarah had feared, Judge Eckersley was less than impressed. Meeting in the judge's chambers without the jury, she said: 'Aubrey Adair? I don't find her anywhere on your list of defence witnesses.'

'No, My Lady. She's not there. But she was interviewed by the police so her witness statement is in the bundle. The defence have always been aware of her evidence but it has assumed new importance in the light of this morning's testimony by her brother, Tom Weston. Very suspect testimony, I think you'll agree. He claims he phoned his sister numerous times and yet there is no record of those calls whatsoever.'

'Yes, I saw that.' Catherine Eckersley was a tall, angular woman in her late fifties. Her thin, bony figure suggested she might have been an athlete – a hockey or lacrosse player – in her youth, and she still looked fit and healthy. Unlike many judges she did not lounge behind her desk in the oversize padded leather chair thoughtfully provided for sixteen stone men, but paced up and down behind it, occasionally glancing out of the window at the ever-widening river which was threatening to cross the road and lap at the edges of the Crown Court itself.

'So what exactly do you propose to ask this witness, if I allow it?'

'My Lady, in addition to her witness statement, we have her phone records. These show numerous calls to and from the same mobile phone number beginning on Friday 26 August and continuing throughout the weekend of 27-28 August, when the police believe Vicky Weston was killed. These calls are very frequent and may have some connection to the murder – if murder it was.'

'I thought you believed it was suicide,' the judge remarked with a thin smile.

'My Lady, I believe nothing,' Sarah replied, as smoothly as she could. 'The defence are merely exploring the possibilities. And whether this was murder or suicide, we think that this woman, and these phone calls, may have had something to do with it.'

'It's a bit late, Mrs Newby, isn't it? Why didn't you list this witness before?'

'There have been new developments, My Lady. Arising particularly out of the probable perjury of the witness this morning.'

'Perjury?' Alex Corder snorted. Standing beside Sarah, he was having some difficulty supporting his huge bulk, and was wishing that the pesky judge would come away from the window and sit behind her desk like a normal person, so that they could have this discussion in comfort. 'That's a bit harsh. Remember, the poor man's just lost his wife!'

'And his phone too, it seems,' Sarah said smoothly. 'Didn't you see his hands fluttering towards his pocket? He's hiding something, My Lady, and the court needs to know what it is.'

'Maybe, Mrs Newby.' The judge examined the large wedding ring on her bony fingers, and cracked her knuckles unexpectedly. 'But we are not detectives, remember. The police are there to investigate, we just examine the evidence. I can't order a search of the man's pockets. Anyway, who is this mysterious number registered to?'

'That's what I want to ask the witness, My Lady. If it turns out to be her brother, then ...'

'Then what?' Corder asked. 'The man was in Scotland, we know that. This looks to me like a wild goose chase, My Lady, I'm afraid. With the greatest respect to my learned friend, she is conducting this defence as if she was on a daytime television show. She insults the court's intelligence by trying to portray murder as suicide, and now appears to be suggesting that this was somehow murder by remote control – both of which are absurd fantasies designed to encourage the jury into wild speculation, and distract their attention from the obvious guilt of her client.'

'My Lady, I am simply asking to be allowed to examine the evidence – evidence collected by the police – as thoroughly as possible.'

Sarah had noticed the expression which crossed the judge's face while Corder was speaking. A frown of irritation perhaps, or distaste; whichever it was, she decided her best tactic was not to respond. Alex Corder was probably not the first overweight male QC to attempt to bully Catherine Eckersley; more than once, no doubt, as a young barrister, she had been in Sarah's position.

'Well, well.' The judge turned to Sarah, the faintest hint of a conspiratorial twinkle in her eyes. 'Do you have this witness in court?'

'No, My Lady. She will have to be summoned.'

The judge glanced out of the window. Low dark rainclouds were gathering and the ubiquitous flood water was pitted by rainfall.

'In that case, I imagine everyone, jurors included, will be relieved to get home early. I'll adjourn until tomorrow morning, Mrs Newby. If you want this witness to give evidence, try to get her here by then, all right? By boat, if necessary.'

* * *

Watching Tom Weston give evidence in court, Emily had had a brilliant idea. He really did look quite like her father. A little taller, perhaps, stronger in the shoulders, and with a mean, distrustful look which she had seldom seen on her father's face, at least not often. Once or twice perhaps, when he'd been losing an argument with her mother, as this man was now.

Emily wasn't hugely concerned with the guilt or innocence of Adrian Norton. It was interesting, of course, to watch her mother conduct a murder trial, but she didn't really care who won. What mattered to her was to rescue her father from his nightmare of false accusations – they *must* be false, she told herself firmly at night, when the doubts sometimes crept in. *My father wouldn't do that!*

But the more she delved into the case the more certain she became that this man Tom Weston was at the heart of it. It was he who had been dismissed by the headmaster, not her dad; his face stared at her out of the old school photograph. And now here he was, amazingly, giving evidence in court. It was an opportunity too good to be missed.

Emily thought of running her idea past her mother but by the time she had come down from the public gallery Sarah was already hurrying away towards Tower Street with Lucy Parsons. At the same time, there was Tom Weston, walking in the opposite direction towards the castle car park. Emily started to follow him but she was only halfway there when he got into a dark green Range Rover, backed it out of the parking space, and drove away.

Never mind, she thought. It doesn't matter, I know where he lives. Terry Bateson told me.

50. Burglar

'I T'S JUST the perfect opportunity, Dad, don't you see? Of course he won't confess outright, but if he just admits he knew those two girls, that'll be a start. Anything will help, at this stage.'

'I don't know, Emily. Remember what Lucy Parsons said about harassing witnesses. I don't want to see you in trouble.'

'Tom Weston's not a witness, Dad, not in your case anyway. That's the whole point. The police are refusing to interview him, so I will.'

'You'll be impersonating a journalist, again.'

'I *am* a journalist, Dad, I've still got my press card. Anyway, he doesn't have to talk to me if he doesn't want to.'

'How do you know where he lives?'

'Terry Bateson told me. The detective.'

'Well, take care, for heaven's sake. I don't want you hurt.'

Emily laughed. 'I'm a big girl, Dad, I can look after myself.' She was sitting at the back of a half empty bus. Rain streaked down the windows out of a leaden sky. The phone signal to her father in Harrogate was intermittent. Twice she had had to redial when it cut out. As the bus approached the stop for Osbaldwick she said: 'I'll call you later, Dad, tell you how it went. It's worth a try, don't you think? Take care.'

* * *

'Welcome back, Terence,' Will Churchill said. 'You know I always believed in you.'

'Thank you, sir.' *Lying toad,* Terry thought, *you were hoping to get rid of me.* He smiled politely.

'How's the arm?'

'Thinner than it was, but it works, that's the main thing.' Terry flexed his right arm gingerly. It felt strange to have it out of plaster at last, inside a proper jacket sleeve, where it should be. But not much stranger than to be here, in Churchill's office, no longer an outcast or a suspect but a visitor. He had been called in to be told that his suspension was officially lifted; now he was only off duty on sick leave.

'When can we expect you back?'

'In a week or so, the medics say. I'm still a bit ... fragile.'

'Well, don't rush. And no more fights with forty ton trucks, eh?' Churchill smiled, picking up a pen to show the interview was ended. 'DS Starkey wants a word, before you go.'

Closing the door softly behind him, Terry thought, that's a first. Anyone would think we were best mates. Though if Jane's trial goes tits up because of what I told Sarah this morning, that'll soon change. Normal hostilities will resume, without quarter.

Dave Starkey actually stood up to shake his hand. Terry winced, but tried to return the grip. 'So, you want to see me?'

'Yes, I've got some more stuff on the Mary Nightingale case – you know, Maria Slavik, the kid who was run over with you.'

'How is she?'

'Walking fine, they say. Back to school. Here, take a look.'

Starkey clicked a mouse and the image of a skinny teenage girl in jeans and a puffy anorak appeared on the computer screen. She had dark hair and a shy, distrustful smile on her face. She was supporting herself with a metal hospital crutch, and behind her, in a school playground, other children were playing.

'She'll be a bit of a loner, after all she's been through,' Terry said. *This child is no older than my Jessica, he thought; yet she's been kidnapped, trafficked halfway across Europe, and prostituted ten times a day. How can anyone survive that unscarred?*

'At least she's back with her family,' said Starkey, sharing his thoughts. 'Let's hope they weren't part of the problem in the first place.'

'Amen to that.' Terry nodded, remembering that Starkey, too, had young daughters. 'So, are you on the track of these bastards?'

'A bit more information, at least. I thought you'd like to see it.' Starkey opened a folder on his desk. 'We've traced the phone records of Alastair MacFarlane – or Aberdeen Angus as he chooses to call himself – which is why you're a free man.' Starkey grinned. 'You don't feature in his address book, not even among his favourites. But someone who does ...' he ran a finger down the list to a number which was marked with a yellow highlighter '... is this number here. See the time and date? A call made just eighteen minutes before you tried to hold up the traffic. So this poor kid, Mary, was almost certainly right. He *was* trying to pimp her to a customer – just not you.'

'So who is he?' Terry asked, his voice grim. 'Have you tracked the bugger down yet?'

'Not yet, but we will. We know he's not some random punter, though. Look here ...' Starkey flicked over a page. '... here, and here. These boys are talking to each other quite a lot. But the number is pay as you go, no account, no name. What we can say, though, is that he was somewhere in York when he rang. Not just on that day, but other days too. Probably lives here. This came through this morning.'

He pulled a document, several pages long, from an envelope on his desk. 'The cell site report. Traces every phone call to the radio mast nearest to the caller and receiver. Most of the time – including on the day of your accident – the nearest radio mast to this fellow was here.' He pointed to a map included with the report. 'The village of Osbaldwick. Know it?'

* * *

Approaching Straw House Barn, Emily was surprised to see how grand it was. Terry had told her the location but not described the building. But it was clearly the right place. As she walked between the wrought iron gates, she saw the dark green Range Rover parked beside an Audi on the gravel behind what appeared to be a circular stone fishpond with a statue of a mermaid on a plinth in the middle, with water trickling down across her knees from a jug held artfully across her breasts. The effect, unfortunately, was marred by the mat of green algae which had spread across the mermaid's thighs and lower belly, fed presumably by the constant flow of water and the lack of attention to cleaning.

The house, nonetheless, was imposing, and Emily felt her nerves tingle with each intrepid step across the gravel towards the doorway in the two storey plate glass wall which filled the arch of the former brick barn. Through the glass, she saw a stone-flagged hallway in which a chandelier made from a converted wagon wheel hung from the ceiling, bright with electric bulbs.

There was no doorbell, so she knocked on the glass door, standing outside while the rain dripped on her head, trickled down the gutters, and splashed little circles in the fishpond behind.

No answer. She tried again, banging harder this time. But nobody came. There must be someone at home; the lights were on, there were two cars parked outside. But however hard she banged her palm against the wet glass, she met the same lack of response.

I haven't come this far to give up now, Emily told herself firmly. She was prepared – indeed half expecting – to be turned away by a man with no interest in talking to the press; but she refused to be rejected by a blank glass wall, however grand. After her fourth attempt at knocking she began to look around. A house this large must have more than one entrance, and perhaps – since it stupidly had no doorbell – there were rooms so far away from the front door that visitors could be ignored unheard.

Looking to her right she saw an ivy-clad garden wall at the end of the house with a door in it. She walked across to it and opened the door with the old iron ring handle. On the far side was a hedge and a rutted grassy track which led round the end of the house towards what was probably a rear garden. Cautiously, Emily walked along it, her footsteps squelching in the rain, which was now falling more heavily. At the far end of the house was what looked like an open garage with a ride-on lawnmower and some garden tools inside. To the left of the garage was a sort of patio sheltered by a roof supported on pillars – a gazebo. In the middle of the patio was – *yes, that must be it!* – a hot tub, covered by a black tarpaulin lid.

Emily stared at it, shivering slightly. Although she hadn't focussed fully on her mother's murder trial she had picked up enough to know that the victim – Tom Weston's wife – had been drowned in a hot tub, or so the prosecution claimed. Well, this must be it. All shut down and covered for the winter, presumably, but even so – a murder weapon, right here in front of her.

She stepped forward onto the patio. It was a relief to get out of the rain, which had been beating on her head. Now it drummed on the roof of the gazebo above her – a noise still loud enough to drown out the sound of any movements she made. She thought of calling out – her aim, after all, was to attract attention, to gain entrance to the house – but somehow her present situation, creeping uninvited into someone's back garden – made her movements more furtive. She moved quietly, like a trespasser.

Beyond the hot tub, still under the roof of the gazebo, was a door with a key in it, leading into some sort of changing room or garden room, perhaps.

And round the corner, away from Emily, light flooded onto a lawn from what must be a window. Was the room occupied? Or had the light been left on here just as it was in the rest of the house? Perhaps Tom Weston was too wealthy to worry about electricity bills. Emily, a long-standing member of the Green Party, frowned in disapproval.

Emboldened by this brief flash of moral superiority, she stepped forward to the door, intending to knock or open it. But as she did so she heard voices coming from the back garden. Startled, she spun to her left, uncertain whether to run or explain herself in a loud, embarrassed voice; then she realised there was no one there. The window, spreading light across the rain-sodden lawn, was half open; the voices were coming from inside the room.

* * *

'Let me see that number again,' Terry said. 'I think – have you got a pen?'

'Be my guest.' Starkey took a pen from his pocket and passed it to Terry, who copied down the number on a post-it note.

'Recognise it?'

'I'm not sure,' Terry said. 'Could be; I'd have to check in the file. Is Jane Carter around?'

'Doubt it. She's in court, isn't she? Watching her murder trial.'

'Yes, probably.' Terry thought for a moment. 'That report on the cell site location – how precise is it, exactly?'

'Well, let's see.' Starkey picked up the report and leafed through it. 'I haven't had time to study it thoroughly but ... yes, here we are. There's a mast just outside Osbaldwick and the next is in Tang Hall so ... about half a mile, they say. The best they can do.'

'So the caller from this number could have been anywhere in Osbaldwick within half a mile radius of that mast, is that it?'

'Yep. Covers several hundred households, at least.'

'What about time? Which period did you ask them to check?'

'Just the day before and after your accident. Why – what do you want to know?'

'If this number is the same as the one I'm thinking of, we'd need them to check back in August,' Terry said. But even as he spoke, he realised he was in danger of sharing too much. He hardly knew Dave Starkey. True, he seemed friendly enough today, but it was not so long since this man, and his old chum Will Churchill, had suspended Terry, making a judgement which could have ended his career. If the suspicion which he had confided in Sarah this morning did lead to the collapse of the case against Adrian Norton, his boss's fury would be rekindled.

He wouldn't be the only one, either. Jane Carter had worked hard on this case, the first murder trial she'd presented. If she thought for a moment that at this late stage he was re-activating the investigation, questioning her judgement, she'd be justifiably outraged. Suspicion wasn't good enough; he needed to be sure of his facts.

Terry looked around the room, saw an empty computer terminal. 'Mind if I use this?'

Starkey shrugged. 'Be my guest. I've got a few phone calls to make.' He grinned wolfishly. 'Some kid's been interfering with witnesses.'

* * *

Creeping closer to the door, Emily wondered what to do. She thought she recognised one of the voices – Tom Weston, the man she'd heard in court this morning. Well, it was him she'd come to see. She looked down at the door handle – there was a key in the lock, that was strange. Probably a garden room, only opened occasionally, mostly kept locked against thieves and burglars.

Like herself.

Don't be silly, I'm not a thief or a burglar, I'm here to conduct a legitimate interview.

And steal vital information, if I can.

Shut up. Just do it.

Her hand hovered over the door handle, not quite daring to turn it. Then she heard the other voice, a woman's, say clearly: 'They called already, this afternoon. They want me to give evidence, tomorrow.'

'Well, refuse,' the man said. 'They can't force you, can they?'

'I don't know. This lawyer woman seemed to think they can. Shit, Tom, what the fuck did you say?'

'As little as possible. It was all right at first, she asked about my quarrel with Vicky and the phone call that night, you know, when you rang me, and the suicide note. She still thinks it's suicide, silly bitch, trying to blame me for it. But after ...'

Silly bitch, suicide note – the words were like a jolt in Emily's brain, an electric shock. *That's Mum he's talking about, the things she questioned him about in court this morning. She'll want to hear this.*

Swiftly, Emily pulled the smartphone from her pocket, and pressed the icon for Record.

' ... she went all sweet and smarmy and asked about you.'

'About me? Why, for Christ's sake?'

'She was just saying what a shock it must have been, did I need comfort, who had I asked – so I said you'd been a great help, well, *after* of course, not *before* ...'

'Thank Christ for that.'

'I'm not that stupid, Audrey, give me credit ...'

'Aren't you?'

'*No*! For fuck's sake! Just listen, won't you?'

There was a pause. Emily's fingers shook, as she held the phone at the end of the wall near the window, where she hoped the sound would be clearest. She imagined the two speakers glaring at each other, speechless with fury, as she'd seen her parents do once. What if one of them turned away in disgust, and flounced out of the door?

'I'm listening, Tom. Just tell me.'

The woman's voice was lower now, much more steely and menacing than her brother's. Emily shivered.

'So all I said was, yes of course you'd been a comfort and a help so I'd phoned you when Vicky went missing and we thought it was suicide and so ...'

'You told her you phoned me?'

'Yes, well she asked, and that's when it started to go wrong. She has our phone records, you see, but not mine of course from that number I always use, for you and ... other stuff. And she's smart, that barrister bitch, she even asked to see my phone. I had to lie ...'

'That shouldn't have been hard. You were lying about all the rest.'

'Anyway that's what she wants to question you about. How could I ring you when there's no trace of my phone number – the one they know about – anywhere on your phone records, she asked.'

'Jesus, Tom. What a mess.'

Another pause. Emily peered back up the grassy track, thinking that would be the best escape route, when she needed one. Out past the cars and fishpond, down the lane and into the village street. Surely she could run faster than a middle-aged couple. Five yards start and they'd never catch her.

'She doesn't know that number, does she? Your second SIM card?'

'No. Well, yes, actually – Christ, of course she does. It's all over your phone records, isn't it, each time we spoke. She just can't prove for certain that it was me. That's why you can't give evidence tomorrow. You mustn't.'

'No. Obviously not. My God, Tom, you don't half screw things up. That first time, with Christine, you nearly dropped me in it.'

'Well, I didn't know you were going to kill her, did I? And I covered up for you then.'

'True, but you were glad enough when it happened, weren't you? Look at this house. All Christine's money. And now Vicky too – she *was* insured, wasn't she?'

'Yes. Though God knows how we'll claim it, if this trial goes wrong.'

'It wasn't going wrong. Till you opened your stupid mouth.'

'That's not fair, Audrey. I had to give evidence. I'm the grieving husband, remember?'

'Yeah, sure. My heart bleeds.'

Another pause. The rain had eased now, into a gentle mist. Emily held her breath, poised to flee. She could hear movement inside the room, footsteps approaching the door. Then they stopped, as though the woman, Audrey, had had another thought.

'It was bad enough when that woman saw me driving the car. She thought I was Vicky, thank God. She said that in court. But this ...Tom, what about the call I made to you that Sunday night. That was to your normal phone, wasn't it? Not to your secret SIM?'

'Yes. You rang me from Vicky's phone. She only knew about the normal number. You sent the suicide text from her phone too.'

'That looks okay then. As it was meant to. But – oh God, what about all those calls you made to me from the train on Friday morning? Running off to Scotland after you'd drowned her in the hot tub – pleading for me to come here and clear it all up? Audrey, please help me – make it look like suicide! Which I did – they were all from your second SIM card too, weren't they?'

'Yes, but they can't trace what we actually said, can they? No one records conversations, and – we didn't send texts. Or did we?'

'Christ, Tom. I don't know. What a monumental fuck up ...'

At that moment, Emily's phone rang.

51. WTF

'THAT MAN Starkey is a pain,' Lucy said, coming into Sarah's office. She shook her umbrella which sprayed drips across the room.

'What's he done now?' Sarah asked, looking up from her desk.

'Oh, it's not about this case. But I suppose you have a right to know, since it's your daughter, not your ex this time.'

'Emily? What's she done now?'

'It's not now, it was a few days ago. Didn't she tell you? She managed to find the main complainant in Bob's case. Emily paid the woman to give her a recorded interview, claiming she was a journalist.'

'Oh my God! Emily? But she's just a student.'

'Student journalist, she claims. Give the girl credit, she's got herself a press card – sort of. But Starkey's not buying it. I've just been on the phone to him for half an hour. Claims it's fraud, harassing and intimidating a witness. He hasn't realised she's your daughter – or more to the point – Bob's daughter, yet. She called herself Helen Beasley.'

'Wonderful,' Sarah groaned, leaning forward on her desk and running her hands through her hair. 'Just terrific. Exactly what I need. Why didn't she tell *me* any of this? Ask my advice, even?'

'She probably thought you were busy,' Lucy suggested. 'Which, to be fair, you are. And it's her father's case, not yours.'

'Even so, she's still my daughter, staying in my flat. I must have some sort of responsibility,' Sarah insisted. 'Even if she is technically an adult. What's Starkey going to do about it, anyway?'

'He was going to ring her, he said, as soon as I got off the phone. I tried to dissuade him, but no dice. He hasn't got her name of course, just her number which the complainant gave him. But even so ...'

'This isn't going to work out well for Emily, is it?' Sarah said gloomily.

* * *

The ringtone – the theme of Wagner's *Ride of the Valkries*, which Emily had downloaded a couple of weeks ago, after watching *Apocalypse Now* – lit up the smartphone and began its inexorable rise to a crashing crescendo. The call coincided with a pause in both the Westons' conversation and the rainstorm. Horrified, Emily crouched over the phone, desperately jabbing her finger at the screen while the horns, trumpets and trombones thundered their menacing triumph across the silent sodden lawn.

It only took a moment, but then, just as she achieved silence, the door crashed open and an arm snaked around her neck, crushing her windpipe and wrenching her backwards off balance.

'In here, you little shit!'

Choking, hands clutching at her throat, she was dragged backwards though the door and flung roughly onto a tattered sofa. A man – Tom Weston – stood glaring down at her. He shoved her back down as she attempted to rise.

'Get down! Who the fuck are you, snooping out there?'

'I'm not ... I wanted to talk ... ow!'

'*What* did you hear, eh? Were you listening outside the door?' The woman, she realised – a skinny, muscular woman, the owner of the forearm which had nearly throttled her – was standing behind the sofa. She dragged Emily back by the hair.

'Talk, you little tart. Quickly. Who are you?'

'I'm ... I was lost. I'm not stealing. Ow!'

While his sister gripped her hair, forcing her to stare up at the ceiling, Tom Weston darted outside, returning with the phone which Emily had dropped. 'Who was this phoning you then?'

'My name's Helen Beasley. Let go, please, and I'll explain.'

The grip on her hair lessened slightly, but it was still painful. Her face was still facing the ceiling. Casting her eyes down as far as she could, Emily could make out the figure of Tom Weston towering above her. Like her father but ten times bigger and a hundred times nastier. With a sister behind who had murdered someone. Wasn't that what she'd said? Both of them killers. He'd murdered his wife in that hot tub outside.

'I'm ... I'm a journalist, I just wanted to ... ow!'

'Bloody hell fire. That's all we need.' Emily saw his eyes flicker away to her tormentor behind the sofa. 'What are we going to do, Aud?'

'Ask her what she heard. You were listening, weren't you?'

'No ... I ... didn't hear anything. I'm sorry, I was lost ... aagh!'

'She's lying, we can't take the risk. This is serious, Tom. A journalist, for fuck's sake! It couldn't be worse.'

'Are you up for it?'

'How? Not another.'

'I don't see we've got any choice.'

Silence. Emily lay there on the sofa, her head stretched back, staring at the ceiling. The thin strong fingers wound tightly in her hair felt as though they would rip it right out of her scalp. Her hands and feet flailing, splayed like a starfish. She raised her right hand, trying to free her hair, but the woman's free hand snatched her wrist and twisted it back over the sofa beside her head. The woman's other hand was still wound in her hair, tugging painfully. All Emily could see was the ceiling. Her two captors leaned over her, silently conferring.

This is my life they're talking about, Emily thought frantically. *Something, I've got to do something.* Her left hand, scrabbling surreptitiously, found something smooth and hard on the sofa. Her phone. He must have dropped it. But what use is that now?

'There's the hot tub,' Audrey suggested, with a grim challenge to her brother. 'That worked fine. You can show me how it's done.'

'Tip her in and hold her legs up,' Tom said. 'Simple – two minutes splashing and kicking, all done. But we'd have to drain the tub to clean it like last time and even then, you know what that bloody pathologist said – salt water in the lungs. It won't look like an accident.'

'So how then?'

'You're the expert on accidents. What did you do with Christine?'

'That was at sea. There's no sea here.'

More silence. Emily's fingers touched the phone. It was so familiar, it gave her comfort. She'd muted it to voicemail. She wondered whether it was still recording.

'Maybe not, but ...' A cruel sadistic pleasure crept into Tom Weston's voice. As though tasting something exquisite, a joy. 'There's the river. That could be an accident. Especially now.'

'What do you mean?'

'We take her to the river, just like you did with Vicky, and in she goes. It's in flood now, haven't you seen it? A torrent. No one could fall in and survive that. A journalist, maybe she came to take a look and – whoops!'

This is it, Emily told herself. *If I don't do something soon, I'm dead.*

* * *

'There's a call for you, Sarah,' the chambers clerk said, his voice oozing tact. 'A Mr Robert Newby?'

God no, what does Bob want now? Sarah sighed, hoping her embarrassment wasn't too obvious. This young clerk was new, he'd probably guessed she was divorced, but didn't know much of her history. Anyway, what did it matter?

'Okay. Put him through.' Lucy had left and Sarah had been about to follow. She switched off her desklamp, leaned back in her office chair and gazed out into the dark of the early evening. Everywhere she looked there was water, lit here and there by floodlights brought in by the Environment Agency. It would be an adventure making her way home across Skeldergate Bridge, if it was still open.

'Sarah?'

'Bob. Hi.' Her voice was flat, cautious. What was it this time? A plea for help, reconciliation? She wasn't sure she had the energy.

'Is Emily with you?'

'No, I'm at work. Why?'

'It's just ... I'm a bit worried, that's all.'

Oh God. She remembered what Lucy had told her earlier. That detective, Starkey, has probably arrested her. And it's all Bob's fault, the idiot.

No, that's unkind. 'What are you worried about?' she asked.

'Well, I tried to phone her, and she's not answering. Her phone goes straight to voicemail'

'So? Does that matter?'

'Well, yes, because the thing is ... do you know where she went, this afternoon?'

'No, I've been working here. Where?'

'She went to interview Tom Weston.'

'*What?* Bob, you're joking!'

'No, I'm not.' As clearly as he could, Bob explained Emily's plan, as she had told it to him. Sarah was appalled.

'That's crazy! And you just let her go?'

'I didn't *let* her go, Sarah; she insisted. It was all her own idea – she's an adult, after all.'

'Even so, you could have stopped her, surely.'

'Really, I tried. But anyway that's not the point, Sarah. I'm worried. She promised to ring when she'd finished, and that was two hours ago. Nearly three. When I ring her phone it cuts off. Goes straight to voicemail.'

'Well, what can I do?'

'Call the police?'

'You could do that yourself, Bob. Why ask me?'

'Yes, but they'd probably ignore me, Sarah. You know how it is. Whereas you know who's best.'

Sarah drew a deep, long sigh. This was the history of Bob, all over again. He seemed like a competent, professional adult – he was a head teacher, after all – and yet in moments of crisis like this he passed the burden to her. Often with good reason, but still ...

'All right, Bob. I'll see what I can do. Ask Terry Bateson, perhaps.'

'Thanks, Sarah. Let me know, will you? I do care.'

* * *

'How do we get her in the car? She won't go easy.'

'Got any rope? Gaffer tape?'

'I think so. In the garage.'

'You get it then. I'll hold her here.'

The woman's left hand twisted Emily's hair tighter. Her right hand was bending Emily's wrist so sharply over the back of the sofa that it felt it might break. She raised her bottom, arched her back to make the position more bearable. As she stared helplessly up at the ceiling, Tom Weston's face swam into view.

'Stay there, you little cunt. One move and I'll break your neck.'

Then a huge, stinging pain as he slapped her face – left, right, left again. Her eyes flooded with tears, her nose seemed so full she couldn't breathe.

'Go out, Tom, I've got her.'

Emily heard the door open and close. She arched her back further to ease the pain. Her feet were pushing against the floor; she was bent over backwards, almost in a bow.

'Let go ... please. I'm a journalist.'

'Not for much longer, you little spy. Good swimmer, are you? You'll need to be.'

As Audrey spoke, she bent forwards, looking directly into Emily's eyes. Emily saw the thin, bony face, weirdly upside down, just an inch above her own. Cold grey eyes glared into hers, gloating. Thin sharp teeth grinning. A drop of spittle fell on her forehead.

Then it happened. Emily twisted her head, arched her back further, and felt the sofa tilt beneath her. As it began to topple backwards, she gave a strong shove with her feet and then drew her legs up, folding herself into a ball which increased the sofa's overbalancing momentum. The ceiling whirled above her and a second later she was on the floor, sprawling on something soft and bony – this bitch, this bloody woman, her tormentor Audrey. There was a brief, frantic scrabbling, arms and limbs everywhere. Emily flung her head sideways, felt a sudden sharp tearing pain, then the fingers clutching her hair were gone. Her wrist was free too. The woman beneath her was bony, strong, but she was winded, twice Emily's age, and her legs were trapped under the sofa. Most importantly, Emily was on top. She had no great skill in fighting but the adrenalin was surging through her. She slapped the woman's face, drove her knee into her stomach, and then gripped her throat with both hands and started to squeeze, thumbs pressed into the windpipe. Audrey's free hands snaked up and scratched Emily's face, nails digging for her eyes. Shaking her head and turning her face away, Emily continued to squeeze the woman's throat and at the same time she lifted her head and banged it hard against the floor, again and again – thump, thump, thump. Audrey started to choke, her eyes red, and her hands flew back to her throat, clawing at Emily's wrists, trying to loosen them, drag them away. But Emily was younger, stronger, fighting for her life and full of a fury she had never felt before. She squeezed until her thumbs almost met, and banged the woman's head relentlessly against the wooden floor, until slowly she realised resistance had ceased.

She stopped banging, released the pressure slowly – eyes closed, no more movement – and stood up, shaking. *Have I killed her? Doesn't matter, find out later. Got to get out of here now.* Looking around, she saw her smartphone, lying on the floor near the door where it had fallen. She picked it up – yes, still working! Had it recorded*? If I die, someone must know.* Just a few quick taps on the screen – one, two, three, scroll – that's it, now run!

She opened the door. Tom Weston stood there, filling the doorway. Emily ran forward, trying to push past him. Then a fist, like an elephant's foot, smashed into her stomach.

* * *

Terry was at the supermarket checkout when his phone rang. 'Hello?'

'Terry, it's me, Sarah. Where are you?'

'Morrisons. Doing the weekly shop, for my sins. You?'

'Walking home, crossing the bridge. It's pretty scary.' He could hear sounds like wind and rushing water in the background.

'Floods still up, then?'

'Even higher. They've closed the bridge to traffic. Pedestrians only, and that won't last much longer. I'll be lucky to get home.'

'Go carefully, then.'

'I will. You should see it, Terry. Like the end of the world.'

He tried to imagine the scene. Darkness, low clouds, a swirling torrent of black water, a few nervous pedestrians scurrying across the bridge. He could hear the wind blustering in her phone too. Just half a mile from the queues and bright lights in the supermarket. A different reality. The woman in the queue in front of him had just finished paying.

'Terry, I'm sorry to trouble you, but I've got a favour to ask. It's about my daughter – you know, Emily.'

'Okay. What's she done now?'

'Well ...' Terry listened, holding his phone to his ear with his left hand while his right – the one still recovering from being in plaster – clumsily packed his groceries into bags as they came through the checkout. 'She went *where?*'

'I know, Terry, it's crazy, but I've only just found out. And I've tried to ring her but her phone doesn't answer. It goes straight to voicemail.'

'Right. It does sound worrying. She's a resourceful girl, though, she'll probably be okay.'

'I hope so, Terry, but could you look into it? Please? I didn't know who else to call.'

'I'll do my best. Soon as I've got this food bagged up. I'll let you know.'

'Thanks. Terry. You're a pal.'

'You go home now. Get off that bridge. That river's no place for swimming.'

His voice, he hoped, sounded reassuring, but the message was more than a little alarming. Since his meeting with Dave Starkey earlier Terry's suspicions about Tom Weston had grown. If the number Starkey had found on the Scottish people trafficker's phone was the same as the number used to call Audrey Weston on the weekend of the murder – as Terry suspected – and that person was her brother Tom, then he might be a very dangerous individual indeed. Not the innocent victim he portrayed himself as – the grieving husband of a murdered wife – but a knowing accomplice to murder, and a child abuser to boot.

Had he really murdered his wife? No, that can't be true, Terry told himself sternly. He was in Scotland, he has a cast iron alibi. But then what was he talking to his sister about that weekend – calls which he's tried so hard to cover up?

Was *she* the killer? Murdering by proxy as I suggested to Jane once? If so, what if she's at home with her brother now?

Not the sort of couple which you'd send an innocent young student to interview. Especially a student with no proper cover story and no back up at all.

Only me, Terry thought ruefully as he wheeled his trolley full of groceries across the supermarket car park. That's what Sarah wants, me to be her back up. A man with a fragile arm.

He thought about it as he loaded his groceries into his car, a black Audi. The sensible thing was to ring the station for support, a couple of uniform cars, proper back up. But Terry had no radio in his car; he'd handed that in when he was suspended and hadn't retrieved it yet. He could phone for support but even that was awkward: after all, no one would be very concerned if he told them a student, a young woman in her twenties, had stopped answering her phone for an hour or two. And if he explained his suspicion that Tom and Audrey Weston might be murderers, the uniform inspector might check with Will Churchill and be indignantly informed that Tom Weston was no murderer at all, but a grieving husband who had just given evidence in the trial of the man who *had* just killed that wife. Added to which, the student who had so stupidly and callously set out to pester him on his own doorstep was herself wanted for questioning by DS Starkey to face possible charges of fraud, impersonation and harassing a witness, in a case where her father had been arrested for historic child abuse.

No, it was all too difficult. He would have to do this on his own.

As he crossed the car park to return his trolley Terry checked his phone. Maybe if he just called Emily she would answer and it would all turn out to be a false alarm. But when he tried it just went straight to voicemail. He left a brief message asking her to phone him and then to his surprise, just as he got into the car, she sent him a text.

Great, he thought. Everything solved. But when he opened the message there was nothing there. No words. Only a little icon to show that there was something else – what? A picture? No, a recording.

He parked the phone in the dock and started the engine. At first there was no sound from the phone – just a sort of rustle and drumming like rain falling through trees. Then a voice – a woman's voice – came through the speaker.

Not Emily at all.

52. Audi

TERRY DROVE towards Osbaldwick with a sense of growing astonishment. At one point he even laughed aloud. This girl Emily was clearly a genius. She had somehow managed to record evidence which had eluded both him and Jane Carter for months. Tom Weston *had* killed his wife after all, just as Terry had suspected all along, but been unable to prove. Here he was admitting it, on tape – discussing the crime with his sister, the accomplice who he'd called in to clear up after him.

'But – oh God, what about all those calls you made to me from the train on Friday morning? Running off to Scotland after you'd drowned her in the hot tub – pleading for me to come here and clear it all up? Audrey, please help me – make it look like suicide!'

His alibi was broken, too. Because all their assumptions had been based on a faulty time of death. Vicky Weston hadn't been killed on that Sunday evening as they'd always believed; she'd been drowned in the hot tub two days earlier, on the Friday morning. Her husband had killed her during their quarrel, before he set off for Scotland. Then, sitting in the train – panicking no doubt – he'd rung his sister, who was still on holiday in Spain, telling her what he'd done, and asking her to sort it out for him. So his sister Audrey had come back from holiday on Sunday, pulled her out of the tub and faked the suicide, using Vicky's own phone to ring Tom in Scotland and then send a text to make it appear she was still alive and about to drown herself.

God, how did we miss this? Terry thumped the steering wheel in frustration. And it was all because of that second SIM card which Tom used to communicate with his sister. He slipped out of the room to remove it that day we called to say we suspected murder. If only ...

Suddenly the tone on the recording changed. There was music – *The Ride of the Valkries,* for some strange reason – followed by a gasp and the sound of a struggle. Audrey Weston's voice, louder, harsh.

'In here, you little shit!'

Then more thumps, gasps, and her brother Tom snarling: *'Get down! Who the fuck are you, snooping out there?'*

'I'm not ... I wanted to talk ... ow!'

That third voice – Emily's – set Terry's heart racing. Appalled, he put his foot down, trying to make progress along the busy Hull Road. But it was hopeless – he had no blue light, and each time he pulled out to overtake there was traffic coming towards him. Don't cause another accident, casualties, months in hospital, that won't help. Terry swung left at the traffic lights, then right through Tang Hall, all the time listening to the screams of pain, the abuse, the threats.

Audrey's voice. *'There's the hot tub. That worked fine. You can show me how it's done.'*

Then, a few moments later, her brother suggesting the river instead.

'No one could fall in and survive that. A journalist, maybe she came to take a look and – whoops!'

Then a discussion about fetching ropes and gaffer tape from a garage. The sound of a door opening and closing. Then the woman's voice again, cold, gloating, menacing:

'Good swimmer, are you? You'll need to be.'

Ignoring the speed limit, Terry sped through a council estate towards Osbaldwick. There were no more words, just the sound of a struggle, someone being beaten. The poor girl! It sounded as though she was putting up a fight – good for her – but against two adult murderers. As he reached the village itself the tape ended. A long continuous hum, then nothing, dead. Which is what Emily will be if they get her to the river, Terry thought desperately. No matter that she's uncovered a crime – two crimes if that talk about Tom's first wife Christine was true; none of that will do her any good if these two devils carry out their satanic scheme and throw her in the river. Tom Weston is right: no one could survive in that river when it's in spate, not even an Olympic swimmer. And the poor kid's probably concussed already, to judge from the sound of the beating they've given her.

Terry swung round the final corner and there right in front of him was a dark green Range Rover, coming out of the track from Straw House Barn. The four by four turned left away from him, swaying slightly into the middle of the road as it did so. For a millisecond Terry hesitated, his foot on the brake, the car disappearing round the corner towards the pub. Which way? She might still be in the house, bound, gagged, in need of urgent medical attention. But no – he knew what their plan was, and he had seen Tom's car. Emily was almost certainly in it, tied up probably on the floor, with Tom Weston driving and that woman's feet on her head. And nobody knows what's happening, only me. If they reach the river and throw her in we can arrest them later, charge them with murder and lock them up and it'll make no difference at all.

It'll always, always be too late.

Sarah asked me to save her daughter and I'm the only one who can do it. Terry put his foot down, swung around the corner, swerved to avoid a cyclist outside the pub, and saw the Range Rover in the distance, turning right into a housing estate, heading towards the Hull Road.

*　*　*

Safe home in her flat at last, Sarah shrugged off her wet coat, and walked into the kitchen to put the kettle on. Outside, rain was drumming steadily on the windows. She took her mug of tea and stood by the glass door leading onto the balcony, peering out into the darkness.

It wasn't all dark. The rain streaming down the glass distorted the floodlights of the police, Army and Environment Agency workers struggling to re-direct the traffic and control the flood. There were lights on the Foss Barrier too, where the pumps, she hoped, were working this year, preventing a repetition of the disaster in 2015, when the floodwater in the Ouse had spread up the Foss, devastating thousands of homes. As she watched, a vehicle with a flashing blue light – police, ambulance? – appeared, the on-off light sending colourful patterns through the streams of water flowing down her window.

Not an ambulance, please, Sarah thought. Anyone who's fallen in down there will have no chance. As she'd crossed the bridge, one of the few pedestrians who did so, she'd been awed by the power of the dreadful dark torrent flowing beneath her feet. The iron bridge stayed solid, but if the stone piers beneath it cracked, started to crumble ... the idea terrified her. She'd drawn comfort from Terry's voice, even while explaining her worries, and been more than happy to be met at the far side of the bridge by a burly man in waders and hi-viz jacket who had extended a protective arm and directed her to the safest, driest route home.

She wondered if she'd been too precipitate, begging Terry's help to find Emily. After all, she was a resourceful girl, she could look after herself. Had it been that other fear, the physical terror inspired by the awful power of the river, which had prompted her call? That, and the anxiety in Bob's voice – but she was used to that.

She turned away from the window, wondering what there was in the freezer. Microwave meals for one – she had a stock of those, dating back weeks. But since Emily had been staying, she'd been making more of an effort. The remains of last night's shepherd's pie in the fridge, enough left for two. I'll wait awhile, she decided, see if she turns up. In the meantime, there's the line of questioning to work on for the final witness tomorrow, Audrey Adair.

If she turns up, that is.

Sarah had spread out her papers and was beginning to work when her phone rang. Glancing at the screen she saw it was Lucy.

'Sarah, hi. I've had an idea. I hope I'm not interrupting your meal, am I?'

'No, I'm all alone. Fire away.'

'Good. It's about Audrey, this woman we've asked to attend tomorrow. Though whether she actually appears is anyone's guess.'

'I hope for the best. I'm writing my questions now.'

'Good. Well here's another one you might want to consider. You know that DVD we've got, with the CCTV video of Adrian on his bike outside the pub?'

'Yes.'

'Well, call me a sad lonely nerd, but I've watched it right through to the end. Played it in the kitchen while I was cooking. Don't think we've ever done that before. We stopped it just after 11 last time, when there seemed no more point.'

'And?'

'Well, it goes on for another hour. Totally boring except for one thing. When everyone's gone home from the pub there's still one car left in the car park. A black Audi. It's been there the whole time, long before Adrian appears on the scene. So I just wondered, while I was chopping up veg, is the owner staying in the pub or will someone come to pick it up?'

'And the answer?'

'Someone does. At 11.18 to be precise. A taxi pulls up, a woman gets out, and drives the car away.'

'So? Why is that significant?'

'Well, I rewound to see when the car first arrives. Twenty to seven, is the answer. Same woman, tallish, thin. But here's the strange thing. She doesn't go into the pub or talk to anyone there. She parks the car at the back of the car park and goes over the fence – there's a stile there and a footpath which dog walkers use – but this woman hasn't got a dog. And the footpath – I checked – goes right behind Straw House Barn.'

'So you think this woman might be ...?'

'Audrey Adair. Well, it could be, couldn't it? That's all I'm saying. It's odd, isn't it? She arrives before seven, walks off across a field, and returns by taxi after 11 at night. All of which covers the time frame when we think Vicky Weston was killed.'

'Does she look like Audrey Adair?'

'Can't say. Never seen her. But that's it, you see. If she does turn up tomorrow we'll know what she looks like. There's a fairly clear picture on the CCTV when she pays off the taxi. Ask if she drives a black Audi.'

'So I could show her the picture, you mean? Ask if it's her?'

'Yes. And if that's her car? You can see the registration, just about.'

'Thanks, Lucy love. You're a treasure.'

* * *

Terry had had the Audi for five years now. Several colleagues had suggested he change it – some couldn't believe he still drove such a relic – but Terry didn't see the point. It was comfortable, spacious, reliable, and his girls seemed to like it, so why bother? Esther had even given it a name – Wilfrid – which he'd thought meant she was fond of it but could, he reflected later, be a juvenile attempt at sarcasm.

The car was due for a service but it was doing well enough today. He slammed his foot to the floor and the engine responded powerfully, so that by the time he reached the roundabout on the Hull Road near the *Inner Space Service Station* he was only a few lengths behind the Range Rover. He flashed his headlights, hoping to induce Tom Weston to stop. But it seemed to have the opposite effect. The bigger car shot out into the traffic, causing a Mini to screech to a halt and the man in the white van behind it to swerve past the Mini on the inside, leaning on his horn and raising two fingers at the furious young woman driver. By the time Terry had negotiated his way past them the Range Rover had shot off down Field Lane, heading past Terry's home towards the university.

It was all Terry could do to keep it in sight. He almost lost it but saw it again stopped at the traffic lights at the end of Broadway, the junction with Fulford Road which led left to Landing Lane, right towards the city and Skeldergate Bridge. Either way led to the river, where Tom and his sister could slide their terrified, bound captive into the swirling, torrential waters. How long would it take to do that? Terry didn't want to find out.

As he drove he was on his mobile, calling out the details of the chase. Never mind he'd recently been suspended, he was still a police inspector, wasn't he? And the concerns he'd had earlier about the trouble this could get him in didn't apply now. That recording was evidence – conclusive, surely – that the man he was chasing was a murderer, intent on killing again. The embarrassment this discovery was going to cause to Jane Carter, the CPS, and Will Churchill was as nothing, compared to the life of young Emily.

'This is DI Terry Bateson, in hot pursuit of a dark green Range Rover registration Yankee Oscar seven three – shit, I can't see the rest – on Broadway, heading towards Fulford. Driver believed to have kidnapped a female student, name Emily Newby, with the intention of murder – repeat murder. Request all available cars, immediate assistance.'

'Got that, sir,' the duty sergeant replied, 'but we don't have many cars available. They're all out dealing with the floods.'

'That's where he's heading,' Terry shouted. 'Turning right now towards Skeldergate Bridge. He says he's going to throw her in.'

'Do my best, sir. Passing it on.'

While Terry had been talking, the Range Rover had shot through the lights, causing another screeching of horns and possible pile-up. He knows I'm following, Terry told himself, I should never have flashed my lights before. But as the lights turned green he turned right to follow it, gunning the ancient Audi past the police station itself and overtaking a bus in a risky manoeuvre which would have had the traffic police hot on his tail if only there *had* been any traffic police available anywhere within three miles. The Range Rover was ahead, going through one green light and then another turning from amber to red which gave Terry the choice – break traffic rules or be there in time to save a life – and by the time they reached Fishergate School he was only fifty yards behind. Then as the inner ring road with the city walls came in sight the Range Rover headed down a slope towards the bridge and the Foss Barrier both of which were crowded with floodlights, men in yellow hi-viz jackets, squaddies and police, with stop signs, portable traffic lights and temporary metal crash barriers and Terry thought, the man must be mad to think he'll get away with murder here, there are hundreds of witnesses everywhere and anyway he'll never get onto the bridge.

Terry flashed his lights again, once, twice, three times, and blew his horn. *Stop, for Christ's sake, stop now! Come on, you guys, look up, this is a killer driving towards you!*

But the driver of the Range Rover didn't seem to care about the obstructions in front of him. With Terry close behind him he speeded up, straight through a temporary red light, smashing the crash barriers aside and scattering startled Environment Agency workers to left and right. There was a lake of flood water a foot deep on the road before the bridge; the Range Rover drove straight through it, water spraying right and left, Terry desperately following.

On either side of the bridge, the river was as high as he had ever seen it. Even with his headlights pointing straight ahead, he was aware of a vast black torrent, sliding inexorably downstream only a few feet below the thin strip of stone and tarmac on which the two frail vehicles were travelling. Terry felt suddenly how small and vulnerable he was, in this tiny fragile tin box. Clearly no person who fell in there would survive; neither would a car, not even one as relatively robust as the Range Rover. It would be crushed, sunk, smashed to pieces in a second if it was swept against the bridge. Or if it went downstream it would vanish instantly, the vehicle and its drowning occupants swirled away to surface later – if at all – miles away, at the Archbishop's palace, perhaps, or further, Cawood, Selby, even swept out to sea in the Humber estuary.

Was that what he was about to witness? Not just a murder but a double suicide? Tom Weston and his sister didn't care about witnesses because they meant to drive the car off the bank on the far side and take Emily with them, the killers and their captive together? And if they did that – the horrid thought flashed into Terry's mind – they would be doing it just in front of her mother's eyes. There were no railings or bollards just there to obstruct them. All Sarah had to do was look out of her window now and watch the tragedy unfolding below.

In front of the Range Rover at the far side of the bridge there were further crash barriers, stopping all traffic. At first Terry thought it might smash through them too, but then men – two, three, six – all in hi-viz yellow jackets with torches came running towards it. The Range Rover braked, then stopped, and the driver's door opened. *No!* Terry thought, *I was wrong, they're just going to throw the poor girl in!* He opened his own door, got out, sprinted the few yards towards Tom Weston, yelling into the wind and rain:

'Stop it! No! Let her go!'

And then realised, as he reached the rear of the car, that something was wrong. He had misunderstood.

The driver wasn't Tom Weston at all. Wrong shape, wrong silhouette. Not a man, but a woman. Young. Someone he knew.

Emily.

* * *

'Keep away!' Emily yelled. 'Come any closer and I'll kill you!'

Then she turned and sprinted away from Terry, towards the men with torches and hi-viz jackets.

'What? *Emily!*' Terry glanced briefly through the windows of the Range Rover but there was no one inside, no one else. Empty. And Emily running screaming *away* from him. What was all this?

Emily hid behind the men in hi-viz jackets screaming: 'Keep him away, don't let him come near me! That man wants to kill me!'

'But Emily ...'

'All right, mate, that's far enough.' Two burly men approached, shining torches in his face. Terry held up a hand to shield his eyes.

'It's all right, I'm a police inspector.'

'That's as may be, but the girl is terrified. And this place isn't safe.'

Terry glanced over the parapet. Now that he was outside the car he noticed the sound of the wind and the rain. And beneath it something else – a splashing and something ... an underlying silence which was not quiet, not an absence of sound, but rather a distillation of it, a menace, a surge just below hearing which gave the impression of immense, overwhelming power. Power that had no interest in humanity at all.

'Yes, okay, but tell her my name, please. It's Terry, Emily – Terry Bateson!'

At first she didn't seem to hear him and they walked in a convoy towards the crash barriers on the far side, his two burly escorts taking care to keep between him and Emily. When they reached the far side he tried again.

'Emily, it's me – Terry Bateson! I'm not here to hurt you!'

'Oh.' She turned, peered more closely over the shoulder of one of the hi-viz men. 'Terry? Is it you? No one else?'

'Yes. Just me. Who did you think it was?'

'Well, him of course. Tom Weston. And his sister.' She stepped out cautiously from behind the men. 'What are you doing in her car?'

'I'm not in her car. That's mine.'

'What – the black Audi?'

'Yes, of course.'

'So it was you then, following me? Flashing your lights?'

'Yes. I thought it was Tom driving, with his sister. They kidnapped you.'

'Yes, but I escaped.' Emily turned to the men. 'It's all right. He's my friend. Not who I thought.'

'All the same, miss. That car shouldn't be there. If the bridge goes you'll lose it.'

'I don't care. It's not mine. It belongs to a criminal – a murderer.' She turned to her astonished rescuers. 'This man – he really *is* a policeman. An inspector.'

'Look,' said Terry. 'We'll move the cars in a minute. Or you can. I left my keys in mine. This girl's mother lives just up there, and I think she's in shock. I'll take her, okay? Then come back for the car.'

'I'll come with you, sir, if you don't mind,' said the largest of the men. 'Just to be sure.'

'Fine. It's only a short way.' As they walked down off the bridge, splashing though another small lake, Terry asked: 'How did you escape?'

'There was a fight. First her, then the man. I knocked him down somehow, stole his keys – he dropped them. Locked them both in the room. But I thought they'd got out, you see. Following me in the Audi.' Emily gave a short laugh, suspiciously like a sob. 'They meant to kill me, you know. Drown me in the river.'

'I know.' They walked quietly on, through a private car park to the door at the back of the flats. Their escort trudged behind, listening no doubt in amazement.

'You *knew?* How did you know?'

'You sent me a recording, remember. To my phone.'

'Oh that! Gosh, did it work?'

'Yes. I heard everything. Well, a lot anyway. Enough to convict them.'

'And you came to save my life, I suppose?' Emily flashed a sudden smile in the darkness.

'Oh no.' They were inside the building, mounting the stairs to the flat now. 'You saved your own life, Emily. You did it – no-one else.'

'And scared you to death in the process. On that bridge.' Another smile.

'Be my guest. Just ... respect the traffic lights in future, okay?'

'He *is* a policeman, you see?' said Emily, turning to the burly man behind them. 'He had to say that.'

Terry rang the bell on the door. After a short pause, it opened.

'You asked me to find your daughter, Sarah,' Terry said. 'So here she is.'

53. Developments

'So, MRS Newby,' Mrs Justice Eckersley smiled pleasantly, standing by the window in the judge's chambers. 'Is your witness here this morning?'

'Er ... no, My Lady. There have been a number of developments.'

'Developments. I see. Such as?' Judge Eckersley raised a quizzical eyebrow. Behind her, through the window, Sarah could see workmen in hi-viz jackets, busying themselves by the bridge.

'Well, the witness, Audrey Adair, is in hospital, suffering from concussion, I understand. Also she has been arrested.'

'Arrested? On what charge?'

'Suspicion of murder, My Lady.'

'Goodness! I see what you mean about developments. The arrest relates to a separate case, I take it.'

'Er ... actually no, My Lady. It's the same case. She is charged with the murder of Victoria Weston. As an accomplice in a joint enterprise with her brother, Thomas Weston – the victim's husband, who gave evidence yesterday morning.'

The judge peered over her reading glasses at Sarah in astonishment. Sarah tried to keep her face as calm and expressionless as possible, but inside she was bubbling with the thrill of excitement. This was the sort of rare moment in her career which she cherished, the instant when everything in a case suddenly turned on its head, and she could – very occasionally – snatch triumph out of disaster.

'You astound me, Mrs Newby.' The judge turned to the prosecutor, who stood sweating silently beside Sarah. 'Were you aware of this, Mr Corder?'

'I have only just been informed, My Lady. It is ... a most unusual development.'

'Indeed. How do you suggest we proceed?' The judge switched her gaze from one counsel to the other, apparently seeking enlightenment.

'My Lady,' Sarah said, 'perhaps it would be helpful if I summarised some of the freshly discovered evidence which has emerged since yesterday. I have just given an outline to Mr Corder and here ...' she passed two pages of A4 over '... is a copy for you. It is my submission that in the circumstances it would be inappropriate for this trial to proceed any further.'

* * *

'How does it feel?' Sarah asked, an hour later, standing with Lucy beside their astonished client in the well of the courtroom. The judge had just pronounced Adrian Norton free to go, and the warder had released him from the dock. Behind Sarah, the disgruntled Alex Corder and his junior were packing up their files and preparing to depart. The jury, who had been dismissed, were filing slowly out of the jury box, glancing towards Adrian with expressions of mingled curiosity, disappointment and – in one or two cases at least – open dislike. *I wasn't going to win,* Sarah thought. *Not if they'd had the final say.*

'Feel? Amazing, of course. Astonishing. But ...' Adrian gazed around him, bemused. 'This is really it, then, is it? They can't change their minds?'

'They could, in theory,' Sarah said cautiously. 'But it's highly unlikely. Not with this new evidence. It amounts to a virtual confession – better, in a way, because it was obtained with no element of coercion. And it explains all the facts, too, the ones I called into question. That neighbour, Mrs Bishop, for example – she really did see a woman driving the car. But it wasn't Vicky Weston, it was her sister-in-law, Audrey Adair. It explains the lack of traces of your bicycle, too. It was never in the car, because you weren't the killer.'

'No. Anyway I can't drive,' Adrian said. 'But I'm still not sure I get it. How can you be sure it was her – this Audrey?'

'Well,' Sarah said patiently. 'Firstly because she admitted it, on tape, And secondly ...' She glanced at Lucy, who took over.

'Because we've got her on CCTV. There she is, leaving her car outside the pub and approaching the house via a footpath just before seven that Sunday evening. We know it's her car – a black Audi – because the police checked the registration this morning – it fits. So she put poor Vicky's body in the boot of her own car – with a blue towel under it, probably, to keep things clean – drove to the river, pushed her in, abandoned the car, and took a taxi back to the pub to pick up the Audi from the car park. The police are contacting the taxi firm now, to see if the driver remembers.'

'So this sister-in-law, Audrey whatever, must have been the person I saw when I cycled past the house that evening, then?'

'It must have been, yes,' Sarah said. 'It wasn't a man, as you thought.' This wasn't the most perfect point, but all the rest of the evidence seemed to back it up. Eye-witness identification evidence was notoriously unreliable – as Corder had insisted against Mrs Bishop – and it had been Adrian's creative attitude to the truth which had got him into this trouble in the first place.

'So *she* killed Vicky, then – this Audrey?'

'No,' Sarah said patiently. 'If you did see Vicky, she was already dead. Left lolling in the tub for three days, poor woman – under the lid, maybe. What you probably saw was Audrey just preparing to pull her out. She disposed of the body and then faked the suicide. Her husband Tom had killed her on Friday morning during their quarrel. Then he went off to his conference in Scotland which gave him the perfect alibi – or so he thought.' She explained Tom's use of the second SIM card to hide his phone calls, and the way brother and sister had used Vicky's phone to send the suicide text which made it seem she had still been alive on Sunday evening.

'So,' she concluded brightly. 'What are you going to do now? With the rest of your life, I mean.'

'Wow! That's a big question.' Adrian drew a deep breath, stretching his arms expansively. He grinned, and loosened his tie. 'Get out of these clothes, at least. Back to my studies. And ...' A sombre thought seemed to strike him. 'Ring Michaela, perhaps. See if she'll give me a second chance.'

'Good luck with that,' said Sarah, somehow managing to temper her cynicism with a sort of blessing. 'She's a feisty girl, I liked her. But if you want my advice ...' She hesitated, wondering if she was presuming too far. *I'm an old lady to this youth,* she remembered. *A granny.*

'Yes?' He didn't look too offended.

'Tell her you love her, if it's true. But always, always tell the truth. Not the imagined truth – the real one.'

Adrian grinned. Sarah had never really warmed to her client, but she could see, especially in this moment of shared triumph and relief, that he was a handsome young man, charming enough in his way. Innocent too, in more than one sense of the word.

'I'll try, Mrs Newby. And – thanks.'

* * *

'But why, Terry?' Sarah said. 'That's the part I don't get. He was heading for a divorce – why murder his wife instead?'

It was a week later. In one of those improbable reversals in the jetstream which make British weather so unpredictable, the weeks of ceaseless rain had been replaced by a welcome succession of days of clear blue skies and midwinter sunshine. The river, though still full, had subsided sufficiently for some, at least, of the riverside walks to be accessible to people – at least those who didn't mind splashing through a little mud and were equipped with wellington boots and warm coats. Terry and Sarah strolled companionably side by side, close but not touching, gloved hands thrust deep into anorak pockets. Fifty yards ahead of them, Jessica and Esther hurried on with Emily, slipping and sliding towards the turning for the vast open spaces of the Knavesmire, York's racecourse, where Terry's daughters planned to fly their new kites.

'She must have found out what her husband was up to,' Terry said. 'And threatened to expose him.'

'Maybe,' Sarah agreed. 'Young Adrian mentioned something like that, about a secret Vicky was going to tell him. Trouble is, he came up with this story so late, it just looked like another excuse, a fantasy. Idiot – it was hard to believe him!'

'Nonetheless, he may have been right,' Terry said. 'I was talking to Dave Starkey yesterday. You know, your favourite detective ...'

'After Will Churchill, Terry,' said Sarah ironically. 'He's my number one. Always will be.'

'Yes, well.' Their eyes met, each recalling the bitter tussles they'd had with Churchill in the past. 'But Starkey's not so bad, you know. Just your dedicated hard man in pursuit of evil. Anyway, what he's found out with the help of the Scottish police explains a lot. You know Tom Weston was in touch with this man Angus, or Alastair, whatever – whom I met at the service station the night of my accident? Well, it turns out they're old mates. It's not just that Angus was trying to pimp this girl Mary to him while he was driving through York; that's the least of it.'

'There's more?'

'Much more. It's true Tom Weston attended a publisher's conference in Edinburgh that weekend – his alibi, remember – but the conference ended on Saturday night. Which left him free all Sunday to hire a car, drive down to Angus's café near Melrose, take his pick of the young girls in the refugee reform school Angus runs there, and drive back to his comfy Edinburgh hotel that evening. They've found pictures, nasty video evidence.'

'While his sister was dumping his wife in the river – the same night? He was shagging teenage girls? Jesus, Terry!' Sarah shuddered, glancing to their left at the remorseless stream of brown water flowing swiftly downstream. 'So he murdered her to avoid being exposed as a paedophile?'

'Looks that way,' Terry agreed. 'And the same thing may have happened to his first wife as well. We're trying to get that investigation reopened too. The pebbles in Vicky's coat came from Budleigh Salterton in Devon, where the sailing accident happened. Audrey's idea of a sick joke, maybe.'

They strolled on for a while in silence. Then another thought struck Sarah. 'What does this mean for Bob?'

'Your ex? Hasn't Lucy Parsons told you?'

'No.'

'Oh. She's probably waiting to have it confirmed. But Starkey told me they're likely to drop it.'

'Really? That's a relief. What's brought him to his senses at last?'

'Your brilliant daughter, of course.' Terry pointed ahead, where Emily was shepherding Jessica and Esther across the road into the vast green open spaces of York racecourse. 'Starkey called Clare Fanshawe back to go through her allegations again, in the light of what she'd told an investigative journalist called Helen Beasley ...' Terry laughed, shaking his head at the memory of Starkey's puzzled face ' ... whom he still hasn't traced, but anyway, he got her to admit that she remembered the wrong man. It was Tom Weston who seduced her – groomed her, whatever – when she was a schoolgirl, not your ex. So she's made a new statement to that effect.'

'So Bob has no case to answer?'

'You know what they'll say, Sarah. No further proceedings due to insufficient evidence.'

'Insufficient evidence!' Sarah's anger flared suddenly. 'How is that supposed to be justice? Poor Bob will never keep his job, will he? Not with a slur like that hanging over him. And all because of a stupid lying fantasist!'

'It's how it works,' Terry said grimly. 'The way Starkey puts it, he thinks he's being generous. Magnanimous, was the word he used.'

'Dishonest, is what I'd call. Pusillanimous, perhaps. Mealy-mouthed.' Sarah sighed. 'That's the trouble with these witch hunts, post Savile. They ruin people's lives. Celebrities, and stupid innocent schoolteachers like Bob. Emily will be devastated. She thinks she saved her Dad.'

'Well, she did, in a way. Not only that, but she exposed the real paedophile.' They crossed the road, and followed the young people onto the grass. There was a sprinkling of walkers enjoying the wide open spaces, a couple of football matches in progress, and dogs racing through wide shallow puddles, putting seagulls to flight. Jessica's kite was already flying, and she was taking giant strides backwards, tugging enthusiastically to keep it aloft. Emily was bending over Esther, helping her untangle some problem with the string.

'You should be proud, Sarah. She's a truly remarkable young woman.'

'Oh, I am, Terry, I am. Hugely proud. And I nearly lost her, too – again. Remember when she ran away as a schoolgirl, years ago?' She looked up at Terry, smiling, a hint of tears in her eyes. 'Thank you for bringing her back.'

'I didn't, Sarah. She did it all herself.'

'Well, thank you for trying, at least.'

She slipped her arm through his, linking him close to her side.

'Come on. Let's join them, shall we?'

I hope you have enjoyed this book. If you have, please consider leaving a short review on Amazon. Word of mouth is crucial for any author to succeed, and even a few positive words can make a big difference.

You might also be interested in some other books listed on the next page. You can find them on all major retailers, or read more about them on my website www.timvicary.com

Thank you for reading.

Tim Vicary.

Other Books by Tim Vicary

Legal thrillers in the series 'The Trials of Sarah Newby'

A Game of Proof
A Fatal Verdict
Bold Counsel

Historical Novels

Nobody's Slave
Cat and Mouse
The Blood Upon the Rose
The Monmouth Summer

Box Sets

Women of Courage (3 historical novels)

Audiobooks

A Game of Proof
A Fatal Verdict
Nobody's Slave

Website: www.timvicary.com

Printed in Great Britain
by Amazon